MW01093817

Reflection

"Who are you?"

Kitty was taken aback. Her wishes never spoke to her before.

Kitty stumbled on her words, but finally forced out, "I'm Kitty Guthrie."

The spell girl nodded. Its dull eyes stayed glued to Kitty's. "Who am I?"

"Well...um...you're a magic spell. A copy. You're just like me. Well, you are me—for just a little while."

The spell girl's words popped out in a rapid fire that slowly rose in pitch as she asked more and more questions, faster and faster. Soon her voice was a whining ring; the questions were barely audible. "Do you really think mom can control herself? Do you like the doctors working with Edith? Do you want dad to come home? What would you do if you saw him again? Where do you think he is?"

"Stop it!" Kitty slapped her hands over her ears. She blinked her eyes hard. Her mind clicked like a button, a familiar feeling at the end of making a wish, and then she felt an uncomfortable pop in her chest as her bedroom returned to normal. Everything started tilting sideways, and Kitty realized she was falling.

DUAL NATURE

PRINCIPLES OF MAGIC

BRENNA R. SINGMAN

Dual Nature is a work of fiction. Names, places, and incidents either are products of the author's imagination or are used fictitiously. Any resemblance to actual events, locales, or persons, living or dead, is entirely coincidental.

Copyright © by Brenna R. Singman

Printed in the United States of America
First Printing, August 2019

ISBN 978 1 0740462 2 4

Brenna R. Singman
Atlanta, GA

www.authorbrenna.com

For the high school girl with the tiny spiral notebook who never gave up on this story.

We did it.

"The whole aim of practical politics is to keep the populace alarmed—and hence clamorous to be led to safety—by menacing it with an endless series of hobgoblins, all of them imaginary."

- H.L. Mencken

"How many people does each of us know who claim to seek happiness but freely choose paths inevitably leading to misery?"

- Theodore Dalrymple

DUAL NATURE

One

Kitty Guthrie's toes throbbed in her boots. There hadn't been a minute to sit for the last two hours. She oversaw the other students in the gym now storing paint, folding tables, and rolling carts of insanely expensive sound equipment back to the storeroom door. After any project was complete, even just emptying the garbage can, Kitty checked off different boxes on her list snapped into her clipboard. Sometimes the pencil found its way back into her lopsided ponytail for safekeeping. More often it was between her teeth as she gnawed on it like a carrot.

WHAM!

Kitty jumped at the sound of metal slamming against the wooden floor. A group of older boys from the high school were egging on their friend who was on his tiptoes at the top of an unsteady ladder. He strained to reach the edges of a brightly painted banner advertising for the Glade Crest Junior High Homecoming Dance while shimmying his feet wider apart for more balance. The banner was as tall as him and taped at an obvious angle against the wall beside the rear exit. Between his teeth he clenched onto the handle of a packing tape dispenser. It wobbled every time he spoke, and the thin plastic threatened to snap in his mouth.

"Ah kud eech it!" the boy said.

One boy doubled over in laughter. "He just said he could eat—!"

Another boy slapped the first around the back of his head. "He said 'Reach it', turd brain. Bro! You're a pipsqueak! You can't reach!"

"You're tiny, Dino!"

"That's what she said!"

More laughter erupted. Kitty shoved her pencil into the knot bound by her ponytail and stormed over to the boys, the sharp pain against her smallest toes almost bringing her to tears. She knew them from the high school's P.A.L.S. program. The Peer Assistance Leaders helped get new students situated at school and organized volunteering with the other public schools for major events. Of course Kitty got the goof offs, and they were challenging her authority.

"What the actual heck are you doing? Cut it out!" she said with a stomp of her heel. The boys quieted for a moment, and Kitty marveled at the power of her boots. She only wore them on special occasions or when she needed to look like the height of authority. She didn't like to admit how the beige leather made her ankles sweat. Important people didn't have ankle sweat. Unfortunately, the boys only looked at each other and laughed again.

"Dino, you're getting us in trouble with the Itty Bitty Kitty Committee," one of the boys said.

A few threw their mocking hands in the air. One boy turned to hide his laughter. A gleaming silver watch caught the light as he controlled himself and flicked his sandy bangs aside. Kitty, trying not to note his handsome blue eyes or any attractive features on the older boys, defensively crossed her arms over her chest.

"You're not goofing off on my watch...Dino." She read from the ID badge hooked to his jeans. "You and your friends can either get to work or you can get out. This place has to be spotless in half an hour or I don't care if any of you miss your late buses."

"Billy-boy here actually walked," Dino said, nudging a thumb towards the boy with the watch and blazing blue eyes. "Not even from the high school. He's one of those fancy homeschool kids. And he still got suckered into this. Get better at poker, kid."

Kitty sized up the homeschool kid for a moment, daring him to keep up the joke, but *Billy-boy* only shrugged and nodded. She rolled her eyes and squeezed her clipboard from frustration.

"I don't care why you're here. Just get back to work. I'm leaving on time and I *will* lock you in."

She spun around, hawk eyes watching out for any other slackers. The boys' renewed laughter trailed behind her along with loud whispers she couldn't quite make out. It was as if some of them wanted her to turn around, to be hurt by the childish hissing. She didn't care if they liked the work or not. They just had to get it done and not kill themselves in the process. Homecoming was too important to be interrupted by a dumb boy's funeral.

Kitty knew most of the students were there for extra

3

credit, and it was only the end of September! One girl dressed in black was whispering to her equally bleak looking friends. She twirled a dried paintbrush that hadn't touched anything in over an hour. Miren Patrick wouldn't have shown up except at their only mutual friend's request. Kitty would have preferred if she just went home. The constant hiss of their voices in Kitty's ears was also grating. Kitty chewed on the end of her pencil again and swatted at her ear as if it would shake the voices loose.

"Stop it, numbnuts," a girl said as she threw a muscly arm around Kitty's shoulder and yanked the pencil from her grip. The metal tip clicked against her front teeth, and Kitty grabbed at her twinging mouth. Becka Hutchinson didn't always know her own strength, but sometimes it was nice to have a best friend that doubled as a bodyguard. Her jeans and baggy tee shirts made her look wider than she really was, which suited Becka just fine. "I told you I'd watch Miren. She didn't break anything yet."

"Ow! Becks, you nearly pulled my tooth out!"

"Then don't act like a human pencil sharpener, Kitty." Becka returned the pencil to Kitty's ponytail and wiped her cut off gloves on her jeans with an overdramatic groan as if they were covered in slobber.

"I can't help it," Kitty whined and found a loose strand of hair to tug. Butterflies battered her stomach as she saw one group of students play fighting with the last two paint brushes out of their tin. Her cheeks flushed at a boy and girl holding hands and standing much too close while a cart of sound equipment went ignored. "This is my big event. This is the thing that's gonna get me a fast-pass out of the Valley one day. Everything is riding on this. I mean, come on! No

4

other student has ever planned a Homecoming party for the junior high. But even the students doing what they're supposed to do don't really care, and this is all gonna blow up in my face!"

CRASH!

Both girls jumped at the sound of shattering glass. Immediately Becka ran over to where a pair of sixth graders were staring at the wet spot on the floor. Kitty held back a minute. Her heart was thumping in her chest. Her head felt foggy, and her dry eyes scraped across her eyelids like sandpaper when she blinked.

Kitty knew the feeling when fear took over. She tried to take a steadying breath, but it shuddered from her throat.

Becka was kneeling beside one of the kids and grabbed the useless wad of paper towel he was sloshing through the water. Slowly rolling a few feet away was an empty glass jar, perfectly intact. Kitty stopped it with her boot just as one of the sixth grade volunteers caught up to it. He saw Kitty's stern face, then shrunk back with the jar and gently placed it on the table.

There wasn't a crack to be seen. Kitty looked down at her hands as if expecting to see lightning rippling across her palms or some movie-style halo of light. She knew it never happened that way. She didn't want it to happen at all unless she asked it to, but sometimes, when she was too excited, she couldn't hold back a wish—the only word that made sense for what she could do. God forbid someone in school saw something! She might as well tattoo F-R-E-A-K-A-Z-O-I-D to her forehead.

"Thirty minute warning!" called one of the teachers loitering by the doors. His voice was slightly strained as if the bow ties he always wore to match his daily suit were a little too tight around his thick neck. Mr. Briggs was the faculty advisor for Kitty's Homecoming event, and her point person for the last nine months of planning, and while he was never cold to her, he still made her nervous. If anything went wrong, he would be the first to know and the first to make her face the music. Her biggest fear was if Mr. Briggs couldn't handle the problem. Then it would go up to the PTO and fall in the hands of the PTO president Angela Smith who was opposed to Homecoming from the start. If Kitty couldn't make Mrs. Smith happy, then all of her hard work would be for nothing.

To make sure Mr. Briggs knew that she heard, Kitty was about to repeat the time warning when more shouts filled the gym, drawing attention back to the high school boys with the banner. Dino the clown was laughing one moment, and then his foot scraped past the edge of the highest metal step on the ladder. His arms flew out sideways, catching the dangling tip of the banner. Kitty watched the world slow to a crawl as he pitched backwards, crying out in shock for help. The banner came loose from his grip like a useless parachute.

Kitty's mind sparked in that familiar way, but she controlled her breathing. A mask of translucent dark green covered her vision. Light blue ribbons appeared around Dino's right wrist where he was certain to fall, and Kitty's mind focused on those. They danced and knotted into a strange design of loops and twists. She felt the silent plea in her heart.

Don't let him get hurt. I'll take it instead. Please. She lifted her arm. Her eyes fluttered back, dry and scraping.

6

Something started listening—Kitty imagined God was tuning in if he was the one who gave her the power to make wishes—and a heavy, but comforting weight settled over her. In that weight were the heartbeats of everyone around her threaded into her own breathing, rustling trees in early autumn overlooking cold steel buses trundling into their parking spots and spewing noxious fumes, spreading further out to the birds in the sky starting their noisy path south. Just before the sensations went past the dewy clouds, Dino slammed into the ground with a short cry. As he made impact, Kitty blinked.

The light that was surrounding Dino's wrist appeared on hers. She felt a terrible pop like cracking a knuckle, and a quick burning pain burst across the joint. The gymnasium swam before her eyes as she sank to her knees. The digitized screen faded as white static crept along the edge of her vision. Then, for what seemed like just a few moments, her world was drowned in a sea of white.

"Kitty?" A girl's voice sung in her ears along with more whispering.

Kitty blinked her eyes open. Her other best friend April Sullivan was kneeling beside her with a bangle-laden arm propping Kitty up. Trails of gold glitter masked the makeup over her dark cheeks, and a smock covered her stylish dress. Kitty didn't know when she started helping herself up like nothing was wrong.

"Hey, hold up," April said, taking Kitty's elbow. "You okay?"

Kitty pulled her arm loose, cringing at another shock of pain in her wrist. She brushed off her sweater with her left hand while her right arm hung at her side, twinging and only useful for pressing the clipboard to her body. "I'm—I'm good."

April cocked her head to the side, and her shining black hair swept over her shoulder. "You fainted, you baby."

"I'm not a baby." The sounds of the gym were quickly returning, and everything took on its normal brightness. Clean up stopped as all eyes were on Dino. He waved off anyone's concern with a giant grin and jumped up to his feet, gelled hair still perfectly in place. Kitty was relieved that he wasn't hurt, but she certainly wasn't expecting that kind of a shock. She was more used to her little sister Edith's bumps and bruises. A sprained wrist wasn't something Kitty wanted to feel again.

"Is that kid okay?" she asked. She was already marching towards the slowly dispersing group around Dino and his friends. April followed closely behind. Her willowy body moved with an unusual grace for being six inches taller than her peers. Kitty used to hold her arms out whenever April hurried anywhere, always afraid her friend would tip over.

"As okay as a dumb boy could be. Why are they always cute but fifteenth level numbnuts?"

The boys were laughing about what had happened, and some were shifting a ladder over to help Dino get back up. Kitty grabbed the metal ladder with her good hand.

"Are you kidding me?!" she said. Her eyes were daggers aimed at Dino.

"What in the world is going on?" Mr. Briggs said, approaching the group. He stood just a few inches taller than the students around him, short and stout, plucking at his bright red bow tie. The students quieted. Some went

8

back to finish their duties while others hung around to watch the drama unfold. "Ms. Guthrie, care to explain?"

Kitty tensed as she turned to look at Mr. Briggs. She hid her useless wrist that pulsed with an awful ache with each heartbeat. "I was just seeing what the problem was myself. I heard a noise and right away I checked it out—"

"A student fell from a ladder, Ms. Guthrie," he retorted, a stern frown growing on his wide face. Kitty couldn't bear to look at it. She lowered her eyes and wished her hair wasn't up in a ponytail so she could cover her burning cheeks. "That's what I saw. Thankfully he seems alright. Are you hurt, son?"

Again Dino brushed it off and performed a small jig to prove he was fine. His buddies kept laughing, lightening the mood for them, but Kitty continued to shake and sway. Mr. Briggs looked him over to be sure, and he was escorted with another teacher to the nurse who probably wouldn't enjoy having her day extended any further. The other teachers sent the students back to their tasks as Mr. Briggs focused on Kitty again.

"You understand this can't ever happen again," he said. Kitty quickly nodded. "You're the student adviser for this event. If you don't set a good example, you won't keep these responsibilities. I have to be able to trust you, you understand?" Again, Kitty nodded. Her face burned and her eyes stung with building tears. "We'll see how we can spin this for Mrs. Smith when we meet with her next week before the Homecoming game. Of all people we need on our side, it's the PTO President. Can I trust you won't let any more catastrophes happen?" A third nod. "Good. Finish cleaning up in here. You're doing good work, Ms.

Guthrie. Don't let me down."

Mr. Briggs returned to where the teachers were gathered by the door. Kitty felt the sparking butterflies in her stomach, the scratchiness behind her eyelids, and felt a small snap as her hair tumbled out of the hair tie that lay broken on the ground. She groaned and snatched it up, stuffing the limp tie in her pocket. Kitty charged towards the bleachers where her backpack waited, noticeably unzipped. She glanced around to see if anyone looked suspicious and might have taken anything from there. She didn't have anything worth stealing, maybe her ID card, but it wouldn't do any students any good without stealing her face or fingerprint too. Still, she peaked into her bag, shifted the books around, didn't note anything missing, but a small addition got her attention. She started pulling out something thin and wrapped in a white paper with small, colorful cakes and gold foil messages of Happy Birthday.

Kitty looked around the noisy gym again. No one was looking at her, just chatting with their friends as they finished up their tasks. Whoever dropped this in there was either pranking her or didn't have better paper to use since Kitty's thirteenth birthday was four months ago.

Another twinge in her wrist made Kitty momentarily dizzy. She wouldn't be able to finish her work in that kind of pain. Kitty laid her clipboard in her lap, pretending to read through her seven month calendar of meetings, events, and student surveys, but instead she rolled up the pink fluffy sleeve of her sweater and winced at the ache and bruising around her wrist. It was swollen quite a bit, different than any injury she had ever gotten before.

Best I can hope for is to get rid of the bruising, she thought as she remembered one science class that taught her how bruises were just tiny bleeding capillaries under her skin. Kitty let her eyes drift shut, feeling the scraping dryness and letting herself fall behind that green, digitized screen. Her heartbeat pulsed in her ears like a drum solo. The murmuring of the gym crackled into its own beat that matched hers, each heartbeat listening in, catching the rhythm, hearing her out. The sensation stretched again to a louder, sturdy pulse from somewhere below the moist dirt of the school's lawn. It reached all the way to the layers of dense air that kept the molecules people and animals needed to breathe from floating off into space. Everything seemed to hear her all in a moment, all in the space between two heartbeats.

Streams of light blue lines swarmed Kitty's wrist and knitted together into strange patterns that somehow Kitty had asked for. She made her wish, wanting to heal the burst blood vessels first. Those lines tied off like neat bows. Then she wanted the rest of the pain and swelling to stop. She asked for her wrist to return to how it was before Dino fell off of the ladder. The lines that followed looked different, hazier somehow, like they didn't fully understand how to be. Her ears filled with a barrage of that whispering again. She never heard outside voices when she made wishes, and she wondered who could be talking. Loosely knit as they were, Kitty could see little symbols, some mix between music notes and the Latin letters on her mother's old sorority sweatshirt, each symbol shivering as it melted into another and broke apart again. The ribbon of light coated Kitty's wrist and sank into her skin. She felt another dull, painful pop as her wrist snapped into place.

11

Kitty blinked hard and could see clearly again. Her wrist no longer ached, the dull roar of students filled her ears again, and she was sitting alone next to her partially zipped backpack. She smiled to herself, glad that if she needed to help her sister beyond bumps and bruises, she could try that now. The smile didn't last as she twisted her wrist to test it out. It was stiff with some remnants of bruising beneath the pink and black plastic that made up her friendship bracelet. Her hand was twisted at a distinct angle, and when she tried to straighten it, she felt like she might as well pop it out of place again.

"Oh junk..." she muttered.

"Kitty!" April's voice trilled from halfway across the gym. "Tell this kid to lay off the disco ball. It's half as big as him!"

Kitty sighed and tucked the clipboard under her arm. Only another half hour. And then just a week to go. She promised herself that when Homecoming was done, she would get better acquainted with this wish stuff.

Two

Just as the five o'clock bell rang, Kitty was alone in the gym scraping up bits of paint and picking up cut ends of streamers. April's mom hurried her out for dinner on one of the rare nights that both of her parents were home before one took a late shift at Glade Crest General. Kitty was counting on Becka to hold their seat on the bus so they could sit together. She still had a few minutes before she had to run out or risk the bus leaving without her. That would be a mountain of trouble.

Kitty shoved the last of the equipment into the storage closet of the Rec Room. It was all safely tucked away opposite the towering stacks of boxes with the Homecoming Game souvenirs. Mr. Briggs had commended her on getting permission to keep the game merchandise so close to the football field to make set up easy. It had kept Kitty smiling that whole day, which she found herself doing again as she shut and locked the door.

Lastly, she jogged a cart of art supplies down the same short, dim hallway that reminded her of a dungeon, but took an adjacent hall that ended in a small art studio. Kitty wasn't artistically talented and had to stop and admire some of the work displayed on the exposed cement walls and some piles of pages on the wooden tables. If they raised enough money from the raffles at Homecoming, more than just the art students would get a great space like that. She ran back to the gym, checking off the last task on her list with some difficulty.

"Perfect," she said, but balancing the pencil in her hand with her wrist sitting crookedly was less than a perfect situation. Kitty shoved the clipboard into her backpack. It bumped against the present someone dropped in there. With the room empty of anyone who could laugh at her, she picked it up. It was thin and rectangular, almost like a necklace box, but it had some weight to it. Kitty gave it a little shake, and something slid around. The thuds against the sides of the box were muffled by whatever wrapping was inside. A single fold card sat on top, glued to the red satin ribbon. On the front it read: KITTY

Well there was no mistaking that this was for her. She was the only one with a name so trapped in the past in all of Glade Crest except for the old people she knew from the senior care center where she volunteered. Kitty unfolded the card.

> *Hi Kitty! Sick Transfer oration btw.* (That sentence was quickly scribbled above the line.) *This ought to help get you familiar with magic pretty fast. It's a Magical Harnessing Device. It's like a tablet on*

steroids. Check out the Initiate Resources and look
me up if you have questions. I'm on the Family Tree.
Welcome to the club. Don't curse anybody!

(And I'm a poet and I didn't even know it.)

-Will Cavanaugh

Kitty read the note five more times before she understood what she was reading. Magic! This person knew about her wishes! She tried so hard to keep it hidden, but someone knew. At least he wasn't threatening her. She looked at the box again, desperate to both tear it open like an early Christmas present and to chuck it in the garbage. If it was a prank, Becka might be able to help her figure out who would do this. She knew a bunch of the less friendly students thanks to people like Miren.

"Becka! Oh junk!" Kitty threw the box back into her bag and ran out the doors that led directly to the grounds.

There wasn't time to rest her aching side until she was on the bus and shoving her bus pass at the driver. The woman briefly raised an eyebrow at Kitty and removed her hand from the door lever slowly, annoyance carved into her wrinkles.

"This ain't signed," the older woman droned.

"What? Of course it is." Kitty took the pass back and looked. Her stomach knotted as she realized the bus driver was right. The section of the pass that required a parent's signature was blank. Kitty forced a stunted laugh. "Sorry, I just—grabbed the wrong one. One second."

The driver grunted. Kitty ducked down and reached

into the small pocket of her backpack where she kept the passes, face growing hot as if a million eyes were staring, watching, judging her. She could have torn her mother's hair out for forgetting something so important, and she kicked herself for letting her guard down and not double checking.

The fat booklet was full of triple copies of passes in white, yellow, and pink for each quarter of the year. Only a few had been torn out so far since the school year had only just begun. Kitty's hands shook as she considered what she might have to do. The alternative was to walk home—a much farther trip since her family moved—or wait in the office while someone called her mother. At least Mrs. Guthrie was easy to reach and Kitty wouldn't get a police escort home instead.

Kitty took a deep breath and stared at the empty signature line, letting her wish sit at the front of her mind. Her stomach buzzed and her eyes felt dry. Her heartbeat hammered between her ears, mixing into a wild chorus of glee, hope, anxiety, and despair from everyone around her. The far out something listened as she wished or prayed.

Please add my mom's signature.

Kitty recalled the loopy scribble her mom only ever used for signing things. She remembered how the top of the 'L' in her first name was never quite as fluid a loop as the bottom. Kitty blinked hard. When she looked again the name Lydia Guthrie was on the pass. She tore off the white and yellow copies and stuffed the booklet back into her bag. Then she handed the copies to the bus driver with a smile.

"Mhmm, take a seat," the older woman said as she hole-punched the copies and placed them on a stack of other passes.

Kitty climbed past students' feet and bags to the three-seater where Becka waited, flailing her arm. Kitty slid in past her and sat beside the window.

"Took ya long enough," Becka said. "I thought I was gonna have to start talking to numnbuts Jennifer Crazy."

Kitty smacked Becka's arm and peeked over the bus seat. Behind and across was a girl alone in the two-seater, but never without company. She batted her long lashes and threw back her head with twinkling laughter at one of her own jokes. There was a lot of time between Becka making fun of someone like Jennifer Casey and once making fun of someone *with* Jennifer. Kitty still got along with her well enough, but neither Becka nor April seemed to want to give her the time of day. Kitty understood that people and situations could change. She understood that painfully well. That didn't mean they couldn't still be friends.

Kitty sat back down. "She's not as bad as you make her out to be."

"Ha! All that perfume made her brain shrink. If there was anything there to start."

"Becka, not cool. Just because you two grew apart doesn't mean—"

"Right. Whatevs. What's she doing on our bus anyway? She's a Crest kid."

Kitty shrugged. "Gemma isn't. She's probably going to her house for the weekend."

"Huh. Speaking of that, April hasn't called for a party weekend in a while. Maybe after Homecoming. And we can sneak Fabio's pizza. Or just go to Fabio's and hide in that little broken booth. All of that sounds more fun than all the homework I'm not gonna do."

The girls laughed.

The bus finally rolled out of the long drive and through the streets of the Crest with its tall, historic looking houses, curling stone driveways, and beautiful, unnecessary gates. April lived among those streets with the other elite of Glade Crest. The bus turned onto Main Street and left the pristine safety net of the Crest to where the houses became a little shorter, the yards a little smaller, but worked to be just as vibrant green with smiling little porcelain gnomes. A lot of families began hanging their autumn decor like wreaths of green mixed with reds and gold. Decorative pumpkins sat on porches or lined the edges of lawns. Dogs yipped for attention or curled up at their owners' feet while the families sat to dinner or watched TV.

These were the familiar sights to Kitty. The swarming trees reaching across sidewalks, dropping leaves into colorful patches as if they had a plan for how they should fall, and the crisp clear air always dragging the earthy smell of someone's fresh cut lawn were the gut wrenching sensations Kitty longed for again. How could something be so wonderful and so terrible all at once? It all made her sick with jealousy.

As Becka got into an argument with one of her classmates two rows ahead, Kitty let herself sulk for a moment, taking in her old haunts of the Slope. One street peeling off of Main led to her favorite pizzeria where she, April, and Becka still met up on weekends when Kitty had time. Lately she had been too busy with volunteering and Homecoming plans to get there often, but even when she could, she could only afford a plain slice and a small soda. She made sure to order only after April and Becka had moved down the counter to hand money to the cashier.

Another stretch of road caused a collective inhale from at least half of the students on the bus. On one side of the road was a high fence blocking a section of forest, the northern tip of the Glade Crest Reservation. On the opposite side was a lonely looking mansion with dark panels and roofing, gutters laced in vines, and windows with drawn, unmoving curtains. It was the last house until Main Street curled back around past the reservation. Legend had it that Mrs. Sommers who lived in that mansion was a witch who cursed the air and anyone who breathed it in. Anyone who believed—and Kitty didn't like to take chances with curses—held their breath until they reached the end of the block where Main Street turned.

Laughs and accusations of who got cursed by the Old Witch flew around the bus, but Kitty's eyes caught on to the next street off of Main. The bus slowed to let some students out, and Kitty could see another small street leading off of the first, a dead end to a cul-de-sac with a sweet little blue cottage house sitting at the bend. There were so many fond memories at that house, all of Kitty's birthday parties, sleepovers with April, Becka, and Jennifer, climbing the sturdy tree out front that reached higher than the roof when she lived there, but the new owners had sheared it down to a stump. But all of the fondness was broken up by other memories like her mom crying or yelling at no one for a long time.

Kitty's eyes felt glued to the corner of the street, and her insides turned frosty. Her life in the Slope was simple and kind, and then suddenly her dad was gone and everything fell apart. They packed up what could fit in an apartment, and they moved to the Valley. The sleepovers stopped, the summers were marked by whirring fans instead of breezy barbecues, and Kitty was stuck in her new home taking care of both her mother and her little sister. At first she wanted to stay outside of the apartment as often as she could, still meeting up with her friends or finding excuses to stay late at school, but her mom was even less okay than she was, so Kitty took charge until her mom became better again.

Kitty sighed and rested her head on the window. *I just wanna go home...*

But I am home. Kitty jumped at the creeping thought in her head. It sounded just like her, and it was a familiar feeling, but it was so cold. *He can't just walk away from his family.*

A phantom haze in the shape of a tall man blurred her view of the lonely street corner, the smooth brown hair, the muscular arms, but he was turned away. He was frozen in time, right on the cusp of turning to face her, but never committing, always regarding her with his disappearing back.

What's taking the bus so long?

She partially pleaded with the bus to keep moving, to take her away from that hurt.

I don't have to go anywhere...

A few blares of a siren outside broke Kitty's reverie and drew the attention of everyone on the bus. Their whispers were loud, some shocked, some giggling and excited. Most of Becka's body was leaning into the aisle. Kitty kneeled on the seat and looked over students' heads, twisting one way or another as the bus driver opened the doors again. Heavy feet clunked on the steps until a tall man in a navy blue uniform appeared and glanced around the bus. Something about the police officer gave Kitty a terrible chill. She could only stare as the officer stepped forward, his dark uniform making him look like a walking shadow. He was a heavyset man with a no-nonsense grimace under his mustache that threatened to take over his entire face. He took off his cap and began addressing the bus driver.

Everyone watched in tense silence as the bus driver pulled out a stack of mostly crumpled bus passes, a fat wad of white and yellow slips with scribbles of parents' signatures. The driver licked her thumb and sorted through the stack, pulling out a half inch thick portion of it, the ones on the bus for the late route. Kitty's skin felt clammy, and something in her gut told her to duck her head or dive for the emergency exit in the back. She couldn't understand where it was coming from; she certainly hadn't done anything wrong.

"Maybe somebody is sneaking on the bus," Becka whispered. "They're gonna get nailed for that!"

The officer skimmed the stack, then held one of the slips in his meaty hand and nodded at the bus driver before turning back to the students.

"This is a standard procedure by the Glade Crest Police Department," the officer said as if he were lecturing them at a school assembly. "I'm Officer Bryant. You were all taught about the Student Protection Act in class, right?" He received a low rumble of acknowledgement. Kitty knew the law well. She had to become very familiar with it when she started staying late for Homecoming meetings so she wouldn't run the risk of dragging her mom out of work to pick her up. It was especially important to know when she asked student volunteers to stay late as well. The tightness in her stomach worsened.

"We take the law seriously around here," Officer Bryant continued. "Students' protection is one of our highest priorities. With a recent string of delinquent behavior, we need to make sure no one here is disobeying the law and getting themselves into trouble. Now any troublemakers better watch yourselves. I may not catch you today, but rest assured you will get caught. Forging a parent's signature is no laughing matter. Now can I please see Ms...Kitty Guthrie."

Kitty nearly fell off the chair as she gasped and lost her footing. More mumbles flew around the bus. Kitty may not have been the most popular girl at school, but she made a name for herself, especially since she took on the responsibilities of Homecoming. She got good grades and took her work seriously—some liked to call her student soldier—but this wasn't what she wanted. Becka looked at her with a mix of shock, awe, and pride.

"Kitty, what did you do?" she hissed.

"Nothing! I swear!"

The officer was quickly standing in front of the two girls, looking between them. "Ms. Guthrie?" Kitty gulped, but stood up to a round of "Oooooooh". Officer Bryant directed her to grab her backpack and follow him. Kitty stared at the officer's back, refusing to make eye contact with any of the jeering students around her. She wanted to argue, to prove that she would never do something like forge her mother's signature. And how would they even know?

Instead, Kitty silently made her way off of the bus behind Officer Bryant. He pointed to the sidewalk right behind where the black police car was parked and ordered, "Stand there."

Kitty did as she was told, painfully aware that Officer Bryant hadn't sent the bus on its way yet. He checked her student ID, tossed it back so quickly she fumbled with it, and went through the rest of her bus pass slips, the regular and the carbon copies. He seemed at least somewhat satisfied to see them blank.

"Where are your folks?"

Kitty opened her mouth to answer, but something about this man made her hands shake as she pasted them to her sides. She wasn't afraid of police officers mostly because she didn't do anything wrong. They were around to stop bad guys, not student soldiers. More than that, the man's presence shook her to the bone. There was a coldness like the one in her thoughts. His eyes were muddy brown, but as he approached, the light played tricks and made the color shift to something darker.

"I said, where are your folks?" The officer spat out each word.

"At home. I mean, my sister is at home and my mom is at work. But there's a babysitter so she's not alone, I promise. I have to let the babysitter go home."

The officer sighed. "So mom is at work. Where's your dad?"

Kitty's eyes dropped, and she only shrugged. Officer Bryant responded with another sigh.

"Why don't you come along with me?" He pointed to the car where the lights continued to flash and spin.

Kitty shoved her ID back in her pocket, not realizing she was also stepping back from the man. A number of

23

fears scrolled through her thoughts. Her mom would get in trouble. She would get in trouble. What would happen to her sister? Was she going to jail? Somewhere in her she knew she was overreacting, but somewhere deeper, in some gut instinct, she only felt fear as her heartbeat drummed between her ears.

The officer's voice lowered to nearly a growl, not at all the same charming voice he used in front of the students on the bus. "Come on, kid. Get in the car. Don't make me ask again." Officer Bryant held a thick hand out to Kitty. Finally she walked towards him. She thought he was going to shove her into the back of the car like on those TV shows, but he made her stand on the sidewalk and face away from him. He gave slow commands to stand still and spread her legs just past shoulder width apart. He lifted her arms and told her to keep them up where he left them. At his first touch around her chest, her muscles took over, and she started to run like she meant to. He grabbed her arm, and she clawed at it like a caged animal. "Please just let me go home!"

"Cut that crap out!" He yanked her back. She tripped and slammed against the sidewalk.

"Hey! She didn't do anything that bad!" Becka called from the bus window. The bus driver shouted something, but her voice was lost among other students whispering and sneering.

"She's in huge trouble!"

"I didn't think Kitty could break the law!"

"I knew she was so Valley," said Jennifer's friend Gemma. Kitty felt hot tears pool around her eyes and slide down her nose as she wished the ground would swallow her whole. Her stomach buzzed and her eyes dried, but a cold gust swept over her, killing that panicked wish in her mind and replacing it with something calmer, but heavy. Her body sank deeper into it as Officer Bryant spoke.

"You're gonna go home, but you need to understand something first." He bent over and pressed Kitty's arms down over her back with more than enough pressure to stop her from moving again. His hot breath rustled her hair beside her ear, and her skin exploded with goosebumps. "There are some nasty folks out there, you understand me? We've got rules for a reason. We've got to keep you safe because you can't take care of yourself. You're just a kid. But you make it difficult when you do dumb things like break the laws that keep you safe. Now I'm sorry I had to be a little forward with you, but I don't want to see you part of our real scared-straight program, you understand? Speak up."

"Y-yes, sir," Kitty said. She felt as small as an ant. Her wet cheek was crushed into the cement.

"Good. You seem like you've got a good head on your shoulders. Maybe you oughta keep away from people who call themselves your friends if they ask you to do something dumb or dangerous. No need to make waves. You understand?"

Kitty quickly nodded. Then she remembered to answer, "Yes sir."

"Okay, good." He slowly guided her to her feet with his meaty arm, keeping at least a foot of distance between them. "Behave. Follow the rules. You'll be fine, kid."

Kitty's entire body shook as Officer Bryant patted her down from under her arms, down her sides, and all the way to her sneakers. He continued between her legs where

April had taken the measurement for the inseam of a new pair of pants. She winced whenever the officer touched her. Maybe he thought she was going to run because he would remind her not to move and squeeze whatever limb he was checking.

"Alright. In you go. I'm taking you to your mother. Where's she at?"

Kitty gave the officer the exact address of Beautician Magicians, one of several salons on Main Street, and began babbling their store hours and special discounts until he scolded her to shut her mouth.

He opened the door for her and guided her inside with one hand always on her shoulder. Kitty bit her bottom lip trying not to cry as she crawled across the black vinyl. It squeaked and puffed as she planted herself on the far side of the car from the officer's seat. After finally waving the bus along, Officer Bryant got into the car, and they sped off. Kitty tucked her head against her bag so Officer Bryant wouldn't see her crying. She held her breath until the mechanical chirps from his radio could cover her sniffling.

The streetlights were brighter through the window as they reached the busier streets of the Valley. The officer parked in front of the building, blocking the cars in the white painted spots. He ushered Kitty to the front door. Immediately, a woman with kinky black hair peeking from a colorful scarf was there. Her plump body was dressed in a stylish black sweater and matching black pants. She gasped as her eyes fell on Kitty.

"Oh Lord in Heaven, what is this about?"

"I need to speak to Lydia Guthrie," said Officer Bryant.

Mrs. Charles, the store owner, wasted no time running

back into the busy salon and returning with a woman who was nearly two steps ahead of her in a blind panic. Mrs. Guthrie was peeling white plastic gloves from her hands and shoving them into the pocket of her black apron. Her messy dark bun was falling apart from beneath her floral scarf. She fished through her wallet with fumbling fingers to show the officer her driver's license with a number matching Kitty's student ID badge. The panic switched to relief and then melted into fury as the officer explained what happened.

"Forged a signature?" Mrs. Guthrie exclaimed. "Why in the world—? Sir, that doesn't even begin to make sense. My daughter would never do that."

"Ma'am, sometimes kids leave passes at home and borrow from a friend. Less than careful bus drivers don't always catch a quickly scribbled signature. They think it doesn't cause any harm, but it's a slippery slope. Children sometimes don't realize a proper signature needs to reach all three layers of carbon copy, and yours consistently have. Until this one."

Mrs. Guthrie looked down at Kitty, the anger mixing with disappointment. "I signed your pass this morning."

Kitty didn't say anything, choked up by her own disappointment.

Office Bryant jotted something on a notepad clipped to his pants and tore a page off, handing it to Mrs. Guthrie. It looked like the carbon paper used for her bus pass. Mrs. Guthrie's face was beet red as she thanked the officer through gritted teeth and apologized for the trouble.

When he left, she spun around to face her daughter. "Sit down. Do your homework. That's it. On my break I'll take you home."

Kitty didn't argue, afraid she would say things she would later regret. She plunked herself in one of the seats in the waiting area as far from chattering ladies as she could get while her mom went back to her client. She might have wished herself away, one of the wishes she had little success with, but that cold, powerless feeling lingered in her belly and kept her where she was commanded to be.

Three

Kitty couldn't focus on homework as she sat in the bright salon. She kept getting distracted by the perfumed shampoos and whatever gossip the ladies in the waiting area were sharing as if she hadn't done this same thing a thousand times already. Then the clients chimed in, and then the stylists. Everyone had some story to tell about a friend of a friend, and no one minded how expertly these women could talk with a pair of scissors dancing in their hands.

"I swear I thought that boy had more sense," a heavyset woman in Mrs. Guthrie's chair was saying. It was her tenth complaint about her son. Kitty was starting to tell the clients apart just by voice while her eyes were glued to her phone and the game level she couldn't beat. "Yeah, he got some problems at school. I get it. But he ain't never tried to hurt nobody before. Then outta nowhere, bam! He's waving a knife around the grocery story 'cause they won't take some old coupon for cereal?"

Kitty let her eyes wander up for a minute. She hated when people lived up to Valley stereotypes.

"He did all that for a little food?" Mrs. Guthrie asked, eyes still on the woman's shining hair as she flattened a section across her scalp and set it with a pin. "He knows he can come by here any time if he needs some money."

"I been tellin' him that. I said to him, 'Marcus, we got a family everywhere we go. We got a blood family and then another family that found their way to us through God's good grace. Just like you, Lydia. You got your beautiful girls and you got us through Ms. Constance and church. Marcus knew that. I don't know how he ended up like that."

A few people shook their heads at the woman's story.

An hour and a half passed with Kitty accomplishing nothing. She was scrolling through Friendville on her phone, ignoring messages from Becka, when her mother cleared her throat right above her.

"Let's go, Kitty. I've got twenty minutes before my next appointment, and you need to relieve the sitter." She looked much calmer, but her tone revealed the smoldering beneath the surface.

Kitty threw her bag over her shoulder and followed her mother out without catching anyone's eye, but she could feel the stares drilling holes in her back.

The car ride was short and silent. Mrs. Guthrie didn't ask any questions or continue scolding her, but she also didn't play the radio or pop a CD into the ancient disc player. The quiet made Kitty restless; it felt like the calm before the storm. Surely her mom would be furious about having to pay Claudine for the extra hours with Edith and whatever punishment Officer Bryant doled out.

Kitty occupied herself by pretending to look through her overstuffed backpack, careful not to tweak her wrist any worse. Her finger grazed something vaguely familiar, the corner of something rectangular covered in smooth paper. She started reaching for it when the car stopped. They were parked in front of a tall gray building that matched four neighboring buildings. Each was weathered and stained with dirt and graffiti tags near the metal fire escapes running down their sides.

Mrs. Guthrie turned around in her seat to look back at Kitty. "So," she said.

Kitty fidgeted with her bracelet beneath her sweater sleeve. "So?"

Her mother let out a sigh that seemed to deflate her anger into exasperation. "Kitty, I need to understand what happened today. I don't want to believe you're out causing trouble."

"So don't believe it. It's not true," Kitty snapped. She stepped out of the car, hoping the conversation could end right there, but the driver's side door opened shortly after. Kitty didn't let herself stop moving even as her mother's long stride let her catch up in a heartbeat.

"Kitty, help me understand then. Why did you sign my name on your pass? What happened to the one I signed for you?"

Kitty felt the words on the tip of her tongue, pure frustration at her mother's seemingly innocent concern when, once again, she let her daughter down and she had no idea. Instead, Kitty kept her mouth shut and walked on.

Mrs. Guthrie held Kitty's shoulders and gently turned

her around, crouching to be at eye level. Kitty stared closely at the small scuff on her boot. "Kitty Eleanor, listen to me. Everyone makes mistakes, and that's how we learn. It's alright if you forgot the pass or lost it. You can be honest with me, but to do something like this...I don't want to see you get mixed up in a bad crowd."

"What, like Marcus Fields? You really think I'm gonna start stabbing people?"

Mrs. Guthrie sighed. "I just want you to be safe. You've always been smart, now I need you to be safe. I hope you know I do my best, but you have to understand how it looks to have my daughter brought to my work by the police. People talk. People judge. And we're good people, no matter where we live." As Kitty kept her eyes on her shoes, her mother let go of her and stood up straight. If she sighed any more, Kitty thought she might completely deflate. "Maybe I shouldn't have let you do all of this Homecoming stuff. Maybe it's too much stress."

Kitty gawked. "Let me? You didn't care if I worked on Homecoming! You don't have a clue what I'm doing half the time! I only told you about it because I needed my late passes booklet. You couldn't even do that!"

"Excuse me?"

"I signed the pass because you didn't! If I didn't fix your mistake, I would've been stuck at school!"

Mrs. Guthrie's cheeks reddened and her jaw set. Her voice smoldered like popping coals. "I have never forgotten something like a way to get my child home from school. I know I signed your pass. I did it last night when I got home. So you can lie to your teachers and your bus drivers, but remember that I pay for it with fines." She pulled out the crumpled slip Officer Bryant handed her. There was a large number scribbled across it.

"Well when I needed to give it to the bus driver, it was blank! Maybe you only thought you signed it because that's what a good mother would do!"

She watched her mother's mouth flop open and shut with a sick satisfaction that she knew she would regret once the ringing in her ears stopped. All she could see was red. The relief of screaming loud enough for some of the window lights to flicker on eased the tension on her chest in that moment.

She deserves it! She's a big fat screw up! voiced a part of her that burst from hiding. *I deserve better!*

Without another word, Mrs. Guthrie stormed back to her car. She slammed the door shut, and the car screeched out of the parking lot. Kitty felt her bottom lip tremble, and she wished she could stop it. As she tucked that hideous voice away, all that was left was regret. Soon hot tears spilled down her cheeks. She ran the rest of the way around her building and looked up at where the ladder to the fire escape was hooked ten feet over her head.

The screen for wishing fell over her scratchy eyes. The ladder jolted and dropped with a rusty whine. Kitty leaped for the lower rungs and climbed, being very careful of her twisted wrist. Her feet carried her three steps at a time to the seventh floor landing by her bedroom window. Kitty forced the window up, threw her backpack into the room, and crawled in after.

The bedroom was small, but spotless. Kitty's purple bed sheets and comforter were tucked in, slightly stretching the wide-eyed cartoon cat faces. Her desk was covered in small picture frames and neat stacks of notebooks, and the rolling chair sat neatly beneath. The sliding closet doors were open a crack, showing a few of the denim skirts and skater dresses she picked from that morning. Beside the head of the bed was a small wooden nightstand and a lamp with a fake crystal chain that lightly clinked against a picture frame as Kitty dropped onto the bed. She fell face first into her pillows, screaming until her lungs burned. Then she pushed herself up, took another breath, and screamed into the pillows again.

Kitty flopped over and lay in bed, staring up at the plain white ceiling. For a long while her mind was blank. She only heard vague static of words that didn't translate from the living room television through her shut bedroom door. At some point she knew she would have to get up and relieve the babysitter. A little part of her wanted to keep Claudine for long enough to make her mom pay for another hour of her time. She turned her head to find the small digital clock on her desk. It was nearing a quarter to eight. Fifteen more minutes and...

With a frustrated sigh, Kitty sat up and pulled her backpack onto the bed with her. She fished for her key ring that had the key to the small lock box in her mother's room. For a moment she felt a terrible resentment again. If they had a normal family, Kitty wouldn't have so many keys to so many important things. She could be with April and Becka on a Friday night. Kitty tossed her bag aside, and the small wrapped box slid out. She paused, staring at it and the bent note attached to it.

Will. The boy knew her secret yet she didn't know who he was. Kitty couldn't resist. She tore open the wrapping and removed the lid of the box. She cocked her head to the side and lifted a thin tablet, discarding the wrapping. The glass screen was spotless and reflected Kitty's puffy eyes and tousled hair back at her. The casing was white, but she couldn't see any logo or brand name. All she saw were too many ports, and she couldn't tell which would charge it.

As a green notification light flashed, Kitty realized the tablet had to have a charge already. She swiped her finger over the perfectly clean surface. The screen shone bright in her dark room, nearly blinding her.

Squinting until her eyes adjusted, Kitty saw what looked like a home screen setup and icons that looked like internet browsers and search folders. One sounded familiar: Initiate Resources. Will's note mentioned it. One had a leaf icon and read Family Tree. Another that caught her eyes said Spell Diagram Search Engine, while another said Saved Oration Shortcuts.

Kitty paused for a breath.

Spells...

Magic!

She was holding a computer's worth of information on all of the weirdness from the last nine months wrapped up neatly with a great big bow. Every dream and nightmare that fueled some wish, the high of sensing so much more than her own body and mind, the terror of that coldness when she wanted to wish for something terrible to happen, there it was.

Kitty noticed an icon at the top right of the screen pulsing to the flicker of the notification light. It looked like a globe with a red thumbtack sticking out of it.

Hesitantly she tapped it, and the browser opened to

reveal a map of the city of Glade Crest with a tiny pinprick of light sitting within a sea of grayish rooftops. When she touched the light, the map zoomed in on a city block that Kitty recognized. Garden Avenue. It wasn't far from where April lived. The spot of light was reading off some kind of code in those same jittery symbols like music notes mixed with a foreign language. The longer she stared at it, the more her lips moved to spell out something that was felt more than spoken

"Will?" she finally said to no one. Whatever that line of coding was, it was about Will.

Next to the light was a word bubble icon with three bouncing dots. It looked like the incoming message symbol when Kitty chatted with Becka and April on Friendville. Kitty touched it, and it expanded to fill half of the screen. A message scrolled across.

> If you're reading this, you figured out how to read a map. Good job! If you need anything, let me know.
>
> -Will

Will seemed to be the way to finally get some answers, but, thrilling as the thought was, Kitty wasn't sure she was ready to run off and meet strangers in the middle of the night. She wanted to find some of her own answers. This was far too complicated to be a prank, but her wrist reminded her that she didn't want to walk into any more trouble.

Kitty's palms felt sweaty, but still she tapped the icon

that read Initiate Resources and watched as a bright window popped up and filled the screen. Words scrolled into place.

> *Welcome, KITTY ELEANOR GUTHRIE, to your Magical Harnessing Device. In the following chapters, you will find details on the history and purpose of embarking in magic oration, the evolution of spells and curses, how to properly harness magic energy using your device, as well as the correct implementation of magic via spell diagrams to oversee adjudications.*

There was that word again: magic. Kitty noticed highlighted text that looked like hyperlinks. History sounded important, but boring. Curses weren't anything she wanted to deal with; she wasn't a witch. She definitely wanted to know more about the diagrams that popped up in her dreams.

Kitty tapped the link over the words 'spell diagrams'. A tiny preview screen appeared above the words with an excerpt from the section. Kitty tapped again and watched the text blink out and reappear on a much further page.

She started to read.

> *A Magistrate's most implemented tool is magic. It is what separates influential Quotists from Magistrates. At its heart, magic is a conversation with the target. Magistrates create well prepared arguments to discuss the reasons for change, change being a constant within the universe, but in order to do so requires precision and understanding*

of the task set before you. This is called Oration. Magic diagrams create the argument and channel the influence to execute successful dictation of intent. The power to influence both sentient and inanimate life is the blessing and the responsibility of a Magistrate. One must be mindful, however, that both spells and curses can influence the universe via argumentation.

It has been so since the first days of the <u>natural state of being</u>. Others have called upon Magistrates and influential Quotists for adjudication of conflict. Magistrates continue this process where their fellows cannot grasp deeper dangers from those who don't only passively influence the constant change in a direction against the natural state of being, but also those who actively aggress upon the natural state of being.

The most important factor in an influential argument to change an entity into something it was not is receiving consent from said entity. No spell oration can be debated without consent from the target entity, although the heart of a curse diagram ignores or actively negates one's consent. One cannot force another to hear what one says or do what one does without threat of violence.

Kitty's eyes were starting to blur, and her tongue felt thick trying to read and reread some of the words she didn't understand. She set the tablet down for a moment and pulled up a dictionary web page. She typed in 'adjudication'.

"Like a judge," she said as she skimmed the first

few entries. "A magic judge. That could be fifteenth level awesome. I could sentence Mrs. Smith to jail for being a capital B." Kitty turned back to the paragraph, looked up a few more new words, and then stopped as she saw another piece highlighted. The natural state of being. It sounded ancient as if these magic judges had been around forever and no one knew. Curiosity led her to tap the link. Another few blocks of text appeared from near the beginning of the entire document.

So long as there has been life in our universes, there has been conflict. Scarcity—Kitty searched the word—*created need for resolution. Peace, collaboration, and kinship were the most fruitful tactics. It is the natural state of being for interaction among entities. When acted upon by an opposing force, it is subject to change with time. Peace is violated by aggressive forces, those that would seek pure strength to dominate, both strength of physical form and boundless will.*

However, this never negates the natural state of being. It is ever present and needs tending and protection. The first entities to sit together among this power became Its Magistrates—wisemen who could turn the worlds' hearts back to their natural state. They could influence the world around them so long as they were permitted to do so or to defend themselves from any <u>entities</u> that would harm them or their work to maintain the natural state. This power is the antithesis of force. Vitae.

A wave of warmth flooded Kitty's mind as she read the strange name. It was powerful and terrifying, but also nurturing and kind. It was the feeling every time she made a real wish, the lingering feeling in a few happy memories that suddenly trailed through her mind. Now it had a name. Kitty found herself longing to feel that way all the time, to flip the name and the sensation around her tongue, and she wanted others to understand how nice it felt. There was happiness in those words. Peace.

Kitty typed the word 'antithesis' into her online dictionary. Direct opposite. She wanted to know who was dumb enough to fight against that motherly power that seemed to bring nothing but good. She tapped twice on the word entities. It brought her to a new chapter of the text. Every word it described left her feeling nothing but dread and horror.

> *Those who succumb to the force against the natural state are driven by nothing else than their own desires. They fall prey to the yearning for safety through control through any means. As is the way of aggression. These become the* Hostilia *who will stop at nothing for satisfaction.*

Kitty shivered. That word...Hostilia. It was the polar opposite of what serenity had been swirling in her chest. Memories of anger and losing her cool flashed through her mind, but surely she wasn't one of those Hostilia. She wasn't perfect, but she liked to think she was a good person. She sought out some telling detail in the pile of information that would prove she could be one of the Magistrates and not one of the Hostilia. There was another link. This one jumped a few paragraphs, and one word stood out. It wasn't written in English, but rather it swirled in the dancing symbols she had come to know when she dreamed of wishes—magic. These letters weren't the soft blue lights that made miracles happen. They were black, sharp tick marks that pulsed in rage.

> *Ever present, as Magistrates assume their duties, is the power bred from the aggression against the natural state. It is the ever lurking enemy that sways the hearts of the best of men. Whether you see It directly or sense It spying from the shadows of spell diagrams, seeking to create a curse, It is present, feigning to be as natural as the original state of being. It is desire for control. It is assumed authority. It demands devotion with vain promises or closed fists.*
>
> *Nefas*

The air in the room pulsed and screeched. The heartbeats beyond her walls were ragged, and cries tore at her heart. Voices begged to make others see reason—their own reason—with lies or with fists. Kitty slammed the tablet against her lap to hide the screen. Her heart sped out of control, body coated in a cold sweat as she buried her face in her hands. That word was so much worse than when she read Vitae's name. It was every fear that brought her nightmares to life. All of the sneers and whispers from anyone who knew her from the Slope. It was her mother in the early dark days after her dad walked away and

41

the shattering of putrid glass. It was screeching tires and screams.

Kitty held her stomach and tumbled off of the bed. She kneeled next to her garbage pail, waiting for the dry heaving to stop. Finally, her breath returned. Kitty rolled back and leaned against the wall. She blindly swiped at the screen to clear it before looking down again.

Kitty's heart leaped into her throat as her door swung open. The metal knob bounced against the wall making her picture frames shake, and a plush toy toppled off a high shelf of her bookcase.

"Kitty!" her little sister sang. Edith hopped into the room with her legs pressed together and her wrists bent forward like a rabbit. Her hair was a mess of golden brown curls tied up into two knots on either side of her head. She turned to find Kitty on the floor. Her enormous eyes darkened for a moment. She nearly tackled Kitty as she wrapped her petite arms around her older sister. A lot of her graceful features came from their mother while Kitty had the misfortune of taking most of her dad's traits. Kitty was shorter for her age and a little blockier than her sister and mother. Before long Edith would be eleven, and more of her mother would show in her. Unfortunately, she would have no idea how lucky she was.

"I'm okay, sweetie," Kitty said as she pet the back of her sister's head like rocking a fussy toddler.

Kitty looked up as she heard someone else walking in much more calmly. Claudine Benoit rested a hand on one hip and was shaking her head with a good natured smile. "You could've come in through the front door so I knew you were home."

"Sorry, Claudine," Kitty said. "I just got here. Mom dropped me off. Long story."

"Okay. But if you're here then I'm gonna bounce. Could you tell your mom to CashApp the money to me? Later, ladies! Don't worry about getting up, Kitty. I'll let myself out. You're busy." She laughed. "Good night!"

"Bye Lala!" came Edith's muffled shout into Kitty's shoulder.

Kitty gently removed her sister. As Edith sat back, she continued to clench her eyes shut and hold her arms rounded and absurdly stiff as if a body were still there. She gritted her teeth, but giggles escaped.

"Edie…You're such a little monster," Kitty said. Edith shook her head wildly. "Yes you are." She started tickling Edith's sides as the younger girl rolled back and shrieked with laughter. "You're the littlest monster!"

Kitty pulled her sister back into her lap. Edith's eyes were rimmed with joyful tears. Just at her hair line a pale scar stretched to her ear; Kitty gave it a kiss as Edith fidgeted. "Not my bad head!"

"You do not have a bad head," Kitty told her, always trying to convince herself of the same thing. She did have a bad head, but it wasn't her fault.

It was never Edith's fault, she told herself. Each word was laced with venom, and her chest felt heavy. Visions of the accident flashed through her mind. The months in the hospital, wondering if Edith's mind would ever be the same, were the worst in her life. *It was always mine.*

Kitty was shocked from her chilling thoughts as Edith threw her arms around her neck and nuzzled her face below Kitty's chin.

"You don't have a bad head, Kitty," Edith whispered. Kitty blinked, staring off at nothing for a minute as she tried to understand what her sister said. Edith had a wild imagination like the most beautiful prison, but sometimes Kitty thought she could understand things better than anyone...like how Magistrates were supposed to.

Could they fix her?

Kitty scrubbed at her eyes to brush the sudden tears away, and she held her sister back again with a shaky smile. "Did you clean up your dinner?" she asked Edith paused for a second and then nodded her head. A cheeky grin pulled at her lips. "Edie, put your dishes away. You know better. And remember to scrape your plate." Edith blew a raspberry and stomped down the hallway. "Don't stomp! We have neighbors!" Kitty shouted after her.

With her sister distracted for at least a few minutes, Kitty picked up her tablet that had slid out of reach. She would have to skip the rest of the tutorial and find Will first. Knowing she could get answers brought back all of the questions Kitty had for almost a year. Why did she get those dreams on New Year's Eve? How did they turn out to be so real? How could she use it to help with little bruises and also broken hearts?

Before Kitty could think too much, she emptied her backpack of everything except the tablet, her phone, and her house keys. Crawling beneath her bed, Kitty slipped a folder from between the crossing metal wires of the box spring. Inside was a small stack of drawings that anyone else would have passed off as doodling. Each one had a different design, but all of them were bright blue threads knotted in different patterns and asking for different things.

A few were crayon drawings from almost a year ago. Kitty had taken the large case from her sister's room and used every shade of blue and white until they were useless nubs. She didn't remember doing it until she woke up with mounds of wax under her stained fingernails.

Kitty couldn't believe the drawing she had made. It looked exactly like the image in her head as she thought about what she wished she could do. The same thing happened a few nights later, and Kitty realized she was starting a collection of pictures that made her wishes come true.

Instead of using up her sister's colors, Kitty borrowed a box of markers from school. She buttered up the art teacher with pretend dreams of finding her inner artist. She got four extra boxes for that, but all she wanted were the blues. Every dream was more vivid and every picture was clearer until she could look at the picture while she was awake and the wish—the magic—would happen.

Kitty flipped through and pulled one of the messier scribbles from the stack. She locked her bedroom door and stared at the picture. It wasn't perfect, but it would have to do. She watched herself in a green-black space like an out-of-body experience, and wished for a second version of herself, exactly the same so no one would ever know. The rush of feelings blossomed around her as that beautiful power listened. In her heart, Kitty promised Vitae she was doing this to make things better. A second Kitty could take on the load of her extra burdens while she figured out wishes.

The wish never worked quite right before. Kitty tried to make time with April and Becka while still going to

Homecoming meetings, doing homework, volunteering, and watching her sister. Every messed up copy was different. Once the second Kitty had a hunch back. Another time, it couldn't be called a girl. As Kitty practiced, the best she got was a version of herself that was too lethargic to do much more than plop in front of the television and watch movies, so she kept that drawing.

Now that she knew what she was dealing with, Kitty was sure she could make the magic work right!

Through scratchy eyes she saw herself sewn together with blue threads. Her boots weaved into her legs which attached to her torso and chest. Her neck sprawled into a fluttering wave of her face and hair. Arms reached out and stretched. In the dream, that second Kitty started running. Now she stood a few feet away staring at Kitty with a slack jaw and dull eyes. Its unsteady lips trembled, and it grunted. The pitch slowly rose from a guttural animal to a young girl.

"Who are you?" it finally spoke. Kitty was taken aback. Her wishes never spoke to her before. It slowly cocked its head to the side, pleading.

Kitty stumbled on her words, but finally forced out, "I'm Kitty Guthrie."

The spell girl nodded. Its dull eyes stayed glued to Kitty's. "Who am I?"

"Well...um...you're a magic spell. A copy. You're just like me. Well, you are me—for just a little while." Kitty coiled her bracelet around her wrist in anxious bursts.

"I'm you?" it said. Recognition sparkled in the dummy's eyes. Then it squinted with pursed lips. "Is that all? What do you like to do for fun? What's your favorite way to do your hair? What's your favorite flavor of ice cream? Do you like your clothes? Do you miss having your friends over?" The spell girl's words popped out in a rapid fire that slowly rose in pitch as she asked more and more questions, faster and faster. Soon her voice was a whining ring; the questions were barely audible. "Do you really think mom can control herself? Do you like the doctors working with Edith? Do you want dad to come home? What would you do if you saw him again? Where do you think he is?"

"Stop it!" Kitty slapped her hands over her ears. She blinked her eyes hard. Her mind clicked like a button, a familiar feeling at the end of making a wish, and then she felt an uncomfortable pop in her chest as her bedroom returned to normal. Everything started tilting sideways, and Kitty realized she was falling. She collapsed to the ground, unable to move or twitch. Breath sputtered from her frozen lungs. She could hear heavy pounding on the door and her sister calling out.

"Are you there? Kitty!" Edith's banging stopped. Kitty could see the shadow of her feet below the door. Panic consumed her as she realized she couldn't answer. She could barely breathe let alone speak. Soon Edith's footsteps scurried down the hall.

In a few minutes Kitty's fingers flicked. The pins and needles feeling spread from her fingertips and toes until she felt like a pincushion. Slowly her muscles cooperated. and her arms and legs flapped against the cold wood floor. She rocked like an overturned turtle until she slumped onto her side. Using the bed frame for leverage, Kitty dragged herself off of the floor gasping. "Okay, no changes this time."

When her breath steadied, she took the diagram

drawing into her shaky hands and let her mind clearly remember the tired version of herself. Another haze of green appeared, and another Kitty stitched itself together without debate.

The dummy blinked a few times, and a hint of life filled her. She yawned and stretched. "I could use a nap."

As Kitty stood upright, she could feel her limbs gently tingle as her energy slowly returned. Wishes had a cost, she knew, but never had the cost been so great as that last mistake. She eased herself onto her wobbling feet.

"Napping is fine," Kitty mumbled. Her lips were still numb. "Just watch Edith, please."

"Sure th—" The dummy interrupted itself with a drawn out yawn. "Sure thing. How about another exciting showing of Hop-Along Princess?"

The dummy dragged its feet to the door and struggled with the locked knob for a moment. Then it shuffled into the hallway to a delighted shriek from Edith.

Kitty stood in front of her window where the mesh curtains wafted, as if daring her, beckoning her, to take those final steps into some new kind of danger. It also promised her the answers to everything she ever wanted. She threw the curtains aside and crawled through the window.

Four

From that high up on the fire escape, Kitty could see a fair amount of the city glittering with little yellow lights. A brief wind blew past her, and she clenched the pages of doodles tightly. She stared down at the top page. It was a series of jagged lines intersecting circles like a cracked dart board. On first glance, the picture was nothing more than a wild doodle, but the longer Kitty stared and concentrated on the direction of the lines, all leading to the centers of those circles, searching for a way through, she could feel pulsing through her fingertips. It was her heartbeat and so much more, softer now as the lives in the city began to wind down towards sleep for the night. Even when her wishes didn't work out like she hoped, they were always a little calmer at night.

Whispers flooded her thoughts as the green screen fell over her eyes.

Where do you want to go? What material are you landing

on? How many people are within five hundred feet of your target? Who are you helping? Why are you a Magistrate?

Kitty didn't have these answers, but before she could think to look anything up, an air of satisfaction filled her, and the questions disappeared, replaced by new ones, all waiting for answers. It was the same bombardment she faced when she tried to make this traveling wish before. The further out she wanted to go, the more questions grabbed at her heart. The very first time she made the diagram in her dream, she woke up in a cold sweat as if she ran ten miles in an instant with a monster chasing her, but was still in her room. Her first real experiment had been into her sister's room. She was a little winded, but it was simple enough. Then she tried reaching Hope Creek Church a few blocks off of Main Street. Kitty lost her balance from dizziness in the Sunday School classroom. Getting to Fabio's pizzeria in the Slope knocked her out for a few minutes. That was months ago.

This would be her farthest jump yet, but Kitty wondered if she was better prepared now that she had read some of the Initiate Resource. She tried to keep in mind who she was dealing with as the spot on the map became crystal clear in her thoughts.

I'm going to Will Cavanaugh's house. He's a Magistrate. I don't know what he looks like, but he seems like a good person because he wants to help me with—magic stuff. He lives on Garden Ave, which is only a few blocks from April Sullivan, who is fifteenth level coolness. So pretty much everybody even sort of related to this is good and wants to do good things. So please take me to Will's house. Oh! Please take me to his backyard so no one sees me! But only if no one is in the backyard.

Kitty spoke over the questions, most of which filled themselves in, but more still that fought for answers she didn't have. Some asked about the geology in this area of New Jersey and what were acceptable levels of disruption to the crust of the Earth. More wanted to know about how life forms from other locations—regional, terrestrial, interdimensional—would handle the same task. Holding the wish to try and answer felt like holding her breath after accidentally inhaling water.

She blinked hard and felt a rush of warmth zip through her body. Her rapid heartbeat didn't blend as smoothly as it had before with the pulse of everything nearby as the world seemed to take in a sharp inhale. When she opened her eyes, her view of the city was blocked. Partially cutting through the metal railing of the fire escape was a wide ring, pure black and about six feet high. The edges were smokey and made the metal bars seem less real. It let out a cold smog.

Weirdness, Kitty tried to say, but, as she feared, her entire body seized up as if she were suddenly a block of ice, and she collapsed to the metal platform. Normally when she opened her eyes she would be standing where she wanted to be, or at least she was falling over in the place she wanted to reach with a nasty headache. She hoped Will had answers. She was already tired of losing control of herself when it came to wish granting.

In less time than it took her to recover from the failed copycat wish, Kitty was crawling to her hands and knees, feeling small in front of the black hole. It seemed dangerous somehow, a giant split as if the air around her balcony bent over too quickly and ripped its pants. Still, Kitty figured if it led to Will's house, then she got what she wished for. With help from the wall, Kitty dragged herself to her feet. She shoved the doodles back into her bag and walked through what she hoped was a good spell and not some witch curse.

Cold gripped her for just a moment, and in that moment Kitty was terrified that she made a terrible mistake. Nothing felt like it did with her other jumps—this was more like walking through a portal like in sci-fi movies—but for all she knew, this could have been the first time she ever did it totally right. She desperately clung to that thought as the cold dissolved into a strange lack of feeling before the magic spat her out into an ungraceful tumble onto a stretch of flat, manicured grass. The yard was twice as large or more from the lawn she had in the Slope. It led up to a towering white house and its beautiful stone slab patio with a few glass tables and umbrellas poking through their centers. There were flowerbeds to one side and a vegetable and herb garden on the other protected by a sheet of chicken wire. A wide, in-ground pool was covered with a tarp, but the white stone tiles surrounding it shimmered with moonlight.

Kitty's hands shook. She was accustomed to rich people and their fancy things; the Sullivans lived the good life. Somehow meeting a stranger who had so much made her feel uncomfortable. She didn't have much of a choice.

A few of the windows were lit including the sliding glass patio doors, but gauzy curtains blocked her view inside. She didn't want to creep around the property and get the neighbors' attention. She took the tablet out of her backpack and found the message from Will. A curling arrow below the message seemed to be her best bet for a reply button. As she clicked it, the words shrunk, and a writing window appeared with a blinking cursor. She thanked God that magic people knew what qwerty keyboards were.

Hi Will,

You said I could let you know if I needed anything so I dropped by your house. I hope that's okay.

Sincerely, Kitty

Kitty continued to burn with embarrassment as seconds stretched on while she waited for something to happen. Whether Will would pop up as suddenly as she did or just reply to her, she had no idea. Her ear tingled as she heard a quiet beep that could have been mistaken for a high pitched bug flying by. Then she noticed three wiggling dots below her own message. Soon more words appeared.

You here now?

Kitty stared at the words, heart pounding. Her mother would kill her if she knew she was out meeting some boy, but it was definitely too late to turn back. Kitty replied.

Yeah. In your backyard.

Got it. Hang tight.

Kk

Kitty hugged the tablet to her chest while she waited in the quiet suburban evening. No cars were speeding around. No loudly talking guys were lighting cigarettes in the parking lot. The air smelled like the flowers, herbs, and freshly mowed lawn instead of gasoline and hours old hot dogs spinning in a corner store. Just as Kitty was wondering if she might have met Will had her family stayed in the Slope, the patio doors slid aside. A boy a few inches taller than her stepped out and shut it behind him. He turned back to her with a grin.

Kitty's heart sank as she locked onto his piercing blue eyes nearly blocked by his sandy bangs. She knew a silver watch was surely sitting on his wrist below the cuff of his plaid button down shirt.

"You're Will?" Kitty asked, barely keeping her jaw from dropping.

"If my mom had a say, I think she wanted me to be a Theodore." Will shrugged. He plopped into a chair beside one of the patio tables. "What's up, Kitty? Good to actually meet you."

Kitty tentatively approached the table where Will made himself comfortable. She sat on the very edge of the chair, feet tensed to bolt. If he was friends with Dino the clown, who knew what he could do?

"Gotta say," Will said again as Kitty finally sat, "you being less bossy is a much better look."

Kitty gaped. "Well I need to be bossy if I ever expect work to get done."

"Relax! Everything looked great. Your party is gonna be great, but that's not important now." Him saying that only made her more annoyed with him. That party was the most important thing. "You're here about magic. How's the MHD working out for you?"

"MHD?" Kitty asked.

"Magical Harnessing Device. Did you look at the Initiate Resources? It's a solid place to start. Good information for beginners."

"I...started looking through it, yeah."

"So you had questions or what?"

"I—I guess I don't—" Kitty paused. In her excitement to meet Will, she didn't know what she wanted to ask. She had so many questions, most that felt too personal to start with, others that were more statements than questions. She just wanted to know whatever he knew so she could do magic right instead of sudden outbursts whenever she got upset. She wanted to help the people she cared about most and, if possible, to have more hours in the day.

"How's your arm?" Will asked, looking at her right hand pressed firmly to the tablet while her other hand had a death grip on the strap of her backpack.

Kitty immediately covered her twisted wrist in her sleeve. "Fine," she said quickly. "Doesn't hurt. How did you know what I did?"

"If you know about magic, it's not too hard to sense when something is happening a few feet away from you. I thought maybe I had a wrong adjudication and you were some kind of pro. All I was told was to hand off an MHD to an Initiate. I've never seen any Mage throw down a transference oration that fast unless they were totally prepared. I guess you might've figured Dino would bust his butt."

Kitty shook her head. "I just reacted. Honestly, I didn't think I was going to reach him in time. So you do wishes slower?"

"Wishes? Ah, maybe you didn't get far enough into

the resources. Magic isn't about wishing, Kitty. It's about doing. Talking. Taking action. You have to know what you want and why you're doing all of this while keeping yourself focused on the oration you're working on. It might sound like a lot at first, but it gets easier each time. It's like building a good habit."

"Sure," Kitty said, finally taking her backpack off and sitting back in the chair. She kept her legs politely together and her hands knotted in her lap over her new device.

"How long have you been doing *wishes*?" Will asked.

Kitty thought for a moment. "About nine months. It was around New Years when my mom—well, when I needed to do anything for the first time."

"Do your folks know about it?" he asked. Kitty shook her head. "Wow. Nine months and no giveaway. Pretty sick. My dad would freak."

"My mom totally would. I don't really care what my dad would say about it. He's not around."

"Oh. Sorry about that."

Kitty shrugged it off and said, "Okay, so I'm just going to be sent home to do reading homework? Then what?"

"Well, then you decide if you want to join up with us." Will tapped the face of his watch. Kitty's scalp tingled like a slight itch, and Will held his hands forward. They didn't look different. Then he grabbed the edge of the patio table and, with one hand, lifted it from the stone as if it were a toy. Kitty sat back with wide eyes as Will lowered the table again. "We do more than that at the Alliance, but I actually really like this oration. It's a good just-in-case kind of thing so I keep it in my Shortcut folder."

Kitty's lips bobbed as she scrambled for words that

wouldn't come. A glaring light in her eyes stopped her thoughts. She heard Will's chair skid along the patio as he jumped to his feet.

"Evening, kids," a man said from behind the beam of light. Somehow the carefree tone in his voice immediately made Kitty's blood run cold.

"Good evening, officer," Will said. He stood between Kitty and the policeman who slowly approached them. "Do you need something?"

"We do, as a matter of fact," said the officer. Kitty shrank further back in her chair. Every word he spoke made her hair stand on end, and something in her gut screamed that everything about him was extremely wrong. It was the exact same feeling Kitty had when the other policeman pushed her around.

"We?" Will made a show of looking behind the Officer, past his flashlight beam that kept dancing across Kitty's eyes. "Or *royal* we?"

Thick arms wrapped around Kitty's shoulders and yanked her from the chair. The tablet clattered to the patio, and Kitty's flailing legs knocked the chair back. She shrieked until the second person slapped a hand over her mouth. As Will turned to her, Kitty saw the first man wrap his hairy arm around Will's throat with lightning speed and enough pressure to make his face redden.

"You're more trouble than you're worth," the officer behind Kitty droned in a deep voice. It was the same warning voice from earlier. Suddenly those hands felt stronger and more cruel. "Didn't I warn you not to be stupid?"

"Ma—gic!" Will choked out.

She saw his fists clenching, but Will couldn't lift his

arms past the officer's muscled grip. A small glint of blue light shone around his hands, reminding Kitty of the magic Will showed her. If he could only reach the cop's face, he could pulverize it. She had to help him break free.

"Turn that Mage," Officer Bryant said. His hot breath beside Kitty's ear made her flinch, but she tried to concentrate as the officer continued. "Or kill him if he's gonna fight too hard. This fresh meat gets to meet the Chief."

"What's he want with a kid like her anyway?" the other officer said, carelessly squeezing tighter as Will struggled.

Officer Bryant scoffed. "Don't you have your own brat? You know how emotional they can get. And she's a special little thing too. Doesn't seem like the forgery or frisking left her uncomfortable enough so I'm sure the Chief will have fun riling her up."

Kitty closed her eyes. The film of digital magic layered them. Her thoughts clouded over as she focused on that one need.

I need to free Will from the cop. She sent the desperate wish out to whomever was listening. Maybe it was Vitae. It didn't matter; they just needed to hear her. *Please let me shoot or blast or whatever it is magic can do! He's gonna choke!*

A hazy diagram appeared over her chest, peeking out from the soft tufts of cotton in her sweater. Soon it looked like a printed design that sat stiffly like her favorite old graphic tee. The questions flooded into her mind. *What is the target? How much of the primary target composition will be destroyed? Designate the distance of return to the primary's shell. Why are you a magistrate? How many life forms will be deducted from the parameters?* Kitty opened her eyes to see the blue shining ribbons over her chest.

Just get rid of those monsters!

Then she blinked. The diagram sank in. Its warmth felt nice against her clammy, tingling skin, like downing an entire mug of hot cocoa in a single gulp.

The officer in front of her was fading into a smothering blur. Kitty blinked hard, eyes still dry, but the swirling black smog around the man was still there, wrapping Will in it. The officer's pale skin creeped with pitch black veins that spread until all of him was a hulking shadow. Against her back, Kitty felt pins and needles, and she saw the same rolling darkness start to wrap around her. She tried to focus on helping Will and on that warmth that spread from her chest and down into her belly, and not on the painful memories attacking her thoughts. She kicked her now burning legs as if that would fend off pictures in her mind of sliding into grass with a little girl wrapped in her arms or Christmas ornaments shattering around an already chipped wall. Her arms started to pulse with sweeping fire as well, as if to help protect her, but the wish—the magic— was moving so slowly.

Whoever you are, get out of my head!

Don't be a numbnuts. It's only me and my thoughts. She felt herself answering her own shouts, but the words were coated with pain. And something else. Something that felt almost safe.

Kitty clenched her eyes, afraid to see more. *I said—I promised I'd be better than that, and I am!*

Kitty pushed everything in her heart against those thoughts and memories that fought her magic. It felt like a physical task to shove everything away from her. She let it reach past her thoughts and outward to the monster clinging to her, trying to drag her away. The feeling barreled past him and towards Will and the other officer. The blackness behind her eyelids became bright gray for a moment. When she opened them again, the world was a blaze of white for a second more. Angry and pained cries filled the air, and two inky black splotches burst before the explosion of light collapsed in on itself and charged back at Kitty. It struck her in the chest where the diagram had been, and with nothing left holding her, she fell to the grass.

The air whined for a minute as Kitty stared up at the dark sky. Her chest throbbed. Each limb burned and itched, but she couldn't move to do anything about it. Her heart thumped weakly, almost too tired to keep doing its job. Soft footsteps scrambled across the patio, and a silhouette leaned over her. For a moment she thought the policeman was back to snatch her up again, but this person was shorter, and he didn't feel like danger.

"Holy crap, kid," Will said, moving his bangs aside. He laid the back of his hand against Kitty's forehead. It was wonderfully cold against her burning skin. "You—are something else."

Kitty peeled her lips apart. "Did you get 'em?" she mumbled.

Will laughed. "Nope. You definitely did. I could've taken those Hostilia, but whatever oration you pulled out of your hat—holy crap!"

Kitty didn't know what he was talking about. She made a wish like she was used to doing. It was definitely more tiring than other wishes, but her mom had told her before that fear could make people do pretty big things. Will sat Kitty up. She groaned in protest and fell over against his chest. The cool touch of anything was more important than her slowly budding embarrassment.

"I think you should maybe talk to a Justice about this," Will said. He slung her backpack over one shoulder, then tucked his arm under Kitty's knees and lifted her. Now the burning in her face had much less to do with the wish she made. His chin sat right over her head as he led her to the sliding doors. She wanted to tell him to put her down or take her home. Her lips tingled and went numb as that rush of fire in her body faded.

Kitty fought to keep her eyes open as Will carried her through the house. He didn't seem to care if anyone might pass them by. He only stopped briefly as voices became clearer. A woman with a soft, charming voice was charging through a story of some social faux pas.

"Of all people to forget her pin for our annual photo, I really can't be surprised it was Regina," the woman said and laughed similarly to Will's jovial laugh. "She is the sweetest woman. I really love her dearly, but I think she needs to start making lists for our important event days."

"She can cook like no other," a man said to the music of light clanking metal on dishware. "I'll give her that much. She brought that roast to your last meeting, right?"

"She did. I think I got the recipe from her, but I'll have to double check my book."

"You did, ma," Will said, but Kitty knew it wasn't the Will holding her and carefully walking in the opposite direction of the dining room. Her tired neck couldn't turn back to try and see.

Will brought her into one of the bedrooms, well made like hers, but filled with a lot more; sports posters and pictures of friends hung on the walls, trophies and awards had places of honor on shelves, a whirring computer sat on Will's desk with an athlete jogging back and forth as the screen saver. Will laid Kitty down on the bed to which she immediately grunted in protest as the deep blue comforter hugged her.

"Oh shut it," he said as he drew the blanket around her. "Whatever you did, you smoked yourself, and I'm not letting you wander back home just to hear you collapsed and died or whatever."

Kitty wanted to roll her eyes, but she was too tired. He helped slip her boots off and placed them on the floor next to the bed right beside her backpack. He looked at her with that grin of his as if he had finished an important job.

"Coolness!" He brushed his hands together. Then he stopped and frowned. "I've got to stop hanging around with those guys so much. Anyway, you want me to call anybody. Your mom or—?"

Kitty thought she was shaking her head, but it was hard to tell when every inch of her was still numb. Will only shrugged and sat in his desk chair, doing a lazy spin before settling in front of the screen.

"When you feel better, let me know."

He unlocked his computer, but Kitty's eyes started drooping, blurring the screen. She only needed a minute to shut her eyes. Then she could leave. Just a minute.

Kitty didn't realize when her eyes had drifted shut and sleep overpowered her.

Five

In Kitty's dream, little spindly-armed monsters wearing Halloween masks of a past president attacked her. She was helpless to do anything about it. Somehow she thought scolding the monsters and putting them in time out would work like it did for Edith. Instead, the monsters sprang forward. Kitty clenched her eyes shut and started praying. Wishing. She needed to be anywhere else, to get away before the claws could make contact. She wanted everything back to normal. Just like it was before—

"Kitty! What the heck!"

Her eyes shot open in a brightly lit room.

Kitty was sitting on her knees around torn off bed covers and facing a wall unseeing. Then she remembered where she was. Will had taken her inside his house after they fought off those police officers. Kitty jumped at the touch on her shoulder. A thin black casing with gold lettering dropped from her hand. Down her pinkie finger and across her palm was a blue smear of compact clay that matched blue jagged scribbles on the wall. They flowed in a familiar way like the doodles she had been drawing for the last nine months.

"You know," Will continued with a lopsided smile, "the MHD lets you do all that on the screen so you don't mark up the walls."

"I—Sorry…" She didn't know what else to say. Kitty clasped her hands together in her lap so Will wouldn't see how they started trembling. Will sat on the bed beside her, and only then did Kitty realize he had a tee shirt tossed over his bare shoulder as if her mess interrupted him getting dressed. Her cheeks burned, but if he noticed, he didn't pay any attention as he reached towards the wall. Some of the blue smear came off on his fingers.

"I'm sure my mom won't miss this eyeliner pen. It doesn't do much for her anyway. You must be sneaky to have grabbed it without getting caught. How long have you been drawing diagrams?"

Kitty only shook her head. Her teeth clamped down on her bottom lip, and she strangled her wrists.

"Okaaay." Will stood up again and finished putting his tee shirt on. Kitty stared at the diagram she drew in her stupor. She only thought of them when she was wishing for something. The blurred symbols spoke of home. It was safe, but for some reason it still scared her. Then a wad of damp paper towels started wiping the eyeliner away. Kitty grabbed at Will's hand to do it herself, but Will kept out of reach. "Chill," he said. "You clearly have enough on your mind. I think you should talk to Leo. He's our local Liaison. I think he'd really want to meet someone who can draw diagrams out of nowhere like that."

"Is that bad?"

Will shook his head and tossed the first wad of paper towel in his trash bin. "Nah. I don't think so. I've never seen it before and I've been a Mage for two years. C'mon. It's still pretty early on a Saturday. If you want some answers, Leo has them. He can also fix your bunked up wrist."

Kitty looked between his outstretched hand and his face to see if anything about the gesture gave away a prank. This was the boy hanging around with that clown Dino yesterday after all. Yesterday. So much had happened between her Homecoming meeting and now. On the other hand, Will was the one who gave her the tablet—the Magical Harnessing Device. She finally accepted his hand, and he helped her as she slowly stretched out her cramped knees and slid off the bed.

"I'll let him know we're coming," Will said. "He's been dying to meet you."

"Me? Why?"

"You're a Magus." Will spoke as he swiped across his tablet screen and stared intently at whatever he was browsing. "He wasn't here when you first manifested any ability so now that we found you, you're his first Initiate since getting back. You're technically under his jurisdiction."

Kitty's eyes narrowed. "You're doing that on purpose, aren't you? You know I obviously don't know what you mean by any of that and you just want to hear yourself talk, huh?"

"Harsh. I'm just telling you what's going on. I don't know what you know or don't know yet. If you were a Magus worth any beans you'd have started looking this stuff up already."

"I told you I did, Mr. Know-It-All."

"Oooookay." Will shrugged with a little grin and went back to typing and swiping.

Kitty stretched her neck, rolling it from shoulder to shoulder like Coach Harris made her do in gym class. As Kitty scooped up her backpack, she felt her phone buzz. In the quiet space it sounded like a jackhammer. Kitty grabbed it before it could alert the whole house.

There were a few email notifications and some piled up text messages from April, all following the same vein.

Hey grl where r u?
Kitty r u home yet
Pls call me aspa!

Then there were seven missed calls from her mother and two voicemails. Kitty's cheeks flushed as she remembered the accusations thrown around, but ignoring her mother was never a good idea. She moved to a corner away from Will and played one of the messages.

> "Kitty—" She let out an exasperated breath that crackled through the phone. "Sweetheart please call me right away. I'm sorry about earlier. If you don't want to say anything you can ask Becka or April to call instead. I don't care. Just let me know you're okay. Okay? Okay. I love you, honey. Please call me. Okay, bye.

Kitty sighed. Her copycat should have been home to avoid that mess, but the damage was already done. She left the first of the two voicemails alone, not needing to hear the rage her mother had spewed as Kitty supposedly left her sister alone in the apartment. Kitty quickly sent a response to April's messages instead.

Im fine. I need a NQC for mom. We had a fight.

Sometimes Kitty didn't have time to explain a situation and that called for an NQC—a No Question Cover—to keep her mom from freaking out. It was a pact the girls had. Any one of them would do it for the others. They would send a cover story, and the best one would be the answer.

April responded quickly. She explained in full detail through text how Kitty's mom had called last night. Kitty started to panic until April further explained that she assured her mom Kitty was fine and wasn't mad anymore. She listed a few movies that the two of them supposedly watched as well as which movie they fell asleep watching which was supposedly why Kitty didn't return her mom's call.

Kitty held back a squeal of delight and relief. She hugged the phone, and her fingers were a blur as she sent line after line of thank you's to April.

April's next message popped up.

Y were u fighting?

Kitty's fingers hovered over the flat keyboard until she thought better of it and closed the messenger. A loud roaring from Kitty's stomach interrupted her. She held her belly with one arm as Will laughed.

"Breakfast isn't a bad idea. Sit down, would ya? I'll get you food first."

Kitty smiled gratefully.

She felt awkward to eat a full breakfast—Will's mother declared it brunch by the time Will was asking for it— of eggs, sausage, bacon, toast, and a peeled clementine as she sat on his remade feather soft bed crossed legged. She held a pristine metal fork as best as she could with a twisted wrist and carefully balanced a decorated china plate in her lap. Will sat at his desk frowning at his tablet. From over his shoulder, Kitty could see him dragging blue lines across the screen, pinching and twisting and rearranging them as his brow furrowed. She wondered if her face looked like that when she struggled to concentrate on a wish.

"C'mon, lousy transit," he mumbled.

Kitty pulled out her phone while she ate and checked her email notifications. The subject line read RE: GCJH HOMECOMING - Poster Confirmation and Important Dates. Kitty began looking through the email, her lips pursing in frustration or twisting into a relieved smile. She typed a drawn out response with every detail her teacher adviser and the others in charge needed. New questions. New ideas. New confirmations. A lot of devices auto-correcting her name to Kaitlyn or Karen. Still, it was a relief that Angela Smith didn't bother to personally respond to the email chain. That was always a pleasant surprise. She was probably busy bragging about her son and the GCJH football team's obvious victory at the Homecoming game in a few days. Her priorities weren't in line with Kitty's, but the PTO President was still the boss.

Without her checklist on hand, she had to settle for

opening up a new "window" and switching back and forth between the email and the list. Kitty was surprised she had gotten to any of her homework over the weekends since school started when most of her Saturdays were spent answering emails, cooking, and watching animated princess movies. Edith hated when Kitty didn't pay attention and sing along.

As Kitty set her fork down on her plate and pocketed her phone again, Will leaped up from his chair with a triumphant shout.

"Yes! Finally! Stupid oration. That'll be another question for Leo."

"What will?" Kitty asked.

Will just shook his head. "Just a spell diagram on the fritz or something. No worries. C'mon. You know how transits work?"

Kitty nodded as she slid off the bed and then stared at the plate in her hands. "Uh, do you want me to put this in the sink or—?"

"Seriously? Just leave it, Kitty."

"But I don't wanna make a mess."

"Just put it down!"

The power bent to Will's strength in a way Kitty had never experienced before. She felt a tingle along her skin like a small itch, but it was brief, just long enough for the air to shiver around them, curl up on itself, and then pop as they went from standing on the hardwood of Will's bedroom to a bumpy concrete sidewalk. The sudden reappearance in a new place was what Kitty expected from a wish like that, and she was grateful not to be dizzy or puking. Will must have been doing magic for a long time already.

"That's all I asked from you, little portal," Will said, mostly to himself.

As they walked up to the steps of the Glade Crest Municipal Building, a long, squat structure with decades of caked on grime and weathered stains, Will grabbed the copper handle on one of the doors. It jerked in place, but didn't open.

"Why are we—?" Kitty started to ask.

Will gripped the handle until it glowed bright blue under his touch. Kitty knew magic when it was that obvious. She checked to see if any passersby noticed them, but no one paid them any attention. The doors let out a soft click, and Will pushed one open. He bowed and motioned for Kitty to go in first. Kitty peeked past the door, suddenly unsure if this was a smart idea.

The foyer was dim. Only the bits of streaming sunlight through the grimy windows and the open front door lit the area. The rays caught specks of dust that occasionally looked like dancing ghosts. Kitty could see the abandoned teller desk and a few shadowy hallways branching away from the foyer. She felt a small push against her back, and her squeak of surprise echoed in the large room. Will laughed as he walked past her and down one of the hallways with Kitty grumbling in tow. Her eyes bounced in every direction as she saw more of those dust clouds trailing beside her.

Will held open the door at the end of the hall for her, and this time she went through without pausing. As soon as she stepped in, a large, jiggling mass blocked her way and knocked her backwards. Through hysterical laughter Will offered his arm to help her up.

"I'm really sorry," Kitty said. "I didn't—oh!" She

clapped her hands over her mouth as she saw who—or what—she smacked into. A gelatinous cube of mostly translucent purple wriggled in place, its slick skin wobbling from the impact. There were millions of floating bubbles inside the cube, most of which were swarming at Kitty's height. Slurping, garbled noises erupted from all across the cube until finally they melted into near perfect English. It still sounded as if it were drowning in its own jelly

"...keep forgetting to switch. Are you okay, little one?"

"I'm—uh—yes," Kitty said. She sent a sharp glare at Will who continued laughing.

"Good. Good. On my way then. Many apologies."

It slid across the marbled ground towards a silver doorway like melting butter, but it didn't leave any trail as it formed an arm-like appendage that pressed into a crash bar and let itself out. The door gave off a blue shimmer for a few seconds and then settled again as it shut. Kitty realized that she was no longer in some abandoned section of the Glade Crest Municipal building. She and Will stood in a brightly lit circular room. Silver door frames lined the black marble walls every five feet. Overhead, the curling track lights made the doors gleam while the walls seemed to suck the light into the void of space with each line in the marble like a string of stars to light it from within. A section of the wall opened into a wide corridor where they could hear trailing voices.

Will led Kitty down the carpeted hallway lined with monitors that displayed information in those spinning little symbols. She thought she could read a few names and—

"Is that a birthday list?" she whispered to Will as if the walls could hear.

"Oh yeah," he said. "I got a cupcake and a singing birthday card this year. The acting Chief signed it. Well, it was a stamp of his signature. Nice touch."

Will had to pull Kitty away from each of the screens displaying news and events that she didn't understand.

At the end of the corridor was a small lobby. A few people, some normal looking and others taller and colored differently than normal, were standing against a wall, talking in hushed whispers that still carried. The ones who spoke English mentioned briefings and vacations after tough adjudications. Others seemed to hiss, coo, and click. Along the far wall was a row of metallic doors with a panel of eight directional buttons. Beside one door, the "Right" button was lit and waiting. Will tapped the "Up" button on the neighboring panel and stepped back. The light above that door flashed green and chimed. The door slid open, and a small wave of people filed out. Some were dressed in nice slacks and dresses. Others wore casual jeans under white lab coats with their faces masked behind silver bottle cap lenses. Kitty's heart raced as she spotted more alien beings in the crowd along with some humanoids that looked perfectly normal until she noticed some inverted legs or hair that was more like copper wiring.

Kitty stayed as close to Will as she could without actually touching him. She didn't want to get lost in this crowd as a few more people and humanoids joined them in the lobby. She accidentally made eye contact with a few who politely smiled and nodded at her.

"You can meet everyone later," Will said as he guided her into the elevator.

"I don't know if I want to," she whispered back before a few others joined them.

The elevator was wide enough to fit at least ten more people. Each of the four walls had another large monitor with more new reports from across the globe and apparently beyond. A second door stood opposite the door they entered, and another panel listed different floors and departments. Hands flew over the buttons in an orderly fashion, and the elevator lurched upward. Or forward.

A few newcomers shared quick greetings. Others who were settled spoke in polite, low tones about something on a monitor. Something about "precautionary awareness of pre-set diagram access points." The words were lost to the music pouring through invisible speakers. Most of it Kitty recognized from the top 40s charts of today and when her mother was young. Then songs in different languages streamed through. Kitty checked her phone again and saw that her cell phone service was disrupted.

Where the heck are we?

After a few minutes of stops and starts, Kitty and Will were among the last riders. The elevator crawled to a stop just one floor from the top. *DING!* The doors slid aside with ease. They stared into a wider lobby than the one below— or behind. Kitty wasn't sure. The floor was checkered hardwood, and half of the walls were towering windows set with stained glass light catchers. The rainbows they painted on the floor reminded Kitty of her diagram doodles as the colors snaked around each other. The other half of the room had some plush chairs beside tables of different heights and assorted newspapers, magazines, books, and disks next to handheld monitors.

Kitty followed Will down the hall to the left with a few labeled doors separated by portraits, water fountains, and trays of bagged and wrapped snacks until they stood in front of an unassuming metal panel with a flat handle. A steel placard bolted to the door read Leonard Q. Baldwin - Local Liaison District 1. Kitty clung to the hem of her skirt with clammy hands. She just realized she was wearing the same clothes as yesterday, dirt stains and all.

"Here we are," Will said as he knocked against the door.

Kitty cringed as the sound seemed to echo down the entire corridor. "Maybe we shouldn't do this. Maybe I shouldn't do this."

"Why not? You want to learn more about magic, right? It's easier than only reading the Initiate Resources."

"I just want him to fix my wrist," Kitty protested.

"Well he can do that too." Will leaned against the wall until a tiny light beneath the placard flashed green. "If you really don't want to go," he added, shifting to stand straight again, "you don't have to."

Kitty bit down on her lower lip, but shook her head and motioned towards the door. If this was some kind of crazy cult kidnapping her, it was too late. She had walked into the lion's den all by herself.

Six

Kitty stepped into the modest office ahead of Will, and the door slid shut behind them. The click of the door settling in place made Kitty shudder. The office looked professional with its filing cabinets and multiple computer monitors crowding one side of the desk along the opposite wall. It also had a homey feel with pictures frames, a few bright plastic stress toys, and a coffee mug sitting on top of the mini fridge that read "#1 Boss".

Then there were the weird things that reminded Kitty that she wasn't in a normal office like her dad's old job where she once visited for Bring - Your - Daughter - To - Work Day. The wall shelving had different shapes and sizes of silver devices and chests with locks that wouldn't fit any normal key. A few glass jars were filled with dark colored powders and one had dried leaves stuffed into it. They could have come from the potted white orchid in the window sill.

A man looked up from behind two of the monitors on

the desk while rubbing his stubbled chin. He smiled a great, cheeky smile, and came around the desk. Every step was purposeful to show off the cut of his suit pants over his long legs and the gleam of his polished loafers that cushioned his wide feet. He had gray-streaked black hair and charming wrinkles around his eyes and mouth. Clipped to the pocket of his button down shirt was a chrome plated badge that read LEO BALDWIN - LOCAL LIAISON.

"Well well!" he said, slapping Will on the back and then shaking his hand heartily. "This looks like you went above and beyond with your adjudication." His voice was thick with a slushy New York dialect. Leo's watch sparkled like Will's with every movement, and Kitty wondered if it was some company policy to use a watch instead of a clock or phone to tell time.

"I tried not to spook her," Will said, "but we ran into a little trouble with Hostilia."

"No fooling," Leo said, scratching his chin. "They're active lately. A lot of unrest, and that's never good for us. I think local Quotists are noticing too. Misery loves company as they say." He turned his focus to Kitty, and immediately his smile returned.

"Kitty Guthrie, huh?" Leo shot out is hand to shake. Kitty carefully took it and was surprised by the gentleness in his powerful grip. "Damn pleasure to meet you. I'm Leo Baldwin. I'm your Local Liaison, which just means you can bug me with questions when I'm available. I'm sure you've got a ton already. But first thing's first. Welcome to the Planetary Homestead, home of the Alliance."

Kitty gave a tight lipped smile. His eye contact was uncomfortable so she shifted her focus to the window and its unfamiliar skyline.

"Come on. Have a seat, you two." Leo returned to the high-backed, cushioned chair behind the desk and gestured to the smaller, egg shaped chairs in front. Will immediately took a seat, and Kitty followed suit, afraid to look silly standing alone by the door. She sat on the very edge of the plush chair and watched Will sink back and let the shape cradle him. "I know this is a lot to take in," Leo said, sitting back and crossing his legs. "I've been told you're at least a little familiar with magic. Been doing this for a while, huh? It's alright. You're not in trouble."

Leo offered her an open glass jar with assorted bite sized chocolate bars. Kitty reached in, first with her right hand until she saw her wrist twisted out of shape. She snatched it back and took the topmost chocolate with her left hand, but she couldn't distract herself by eating it; she hated peanuts.

"Thank you," she murmured.

"And polite to boot. Ain't that something." Leo replaced the candy jar on the corner of his desk. Will jumped up and grabbed a few pieces. "Alright, if I'm not going to be bombarded with the Initiate Dozen, what can I do for you kids?"

Kitty could feel Will's eyes drilling into the side of her head, but she kept staring at the softening chocolate bar in her lap. Magic wasn't her comfort zone. Give her homework or family drama any day. She could tackle that and still plan the first ever Homecoming Dance for her school. No one ever attacked her for any of those things. Not with their fists anyway.

Will finally spoke up after a few lazy spins in his chair. "Well my adjudication from Justice Paulson was to hand off

Kitty's MHD. And I did. But then I saw she was able to do magic without one. Not just the bursts that Initiates get, but she's done complete orations like she's already a practiced Magus. She drew a transit diagram on my wall."

"I didn't mean to!" Kitty said. "It was just a dream!"

Leo turned to her, thick eyebrow raised. "A dream? What about?"

Kitty looked back at him trying to find the words while fidgeting with her sweater sleeve. She never had to explain what happened before. She felt like a freakazoid, and she was thankful that she never fell asleep in a class before.

"Um...well, I don't really remember most of it this time."

"This time? So you've done this before?"

Kitty cringed for giving more information than she wanted to, but she nodded. She started fishing through her backpack as she explained. "Sometimes I would be running somewhere or I'd wish I could be in two places at once. Then when I woke up, I was drawing something." She shyly pulled out the small stack of notebook paper with blue crayon and marker; she could see them flutter in her shaking hands. Still Leo smiled and accepted them. He carefully looked over each one. One diagram he immediately flipped face down on the table. Kitty noticed it was her dummy.

When Leo had gone through the entire stack twice, except for the flipped page, he returned them all.

"That's really impressive, Kitty," he said. "It could also be dangerous. How have your orations worked out when you executed any of these?"

"Uh...okay, I guess. I've made some jumps—transits or

whatev—but it took time to get anywhere I really wanted to go without throwing up. It's not perfect, I know, but it got the job done. Except one—well, nevermind."

Leo's fingers danced over a few keys on one of his monitors as Kitty spoke, but he quickly looked back at her. "No one is expecting perfection from you as an Initiate. Certainly not from making diagrams this way. Your Magical Harnessing Device is there to help you form properly functioning spell diagrams. Have you had a chance to read through it?" Kitty slowly nodded. "But not much, I imagine. That's alright. You have plenty of time. It's a much more modern way to form these diagrams. The old ways were drawing lines in dirt and chanting at the moon in a circle of lavender and iron filings. I promise this is preferable, but some people still like to dance in the woods these days. I don't care as long as their intent is clear and good."

"Like witchy stuff?" Kitty asked.

"Can't blame the pilgrims for not having internet in the 17th century," Leo said with a shrug. "And some people are very retro when it comes to magic. With the way it works, it's best to do what you're most comfortable with. You, however—" His intent stare returned. "—You're a young woman of the modern world. I think the most up to date version of a Harnessing Device will suit you nicely. You probably can't even write cursive anymore."

Kitty frowned a little. Her words per minute was getting close to 70. So what if she couldn't write her name with so many loops no one could read it?

"So which oration was giving you trouble, Kitty? Maybe we can suss it out with your MHD."

"Well—I mean—" Kitty looked through the stack

and all of the dreams washed over her again. Fixing her sister's bruises and bumps. Fixing broken glass. Sewing a kingdom's worth of stuffed animals. Being in a thousand places at once. Running away.

"We don't have to look any further than you want to," Leo said. "That's the beauty of magic. It isn't some mysterious, wand waving bull crap that Quotists like to make movies about. It's very straightforward. I keep suggesting we rename it ultra-science, but it hasn't cleared the High Advisory Council. Oh well." He chuckled, and Kitty felt her shoulders relaxing. "Magic is a conversation, and we Magistrates are the ones who get to have it. No more, and certainly no less. That's why it's called oration. Any time you even just activate a spell diagram, you're speaking and listening all at once with your target. Creating a spell to fix shattered bottles like you have there, or to create toys from seemingly nothing, means you are telling the world around you, 'Hey, there is another way you should be. You were that way before or you could be that way for the first time, and it's better than what's in front of you now.'"

"The natural state of being?" Kitty asked.

"Exactly! You pick up quick, kid. Most Mages can be quite persuasive. When you've tasted the fresh air of freedom that comes with knowing the way things are, it's hard to look back. Can't really un-know what you know. The world needs reminders mainly because there are those who would take advantage of people not fully understanding the natural state of being. If you don't know how good you've got it, of course you could be told something worse is actually something better."

"Hostilia do that, right?" Kitty asked, hoping for

another bit of validation. She grasped at what bits of wishes and magic made the tiniest bit of sense.

"They definitely make things worse," Leo said. "Hostilia aren't so much the problem as they are the result. You're never too far gone to remember how the world oughta be, but each decision you make in one direction— for better or for worse—makes the next decision easier. If you believe negotiation and compromise trumps strong-arming someone to get what you want, then you'll do more of that. But the opposite is also true. If you think the way to live better is to take from others and morals be damned, then that's the road you're building for yourself. It's an ugly one. I don't recommend it."

Kitty blanched. "So those were really people? But they—blew up!"

Will made a noncommittal hum. "They were much less people at that point."

"Don't they have families wondering where they are? Oh my gee, what did I do?"

"Chill, Kitty," Will said. Leo sent him a relatively stern look. "I mean, it's not something to be super chill about. The way they were, which you don't see every day, they'll be missing or sometimes their real bodies are still where they left them before they got orders to attack. They made a lot of bad choices to wind up like that."

"Oh no! How bad? Like forging my mom's signature on a bus pass bad?"

Kitty didn't appreciate the smile Leo was barely concealing as she stole glances at her limbs to make sure they weren't turning black. "I wouldn't make a habit of forgery," Leo said, "but it's not going to be what makes someone turn rotten. The rules to make kids have signed bus passes might be helpful, but it's not grounded in such a way that Vitae considers them a violation of self. You haven't harmed anyone. Don't freak out over this. Hostilia come from people who surround their lives in their own misery and the misery of others. Think dictators. Sociopaths and serial killers. But also your neighbor that would happily dominate you and your family from his own fears. Strangely more common these days. Fear can make you justify a lot."

Still mostly unconvinced, Kitty said, "I don't get it. Why would anyone want to be one of those things? How do you get like that?"

"Don't think it happens overnight, Kitty. It's hard to believe and it's hard to see, but this takes years, generations, lifetimes. It's a subtle beast that creeps into your life with one little nudge here and a justification there." Leo stood and paced towards the window. "It's an insidious whisper in your ear telling you to take what ain't really yours. It's Nefas."

Immediately Kitty held her stomach as the nausea returned. The ringing in her ears and the white flashes in front of her eyes made her sit back in the chair and cringe. She peered one eye open and saw both Will and Leo looking at her, faces creased with concern.

"I'm okay," she squeaked, but she continued to let the chair cradle her. "Just a little dizzy."

Leo offered her a bottle of water from the mini fridge. She guzzled half of it before she realized how disgusting she must have looked. She covered her mouth with the end of her sweater sleeve as Leo eyed her from his new perch on the edge of his desk.

"You're an interesting one, Kitty Guthrie," he said. Kitty could hardly see how nearly fainting from hearing a word was *interesting*. "I may have an idea of why you had trouble with certain orations."

"It's all of them," she muttered. Then she regretted opening her mouth, but she explained what happened at the Homecoming meeting and how she tried to fix her wrist afterwards, but the magic wouldn't budge. She told him about the many times she tried to make a dummy of herself including her most recent attempt shouting questions at her, but she kept the rest of the incident on a need-to-know basis. Leo went back to his desk and started typing.

"So the orations still worked out in the end?" Leo asked after Kitty's last example.

"I guess so. Maybe not that dummy. I had to make a second one, but that must have fallen apart too since my mom realized I wasn't home."

"Could I see your MHD?"

Kitty handed it over, and Leo quickly found what he was looking for. He showed Kitty the dark screen with light blue jittering symbols tied to each other and forming long webs. "Does this look familiar?"

"No."

"It should. Take a closer look. What does this diagram seem to be trying to explain?"

Kitty looked at the whorls and loops that defined the spell diagram like fingerprints. In fact, the picture it drew in her mind sort of looked like fingerprints when she stared at a certain section. Others gave her an image of brown hair often shoved into a ponytail, but sometimes clipped with a grocery store barrette. Dark brown eyes. Eyebrows a little too thick for her liking. It talked about a girl who didn't mind skipping breakfast when she could chug water to get her through her morning classes. She always offered bigger portions of dinner to her little sister so she would be happy. And then there were blurs that seemed to fight over what to tell. Joyful or depressed. Sometimes both. Thinking about friends that made her excited and scared. Memories of home that were different every time she crossed that same part of the diagram.

Kitty's mind roared with questions as if the dummy were shouting them at her all over again. She lowered the tablet and rubbed her eyes on her sleeve.

"I don't like that spell," she said to no one in particular.

"Spells are just one of the two principles of magic," Leo clarified. "This is a spell diagram and the magic itself is an oration. Maybe you should like this oration a little more. It's you, after all. It's almost exactly like the one you drew there with that dummy. That's why it didn't work. As much as we wish it, we can't actually be in two places at once in a universe. The universe wasn't built to handle that. It's likely the oration simply stalled and was waiting for you to correct it before you terminated it and restarted."

Kitty wasn't so sure. She blinked the magic into life like she always did before. It felt the same as she pinched it off like a gum bubble. But Leo was the expert.

"As for your other diagrams, I have two thoughts here," Leo continued. "One is that you've been doing magic without an MHD, no real means of focusing your energy. It's like coming up with an entire lecture on the fly and that ain't easy. It's going to be a struggle to orate magic that way. Planning and crafting your argument to convince the world that you're correct is difficult, but it is key.

"The second thing is that I suspect you might be a natural with oration. Or at least you've become excellent at convincing. I'll bet if you concentrated hard enough, you could even convince people to do things they might not otherwise have wanted to do. My concern with that is how you do it. I think you pull on heartstrings, Kitty. You draw on emotional support over facts and logic, and that's powerful. It's also extremely dangerous."

The words pierced Kitty's slowly growing ego.

"I suspect you're an Empath," he continued. "It's not the hocus pocus of supernatural reading into people minds and feelings. No, this is something developed based on your own consciousness. You've developed habits that, combined with an affinity for oration and maybe some natural leadership capabilities, allow you to influence the world in an incredibly powerful way. I'll tell you right now, that has to stop. The pictures have to stop. Something as fragile but enormous as our world can't be influenced with dueling sob stories or we'll wind up with more Hostilia than we can handle. And they would have a field day with you on their side. However you decide to continue using magic, with our agency or independently, please do everyone a favor and use the MHD. Emotional pleas over true understanding is the fast track to Hell. You get me?"

Kitty nodded, but the words were still a blur in her mind. Was she really good at magic and didn't know or was she really bad at it and putting people in danger? Sometimes she couldn't control it at all so would that also hurt her? Would she turn into a monster?

"It's a lot to take in, but it's a good starting point as you get to learning more about yourself and your fellow Mages.

Keep a sound mind and those emotional bargains you've been doing before shouldn't be turned against you. I think we at the Alliance would be a great help to you, Kitty. And you'd be a tremendous help to us if you decided you'd like to join us as an Initiate."

"Join? Like a club?"

"More like a mom and pop shop. Our product is tourism back to the natural state of being. We show people what it's like by living the example." He turned to the wall behind him and laid his hand over it. It jolted as a seam formed beneath Leo's palm and a portion of the wall pulled apart, revealing another monitor. A digital globe spun slowly surrounded by tiny stars and the occasional distant planet that shared the solar system. Leo touched part of the globe, and a million little lights blinked to life. "These are territories where we have Magistrates and Justices signed with the Alliance."

"That's a lot," Kitty marveled, leaning forward in her chair.

"It looks like it, don't it?" He tapped on North America, and Kitty felt like she was about to get a history lecture. The screen zoomed in and instantly darkened as the lights spread further apart. There were clusters of them across the United States. The numbers dropped significantly north into Canada. The United States was further split horizontally as if the Civil War were still happening. The north end, including New Jersey, had scattered clusters of these lights. One bright spot flashed in Washington D.C., and a familiar star icon sat over it. Some scrolling text in blue seemed to read "YOU ARE HERE."

"A little less impressive now, huh?" Leo said. "It's a

couple of tens of thousands of us. Which might sound like a lot, but considering there are seven billion people around the world, you start to put things into perspective. These are the Mages we can call on if there is any trouble. This is it."

"What kind of trouble?"

"You wouldn't necessarily have to deal with anything monumental, don't worry. But Mages could get adjudications for anything from political leaders influenced by Nefas—sorry, Kitty." He watched her chug from her water bottle again until the plastic crinkled and collapsed into itself. "Or it could just be helping your neighbors reconsider tossing a candy wrapper on the ground when there's a garbage ten feet away. They're simple choices that anyone can make, but when you're conscious of it, now it's a responsibility you're very aware of."

"So I don't really have a choice about joining if it means that *Thing* won't run around making more Hostilia," Kitty said.

Leo sent her a sharp look. "No no no, don't ever say you don't have a choice. You always have a choice. That's the challenge. That's the responsibility and the danger. But you don't need to be part of the Alliance to make that choice. We'll gladly let you test drive our services, see what we're about and how we choose to turn things around for the better. If you like it, we'll bring you on as a Magus. In time you'll become a full fledged Magistrate, and your responsibilities will grow as you do. If it's not for you, keep the MHD, contact us if you need help, but otherwise just live your life graciously."

Kitty looked back at the map and the brightest flash

of the screen as her mind swirled with too many thoughts.

"How did you hide a place like this in the middle of D.C.?" she blurted out.

Leo smiled and sauntered towards the window and the beautiful cityscape beyond it. Kitty could see some towering skyscrapers and one tall, thin structure she knew from her history class. It was the Washington Monument. It looked out of place so near to the tall office buildings, nothing like the pictures.

"The Planetary Homestead is only anchored in D.C.," Leo said. "It's a very useful oration. The Acting Chief Planetary Justice helps maintain a sort of pocket dimension called a Dimensional Hold. It acts like a buffer between worlds, dimensions, universes, and the like. No need to test what would happen if two expanding universes collided with each other so we keep a safe distance. That's also why non-sanctioned transit orations are absolutely forbidden to and from the Homestead. The type of oration that could bypass that work—well I sure don't wanna know it. That could cause all sorts of havoc if it weighed down the Hold in the wrong way."

Kitty suddenly felt unstable sitting in the unassuming office with the two men who could make such transits. Worse yet, she realized why the monument looked out of place: it was mere miles away from the Empire State Building! She heard Leo laugh, and the light churning of gears shifted the wall closed.

"Dimensional Holds tend to skew the worlds they mimic like looking through a glass bowl. We only need so much space to do our job. Just remember there have been Mages for eons, and we know what we're doing. Don't look so pale, Kitty. That being said, I'll give you some time to digest all of this before you tell me if you'd like to join us. Until then, get to know magic a little more. Have Will here help you out. Is that okay, Will?"

"A mentee?" he said, eyes widening. "Dude, seriously?"

"You've gotta start somewhere, huh? Welcome to being a Magistrate, Mr. Cavanaugh." Will saluted him and started typing on his tablet using an icon Kitty couldn't see. "So Kitty, if you have more questions, you can ask Will. He's become pretty ace at this business after two years so he can certainly help you with the basics. Share numbers, but in case you can't get to your phones, I've got one more thing for you." Leo fished through one of his drawers and pulled out a delicate silver casing the size of a thumbnail. It was attached to a plastic hooked wire that gently bent in his grip. Leo handed it to her. "It's a Chameleon Ear. Slip it over your ear like a wireless phone, and in a minute it should look like nothing is there."

Kitty carefully wrapped the wire around her outer ear and pushed the small receiver in. It felt cold for a moment, and then suddenly felt like nothing except maybe a tickling hair. Leo inspected it and nodded.

"Very good. It re-formed to line your inner ear like a hollow ear plug. If you need to contact Will or myself, you can use that handy little device. It picks up on the active synapses in the part of your brain controlling language and communication. It's sensitive to thought, so be mindful not to shout. We'll keep our versions of it open to you. When you upgrade it—should you decide you'd like to join us—that is also where you'll hear about any assigned adjudications from the higher ups." He held up his hand to stop the questions sitting on Kitty's tongue. "Yeah, yeah, kind of like being a secret agent."

"Mr. Baldwin—" Kitty started.

"Leo. Please. I like to keep things casual. We're practically family."

"Uh, Leo. Are you sure the dummy spell—magic—oration didn't work?" She held up the diagram again from her stack of doodles.

Leo shook his head. "What you were designing was much too close to you, questions, blurs, and all. You don't need to show that to anyone if you don't want to, by the way. It's very personal. The diagram simply couldn't create a second Kitty Guthrie no matter how much of a smooth talker you appear to be." Kitty lowered her head, and hit her lip. "But if you're very concerned, and since you're an Empath that can do God-knows-what, I'll take a closer look, huh? Sound good? Just be prepared for a handful if you did manage a dummy oration like this."

"Yeah. Okay." Kitty fumbled with the pages to fold them back into her backpack. She winced as she forgot the limits of her right wrist again.

"That looks nasty," Leo said, pointing to her arm. "I can take care of that before you go."

It would be really difficult to explain the injury to her mom. Kitty stopped trying to hide the sprain under her sleeve and just nodded. Leo kneeled in front of her, taking her wrist in his palms. He looked it over and ran a finger along the nub of bone where there hadn't been one before. It felt warm for a moment as Leo looked at the face of his watch. The minute and second hands were gone, replaced by streaming blue letters.

"Alright, this should be quick, but I can't say painless." He looked back up at Kitty with his Hollywood grin, and she felt her own lips twitch towards a forced smile. "So one of the key concepts when using magic is understanding what you're changing. Knowing who you're talking to. It looks like you knew the basics of a sprain, but not the details of *this* sprain. I'm going to have to undo the healing and heal it again. I'll count to 3 so you're ready, okay?"

Kitty tensed up, bracing for the same shock of pain that nearly made her pass out.

"First, tell me something, Kitty," Leo continued as he pressed his thumb around the stiff muscles in Kitty's wrist. He worked around the spiraling pink and black cords of her friendship bracelet. "What school do you go to?"

"Hmm? Why?"

"Just getting to know my potential new Initiate. Haven't had a chance in a while. I've been away for my own studies."

"Oh, uh, I go to Glade Crest Junior High in New Jersey."

Leo placed his thumb and index finger on either side of Kitty's wrist, and she winced. "Got a favorite subject?"

"Probably English. I'm doing the best in it. And the homework is easier. For me anyway."

"Easier than—math?"

"Fifteenth level easier—aah!" Kitty shrieked as pain jolted through her arm and left her fingers tingling. She snatched her hand back from Leo and glared at him. "What the actual heck!"

"Sorry." Leo stood. "It's easier when you don't see it coming. I've had my fair share of bumps and bruises before

I knew about magic. But you should be all set. Test it out. Make sure you're okay."

In fact, Kitty's wrist felt perfectly normal again.

"Uh, thanks," she said.

"You're quite welcome. Well, you two know where to find me if you need anything. Kitty, I look forward to your answer about joining us. You would be an incredible asset to the Alliance. Will, could you hang back for just a minute?"

Kitty's shoulders stiffened as Will spun another lazy circle in his chair, waiting to speak to Leo privately. She made her way to the door by herself, but still felt less alone than she had in years.

———◆———

Kitty silently praised herself as she walked without flinching through the sea of unique people who she now knew were Mages. She couldn't focus on them much except to make sure she didn't bump anyone as she passed through the lobby with Will guiding her by the elbow. Her mind was churning. All of the pictures from her dreams were stored like professional artwork on her tablet. Instead of guessing what she wanted, she could scroll through a search menu and find it.

Or I can perfect old spells—orations, she thought.

She would figure this magic business out.

Before she knew it, Kitty was standing beside Will at the door of the still abandoned Glade Crest Municipal building. The dancing dust particles that looked like swirling ghosts still followed them around. Will held the door open.

"So, you up for a little practice?" he asked. "It's still

early and we could probably get to some of your doodle magic easy enough. Could I see them again?"

Kitty fished out her stack of drawings from her backpack just as other voices started to fill her ears. It was that relentless whispering, but the voices weren't just heavy breathing over a phone line that made them crackle and scratch her eardrums. They were quiet feelings. Some words broke through; most others were simply senses. Something was reacting, and all Kitty could tell was that the something was unhappy.

"Earth to Kitty. Come in, Kitty." Kitty looked at Will who was leaning against the door. "Lost you there for a second. Are you *hearing*?"

She shook her head and handed Will the drawings. "Yeah, I hear you."

"No, I mean, are you *hearing*?" he said. "It's what happens when an adjudication is trying to come through. Usually you don't get notified until you sign up as a Magus, but maybe being an Empath has you hearing what I hear. That could be good practice, but before we follow the breadcrumbs, you might want to keep your new toy a little discreet. Let me send you something. You can customize it how you want."

Will swiped through his tablet. A few seconds after, Kitty's device beeped. She saw the messenger icon—a closed envelope with a seal that had her initials on it—with a blue dot in the upper right corner. Kitty tapped it, and Will's message appeared. It was a simple diagram with only a handful of circles that read a basic description of a wrist-sized silver band.

"I keep mine disguised as a watch I got for my

birthday a few years ago. You probably don't want to copy me so you'll need to make it fit for you. That can be our first project."

"Sure. Easy enough. I've done bigger...orations."

"It's not about the size."

Kitty didn't respond to what she would have assumed was a gross joke. Her eyes fell on the clock in the opposite corner of her battery life. She didn't dare believe it. Kitty took her phone out of her backpack and saw two more missed calls from her mother as well as more email responses piling up from when she didn't have service in the Planetary Homestead.

Oh no…

She confirmed the time. It was after two o'clock and her mother needed to be at work an hour ago! It was one thing to disobey her and run out in the middle of the night to meet some boy when she knew nothing exciting was going to happen—at least not between her and the boy. It was another thing to keep her mom from work. Kitty ran out the door.

"Wait!" she heard Will say.

"I've gotta go!" Kitty called over her shoulder.

"At least let me make a transit for you!"

"Thanks, but no thanks!" Her apartment complex wasn't more than ten minutes away from downtown, and she had come by this way so many times before. Most importantly, after seeing Will's house there was no way she would let him see her apartment. In her rush down Main Street, past Beautician Magicians, she nearly bowled down Mrs. Constance.

"Kitty, your mama—"

"I know! She's coming!"

Kitty's feet and stomach ached by the time she saw the gray towers past the short chain fence. She slammed her key into the lock to get into the lobby and took the stairwell two steps at a time rather than wait for the rusty old bucket of an elevator to come down and greet her. Kitty only paused as she approached her apartment door. Just as she raised her house key to the lock, the door swung open. Her mother stood there with a small purse slung over shoulder and a light jacket in the other arm. Her blouse was half tucked into her black slacks and her faint purple lips were pursed. Behind Mrs. Guthrie, Kitty could hear her little sister laughing and playing with a whirring, singing toy that her neighbor was holding.

"We'll talk later," her mother said with daggers in her eyes. "Get inside."

"Yes, mom," Kitty said, still panting, and stepped out of the way of her mother's warpath towards the stairwell. Kitty frowned as her mother left. She never liked to feel like she let her mom down. There were some things she just couldn't do even when she was mad. She had to be the bigger person and set a good example for Edith.

Kitty wished a quick goodbye to the sweet neighbor lady with bits of balled up paper tangled in her white hair. For Edith, she made a sandwich with the last slices of ham and cheese and plopped her in front of the television. A few slaps to the side of the box got rid of most of the static. A furry purple rabbit with a golden crown shaped like three carrot stalks was waving at other brightly colored animals. Edith balanced the paper plate in her lap, held the sandwich with one hand, and wrapped her other hand around Kitty's arm.

This was her real life. She nearly forgot. Edith laughed

and sang along with Hop-A-Long Princess and her friends, and Kitty couldn't help smiling. She kissed the top of her sister's head and freed her phone from her pocket. At least she enjoyed that part of her normal life. She could get back to being a Mage in another hour and a half when the movie was done. Her sister always came first.

A green light flashed, reminding Kitty of her missed messages. Kitty scanned through the email thread about Homecoming to catch up and answer the questions of her naysayers. It looked like someone was answering for her. She wished they wouldn't do that. Every time one of the teachers or parents from the PTO tried to assume her ideas, they were always wrong.

"And they still don't know my name." Kitty sighed as she saw an actual response from Mrs. Angela Smith to *Kaitlin*. "Whoa, I never told her to shut her mouth!"

"Shhh!" Edith said, tugging on Kitty's free arm.

"Sorry, sweetie."

Kitty's heart raced as she scrolled slowly through the messages. Someone definitely responded to the questions under Kitty's name and in Kitty's tone if she didn't have a filter. That someone definitely told Angela Smith to shut her mouth about her poster design. Kitty never typed so quickly in all of her life as she did apologizing to the teachers and staff about whoever must have stolen her phone. Her hands shook as she imagined the scolding she was going to get come Monday.

Now that she had her Harnessing Device, a little tablet that felt like a ton of bricks in her backpack, she thought maybe she could pull off the stunt of a lifetime, second to the Homecoming Dance. She made a note to start practicing her dummy diagram right away. It would be really convenient to be in two places at once.

Seven

"...Jesus is my doctor, and he brings me all my medicine..."

Kitty shut the door to the Sunday School classroom and cut off most of the sound from the sanctuary upstairs. The stomping feet and "Hallelujah!" shouts still found their way down.

Mrs. Guthrie made church a weekly demand for nearly a year. Kitty wouldn't say her family was very religious, but it was nice to spend time with her mom and sister with such neighborly people. They were always so excited too. Kitty really believed each one of the church attendees wished her well and wanted God to bless her. She didn't know what to think when she sat in the pews tapping her polished shoes on the carpet while everyone else shut their eyes in prayer. It was normally a good time to decide what homework to finish first.

Sunday evening at the church was more unusual.

Kitty was only there for her weekly volunteer shift. Mrs. Constance, talented in both hair styling and organ playing, asked if Kitty would switch to the evening instead of normal hours to help with the special service for Reverend Al Houston. He was leaving Hope Creek Church for a new church opening on the other side of the Valley. His face was plastered all over the walls upstairs, shaking hands and leading the humble group in prayer time and time again. He was a balding, dark skinned man with shiny cheeks. What was left of his hair past the tall widow's peak were sparse tufts of wiry gray. His cheekbones were high and sharp and made his already wrinkly eyes crinkle more in each smiling picture. Kitty liked Reverend Al. He was welcoming and never made her participate in any hymns she didn't want to. Volunteering at the church was partly to thank him.

Kitty flicked the light switch. A faint humming started that seemed suddenly louder when the song from upstairs died down. The classroom was bright with construction paper signs and worn down cutout letters thanking God. The air was humid, and the old pipes behind the cracked ceiling tiles gurgled and thunked. The sounds used to fill Kitty with dread. She thought giant rats were nesting and having giant rat babies that would fall through the ceiling during services. The way everyone talked about the Valley, she thought that was a perfectly common thing when they first moved. Now she knew the sounds were nothing more than proof that the church needed more donations.

Kitty started her volunteering shift by wiping down the colorful plastic tables and chairs where the little ones had been earlier for Sunday school. She wadded up some paper towels and doused them in hand sanitizer. The smell of the alcohol in the oozing gel made Kitty's nose sting.

Then she moved on to the wooden cubbies with names like Becky, Michael, John, and Sarah stenciled onto sheets of construction paper. After wiping down a few more spots in the room, she stepped back to look at a job well done. The room shone even in the dull light. Religious or not, she was happy to help at the church. A job well done soothed her. She sat in one of the bright plastic chairs that came up to her calf. Above her she could still hear the congregation slamming their feet and clapping their hands to a lively hymn. She supposed she could go up there and join them to pass the time. Some of the songs were catchy. Some made her wonder if she should pay closer attention.

Then Kitty thought of a better way to spend the next free couple of hours. If God gave her a gift that let her make wishes come true and a mentor to show her what to do with it, she could hardly ignore that. Kitty focused on the bit of wire secretly looped around her ear.

"Will, you around?"

There were a few seconds of silence that made Kitty wonder if she was using the Chameleon Ear correctly. She winced as the concern bounced through the connection as if she shouted into an empty room.

"Didn't Leo tell you to watch out for that?" Will finally said. *"Thought you were at a thing today."*

"There's time before my mom picks me up."

"Ah. Cool. Yeah, gimme a few minutes."

Before long, Kitty felt a familiar little tingle against her skull, an itch just out of reach, that said something big was changing. She looked around and saw the air beside the classroom door waver like heat lines and then quickly sharpen. What looked like a pile of notebooks and papers with legs suddenly stood there. A sneaker tapped against the floor. Kitty only realized someone was holding up the pile when Will peered out from behind it and grinned.

"Good evening, Mentee!" he sang. "Welcome to your first official magic lesson!"

Kitty's eyebrow perked as Will marched to the short plastic table and dropped off his armload. The table wobbled beneath the weight. Will grabbed a chair near Kitty's and whirled it around, sitting backwards with his knees bent by his chest.

Kitty looked at one of the pages loose at the top of the pile. It was a blue drawing of woven threads and coils creating different shapes in a patterned diagram. "Hey! That's mine!"

"Well yeah," Will said, sliding the pages over to her. "You forgot them when you ran off yesterday. I figured if you were determined enough to draw your own spell diagrams like the hippy Magistrates, you'd probably want these back."

Kitty looked through the stack and found the dummy's diagram on the bottom, hidden from any unwanted eyes. She didn't realize it was such a personal drawing; showing it was like writing her student ID code on the bathroom stalls at school.

"I thought you might want to try that one again," Will said, "but I suggest starting small. Where's your Magical Harnessing Device?"

Kitty went to one of the cubbies that didn't have a child's name on it where she stowed her backpack while she cleaned. Hidden in the main pocket between some of her own notebooks and folders was the white tablet. Kitty slipped it out and returned to the table where Will had organized the notebooks by size and started filling in a binder with some looseleaf paper. "What's with the mobile classroom? I don't actually have to take a bunch of notes by hand, do I?"

"It's better for memory," he said without looking up from yanking the stiff binder rings apart. "You don't have to draw more diagrams by hand. That would be crazy. But I was doing some research on Empaths and took some notes. Did you look it up yet?"

Kitty's cheeks warmed. "I mean, I didn't really have time."

"Write it down. I'm telling you, it's awesome for remembering things." Will slid her one of the smaller notebooks and a pen.

Kitty rolled her eyes, but she flipped the notebook open to the first page and made a bullet point. "Look up 'Empath'. Okay."

"Good. So Empaths are really good at noticing emotions. It could be their own or people around them. But for you, it's not just people with emotions, but the whole world! When you become a Magus and get your own NAP, you'll probably—"

"Wait. Get a what?"

Will tapped his ear. He didn't have the slim metal hook that secured a tiny pod in place. In fact, nothing seemed to be there at all. "It's called a Nano Aural Processor. It's like a tiny earbud, but it lets you hear adjudications and stuff. That's what Leo meant by upgrade. You don't have to worry about that. It's all technical stuff for when you decide you definitely want to be a Magus."

"You don't know that I'm going to decide that," she said, crossing her arms. But now she really wanted to write down what Will had just told her.

"I think I do. It really seems to suit you." He shrugged. "You'll make the right call once you know how all this works. But anyway—Empaths. You're hyper aware of feelings, which is great for listening out to what the world is asking for to get back to the natural state, but also pretty dangerous if you lost your cool or something."

"So I'm like a walking time bomb? I've gotten mad before and nothing happened."

"Nothing that you know of," Will said. "You're allowed to have emotions. Just don't, y'know, beat yourself up over everything. Don't let the little things get you down. All the usual stuff your coach says to you."

"Thanks, Coach." Kitty picked up the pen and started jotting down what NAP stood for. Below that she wrote, "Be a magical robot or else you'll explode."

Will sighed. "Very funny. Just remember what I said. Don't wallow. Girls think they're cute when they do that."

Kitty made to kick him under the table, but he seemed to predict it and moved his leg aside so she hit the table leg instead. Her face wrinkled in a pout. "Whatev. What's next, Coach?"

He took one of the books with dog-eared pages and flipped it open. He read a passage. "If you do get angry about something, try to write down what made you feel mad. It's easier to make sense of your feelings if you look at the words than trying to sort out the emotions in your head. If you can figure out what made you mad or sad or anxious, you can figure out if it's worth feeling that way."

Kitty put the pen down and sat back in her chair. "I thought you were my Alliance mentor, not a counselor."

"I didn't say to tell *me* what made you mad," Will said. "I just said write it down. Emotions can get in the way of orations. You're trying to be reasonable. Logical. Not cold, but not a pushover or a dictator. Leo said you were using emotions to do orations without your MHD. That totally can't happen anymore. Got it?"

Kitty jotted down a few more words. "Don't be emotional. Don't be a robot. Okay."

Will shook his head. "Whatever works for you, Kitty. Just remember to take a deep breath. Orations aren't all easy. Some of them ask a lot of questions, but you still have to understand what you're trying to change if you want to get the results you're after. We're going to start easy."

He held up his wrist with the silver watch. Its band was thick, and the face had black, sharp numbers against a gray backing that looked like crushed diamonds. Will tapped the glass disk protecting three frail metal hands steadily making their rounds in hours, minutes, and seconds. It flashed as if he held it in a beam of moonlight. A breath after that his right hand sparked in the same way, and he was holding the casing of his Magical Harnessing Device.

Kitty's eyes widened. "Okay, how...? You didn't even open a diagram or anything!"

"That's a pre-set function," he explained, spinning the tablet over the table. "It's a shortcut you can make for yourself once you have a diagram exactly how you want it. This is my disguise so I can keep my MHD on hand wherever I go without having to carry it. You can always make changes, of course, but some things are in style for a long time." He tugged at the collar of his plaid shirt and rolled his shoulders to easily adjust the sleeves. His watch glinted. Somehow Kitty had expected the watch to disappear, but when she looked closer at it, she realized the seconds hand was gone.

"That's...pretty clever," she finally said. "So that's what I get to do today?"

"Is that what you want to do?" Will asked. "It's definitely handy. I'd recommend it."

"Then yeah!"

"Okay. You should still have the basic diagram I sent you yesterday."

"I want to make it myself," Kitty said.

"No need to reinvent the wheel."

"Well your wheel is for numbnuts. I'm going to make a better one."

Kitty swiped her finger across the screen to activate her tablet. A little smiling face greeted her in a text bubble before it blinked and vanished, leaving the home screen and its few icons and resources. Kitty selected the Spell Diagram Search Engine. A single empty search bar appeared at the top of the screen with a magnifying glass icon at the end of it. In brackets beside the search bar were the words INITIATE MODE ACTIVE.

"What does Initiate Mode mean?" Kitty asked.

"It's sort of like browsers that have a safe search so you don't accidentally get gross pictures. But in this case it's more so you can keep your search narrow. No need to overwhelm yourself. I almost did that. I was two seconds from sending myself to the moon without a helmet." He laughed. "You can turn it off by tapping where it says that.

But not right now. It's only day two, my young mentee."

"Right, right."

Kitty stared at the blank bar with the blinking cursor. She needed a way to hide her Magical Harnessing Device so she could carry it around and not be accused of stealing. It could be invisible, but then she might lose it. She could make a watch like Will's which had to be easy enough, but Kitty didn't like to wear watches, and one that looked like his would be too big for her wrist anyway. A bracelet, on the other hand, would be perfect. She looked down at her wrist and the coils of pink and black plastic. Kitty, April, and Becka wore friendship bracelets with the other two girls' favorite color.

Kitty typed the word 'Disguise' into the search engine. The bar slid off the top of the screen as a wheel slid up from below and settled in the center. One option took up most of the screen on one panel of the three dimensional looking wheel, with an option above and below it slightly bent along the curve. The current option she was looking at described disguising a person of a certain range of height and build considered medium. Kitty scrolled and found more options for disguising people or animals and other living life forms. Those seemed to be more popular searches.

"Wanna try something more specific?" Will offered.

"I'll get it," Kitty said, leaning over the table so her hair hid the screen from him. She ignored his snicker as she tapped a small arrow pointing to the left, a commonly used symbol for going back one page. She typed a full question as if it were a search in a normal web browser at school.

'How do I disguise my Magical Harnessing Device as a bracelet?'

The wheel returned with search results broad in range of size and difficulty. Some were simple designs like chains or laces. Others were far more complicated and gaudy than anything Kitty would ever need unless she was going to Prom. Maybe Homecoming. While she couldn't read the symbols that explained different uses of the diagrams, she could feel the descriptions on the preview screen. Kitty gawked at the diamonds, sapphires, and more embedded in gold. It looked so unnecessary, but she also hadn't met any other Mages except Will and Leo. Maybe some of them were hiding in plain site at mansions in Beverly Hills or penthouses in New York City.

Kitty might have considered some of the nice jewelry options if she still lived in the Slope. Jennifer Murphy's parents hosted a lot of parties, and Kitty went to a few. With an ache in her chest, she remembered the dress her dad bought her so she could look like her friends with jeweled barrettes in their hair and colorful gems in their ears.

Instead, Kitty found the simplest diagram with some images of thread or plastic in the preview screen. She tapped a button that read ACTIVATE, and the panel darkened before blinking away, replaced by a screen of a green so dark it was nearly black. In a smaller box to the left, there were faint blue lines drawn out in a simple, circular pattern with a few loops at three evenly separated spots along the line. One extra line cut through the circle from the top, and as it hit the center where a diamond shaped design lived, it abruptly bent into an angle and exited the circle directly between the bottom and right smaller loops.

"Got your basic diagram?" Will asked. Kitty nodded. "Great. Now you can adjust the diagram to fit what you want. Think about exactly how you want the disguise to look, why you picked that one, things like that, and the MHD can do a lot of the rest for you. Leo is right; It's so much easier than how the hippies do it."

Kitty pictured the bracelet around her wrist, the pink and black plastic threads winding around each other for eternity. The stiff material could still bend comfortably around her wrist. She remembered that on some days when she wasn't paying attention, she would find twisting red imprints against her skin from where she leaned her wrists while typing or taking notes at school. Sometimes she kept the bracelet on when she showered or slept, and the scents of her soap or the laundry detergent from freshly washed sheets would stick to it.

Her favorite part of the bracelet was the little metal charm, the jagged lightning bolt that fit neatly between two curved pieces to form a full heart. In the center of it was a carved out K, while April's and Becka's had their initials. April's charm still gleamed like it was brand new. Kitty's and Becka's had darkened some over time, but that made it look loved.

The more vivid Kitty's memories became, the more the preview diagram shifted before it finally settled into place. Kitty jumped as a tangle of threads appeared on the dark screen like dropped spaghetti. She heard Will laugh again and shot a glare at him.

"Sorry. Sorry," he said. "You were so in the zone, I didn't want to interrupt, but yeah. Once you're done, the MHD will let you go ahead and build the diagram."

"Build it again? I thought I just did that," Kitty said.

Will shook his head; some of his bangs fell over his

eyes, and he brushed them away with a quick swipe. "This is the oration part. Think of magic like giving a speech. You wouldn't want to give a very important speech without preparing and rehearsing it a few times, right? Well this is more important. Even simple orations are still changing something from what it was to what you want it to be. That's a big deal. You're convincing it that you're bringing it back to the natural state of being. And you are. Things touched by spells always seem better off. Unlike curses." He flicked away a piece of dust that had wedged itself between some of the books in the pile on the table. "Curses only make things worse. Both are magic and both are powerful, but if you don't control how you orate, you'll wind up making things worse.

"But you'll be fine," he quickly added as Kitty's face dropped. "I'm looking out for you. I'll warn you if you start acting like a brat and if any Hostilia vibes come off you. Anyway, go ahead and rebuild that diagram using the strands. Think of them like the sentences in your speech. Make sure you're reciting them clearly. You want to hit all of your talking points, and they should make sense. You're not just begging the universe to listen."

Kitty looked back at her tablet and the little bundle of lines with those shivering, beautiful symbols floating on the screen, waiting and listening. "Do I just—I mean, how—?"

"Move them with your fingers," Will said. "Slide them into place to match the diagram. This is a simple oration so it shouldn't have too many questions."

"Even with the MHD it has questions?" Kitty tapped the screen, and it was warm under her touch. She lingered on the loose threads that curled around each other. When she slid her finger along the screen, she could feel more of the warmth, and she could sense the threads and their curiosity. She pulled her hand back again. "Of course it does."

Will motioned for her to continue. "There's a lot more where that came from. I don't know what you were hearing before, but it's gotta be wild to hear it as an Empath."

Kitty figured this a simple enough puzzle. Connect the dots. Paint by number. She could do that. As her finger grazed the screen, one line of thread she had her eye on followed her. It described what she wanted the shape of her tablet's disguise to be. Round, 6.92 inches in length, something Kitty never thought of, but because it was tailored to her wrist, it was fitting itself to her. Kitty dragged that line so it created a downward arch from the top of the main circle towards the left. Another line, shorter than the first, specified colors and how hard the plastic strings were. It fit neatly as part of the slashing line that cut through where the rest of the circle would be.

How often will you wear it? The question scrolled along Kitty's thoughts. She considered that she would wear her bracelet very often if she was going to get herself tangled up with the Alliance. After Homecoming, she would gladly sit through more of these embarrassing tutoring lessons with Will. Hopefully he really meant it that she wouldn't have to show him anything she wrote down. She wasn't sure if she wanted to write anything at all. Diaries never interested her much. They took up time she could be using for homework or hanging out with her friends.

How much physical impact will it endure? What amount of pressure is required for shape stability? Is pink really April's favorite color? Do I know for sure? Why not have all three colors? Why am I a Magistrate? Do I like blue? How much do I own that's blue? Is my wrist too big? Is my wrist too small? Would I like a new bracelet for my birthday? Would that make me happy?

Kitty faltered as the questions bombarded her, and the threads seemed to snag and tug under her fingers.

"Deep breath," she heard Will say.

Kitty's heart skipped a beat at the sound of his voice. She had forgotten he was there for a second as she was lost in the dark with those threads and all of their questions. They moved as if Kitty eventually gave them an answer without realizing, but it was a slow process, and they fought her each step of the way. A cramp grew in her neck and shoulders as she got about half way past completing the spell diagram.

"Wow, that's a feisty oration," Will said, glancing at her screen. Kitty wanted to cover it up again, but felt childish.

"These are a lot of weird questions," she said. "If having a new bracelet would make me happy? I wouldn't be doing this if it wasn't what I wanted."

"Hmm. Could be the Empath thing kicking in."

Kitty sighed. "I'm almost done. I can do this."

"Take a quick break. You've been staring at it for like half an hour."

"No, I can finish it. It's almost done." She rubbed her neck and rolled it from shoulder to shoulder. She took a deep breath and looked back at her progress. Only a few threads were left tangled among themselves while the others were pushed into the shape of the image to the left.

The questions returned. Obscure questions about weekend holiday trips to the beach with her mom and sister and if the bracelet left funny tan lines. Could the plastic snap if she were too cold in the winter? Would that make her friends hate her? Would they move on and forget about her? Finally Kitty seemed to satisfy the diagram and its boundless questions as the last thread tugged, but slipped into place.

"There!" she cried in victory. "I did it!"

Will nodded. "Great job. So go ahead and execute it."

At the bottom of the screen was another small dialogue box that was previously grayed out. Now it shone in a bright green and asked, EXECUTE? [Y/N]

Kitty tapped the affirmative. The connected threads grew bright. Her wrist warmed and itched for a moment, and the little symbols projected from nowhere and wrapped around her wrist. As they took hold, Kitty felt that reaching sensation that started in her chest and flared out to capture every pulse and breath around her. Everything seemed to inhale deeply as the magic shifted the very air and reworked it into something better, sharing happy memories with her and letting that moment be the beginning of new ones.

In a flash, plastic threads coiled together on Kitty's arm with a small metal charm dangling from a hook in the circle. She held out her arm with starry eyes, admiring her work that sat right above the original bracelet. It was her first real bit of magic—one that wouldn't get her in trouble.

"Nice!" Will said.

Kitty couldn't answer for her squealing. She sprang from her chair and danced with her arm out. She flicked at the metal charm to make sure it was real. The small sting beneath her fingernail confirmed it was. She went back to the table and smoothed her hands over where the

112

tablet once sat. It was gone. Then she jumped for joy again, bouncing all around the table and dancing to a chorus only she could hear. Somewhere beyond it, Will was laughing. She couldn't care. She did magic—a spell to be precise. It was unforced; she answered all of the questions, and there it was.

"And it looks so perfect!" she cooed as if talking about a beloved pet. She took off the original bracelet and held it beside the new one. "You're just the greatest little oration ever, aren't you? Yes, you are!"

"Alright, magic ninja," Will said, "This is just the beginning. Come over here so we can practice something else. You have time, right?"

Kitty stopped bounding across the room when he mentioned the time. Pulling out her phone, she considered it. The service would be going on for another hour or so, and then everyone would stick around to chat with Reverend Al. The pastor wasn't likely to check up on Kitty, trusted as she was.

"Maybe one more," she said, crossing back to the table, and then she felt her shoe catch in a sticky spot on the floor. The spot was mostly clear, but now she could see the imprint of her shoe in it.

"Gross babies," she muttered on her way to the closet for a mop. The sticky pull followed, making her walk on the outer edge of her right foot. She tried to brush some of it off on the play rug, but only managed to lift the corner of it with her. Will didn't bother holding back his laughter.

"Missed a spot," he said.

Kitty yanked on the metal handle to the closet, but it stuck in place. She wondered if the same ick on the floor was caught in the door frame. She didn't mean to feel so grossed out, but she was really missing the Slope where doors opened when they were supposed to.

She tugged again.

Nothing.

As if to cheer Kitty on, stomping from upstairs shook the ceiling. She used her sticky shoe against the wall for leverage, and with another powerful yank on the handle, the door unjammed and sent Kitty toppling back onto the play rug. Will was at her side in an instant, helping her to stand as she shook off the sting in the back of her head where it bounced against the floor. That was when Kitty saw the pile of broomsticks and mop buckets half burying an arm in a pink sleeve. Immediately she threw the supplies aside, but before she could help the girl up, she saw a familiar wavy knot bunched at the back of her head, an unstained denim skirt, and a stylish pink sweater that Kitty was positive she had tossed into a laundry hamper last night.

"aHA!" she cried with a triumphant grin. More stomping agreement followed from upstairs, and Will cocked his head aside. "Leo was fifteen levels of wrong! The spell thingy totally worked!"

"No way," Will said. "You couldn't make that dummy. It was too—"

Kitty kneeled beside her dummy oration where her head was turned. Looking at her own face would always feel weird. What Kitty didn't see on her dummy was a plastic pink and black friendship bracelet she had been wearing when she executed the oration. Had dummy lost it as she got stuck in the broom closet?

Kitty pinched the little charm dangling from her

bracelet. It flashed between her fingers and then her left palm sparked as the MHD appeared. A raspy burst of sound in her ear tickled her.

"No need to have you running around if I'm already here," Kitty said, bringing back the home screen of her tablet. "Now where do I turn off orations? And how'd you get to the church anyway?"

As if to answer her, the girl on the floor groaned and started to turn her head. Her arms and legs quaked from the effort of slowly moving out of the pile. Kitty, in a moment of sympathy, laid a hand on dummy's arm to help her up. As she touched the sweater, a terrible shock ran up her arm and down her spine. She yelped and jumped back, losing her balance and tumbling back into Will who barely kept on his own feet. Her Harnessing Device skid along the ground towards the cubbies.

Kitty looked at the tender red mark on her palm. The girl on the floor groaned again and started pushing herself up to her hands and knees. She hissed in pain and started favoring her left hand. The knitting on the sweater by the dummy's left shoulder was slightly singed.

The girl finally looked up and gasped at the sight of Kitty. Her mouth bobbed as she floundered for words.

"Dummy?" they both finally said then clapped their hands over their mouths.

Will kneeled down to look closer at the second Kitty who turned to stare back at him with the same bemused face. "Whoa. No way. I mean, I don't doubt you could make an awesome dummy diagram, but—Okay, let's just be perfectly sure."

Will picked up his tablet and flicked across the screen

before selecting something. He stood next to Kitty again and held the screen out so she could see. "The scanner is another useful function. It lets you see what oration is active unless the Magistrate is hiding the use for some reason."

Kitty could see her dummy on the screen as if looking through a camera lens. Will tapped a circular button, and the screen clicked. The dummy's wary glance was frozen in front of them until it started to dissolve into lines of shivering symbols. Kitty looked for what she wanted to see. Her dream doodles looked like her, but the way the letters sloped and shook talked to her—she now knew it was a conversation—about looking in a mirror. She was reading herself, but not really herself. Someone who was just like her, but that dummy version didn't know everything about her. Not like the real Kitty knew herself.

Kitty squinted at the letters and waited for them to stop shivering. Will let out a confused huff. He shook the tablet for good measure, but it didn't help.

"What are you doing?" the dummy asked with Kitty's borrowed voice. She had her hand hovering over her forearm now. Over the sweater sleeve was a silver casing that stretched to her elbow. "And...how did you get here?"

"Me?" Kitty shook her head. "How did YOU get here? I thought the oration didn't work. Leo said it didn't work." She finally got to her feet and looked back at Will's tablet, but all she got was a blurry string of blue letters. Will didn't say a word. His wide eyes never left the screen. "What the actual heck is wrong with this thing?"

"Nothing!" Will protested.

"Dummies can't orate," the other girl said, dragging herself to her feet, "but I guess they can make friends. Zack, what's going on? Why are you with my dummy?"

Both Kitty and Will turned back to the girl rubbing at her shoulder. She stopped as she took in their looks.

Before anyone could answer, they all jumped at the thunderous crashing from upstairs. It shook the ceiling and walls and knocked a few Bible Tales books from their shelves. Kitty knew the church goers at Hope Creek were noisy, but never to the point where someone could mistake it for a rowdy party. Distant shrieks and thuds continued.

"Raquel, if you're already here, we should see what that was about," the second girl said. "It could be connected to this weirdness."

Kitty shook her head. "That's not my name."

"Oh my gee, are you really trying to tell me you're not a dummy diagram?"

"Of course I'm not! I'm Kitty. You're the—"

CRASH!

Will raised his hands. "Never mind that now! Both of you, come on."

Will ran for the door. Kitty hurried after him and heard the copycat Raquel following close behind.

Eight

At the end of the hallway, they climbed the creaking steps, and Will threw himself at the door. It barely budged. He waved the girls over, and together they shoved. The door crawled along the floor until it pressed against something solid. Through the crack, Kitty could see a tipped over pew blocking their way to the sanctuary where the sound was deafening. People were shrieking and hissing. Thuds of blows with fists and feet filled the air. It stank of sweaty bodies.

"This door is jammed good," Kitty said after one last shove.

"I'll push," Will said. "You squeeze through. Then get the door for us."

Will and Raquel hoisted their shoulders against the door and shoved while Kitty crawled over the fallen pew. As soon as she stumbled to the other side, she froze.

The church was a warzone. Women were pulling at

each other's hair, jewelry, and eyes. Men had torn suits and crumpled hats that were stained with red to match their faces and chests. Kitty flattened herself against the wall as a man flailed past her and crashed to the ground, groaning with a bruised cheek. A cloud of dust sprayed beneath him and more sifted from the walls as people were hurled against them.

"Kitty, let me out!" Will called from behind the door. In that instant, Kitty had nearly forgotten.

"I've gotta move these pews," she said. "One of you needs to call the cops or something!"

As she fumbled for her cell phone and passed it to Raquel through the slit in the door, her own words made her uneasy. She hoped whoever showed up wouldn't be a Hostilia in disguise. Kitty inched around the fallen man and grabbed an end of the first pew, dragging it from the door. Will and Raquel started climbing past. Raquel was speaking in a shrill, nervous tone to someone official on the phone just as a set of hands clamped down on Kitty's shoulders.

"You ain't no real Christian, you little brat!" a husky male voice growled. The man with the bruised cheek had gotten up and started dragging Kitty away from the door. He flung her to the ground, and she crashed into one of the upright pews. She bent her knees, ready to kick at the man if he came any closer, but a woman involved in a different scuffle bumped into him and then slapped him across the face, steering his attention away.

Now Kitty could see Will flagging down a few scared patrons, including Reverend Al and Mrs. Constance who were perched behind a wall with the Reverend blocking the woman from the sights. They skirted across the wall

119

and joined Raquel behind the door to the classrooms. Kitty looked for anyone else unaffected by whatever madness was going on. A young boy and girl were hiding under the church organ. The boy hugged the girl close as her shoulders bobbed from crying. Kitty recognized them as Joey and Tara Marsh, the only other kids who regularly attended Hope Creek.

Kitty turned to tell Will, but he was already moving to separate some fighters who were handling weapons from the kitchen. She was on her own.

Kitty started crawling, ducking into rows whenever anyone got too close. She made it down the side aisle, but still had to climb to the stage and across another fifteen feet to the giant instrument. Kitty waited for a moment when she thought no one would pay her any attention. Then she skimmed the diagram resources in her tablet for anything useful. She could put everyone in the church to sleep. Too complicated. She could make herself invisible. But how would she explain that to the boy and girl? When Kitty's eyes landed on the transit orations, she figured that could work. Who would notice anything like popping up somewhere different in all of the commotion?

"Okay, oration number two," she muttered, "don't let me down."

She activated the spell diagram and watched the strings of light blue text like so many ribbons wrapping around her screen into changeable shapes and forms. She felt the letters asking her questions, begging for as much detail as she could give. She spoke what she wanted in her mind and slid her fingers across the screen, but the questions fought back. They repeated themselves like a child on an endless loop of asking "why". Kitty pushed ahead and insisted her answers were enough as the ribbons of text finally locked into place where she wanted.

EXECUTE? [Y/N]

Kitty pressed the 'Y' furiously. The air directly between her and the back of the first row of pews wavered like heat lines before it darkened into a black cutout just tall enough for Kitty to crawl through. Her breath caught in her chest, and the magic reaching out around her twanged with the gasp of the world changing. She felt the cool splash of nothingness as she crossed the threshold and found herself crawling from worn carpet onto the wood of the pulpit with no one in between her and the church organ. She sprinted down the steps and dove under the keys where the boy was whispering to his little sister.

"Are you alright?" Kitty asked. "Did anyone hurt you?"

Joey shook his head. Kitty wrapped an arm around him and looked out at the sanctuary. Now that she was on the stage, she wasn't sure how to get back without getting caught in the fray; there were at least double the attendees that night for the special service. She spotted another door at the bottom of the stage steps. If they couldn't get back to Will who was wrestling a man off of a screaming patron, they could at least get that far.

Kitty looked back to the boy and his still sobbing sister. "We're gonna have to run and keep our heads down. Can you do that, Joey?" He nodded. Kitty rested her hand gently on Tara's back. She couldn't be more than five years old in her bright pink dress and glitter hair ribbons. "Hey sweetie, your big brother is gonna take really good care of you, okay?" Tara sniffled in response. "Alright, on the count of three. One." Kitty took Joey's hand, and Joey took Tara's. "Two." They all inched out from under the organ. Kitty pulled the short bench to block them from view a moment longer. "Three!"

They crawled out from their hiding spot and raced across the stage. The old wood creaked and dipped. As they reached the top of the steps to the seating area, a woman thrown forward from the aisle caught sight of them. She hissed and spat past her fattened lip and started scrambling up towards them. Kitty kept Joey and Tara behind her as the woman clasped her hand around Kitty's ankle and dragged her down the steps.

A familiar green haze like a computer program fell over Kitty's eyes as her heartbeat pounded between her ears.

I need to be strong enough to keep this squirrelnuts woman away from me and the kids. I need to protect Joey and Tara!

As the green vision cleared, Kitty reached her hands out, now coiled in blue streams of light that quickly melted through her skin. She pried the church woman's hands from her ankle and shoved her back. With wide eyes, Kitty saw her arc through the air and crash into one of the middle pews. There wasn't time to stop and stare. She waved Joey to bring his sister, and the three of them ran through the door.

They hunkered down in a small serving room that looked like a tornado passed through. Tinfoil trays of macaroni, ham, baked and fried chicken, collard greens, and string beans in thick red sauce were tipped and splattered across the floor. A few women in aprons were unconscious, stained from head to toe, and had some nasty bruises forming on their faces.

Kitty waited for a few minutes in hopes that the heavy thuds and growls outside the door would die down. Just as she was losing faith, Will's voice streamed into her ears, *"If you can hear me, close your eyes!"* Everything in his words told her he was about to do a big piece of magic.

Kitty's relief quickly turned to panic as she drew Joey and Tara in and held their faces to her neck. She squinted her eyes shut just before a bright flash spilled under the door frame and made the floor glow around them. Kitty's mind felt scrambled, a torrent of anxiety and sleepiness slapped her brain, but she kept her thoughts on staying awake and keeping Joey and Tara close. After a few seconds the pale gray beneath her eyelids darkened to a normal blackness. Kitty peeked one eye open. Everything looked the same, but the sanctuary was ghostly quiet. The children in Kitty's arms began to fidget. She let them sit back as she inched the door open.

From the small crack, nothing moved. She dared to open the door the rest of the way and saw nearly all of the congregation on the floor or lying over benches. Then Will walked in from the front lobby swiping on his MHD and walking toward Raquel, Reverend Al and Mrs. Constance.

"We called the police," he said to the older man. "Are you alright? Do you need to sit?"

"Oh...um...right. Yes," Reverend Al stammered as he took in the view of his congregation. "Uh, yes, all the ruckus. Everyone gettin' in an uproar. Power of prayer can be...pretty overwhelmin' sometimes, I've gotta say."

"Absolutely," said Mrs. Constance with a rarely heard

hesitation in her voice. "Even these godly folks can forget themselves."

"Kitty, why don't you get them some water while we wait for the police?" Raquel stared at him with her head slowly tipping to the side. Will patted her shoulder. "I know this was pretty crazy, but I think the Reverend could really use some water, huh?"

Raquel shook her head rapidly. "Yeah! Oh, of course."

"I ain't forgot myself that much," Mrs. Constance said. She righted herself and pulled out a wooden fan from her loud floral dress. "You sit tight. I'll do a look over and get us some water. Reverend, you get comfortable. Kitty, sweetheart, you call your mama and have her come get you. I don't want you walkin' home with nobody actin' the fool."

"Now Constance," Reverend Al said, "I will help you. I won't hear any fussin' about it."

The two adults made their way towards the kitchenette where Kitty was hiding. Kitty ordered Joey and Tara to sit tight until Mrs. Constance came for them. Then she crawled out through the door and under one of the rows. When the kitchenette door swung shut, Kitty stood back up and pulled Will back down the stairs to the offices and classrooms below with Raquel in tow.

"One day with the MHD and you've got churches blowing up around you," Will said when they were secured back in the classroom.

"Oh shut it, Will."

"Zack, this joke is going on way too long, don't you think?" Raquel said. She shoved her hands on her waist with a pout. Kitty and Will took in the seriousness of her face. Kitty had seen that look so many times staring into her mirror when she gave herself pep talks to get through school and Homecoming plans. She was serious. She was crazy. Could orations be crazy? In the silence, Raquel shook her head. "Fine. You're so obsessed. I'll just terminate the dummy."

"I'm not a dummy!" Kitty cried. "Will, did the scan work yet?"

"Uh...well, it worked. And to make it clear, I only looked at the full thing because you wanted me to." He revealed his tablet again and returned to the screen with the unsettled symbols.

"Because it's fiftieth level weirdness!" When the scan began floating across the screen, Kitty pointed frantically at all the bizarre spots on the diagram that wouldn't form properly. The little symbols shuddered and spun out of control. The only clear parts were the sections of the oration that spoke about mirror images and half truths about herself. It was as if the diagram only dared scratch the surface of what Kitty expected to see about herself.

"What the heck?" they heard Raquel say, slapping at the silver casing. "Where's the active oration?"

After a treacherously long moment of peering and inspecting, Will finally asked. "Kitty, are you feeling okay?"

Kitty threw her arms up and groaned. "What kind of question is that? Just tell me what kind of magic she is. What oration is active right now?"

"What magic I am?" Raquel scoffed.

"...Kitty," Will looked back at her. "This isn't an active oration...this is your frequency." Will looked her in the eye and tapped on the MHD with his knuckle. "This is you."

Kitty stared. She kept staring. She looked from Will standing in front of her to Raquel staring back. Kitty's lips parted to speak, but no words would form right away. Finally she said very simply, "No."

"Kitty—"

"That doesn't make sense," she continued. "What's the name of the tool? I'll do it myself.

Will pointed out the scan, a camera lens with a single blue symbol in the middle. Kitty selected it and stormed over to where Raquel was now glaring at the two of them from eerily familiar eyes.

"What—?" the other girl started to say as Kitty held the tablet in front of her and snapped another scan like retaking the thousandth picture of herself for her Friendville page. Raquel's confused face appeared on the screen again before becoming enveloped in a grid and broken down further into loops and swirls of jittering symbols. Kitty thrust the tablet into Will's arm with a smirk and then crossed her arms.

"Now what, numbnuts? Tell me what it really says."

It was Will's turn to stare. He looked between the scan, Kitty, and Raquel. One hand kept scratching through his sandy hair. He looked at Raquel, forcing an imitation of his usual cocky grin. "Hi, I'm Will Cavanaugh, by the way. Who are you?"

"Seriously?" Raquel said. "What the heck did you do after I left? Did your runner friends give you something to smoke?"

"O...kay..." Will looked at the scan once again, holding the tablet at every angle, but the screen only rotated to the new view. "Well this says you're Kitty Eleanor Guthrie."

"Will, I am warning you—" Kitty shot him a nasty

126

glare. Her face flushed making her more uncomfortable in the humid room.

"Don't blame me for whatever you did. You couldn't have broken your MHD that fast so how is it that there are two Kitty Guthries standing here right now? That's gotta be a bad sign."

"There aren't two Kitty Guthries," Raquel said. "I'm not Kitty Guthrie. I don't know anyone named...Kitty. And you don't either! Enough with the dummy already!"

The distant toll of police sirens stole their attention. They all remembered the commotion from just a few minutes before. Will pulled the stiff cloth curtains aside and was met with the velvety blues of dusk.

"Maybe we need to figure this out somewhere else," Will said. "I don't want to be involved in police business. We can go to my house if we're gonna talk magic stuff."

Kitty looked at the other two with a strange feeling in her gut like at any moment the world was going to crumble around her. The blaring police sirens reminded her of Officer Bryant's warning to stay out of trouble. She couldn't imagine how much worse things could get than breaking the rules of nature.

Nine

Mrs. Guthrie was never an easy woman to convince to switch schedules around. She had a tight grip on where she needed to be, who else needed to be somewhere, and how much it would all cost.

"You suddenly remembered to tell me about this project due in two days?" Mrs. Guthrie scolded over the phone as Kitty silently packed a duffel bag with pajamas and clothes for school the next day. Her sister was finally asleep in the next room, and Claudine was watching a movie down the hall. Kitty was surprised to hear Edith wailing as the transit let her out on the fire escape outside of her window. It took a lot to put the ten-year-old in a bad mood. Every instinct told her to run and hold her, but she couldn't be seen at home if she was meant to be at the church for another hour. She just needed to pack some overnight clothes in case figuring out her latest problem took longer than expected.

"I've...been really busy," Kitty mumbled into the

phone. Balancing it against her ear was getting harder as her tense shoulders ached. She zipped up the overnight bag and readjusted her phone as her mom answered.

"...everything to Homecoming when you've got homework. Amazing as it'll be on a college application, you still need to get through five more years of school."

"I know, mom. I know. I've gotta run. April's mom is gonna pick me up."

"What? That's nonsense. Kitty, I'll come get you. I just have to check in with the sitter. Edith has been a handful this weekend. Nothing seems to stop her crying."

"No! It's okay, really! I don't want to bug you."

"Kitty Eleanor, stop it," her mother hissed through the line. Kitty stood still from sheer habit as if her mother were right in her doorway. "You are my child, and if you need anything, my job is to help you. Don't let me hear that you're keeping anything from me because you don't want to to bug me. That's ridiculous."

"...sorry, mom, but she's already here. Thanks anyway."

Kitty mumbled a goodbye and hung up. She withheld a frustrated moan as she hurried back out the window to the fire escape. As she shouldered her bag more comfortably, she sent a quick text message to April.

NQC sleepover for skool prjct

Immediately her phone buzzed with a response.

k. subject due date
sci tues
Kk

129

Kitty slipped her phone in the duffel bag and pulled out her tablet. She scrolled to find a transit and looked it over. Just one day into being a Mage and she was lying to her mom. Dodging the truth was one thing, but lies made her uncomfortable. It was one of the loudest things her mom yelled about in her early stupor after her dad left. Lies. Late nights. Maybe she was more like him than she wanted to think. More than she could remember.

He ruins everything. The thought floated through her mind as she tried pulling strands of blue light across her tablet screen. They slipped from beneath her fingers or tugged against her prodding. *Why couldn't he be like April's or Becka's dad. Normal and not a twentieth level jerkface.*

Kitty found herself wanting to slam the tablet into the metal. Her face was flushed, and in her head, she was yelling answers at the questions popping up with each loop in the diagram. It fought back each time. She plopped down ungracefully onto the fire escape stairs and took a deep breath.

With magic I could find him and make him pay, said a tiny part of her heart. It shocked her how much she wanted to listen to it, but she shook her thoughts clear and looked back at the diagram. She directly input Will's address and gave the oration permission to use up the energy it needed. Most importantly, she started answering who she was and why she was asking for the world to take her from one place and drop her in another. The sooner she could get to Will and resolve the situation with Raquel, the better everyone would be. She just knew it.

Still the text didn't yield right away, but the strain didn't come from her. The magic itself seemed to struggle to understand part of the diagram. There were parts that she didn't know like how exactly space moved her or moved around her when an oration happened. She didn't think she would need to know that part if it was set into the base diagram, like how she didn't know the inner workings of her school tablet, but she could still type in a web address.

Suddenly the diagram stopped fighting her as if it were just being stubborn, and Kitty executed it. The air by her window warbled and faded to black. Kitty missed the days of her snapping from one place to another. The little portal circles made her nervous, but still Kitty stepped through and felt the splash of cool nothing against her face and body. Somewhere behind her she thought she could hear her sister crying. She hoped Claudine wasn't in over her head tonight.

She stood in front of Will's bed where he was lying down and throwing a wadded up paper towards the ceiling and catching it. Raquel was in the desk chair staring at her phone in its pink casing, but stopped as soon as Kitty appeared.

"That's never gonna feel normal," both girls said.

"Neither is that," Will added as he sat up. "Have you been practicing your transit diagrams, Kitty? That was really quiet. Nice job."

Kitty only shrugged. "Thanks."

"Yeah. Anyway, now that the whole gang is here, let's figure this out so you can stop with the twin weirdness. I already had to convince Raquel that I'm not this Zack person she kept mentioning and she doesn't live on Crystal Avenue."

Kitty started at the street name. "On the Slope?"

"Yeah. Like ten minutes from here. Why?"

"That's...where I used to live, before we moved a few years ago."

"It doesn't make sense," Raquel said, dropping her eyes. "None of this makes sense."

Kitty put her duffel bag on the floor and sat on the edge of Will's bed. "How do we fix this? An oration shouldn't have the same frequency as me, right Mr. Mentor?"

Raquel glared, "I am NOT an oration!"

Will shrugged. "Nothing can change someone's frequency, but it can be hidden. Not a Magus'. Definitely not an Initiate's, but a Justice's could. Raquel, can you tell us how you ended up at the church?"

"Just a normal transit diagram," she said, and she started spinning in the chair, refusing to make eye contact. Kitty could see her anger and anxiousness with each kick. "He—Zack and I were going to an adjudication. I was going to go straight there from my friend's house, but I wanted to go home first. Just to check in. The diagram was normal, I'd done one a million times. But...once I executed it, this weird sort of dark circle showed up right above me. I felt like I was pulled up and away instead of just..." She clapped her hands together, and Kitty understood. The feeling of what she called her portal wishes was like her body snapped out of existence and showed up somewhere else. But if the dark circle wasn't supposed to happen... "Then I blacked out. I woke up in the church with you two standing over me."

Kitty looked at Will, but he turned his head from Raquel back to his ceiling, folding and unfolding the wadded paper as he thought.

"What about you?" Raquel asked, staring at Kitty with

an accusing glare. "Did you do anything weird that might have messed with my transit?"

"I only got this thing yesterday!" Kitty protested.

"Only takes one oration to do some crazy stuff," Will said.

"Whose side are you on, anyway? What kind of a mentor are you?"

Will held his hands up defensively. "No one said anything about sides. Did you try any weird magic since you've had the MHD?"

"No!" Then Kitty remembered what happened two days ago. That strange dummy oration started yelling its questions just like Kitty had to yell to make the transit to Will's, trying its hardest to be heard over everything else. Kitty's jump worked. The dummy didn't. At least that was what Leo said.

"Yes you did," Raquel said. She stood up so quickly that the chair kept spinning. "I know that face."

Kitty looked at Raquel; she also knew the face. She thought she might get a stern talking to as if she colored on the walls with crayons or refused to eat her brussels sprouts. There were small creases on Raquel's forehead, but her muddy brown eyes were more pleading than scolding. She was about to be extremely reasonable, and Kitty couldn't handle it. She shouldn't have made the oration this realistic.

So she told Raquel and Will everything about the dummy diagram. Her gut told her something about that bit of magic was wrong. The way it yelled and popped wasn't like anything she had ever seen. The point was to make an exact copy. She needed to trust that the dummy wouldn't give her away. Kitty needed an extra Kitty.

Will gave a low whistle. "Weirdest dummy I've ever heard of. It couldn't have worked. Like Leo said, if you were trying to make it exactly like you, it wouldn't execute. There can't be two..."

Will quieted. The room became deadly silent as Raquel and Will stared at Kitty. She lowered her head and sank to the floor, but she could still feel their eyes burning into her skull.

"What did I do?" Kitty whimpered.

"You didn't necessarily do anything wrong." Will got off the bed and crouched beside her. "You're only an Initiate. There's a lot to learn. You could have accidentally stumbled on the greatest discovery ever. A perfect dummy oration."

"I swear to God if you call me an oration again—!" Raquel leaped to her feet. "I am a real person. I'm alive. I'm not magic gone haywire! Stop looking at me like that!" Kitty and Will immediately looked at each other instead of Raquel and her glassy eyes that threatened frustrated tears. Whatever she was saying, she fully believed it. Kitty wondered if it was okay to terminate an oration that felt so much like a real person. "My house is full of strangers and my partner isn't answering his E-Com and I can't make calls to him or even my friends or my family! I'm not squirrelnuts. I'm freaking out!"

"Sorry, Raquel," Kitty said.

"Of course you are! This is your fault!"

Kitty blushed and looked back down at her lap.

"Look," Will said, stepping in, "if a transit got Raquel here, a transit ought to get her back, right? Go ahead. I'll lend you any energy boost you need."

Will caught Kitty's eye with a raised eyebrow. Her ear

tingled as her Chameleon Ear switched on, and she could hear his voice continuing to say, *"Play along!"*

"Yeah," she said. "Me too."

Will got into a comfortable sitting position against the foot of his bed and touched the face of his watch. It glinted for just a moment before the shine reappeared in the palm of his hand as a white-cased tablet. Kitty pinched the charm on her friendship bracelet, and it grew bright under her touch until that glow blinked and became an identical tablet in her hands.

Raquel's eyes flickered between the two of them, her mouth set in a tight grimace. Then she nodded and tapped on a bracelet under her sweater sleeve. It also flashed and grew into a bangle the length of her forearm that left just the tip of her sweater poking out. A screen popped up, and Raquel skillfully tapped a few keys. She started to manually input information about her home as Will peaked over her shoulder. The more she typed, the more Will shook his head and glanced back at Kitty.

Raquel paused, shooting a withering stare at the device. "Why….? Okay, super weirdness. The oration normally fills in basic stuff. Like, the stuff we don't think about because it's so basic, but it's not filling in right. See? There. It's glowing like it wants to be changed, but that's a part I don't ever change. But it doesn't look right either. What is wrong with this place?"

"Let me take a look. Can you send it to me? William P. Cavanaugh on the Tree."

"Uh...I don't see you here."

"Huh." Kitty could hear the forced shock in his voice, but Raquel didn't seem to notice. If she did, too much of her energy was trained on scrolling the names in the Magistrate Family Tree. "I'll bring it up on my own MHD."

Kitty dared to peek as Will put this new diagram side by side with his basic transit diagram. Kitty could see the faint glow around certain areas. They called out with very scientific sounding questions. Things teachers didn't bother to explain like the fact that air was all around and gravity kept people from floating off into space. It was common sense, and the details didn't seem important for wherever regular transits were leading. The new oration demanded to know more about the world at large.

"Can't you copy and paste it?" Kitty asked from over Will's shoulder. "It's that common stuff the Initiate Resource talked about."

"Trying to suck up to teacher?" Will said as he nudged her with his elbow. "I'm working on it now—huh?"

All three Mages watched as fat red exclamation marks started flashing across the screen. One after another, they blocked the view of the diagram behind it. Will tapped one, and it shrunk to a message.

ERROR: UNAUTHORIZED LOCATION.

He tapped another.

ERROR: SYNTAX MALFUNCTION.

ERROR: PLEASE INPUT JUSTICE AUTHORIZATION FOR DESTINATION.

Wherever the faint glow appeared, more of the errors

appeared. Kitty, Will, and Raquel sat back as nearly the entire diagram flared to life with red warnings and each message said something similar. The transit they wanted wasn't allowed.

"That's...never happened before..." Raquel said, her eyes never leaving the screen. "And it's not done yet. I didn't even add anything else!"

The parts of the diagram they could see past the newly sprouting error signs weren't settling into place. The information Raquel shared with it kept fussing. Kitty could feel faint whispers like a child shouting from down the road asking his mother why and not caring what her answer was. The oration shivered, and each movement created new errors. Kitty wondered if the oration had given Will's tablet a virus. Hackers would be sitting on a fortune if they could break into a computer with magic.

"Okay, this is definitely not normal," Will said. "It's not like we're trying to go to space. We're supposedly just going a few blocks away." Will looked at the diagram closer, tapping past each new error message.

Kitty started getting dizzy trying to read them. "Maybe we should ask Leo about this. Oh junk. Do you think he'll take my MHD away?"

Will didn't answer as he continued staring down the tablet screen. Then he looked at Kitty with a sudden grin. "Alright, mentee! We've got a problem to solve. Let's do it."

"Huh? Will, is this really the time to—?"

"It's perfect. A teachable moment! I'm sending you what I've done on the oration so far."

With a few swipes, Kitty's tablet beeped. She opened the message from Will and watched the sprawling mess of blue lines and red exclamation points cover her screen. She popped each error message so she could look at the diagram herself and muttered, "Numbnuts."

Just as before, everything Raquel added to the spell diagram was glowing and shivering. Every few seconds a new error message appeared.

Raquel leaned over Kitty's shoulder. "Does it look different to either of you somehow? Not in the 'duh' way, but different than just a few minutes ago?"

"Yeah, a little," Kitty said. She pointed to a spot describing a house. It still seemed to say the same thing, but the voices asking questions sounded a touch louder, and the image they described looked a hair bigger. Raquel leaned closer and pointed at another spot. The air between them buzzed and made Kitty's skin itch. It was describing a familiar smell about the transit diagram's destination. Something normally comforting, but occasionally it stung like something rancid. Somehow that entire description felt bigger than it had minutes ago.

"It seems like—" Kitty fumbled for words. "Okay, so when a spell diagram is ready to execute, it chills, right? It stops moving around?"

"Well, it only moves under your oration," Will said. "Normally. Okay, yeah."

"So this diagram isn't ready to execute because it's like Raquel started giving it her oration and it's still, I guess, trying to ask questions so it understands. Or maybe it's getting its answer, but every answer is something we can't do. Why, I don't know. Leo never said there were orations we couldn't make."

"But there are places that take too much energy for one

person to execute," Will reminded her. "If you don't have the strength, you'll get a warning."

"These warnings aren't saying that." Kitty pointed at a new error that popped up.

ERROR: UNAVAILABLE DESTINATION COORDINATES.

ERROR: AUTHORIZATION REQUIRED.

"My house isn't unavailable you stupid computer!" Raquel growled. She sat back and pressed the keys on her wrist computer with more force than before.

"Wait!" Kitty said. "Look! The errors are stopping."

On Kitty's screen, the wave of red exclamation marks slowed. Each strange message blipped out of sight until only one last exclamation point appeared. Kitty tapped it, ready to quickly close it and try to activate the diagram again.

ERROR: ACCESS DENIED. AUTHORIZATION REQUIRED FROM ORATOR FOR DIAGRAM ACCESS.

Silence fell over the room again. Kitty let the MHD rest in her lap and stretched her stiff arm.

"Someone's diagram is stopping me from making a transit back to my house?" Raquel wondered aloud. "Who would do that?"

"You make any enemies?" Will said playfully, but his drooping eyes gave away his own concerns. Raquel shook her head.

Kitty watched the screen. She read and reread the error.

Then she wondered not so much about who was trying to keep Raquel from getting home—whether that was down the street or somewhere in Kitty's head—but what that person was using to do it. She picked up the tablet again, but dropped it as her stomach wrenched with nausea. Her face broke into a cold sweat, and the room filled with a numbing haze.

"...Kitty, you're alright," she heard Will say.

"She's really pale."

"Just lean over the garbage."

As the haziness cleared, Kitty was head first over Will's garbage can, gripping the sides with shaking hands. Her stomach was still tight, and she could feel wetness pooling under her eyes and streaking down her cheeks. The nausea struck again. Will patted her back while Raquel pushed her hair away from her shoulders. A tingle buzzed along her scalp which didn't help settle her stomach. Raquel quickly let go.

"Check—the spell—please," she said before dry heaving. She heard someone pick up her tablet, and both Mages groaned and started tapping away more error messages.

"Wait, these are different." Will said. "Error: Adjacent spatial lock. Activation timed out. Error. Interference in activation coordinates. Error...okay, maybe we should talk to Leo. Now they're all junked up. It's not even English on these warnings."

"Not Spanish," Raquel confirmed. "Super grossness to look at. Will, can't you make it calm down again?"

"I don't know what we did the first time. Definitely looks like the diagram is changing again."

"But, like, double time."

Kitty moaned as her stomach kept churning. She hadn't felt this bad since Leo introduced her to—

"Nefas!" they all shouted. Kitty vomited again. She felt Will's hand on her back as he kept talking. "Kitty has a sensitivity thing," he said to Raquel.

"Like a gluten allergy?"

"Sure. Just don't say, uh, Cursed Boss' name, but that's definitely some of Its bad juju warping this diagram. Either It or maybe whoever made the diagram blocking us is affected by It."

Raquel seethed. "Why won't It let me go home? What oration is It using to block our transit?"

"Exactly…" Kitty croaked as she slowly sat back. "I was going to see what oration was in the way."

They closed the diagram, and Will scrolled for any active orations that might interfere with theirs based on that error report. One pinged, but Will couldn't select it. A tag beside it had a curling line that indicated it was signed by very high ranking Justices. It was nothing for a few low level Mages and an Initiate to bother with, but at least it didn't look corrupted with that horrible blackness.

Will tweaked his search to locate any other transit orations that could be active. Kitty wondered if this was playing too far into Raquel's make-believe that she wasn't just a perfected dummy oration. It would make sense that a transit wasn't authorized for a girl made of magic to return to a home that wasn't entirely real. Could transits be made into people's bodies? Their minds? Their hearts?

"Okay! Now we're talking," Will said. His tongue jammed out from the corner of his lips as he selected an oration type in the search engine. A handful of hits appeared in a neat list before some blinked away. Kitty moved closer, pulling the garbage can beside her just in case. There was an unsettling aura about those transit-like diagrams.

Another one disappeared, then another.

"Transits don't last after you execute them, right?" Raquel asked.

Will nodded. "I've also never heard of an active transit getting in the way of anyone else's no matter how close. Maybe it's good that they're getting scratched from the list."

"Wait, see where they are before they all go," Kitty said. "If Cursed Boss is involved, we should definitely tell Leo."

"Yeah."

Will tried to select the remaining orations, but they were only static text on his screen. He shut his eyes for a moment. As if struck with sudden inspiration, he looked through the functions of this search and found a wider display. Hovering tutorial blurbs explained different buttons he hadn't used before. He clicked an icon that looked like a globe, and the screen blacked out, replaced by a satellite view of Will's street and a few neighboring streets in every direction. Arrows to the side zoomed in and out of the image. This one showed grayed out blips with blurbs beside them as the tutorial activated.

ACTIVE SPELL FUNCTION. OUTSIDE SEARCH PARAMETERS. OWNERSHIP TAG: JESSE G. HEWITT (Magistrate). PERPETUAL ENVIRONMENT DETOX FUNCTION. OPEN PARTICIPATION UPON REQUEST.

Will zoomed out until he could see all of the Crest and the Slope when finally a lit up blip appeared.

ACTIVE S__L_ F__N_T__N. ERROR. NO ORATION(S) WITHIN SEARCH PARAMETERS.

Kitty grabbed her stomach again. The light blinked out.

"They're all gone," Will said. "But if they come back, we can figure out where they are at least."

"If they don't, I can go home, right?" Raquel said.

"There's still that ownership tag oration we can't look at. How about I talk to Leo in the morning. It's getting late. Raquel, you can hang here in one of the guest rooms."

Kitty found her phone and checked the time. It was nearly 11:30, and she had an anxious text from April.

Wre r u???

"I'll meet you two after school tomorrow," Kitty said, grabbing her bag and tossing it over her shoulder. She looked back at Will and Raquel with backless words of encouragement on her tongue. She didn't realize the consequences of recreating a life until it turned to her for help.

Ten

The wafting smell of eggs, fried bacon, and buttered toast woke Kitty and April. They peeled themselves from the bedsheets, showered, and dressed. Kitty only paused for a second after tugging on her sock to watch April pin her hair and start applying some lip gloss. She had been quiet all morning when normally she would be talking Kitty's ear off about what to wear. She didn't say more than "Good morning" or share more than brief smiles when they passed each other.

They waited in the breakfast nook, scrolling their Friendville accounts on their phones, as Mrs. Sullivan poured glasses of orange juice on the kitchen island. She was a stocky woman with fair skin and raven hair pulled back in a simple ponytail. She set the food and drinks down in front of the girls and untied her apron. Where April had a keen eye for fashion, her mother made it clear that if she looked just professional enough in some black slacks and an unwrinkled blouse, she could do her job.

"I hope you two got a lot of work done," Mrs. Sullivan said. "Kitty, don't let April bully you into procrastinating on projects."

"Mom, puh-lease," April said, stopping her polite bite of food. "Kitty's the one making us late on everything. She's got a bazillion things to do, but somehow gets straight A's."

"Because she works hard, but what did your father and I tell you about grades, Flower?" Mrs. Sullivan pulled out a little booklet and a pen from a drawer along the kitchen counter. She laid it down and started filling in the pages.

"They're not an accurate representation of learning," April droned around her fork. "But they worked good enough for you and dad. Doctors get straight A's in school. Fashion designers can settle for B's. Math is only important for lengths of fabric."

"And maybe doing taxes," her mother retorted.

After breakfast, Mrs. Sullivan drove the girls to Glade Crest Junior High only a few blocks away. Another perk of living in the Crest was getting to sleep late, eat breakfast, and still get to school on time. The girls crossed the lawn, letting Mrs. Sullivan avoid the traffic jam near the bus lanes. April gave Kitty a stiff hug before they went separate ways to their lockers before homeroom. Kitty frowned at her retreating back. She looked forward to eight hours with an excuse not to think about Will or Raquel, but now she wanted to know what April's problem was. She had already apologized for showing up later than expected, but NQC meant no questions about why.

"Hey, Kitty!" Jennifer Murphy's singsong voice always rose up over the crowd in the hall. Kitty snapped to attention and saw where the taller girl was waving her down from a nearby door, brown hair bouncing and arms free because the girl next to her carried her books. She skipped over and leaned against the door of the locker next to Kitty's, ignoring the other student who was just about to attempt to unlock it.

"Hey, Jen." It was a bit of a surprise to talk to her, but Kitty smiled. Their friendship changed after Kitty moved out of the Slope, but she wouldn't let something stupid like living in the Valley dictate who her friends could be. April and Becka could use that lesson. "I like that top."

"Oh this old thing?" Jennifer tugged at the strap of her sleeveless blouse. It was form fitting under the cropped cardigan and Jennifer was one of those early bloomers. The hem was dangerously close to violating school policy. Kitty figured her friend had no intentions of raising her hands in class and testing this anyway. "It's from like a million years ago. But your dress is new, right? Tenth level super cute."

"Oh, yeah. Thanks. Not really new, but it's one of my favorites. Goes really well with this pair of brown boots I have."

"Coolness!" Jennifer said abruptly and clapped her hands together. "So anyway, I have a question for you. More like an idea. For Homecoming—which, oh my gee, I cannot wait for! But I was thinking, what if we did something like a traditional Homecoming King and Queen?"

Kitty fidgeted with the dangling buckle on her backpack strap. "Uh, I had an idea like that early on, but it didn't seem right for this kind of party. For high school maybe, but this is more about everyone getting together, not really about picking people out over the crowd."

"Oh no, I totally get that," Jennifer said, "but it's not

really about picking people out. It's about friends showing how much they care about each other. And, like, thanking people who really bring the student body together. You know our cheerleaders work super hard to raise everybody's spirit *and* raise money. We're like a step above Spirit Squad. The sports teams show how tough we are and all that. Our nerdy smart kids show how smart we are. Everybody really gets a fair chance, honestly. It doesn't seem fair that one person can just decide not to do something that could be really good for the school, y'know?"

"I mean, I don't decide alone. I just—"

"Oh by the way, Kitty cat, what was up with Friday?" Jennifer's eyes widened, and she covered her mouth with a manicured hand. "That cop looked really intense. What did you do?"

"Nothing!" Kitty protested. Her cheeks flushed when her voice came out louder than she hoped. "It was totally nothing. A huge misunderstanding.

"So squirrelnuts. I'm sure you'd never do something like forge your mom or dad's signature. Well, duh, not your dad's, but totally not your mom's. Anyway, could you be amazing and ask Mrs. Smith about the king and queen idea? That'd be, like, fifteenth level awesome if you could."

Kitty strangled her wrists and let her attention drift back to her locker. If that incident got back to Mrs. Smith, she would never let Kitty stay the face of Homecoming. "I—guess I could bring it up again?"

"Oh you are the best in the universe, Kitty! Hug hug!" She wrapped her arms around Kitty's shoulders. "Later!" Jennifer skipped back to where some boys and girls were waiting for her, and they strolled off. For one fleeting instant

Kitty imagined what it might be like to stand in front of the whole school with some enormous tiara, voted for by the entire student body. Everyone thanking her for putting Homecoming together. Thanking her for funding new after-school programs and clubs. Maybe Preston Smith standing next to her.

Her cheeks reddened. She shook the thought away and ran to class.

Kitty suffered through the most normal feeling day of school in a long time. Everything fell into place as if the weekend never happened. As if being a Mage was still left to movies and books. At lunch, she was practically smiling from the monotony of correct answers and easy pop quizzes meant to catch students unaware. She sat her tray down at her usual table, and it took her minutes to realize that both April and Becka were staring at her and not eating their own food.

"...what?" she finally said, putting her sandwich down. "Who's talking about me behind my back?"

"No one," April said. "I just want to remind you first that neither of us break NQCs."

Kitty stiffened. "Um, okay?"

"We don't break them for a reason. So we're not gonna do it now. This isn't just about showing up at my door at midnight and I had no idea what the actual heck I might tell your mom if you were hurt. Like, seriously? Two NQCs in two days? But that's not the point. It's not the whole point. This is about every day since, like, the summer."

Becka laughed a short, rough laugh. "You know it's been every day since she went squirrelnuts with her Homecoming planning last year."

"Kitty, we're just worried. You pile up your to do list so much that it's as heavy as Laina Turner. We all know you're really smart and you can do anything you set your mind to, but don't you think maybe you're...doing a bit too much?"

"If it were too much, I wouldn't do it," Kitty said. She stuffed her sandwich in her mouth, narrowly avoiding her finger. She didn't need scolding from them any more than she needed it from her mother.

"We've barely hung out since all this started," Becka added.

Kitty rolled her eyes and swallowed the oversized bite. It scraped down her throat. "Like I don't know that? It's not on purpose. I'm busy. Homecoming is Friday. Then everything will be back to normal."

"Will it?" April asked as she picked her fork through a mound of wet rice. "Or will you find something else to be busy with? Suddenly besties with Jennifer Murphy again even though she hates our guts? Like, are you trying to ditch us? Just tell us if you are."

Kitty gaped. "What? No way!"

"Then I don't get it. It's like you've got something to prove and I don't know who you think you have to prove yourself to. The teachers already know you're great. We already know. So who doesn't know? Why drive yourself squirrelnuts like this? Who are you doing this for?"

"It's for the school. It's...it's for me too. It'll look great when I apply for colleges. I could go to any school I want. ...do I really need to explain this to you of all people? You think my mom is gonna be able to help? My dad? My grandparents aren't rich. No lucky millionaire aunts or uncles. No war hero uncles—"

"Hey!" Becka said.

"—and I'm not about to get adopted into a family of doctors!"

April crossed her arms. "Not fair, Kitty."

"Well no one else is gonna help and no one is gonna do anything like this so why shouldn't I?"

Becka and April glanced at each other, faces twisted with frustration. Becka only shrugged, but April continued, "Sorry, Kitty. I'm not trying to attack you or anything so don't bite our heads off. You just look so—"

"Mad?" Becka offered. "Fifteenth level squirrelnuts?"

April whacked her arm. "Unhappy. I was gonna say unhappy. Just don't forget that we're here to help you with anything. You don't have to just bark orders at us at these meetings and stuff. We can help with other things. We did everything you said on Friday."

"I made the sixth graders clean all the paint brushes," Becka said with a proud smirk.

"Yes, Becks terrified some sixth graders." The girls laughed. Kitty felt her chest and shoulders loosen. "Promise you're not gonna turn into a total freakazoid, Kitty cat? Don't keep things from us."

Kitty forced a small smile. "Promise."

"Best friends forever." April held out her arm with her yellow and black bracelet and the left side of a heart charm donned with the letter 'A'. Becka did the same, showing off the yellow and pink thread with the jagged charm and the letter 'B' in the center. Kitty laid her arm out over the table showing her pink and black bracelet with the center piece of a heart and her initial in it.

Kitty's eyes landed on her charm and the K that glinted in the dull cafeteria light and lied right in her friend's faces.

———————◆———————

"Kitty we've got good news," Will said. His voice sprung into Kitty's mind through the nearly invisible Chameleon Ear. *"Weird, but good. Still coming after school?"*

"Yeah, I'll be there."

Kitty sat perched on the tank behind the toilet of the girl's bathroom. Outside of the bathroom, she could hear students' murmurs and rushing footsteps to catch their buses. In her lap, Kitty swiped across her MHD screen that didn't show a single fingerprint no matter how many times she touched it. She stared at the spell diagram that now made her more nervous than she ever felt. She would rather tell off Angela Smith to her face than have to deal with this dummy diagram again. But she needed to get it right. It had to be perfect. At least, it had to be perfect enough.

While transferring her doodle to the MHD, Kitty customized the diagram to the left of the screen. Where it asked about changing personality, Kitty prepared an answer that explained how she would react in some basic stressful scenarios, both good and bad, and she made specific references to the Homecoming meeting that dummy would attend. She explained the missing empathy and understanding. The dummy needed to show emotions as she did. Mimic, not reinvent. The dummy also needed to be active in her own life, but not invasive. She could take it easy, but not so relaxed that she was tired and unresponsive.

When Kitty was satisfied with the changes, she activated the diagram and began pulling the threads to line up with her drawing. The questions she predicted began to pop up in her mind, and she fed her answers to them through the magic swelling in her chest, echoing her heartbeat, watching the diagram shift and adjust to her touch. It still took longer than she would have liked as she felt a kink in her neck forming. Finally it was done, and Kitty hit EXECUTE.

The diagram reappeared right by the door of the bathroom stall. The light stretched to form sneakers, legs, a body hidden beneath a cotton dress, arms, neck, and a head covered in slightly frizzy brown hair. Kitty stared at the dummy version of herself as it blinked and gained consciousness.

"Hey!" it said as her eyes landed on Kitty. "We've got a busy afternoon, huh?"

"No kidding. Will you please sit in on the Homecoming meeting? We're in the final touches stage so it shouldn't be too bad."

"Sure, except Devil-a Smith is supposed to be there, right?"

"You can handle it. We can handle it. She'll harp on my ideas because she wishes she were as smart as me and then we'll move on. I have to help get Raquel home."

"Good luck!"

Then Dummy hurried out of the stall.

The fight with the transit diagram was now a normal part of the activation for Kitty. She finally stepped through and walked out into Will's backyard. She messaged him, and in a few minutes he was at the patio door and leading her back to his bedroom. The house was quiet this time.

"Dad has to commute to the city," Will explained. "And mom had to run to the grocery store for more *Sazón*."

"What's that?" Kitty asked, putting her bag down

while Will sat at his computer and kept scrolling through his Friendville account. He squeezed a baseball shaped stress ball in his free hand. As he clicked through a photo album, Kitty immediately recognized the track field from Glade Crest High School with Will smiling in the middle of a group of boys of mixed ages. They all wore the loose blue vests of the Glade Crest Mountaineers track team. Another boy stood out in the photos: the clown Dino who nearly broke his arm goofing around last Friday.

"It's a really yummy spice," Kitty heard herself say, but it wasn't her speaking. Raquel leaned away from the wall and flopped off of the bed. "Mom started cooking with it more once Manny entered the picture. Anyway, looks like the gang's all here. Can we get going?"

"What did Leo say?" Kitty asked.

"Well…" Will grabbed the white tablet from his desk and swiped along the screen. "Okay, I've got good news and bad news. Which do you wanna hear first?"

"Start with the bad news."

"Dang it. Alright. I messaged Leo and told him you were still convinced that the dummy diagram actually worked. He said if it did, that would be incredibly dangerous. It would be an almost perfect copy, perfect enough to possibly fool the natural state of being to accept that it's housing two of the same person in one…temporal location." He searched for the words from the conversation. "He didn't go into details about the problems that would cause, but he said they would be really bad. Like Earth shattering kind of bad. Any oration like that would need to be immediately terminated."

Kitty's heart leaped into her throat. She didn't know if

she could terminate an oration so realistic. Raquel dropped back onto the bed and hugged her knees to her chest.

"So I'm not saying Raquel is this dummy you tried to make," he said. Kitty got a feeling he was talking more to the anxious girl on the bed in that moment. "But if she's here for any reason connected to that and she reads like your spell diagram...maybe we just need to get her back where she came from as quickly as possible."

"Wherever that is," Will added through Kitty's Chameleon Ear. He finally believed Kitty pulled off a terrible miracle and made a perfect dummy oration.

"Which leads me to part two of the bad news. Getting Raquel home is gonna be way harder than just a normal transit home. Not only do we still have those weird interfering orations that pop up, which I snagged a picture of, but just the size of that diagram...We're talking layers upon layers of knotted Christmas lights in the attic worth of oration to make the diagram work."

With a few quick motions, the white ceiling was smothered in twists, knots, and whirls of blue thread made up of shivering little symbols. Kitty's eyes followed lines of oration all the way across until she nearly lost her balance.

"Yeah, I fell on my butt," Raquel mumbled. "Good idea being near the wall when Will sprung that on you. He didn't warn me."

"Don't be such a baby," he said.

"Okay," Kitty interrupted. "So what's the good news, buzzkill?"

Will's eyes drifted back up to the ceiling where the diagram waited for conversation. "I mean...just look at it! It's a big, beautiful speech waiting to happen! How awesome is that? Ow!" He rubbed his arm where Raquel smacked him with the silver casing along her forearm. "Also, whatever tagged oration was blocking us seems to have changed or gone way. And at least it's still just a transit diagram. It's layered and detailed, but it's still based on the same basic principle we all seem to understand. If we take this one bite at a time, I think we can get Raquel home in no time. But no distractions."

Kitty blushed as her phone buzzed in her pocket.

"But I have a dummy on the loose," she pleaded. "Not you, Raquel."

Raquel's glare softened into a stern annoyance.

"No phones," Will said. "One screw up and Raquel could end up in the middle of space." Raquel's eyes widened. Then Will's voice crinkled in Kitty's ear as it traveled through the Chameleon Ear. *"And we won't have much time before Leo definitely starts looking into this. He started to sound convinced. Wouldn't tell me why exactly. Just a lot of Hostilia active in our area, but that could be because a new Mage popped up. You don't want to hit the terminate button, and I don't really want to, but I think he will."*

Kitty resisted the urge to reach for her backpack and prayed dummy would stay out of trouble.

"Now before you two wet yourselves over this," Will continued, "let's take a step back. This isn't impossible to execute right. But like I said, it's layered on top of itself. We need to carefully handle the layers. Oh! Another teachable moment. Kitty, anything up there look familiar?"

Kitty cringed, but if Leo thought this was helpful to learning more about magic, she supposed she just had to deal with Will being a know-it-all. Everything on the ceiling was a big jumble of blue. Faint glowing edges separated overlapping lines like lit up shadows. It looked like it belonged in a modern art museum. "Not really."

"You sure?" Will drew out the question with a hopeful glance. "What do we already know about this diagram?"

"It's messy?" Kitty offered. She scanned for anything she ought to know. Maybe something Will mentioned yesterday that she forgot in her daze. Then something struck her as she peered at the edge of Will's ceiling over his doorway. She vaguely recognized coordinates that had been shoved in her face when she first met Will.

"We know it's a transit," Raquel said, pointing to a spot towards one corner of Will's ceiling opposite the door. "That's where my home coordinates are."

Will pointed at her. "There ya go. Every spell diagram has its base design. So does this. We know what home looks like and Raquel knows what her home looks like. We can split up the responsibilities on this diagram and we'll have it figured out in no time."

Kitty felt a genuine smile for the first time in what felt like days. They could do this. They could get Raquel home and not worry about bringing on a science fiction apocalypse.

The Mages slowly analyzed and dissected the diagram one layer at a time. Will was able to direct them at the start. If Raquel was even remotely like Kitty, her heart was pounding hard enough to bust out of her chest. Will never actually pointed out where the recognizable parts were for Kitty, but his hints were so strong he may as well have just said it out loud. She had to admit there was a pretty big sense of satisfaction to feel like she was able to pinpoint the areas of the diagram that she thought she could manage.

After a few hours, the diagram was circled, snipped, and rearranged on three different harnessing devices. Then they were interrupted by a knock on the door.

"Sweetheart?" Mrs. Cavanaugh's melodic voice passed through the door. Kitty and Raquel froze. "Dinner is just about ready."

"Sure thing, ma!" Will said. "Uh, some friends might swing by. Is that cool?"

"Oh of course," his mother sang. "Dino and the gang?"

"Some other friends. They work with P.A.L.S too."

"Sounds lovely. Hurry up, please. Your father wants to eat on time."

Mrs. Cavanaugh's soft steps disappeared down the hall. Will let out a long breath of relief and leaned against the door. "It doesn't make sense to keep the Alliance from my mom except that I know she'd tell my dad. They give me a lot of freedom, but this might be a step too far. Anyway, here's what I'm thinking: a transit diagram this big, especially being temperamental, could be dangerous to execute. I wanna look into making a mini Dimensional Hold for us to execute it in. You two can start looking into these interfering diagrams. There are only a few of them on our list. Deal?"

Kitty and Raquel nodded. Then both of their stomachs growled.

"Okay, food first. Then go."

Eleven

Kitty tapped her feet against the tiles of Mort's deli. She was only one of a few people there that evening. A lot of times students from the high school would go there on their lunch breaks if they could sneak past the security guards. That's what Miren Patrick reported to Becka anyway, claiming she had high school friends. What she didn't have that Kitty did have was a way to wish herself to Mort's without being seen by anyone. It was one of her early tests of how far she could make a transit. Mort's was right at the edge of her range before getting her MHD.

While Raquel got to scout out Sportsplex for the strange oration and probably get some games in to ease her mind a little, Kitty didn't mind searching Mort's and getting a little extra snack after Mrs. Cavanaugh's delicious dinner. Neither she nor Mr. Cavanaugh seemed to think it strange that Kitty joined them for dinner. Will kept their relationship vague—acquaintances through the P.A.L.S. program in Glade Crest. It wasn't a lie; that was how they met. Mrs. Cavanaugh proceeded to ask questions about what Kitty liked to do outside of school while Mr. Cavanaugh inquired about her high school plans.

It was so normal, Kitty could have cried. Will excused himself and Kitty right after a brief taste of a lemon meringue pie that Mrs. Cavanaugh made. Kitty almost protested.

"You can come over any time for more pie. We have work to do, remember?"

Will led her to the backyard where she said she wanted to activate her transit diagram out of sight.

The jump didn't cost any extra energy, but it fought her like other diagrams recently. She felt something more than just the regular resistance of her diagram acting up and ignoring what she thought were very clear intentions. Each loop and weave that she customized for the coordinates felt different. They were thicker or heavier somehow. It made the threads of light harder to move. She had gotten so lightheaded that she nearly banged her head into the wall of the alley next to the shop when she stepped through the portal-looking shape that acted like her transit diagram.

Inside she sat for almost an hour listening to the television report on some breaking news while she chewed on a day old bagel and searched for any active magic in the deli. Mort sometimes let the kids get away with a free bagel from yesterday's batch if they were nice enough to him. When her search turned out nothing, she tried to look around for anything unusual. The walls were covered in photos of Mort Goldblum, sometimes his wife, and different family members or important figures. Some school team pride banners hung from the ceiling. The array of pastries and brunch items lined the long granite counter, but it looked perfectly normal.

Kitty pretended to drop the plastic wrap from her bagel and searched the tiled floor and the bottom edges of the walls. All she could see was a black line along the grout that Mort would probably power clean when he closed up. She walked her way slowly towards the garbage, dropping the plastic again in hopes for another quick search. Nothing looked out of place.

Kitty sighed and sat back in her seat, scrolling the Diagram Search for the equivalent of hand sanitizer. As she dragged her lines of argumentation across the screen, each describing the breadth of the cleansing over her skin, the drumming of her heartbeat that started blending with others felt the most meager loss. The spell called for ending the growth of bacterial life on her skin. She was thankful to feel part of the oration fill in something for her she didn't fully understand, but it seemed to answer her concern about magic turning her into a tree-hugger.

> *Micro-organisms fulfill their own operatives within the natural state, but do not hold the capability of logical reasoning nor the potential for said logic —*

Kitty could figure it out later. She tore into her second dinner slathered in cream cheese and watched a clip of a disgruntled ex-employee of a bank trying to rob the place. He swung a baseball bat in his work suit that still had an ID badge clipped to the pocket. His face wasn't covered, and he seemed to be raving about an arcade stealing his hard-earned money that he had given his son to win prizes.

"People are freakazoids sometimes," Kitty said to herself. "That guy looks like he's got a ton of money. What's his problem?"

She nearly choked on another bite of the bagel as someone slammed through the glass doors. He was an older man in black slacks and a button down shirt that contrasted his dark skin. The hair he had left above his very tall widow's peak was wiry and silver. He pulled a knife out of his pocket and stormed up to Mort at the counter.

"Every last penny you've got back there, hand it over!" He thrust the knife dangerously close to Mort's face.

"Jeez, alright. Take it easy, fella." Mort kneeled down and leaned like he was reaching for something.

"Hurry up!" the man screamed and slammed his wrinkled hands on the counter. He looked back at the few people in the store. Kitty had pressed herself to the wall like the others and didn't make any sudden movements. "You keep your mouths shut! Put those phones down! Put 'em down!"

Kitty slid her tablet away. The woman with her daughter put her phone down as well and hugged the young child close. Kitty thought she recognized the man, but most of his face was covered by the tall collar of his leather coat. Mort brushed his hands on his apron and then fumbled with a key to the register. The robber grabbed one of the bagels from the display counter and took a bite. He immediately spat it back out.

"You call these bagels?" he said and chucked what was left at Mort's head. "It's as dry as the Eucharist!"

"Reverend Al?" Kitty said as the thought clicked in her head. The robber turned to look at her. His eyes were unfocused as if she were in three places at once. He started to walk towards her with his head cocked to the side and his mouth fumbling over words. Kitty was afraid to move and startle him or make him mad.

"Leave her alone, you hear me!" Mort waved a grocery bag that was weighed down. "You want money, fine. Just take it and get out." Reverend Al spun around and dove back towards the counter. He snatched the bag and kept yelling about more money.

Kitty slid her MHD back to her and looked for the first diagram that came to mind. She didn't want to hurt the reverend, but she also figured she had a duty not to let him run around acting this way. The panels of the wheel described slick surfaces of ice or erased friction. Kitty picked one and the diagram laid out on the left of the screen. She fed it some further direction about the where and how much until she was satisfied and activated it. Quickly as she could, Kitty dragged the strands of magic, practically snapping her answers to its ridiculous questions, until she hit EXECUTE.

The floor below Reverend Al's feet shimmered for a moment, and as he turned away with a second grocery bag fit to burst, he took one step and slipped. He cried out as he slammed into the ground. Kitty ran over to him to make sure she hadn't hurt him too badly while Mort laughed and ran to the back yelling about getting the cops. The mom and her daughter sprinted from the store.

"It's too big," Reverend Al was mumbling. His eyes were so dark they looked almost black. "It's too heavy."

"Are you okay? Are you hurt?" Kitty asked.

"Kitty? What are you doing here? What am I doing here?" Kitty wanted to tell Mort to call an ambulance instead of police. Reverend Al sat up slowly and looked around. Finally he found Kitty with soft brown eyes. "What's going on?"

"Nothing really. I think maybe the...cold weather is getting to you. You were just heading back to the church. That's what you said anyway." He nodded along to her words. She helped him stand and heard Mort yelling on the phone in the back. "You need to leave though. I think the owner got upset about something. I don't know. It's just a bad day to be here."

"Oh. Um, alright. I guess. Have a good evening." Reverend Al slowly walked out of the bagel shop. Kitty saw the knife he left behind and picked it up with the tips of her fingers. She tossed it in the garbage and made a small transit appear with the easiest coordinates she could think of. Somewhere a few miles away, a knife and a lot of plastic wrappers were suddenly dumped onto a fire escape.

Kitty didn't want to hang around, but she hated that she couldn't find the oration she was looking for. She stepped back out into the alley and called Will and Raquel. Immediately a wave of confusion and fear crashed through the Chameleon Ear.

"Uh, can someone meet me?" Raquel said. *"I think I found the problem."*

———◆———

Sportsplex was one of Kitty's favorite places in all of Glade Crest. Some people thought the giant rotating smiley face with a football for one eye and baseball for another was creepy. Some found the constant neon glow over the maze of flashing and singing machines to be a headache. Those people didn't spend enough tokens to get lost in the battle with the plastic, spring-loaded moles or shriek at the sight of a zombie creeping around the corner of your tunnel vision. It was a thrill Kitty couldn't get anywhere else. She didn't have game consoles of her own or even DVDs except what Mrs. Constance had gifted them for Edith. Her cable stations were limited to soap operas and public access.

Kitty felt a sense of betrayal walking through the glass doors and into the deafening echoes of giddy patrons without Becka and April at her side. She reminded herself she wasn't there for fun. Raquel was terrified of something, and Will stayed home to work on his part of the project to get Raquel back to wherever she came from. Kitty was still a little scared to know what was on the other end of the transit they were unblocking.

An older boy with scars from old acne and over greased hair looked up from his phone. Kitty flashed her month pass code from her cell phone and got a stamp inside. She pushed through the turnstile. The weekday crowd didn't tempt the maximum capacity of the building the way a Saturday crowd could, but still Kitty tread carefully to avoid bumping into too many people or finding ice cream drips or condiments on her clothes. She followed the main aisle, ignoring the empty, beckoning machines that rang and buzzed as she passed by. Towards the end was a cluster of fighting games, each one with a different enlarged plastic weapon or with pads to strike at the right times.

One of the cabinets was taped up with bright yellow caution tape and a sign that read OUT OF ORDER.

"Raquel?"

"I'm behind the machine. Security is pretty lax here. Just be careful stepping around."

Kitty checked to make sure attention was off of her and stepped towards the machine Raquel mentioned. It was a tall metal cabinet painted to look like a stone building with a bamboo roof and golden charms hanging from its rafters. There were Japanese symbols painted just below the screen that mimicked a darkened doorway, and right above the screen printed letters read Shinobi Surprise.

Kitty peeked behind the machine where a mess of cables were curled up on the ground and partially piling up the wall. Raquel balanced precariously on the wires with her arms crossed and silver band activated. Kitty ducked and crawled between Shinobi Surprise and the superhero fighter sim beside it. The whir of the machines' vents grew louder and hot air filled the little hideout.

"Careful!" Raquel hissed. Kitty froze.

She wouldn't have thought twice about the wires on which she meant to rest her hands until she looked closer and saw some of the coiled lengths of plastic were dipping far into a shadow on the ground. The edges smoldered and revealed melted bits of wire. Kitty dragged herself closer to the back of the broken machine and slid along its cool, unused vent until she was beside Raquel.

"What the actual heck is that?" Kitty asked.

"I think...that's the interfering transit. Take a look at this."

Kitty sidled beside Raquel, feeling a static cling raise the tiny hairs on her arm. The screen of the armband displayed a diagram of sorts, but it wasn't loading up and awaiting activation. Certain chains of symbols were becoming very familiar to Kitty for how often she relied on transits the last few days. Some of those same symbols roped through that diagram that described itself with a dark, sniveling sound like a rat if it could talk. It described a jump like a transit, but it didn't have a proper destination. There was a parting in the air, but this was frayed and yanked instead of cutting cleanly through space.

"That...is, like, twentieth level grossness," Kitty said.

Raquel shimmied over the cables to get closer to the jagged shadow. She looped up a bundle of wire, careful to avoid anything dragging against the ground. "It's not even a real transit. It doesn't go anywhere. It just melts whatever goes through. It's like a tear, but I guess it's close enough to a transit to get in the way of mine. I can't believe that thing didn't melt me into a puddle when I went through and wound up here."

Kitty held back answering. She still wasn't sure how much of the story was true or a very clever dummy oration. She could at least confirm that the black holes were dangerous, but the transits she made didn't melt her. "We have to get rid of it, but if it's not an oration that we can terminate, what do we do with it?"

Kitty helped Raquel move any undamaged wire from the shadow. Now they could see the entire tear clearly. It was a black stain on the rough carpet about a foot and a half long. Swirling blue-black tendril hungrily reached out as far as they could around the edges. Its surface seemed to eat any light spilling from the neon bulbs above.

"How goes it?" Will's voice popped into their heads. Kitty felt the light itch of the Chameleon Ear turning on and creeping into her thoughts.

"Well we found the thing," Raquel answered. "You should probably take a look."

Kitty sent the scan to Will, and they listened to his churning thoughts and confusion.

"If Nef—if Cursed Boss is involved here, why would It make a useless transit like this? It's just like some hole in the middle of nowhere. Hold on. There has to be a reason for this."

"Yeah, he wants to cause problems," Raquel said. "Problems breed anger. Anger breeds Hostilia. And as usual he's doing a fan-freaking-tastic job."

"Well don't get yourself worked up like that or you're playing right into Its hands. Hang on. Let me see something." Will's thoughts across the chameleon ear gave them a spotty map of his ideas. He was checking the interfering orations again for anything in common other than missing an end point.

The girls both jumped back in surprise as a flare of sparks burst in front of them. Wires that they had pushed aside were dangling and burned. "What the actual heck!" Kitty hissed.

Raquel looked at the swirling hole and back at Kitty. "Did it get bigger?" "Will, is this thing growing?"

"Growing? Crap, I hope not. Hold on. Where did they go? There were new ones—no. It's like these holes aren't always here, but when they are, they're just there for a few seconds."

"Oh it's here," Kitty moaned, fanning the acrid smoke from the charred wires. "It didn't go anywhere."

"But I can't see it anymore. Maybe…"

Raquel turned to Kitty. "Okay, while he figures out what the heck is happening, can we figure out how to make it go away?"

The girls made sure they were a clear two feet away

from the mess before taking their eyes off of it again. They looked over the scan. It continued to show the start of a transit-like diagram, but then it withered into nothing. It was a directionless oration that kept cutting off its sentences with the sound of gnashing teeth.

"If it's a hole," Raquel finally said over the sounds of a neighboring game machine whirring and ringing a bell, "can we fill it in or something? Or patch it up?"

"Maybe," Kitty said. "Oh, but if this thing eats through whatever touches it, it might just eat through the patch. Or someone could come back here to fix the game and accidentally touch it."

"True. That would be a mess to explain. How else do you get rid of a hole. I mean, if it's anything like jeans you could—"

"—sew it," they finished together. They looked at each other and then burst into a laughing fit. The Chameleon Ear and Raquel's version of a NAP both envisioned the floor like a foldable piece of fabric that they could accidentally sew to the clothes they were already wearing if they weren't careful. Then the laughter died down and their faces softened into pensive frowns. "But what if we could," Kitty said.

"Sew a hole in space? For real?"

"You got any better ideas? Let me know and I'll stop searching." Kitty touched the charm dangling from her bracelet and let it reappear in her hands as her Magical Harnessing Device. She tapped for the spell diagram search engine and paused as she wondered how to phrase such a search.

She started with the word 'sewing' in the search bar.

A wheel of diagrams popped up with lists of names. She daringly refined her search with the word 'time' as Raquel leaned over her shoulder. Kitty's skin tingled.

The wheel was still enormous as it showed orations for encouraging material to knit together faster or slower. Some orations were for creating specific knitted patterns for certain times of year and referenced holidays that Kitty couldn't pronounce.

"How to knit a hole in space," she muttered as she typed. To her dismay, it sounded as ridiculous as she figured. Twin gasps followed the appearance of a significantly smaller wheel of options. They all sounded more complicated with each twist of the wheel so Kitty picked the first one and watched the diagram display itself.

Beside the template diagram, a blurb appeared explaining common uses for the oration. The fact that it had common uses was frightening enough.

> *Magistrates have reconfigured spatial lesions after mistimed transit orations crossing temporal boundaries. These stretches and tears can cause temporal and spatial boundaries to become unstable, particularly around anchors for Dimensional Holds, time lock accesses, and similar orations and active devices. Spatial lesions should be immediately repaired as a top priority adjudication.*

"That sounds serious," Raquel said. "Good thinking, Kitty."

"We both thought of it. If this works, the other few should be a breeze."

Kitty described the size of the tear and then activated the diagram. A warning appeared about the amount of energy her MHD predicted she would need. Raquel waved it off and prepared an oration to share energy. Kitty started maneuvering the threads, trying to swallow the panic as her eyes flickered towards the hole. If it kept growing, they would be in big trouble. As if to mock her fears, the diagram fought back with more and more detailed questions that she couldn't immediately answer. Default explanations about the structure of the very atoms surrounding them filled in, but it childishly refuted her and made the lines of oration stick and pull. How did other Mages make magic look so easy?

They don't have problems like me, a harsh voice contended. *I'm busy with school and Homecoming and stupid dummy orations. Who has time for this? I could practice if Raquel would just go away.*

Kitty clenched her eyes shut to silence that cold thought.

Raquel moved Kitty's hands away from a particularly frustrating part of the diagram, and they worked together on the rest, easing each other's doubts, tuning out the bells, whistles, and laughs around them, and keeping their eyes away from the tear. Finally the girls nodded to each other. Kitty pressed EXECUTE.

The lines and layers of blue sank into the heart of the tablet. Identical threads formed in tightly wound balls above Kitty's and Raquel's hands. They stretched like dough into half inch thick rods radiating a soothing warmth. The base flattened, pinching a small piece into a rounded nub with a blue thread wound through the eye leading back to Mages' chests. The other edge of the needle spun into a sharp point. Kitty wrapped her hands around one of the sticks as it gleamed and solidified into something that looked like steel. Raquel grabbed the other.

"Do we just...?" Kitty looked back and forth between the enormous needle and the hole in the ground.

"If the shoe fits..." Raquel crawled closer and held the point of the needle over the dusty carpet an inch away from the grasp of the hole's swirling edge. She pressed her lips together and slowly pushed the needle point into the carpet. The ground rippled as the pressure of taut air was released and the tip of the needle pressed through. The girls balked at the remaining half of the steel rod. Words weren't necessary. Neither of them thought the oration would work that way, but they both let out relieved sighs.

"Can it come back through?" Kitty asked. She watched Raquel dip the needle towards the tear as she would looking for the right place on a piece of fabric. Kitty recognized the simple pattern of a whip stitch. It was the only stitch April was willing to teach her. A quarter inch from the edge of the tear on the other side, a spot of blue-white light appeared and with another bit of pressure, the air released again and the needle poked through. Raquel carefully guided it back around.

"Start on the other side and we'll meet in the middle," Raquel said.

The girls set to work. Kitty took a few passes to get used to the pressure she needed and the sensation of puncturing air like it was leather. Her hand always stopped at the carpet, scratching against the rough surface as she dipped the needle so it reappeared around the tear. Each time she pulled it out, the thread followed in a crooked, tapering line. It was definitely ugly, but it held. Once Raquel was home where she belonged, Kitty could tell Leo about this so he could fix it properly.

A few inches towards the center, the girls saw the lightly flopping thread start to tighten. As the strands went taut, Kitty felt a pinch behind her eyes like a clamp on her skull. She could see Raquel squinting too, but there was more to do. They fought through the pain and willed the thread to reach far enough to knot off the stitch. Kitty's fingers tingled. Her heart raced. She suddenly felt like she hadn't eaten in a week. But shortly after, the girls pulled up the final stitch and tugged until the tear was practically invisible. Only a faint trace of light remained where the thread bound the tear shut. Kitty's stomach churned, and she took a minute to lean back against the broken machine.

"We're almost there," Raquel said. Droplets of sweat lined her forehead. "Just gotta knot it off."

Kitty pushed herself up long enough to make a few small passes with the needle and formed a clumsy knot to the side of the tear. Then the thread and needles dissolved and the girls collapsed back to the floor. The carpet looked almost perfect if a little jagged, but no one would think twice about a rough seam covered by cables. In a few minutes, the girls crawled out from behind the games.

"I can't believe that worked," Kitty said, beaming despite her tired muscles and using the wall to hold herself up. Every part of her was sore. Her Magical Harnessing Device calculated that the oration cost a little more than a quarter of her energy in one shot. It would have been more if she hadn't shared it with Raquel. "That was...holy cow. Twentieth level amazing."

Raquel nodded as the girls made their way to the exit. "Magic is pretty great. I can't believe I almost passed this up."

"Really? What made you not want to be a Mage?"

"I guess…" Raquel shrugged. "I guess it was just really freaky. It's a lot of responsibility. Excuses don't get you anywhere except in big trouble and a lot of people rely on you and don't even know it. They don't know why they're in danger and how can you explain, 'Yeah, you're pretty much your own worst enemy by ever wanting to slug someone in the face instead of talking out your problems.'? It's a challenge, but it's worth the worry."

Kitty almost forgot that those thoughts were likely borrowed from her. They were some of the things bouncing around her mind as she wondered what she would tell Leo about becoming a real Magus. He told her she had a choice, but knowing that her anger, her moments of wanting to get work done the easy way instead of the best way, could be causing disaster all around her was hard to ignore.

Kitty and Raquel stepped out into the oncoming dusk, backlit from the neon glow inside the arcade. The air was refreshingly cool compared to the warmth of bodies and machines from inside.

"It's getting late," Kitty told Will and Raquel with the Chameleon Ear. *"I need to make sure dummy got home okay and fed my sister."*

"So you got the hole fixed?" Will asked.

"Yeah," Kitty said, *"but we're super exhausted. Think we can tackle the others tomorrow now that we know what to look for?"*

"I can get to one more today." Raquel stretched and

circled her neck to loosen it up.

"The sooner the better," Will said. *"My eyes are going crossed looking at this Dimensional Hold so I'll help you, Raquel. Maybe seeing these things in person will make sense of why the MHD only sees them sometimes."*

"You're in for a trip, dude."

"Cool," Kitty said. *"Later, guys!"*

Kitty waited for Raquel to vanish through a transit and then executed a pre-made transit to her fire escape out of view of the window. The dark circle sent a chill up her spine, but it still couldn't compare to what they found in the arcade.

The curtains were drawn, but a warm light spilled through from Kitty's desk lamp. No sounds. Dummy was probably stuck watching Hop Along Princess for the third time with Edith in the living room. Kitty made a mental note to get a garbage bag for the wadded papers on the fire escape before anyone noticed.

She pushed the window up with a small grunt and slipped inside, tossing her backpack on the bed. She sat for a minute and enjoyed the rare silence. The television was either off or turned low. No one was scrambling around the kitchen. Edith was settled in. Kitty smiled at the dummy's job well done.

Still, a nagging feeling tugged in Kitty's brain. She figured it was her ignored homework. With enough on her plate between school and Homecoming, while Raquel's presence was helpful for learning magic, it wasn't exactly a welcomed one. If she didn't collapse from exhaustion after her homework, Kitty planned to do a little more scrolling through the Initiate Resources. Her stomach growled, and

Kitty realized that oration really drained her. A quick third dinner first.

Kitty listened through her bedroom door, again struck by the quiet. She crept the door open and saw the dark hallway. The living room was empty. The nagging worry clamored in her head now. She quickly walked to the kitchen, no dummy there eating a peaceful dinner alone or studying. The bathroom door was ajar, not in use. Her mother wouldn't be home for hours. Kitty held her ear to her sister's door. Quiet. She nudged it open.

"Edie, hun?" she called. No answer. The room was softly glowing from the unicorn nightlight Edith loved. The lampshade spun like a carousel creating shadow animals that danced along her walls. The pink canopy bed took up half of the room, an ill fit from their old house, but Edith would scream without it. Toys lined the bed in the familiar theater style when Edith entertained herself by putting on a show for the royal court of her fantasy land. Dummy should have been entertaining her. Maybe Edith got scared of being alone and hid under the bed. "Edith, I'm here."

The covers were askew, spilling over the far side of the bed. Kitty was about to shake her head at the mess when she noticed part of the blanket quivering.

"Are you hiding from me, little princess?" She tried to make her voice playful in case dummy had somehow upset her, but the nagging worry was now a thunderstorm in her mind. She quickly stepped around the bed. Then she froze.

A ten-year-old girl with loopy waves sprawled around her head like a halo was lying on her back on the floor. Her arms and legs spasmed. Her neck rocked and her head jolted. Pale bile dribbled from the corner of her lips as her light brown eyes rolled back as far as they could.

Kitty shrieked and dropped to her knees, tilting her sister's head to the side as she continued to seize. Tears burned at her eyes as she willed for her phone to appear. The familiar green haze covered her vision. All Kitty could do was beg and reach her hand out until it clasped around her cell phone.

"911," came the static voice on the other line.

"Please hurry! My sister is sick!"

Twelve

Sometimes Kitty hated to dream. She would be so caught up imagining herself drowning in tipped over lemonade or freezing alone in an ice block that she didn't remember she could just open her eyes and end it. Sometimes she dreamed about more realistic things like her mom, red in the face and yelling about something that didn't exist. She might be sitting in the kitchen crying with a broken glass in her hand, and when Kitty's legs forced her into the dark room, her mom would turn to her with no face at all.

The worst dreams were of her whole family. She and her sister would be swinging on the playset in their old backyard. It was one of Kitty's favorite memories. Her mom would come out with plastic cups and a pitcher of lemonade that she put on the patio table. It would help hold down the tablecloth with the smiling lemons when a breeze started to blow it away. Kitty would look at her sister swinging beside her, and she would slow her own swing down just enough so she could pretend to leap off. Edith giggled and started fidgeting in the harness until Kitty let her out. The two girls would run to the patio just as the door to the house slid open. By the time Kitty looked up, her father's back was always turned, shutting the door behind him.

Kitty grabbed the edge of the tablecloth with baited breath. He never turned around. Wisps of his smooth brown hair would dance in the breeze. Then it suddenly stopped. Everything froze, even Kitty. She stood like a portrait waiting for a moment that would never come. Somewhere in the distance she would hear a screech of car tires and her eyes would shoot open.

And so they did.

Kitty stared ahead at a large bed with bolted railings and buttons along the sides. The stark white sheets were tucked in around her sister's petite body as she continued to sleep. Kitty had been jolted awake by the arm wrapped around her shoulders. Her mother smiled weakly at her from soft purple tinted lips and dark smudges clouded her red-rimmed eyes. Locks of hair were loose from the pinned in scarf, and her dress had pale stains from helping hold her sister in another throw of fits.

"You should sleep at home, baby," Mrs. Guthrie said, rubbing Kitty's shoulders.

"I don't want to."

"You're just going to be sore when you have to get to school tomorrow. Don't argue with me right now, Kitty. Please."

Kitty sighed and shrugged her mother's arm from her.

Mrs. Guthrie countered with a louder sigh and pulled out her phone. Without a word, Kitty left the hospital room and slammed the door shut. She made her way down the elevator with a few roaming patients, nurses, and family pushing the limits of visiting hours. One of the nurses, a young man a full decade older than Kitty smiled softly at her. He always seemed to be smiling, which Kitty liked. He was muscular beneath the blue scrubs, and his dark skin always reflected the lights like he was oiled down. If she weren't so distracted, she might have started blushing like she did when she caught sight of him on a break kicking a hackey-sack around that was knitted to look like a soccer ball.

"Late night for you, Kitty?" he asked. His employee badge clipped to his pocket read Ubi Azikiwe. Kitty's face was familiar at the hospital, and a lot of the staff greeted her kindly. Edith had frequent treatments and occasional emergencies that brought her family to Glade Crest General.

"Edith had a seizure a few hours ago," she said quietly.

Ubi shook his head. "Your mom called over the weekend saying she was worked up. I promise you we'll keep an eye out for anything like that again."

"I know."

Ubi patted her shoulders and leaned down towards her. "I know you know. You might be the hardest working sibling I've ever seen in this hospital. Edith is lucky to have you."

Kitty didn't see whatever Ubi saw.

Outside of the sterile building, Kitty only had to wait a few minutes before a silver sedan pulled up with the RideFellow sticker in the window. She scanned the driver's

ID with her phone, and in a room four floors up, her mother's phone pinged that she was picked up by the right person. Kitty refused to make conversation. She grunted a short thanks and got out of the car at her apartment. She stared at the buildings in the dark and felt like a stranger, like at any moment another officer was going to pull up and arrest her for trespassing. What was she coming home to?

Kitty sat on the curb under a street light. A chill breeze reminded her that autumn was near, and she hugged her knees close to warm away the goosebumps. The charm on her bracelet glinted. As she grasped it between her fingers, it grew warm, and immediately she was holding her MHD.

Before she got the tablet, Kitty's magic was a small nuisance. She might get a little dizzy as she wished for something, but it didn't get in her way. One day with it and she made a dummy so real it thought it was a Mage. When Leo discovered what she did... If she couldn't figure out how to make magic stop fighting her, it wasn't any good to her anyway.

The little greeting blinked at the top of the screen.

WELCOME, KITTY.

The gnawing ache of failure made her stomach clench. She wasn't a failure. She wasn't a quitter. But twice now her dummy let her down, and this time her sister could have been really hurt. That was where she drew the line; magic wouldn't put her sister in danger. She threw the tablet across the concrete and watched with sick satisfaction as it clattered and skid. It would be the last night she had to deal with it.

Something felt off the minute Kitty entered her homeroom class the next day. She felt everyone's eyes on her. Her seat neighbor, a pudgy boy with bent metal glasses, stole small glances. Every time she looked back, he would wheeze and look away.

Did the whole school find out about the bus pass? No way anyone could have found out about magic, she assured herself, but the fear made her heart icy. School was the one place she could count on to do well.

"Kitty, could you come here?" Ms. Bailey said as she poked her head in from the hall. A low 'Oooooo' filled the room, but it was squashed by a stern glance from their teacher. Kitty stood up. "Bring your books too, please."

Kitty's face flushed as she scooped up her morning text books and met Ms. Bailey in the hallway. A school security guard stood beside her, wide arms folded. He briefly said, "You'll need to come with me to the Principal's office," and then started walking before Kitty could argue. Ms. Bailey motioned for her to follow. Her brows were creased, but she didn't say anything else. Kitty bit down on her lip and walked a few paces behind the security guard. She wished she could curl up and disappear every time someone glanced in her direction with a questioning or giggling face. The guard didn't say a word until he opened the door to the office lobby.

"In you go," he said. Kitty obeyed, and he shut the door. The clang echoed.

The secretary didn't look up from her typing as she took a phone call. Every seat lining the office was filled with students sprawled and bored or angrily kicking the chair legs with their heels. The boys all had sagging jeans and stained sneakers. The girls wore skirts that barely complied with dress code or had more piercings than April's sewing projects. Everyone had some kind of cut or scrape or bruise, and some of the girls had tousled hair yanked from a ponytail or headband. Kitty wasn't part of this crowd. Still she took the one available seat between two abrasive looking girls and waited as students were called in one at a time.

"Kitty Guthrie," the secretary finally droned when more than half of the seats were empty, "Principal Shepherd will see you now."

Kitty's feet dragged to the door behind the secretary's desk. The gold placard rattled as Kitty opened the door. Immediately she felt like she was walking into a prison cell. The office was small and cramped with bursting filing cabinets and stacks of paper on every surface. A thin, balding man had his pale forehead nearly pressed to his screen until Kitty shut the door, earning his attention. What shocked her the most was the second man in a chair beside the principal's desk. She immediately recognized the blubbery jowls and squinting eyes of Mr. Briggs, her event adviser.

"Kitty, have a seat please," Principal Shepherd said. His voice sounded less bored than the woman out front. Kitty quietly dropped into a chair slightly hiding the principal's face behind the computer monitor. "So tell me what's going on."

Kitty blinked and hugged her books closer to her chest. She glanced at Mr. Briggs for some guidance, but he mimicked the calm, but painful disappointment on the principal's face. "I...honestly have no idea."

Principal Shepherd shook his head slowly. Mr. Briggs did the same. "Kitty, you don't just hit people for no reason. Certainly not someone like you. I must say, I really expected better, no matter what the provocation may have been."

"What?!" Kitty jumped from the seat so quickly the chair teetered back. "I never hit anyone!"

Principal Shepherd turned his monitor to face Kitty. It showed a gray still image of the school's front lawn. He clicked the play button. A camera monitored silently as Kitty watched a girl with long brown hair pulled back in a ponytail leave the front doors of the school. She had a familiar denim skirt and loose sleeved blouse like Kitty had worn to school the day before. Another girl wearing all black approached her and began waving her gloved hands very close to the Kitty look-a-like.

Kitty imagined what she would have liked to do to Miren Patrick in that situation. Her fists curled. She could hear the taunting in her head. How Kitty pretended to be cool. How she had fallen from grace. How being a teacher's pet wouldn't make her any less of a Capital B wannabe. How it was no wonder the PTO president didn't even want Homecoming to happen. Then Kitty saw herself get pushed and stumble in the video. Rage boiled her blood.

If I could just reach into that video and show her what's what.

Aren't I lucky then, returned the thought as Kitty watched her oration spring forward and shove Miren to the ground. First her fists crashed down into Miren's nose. Then her clawing fingernails tore at her cheeks. When

Miren seemed to realize what was happening, she shoved the dummy off, but the dummy clutched at her shirt and pulled her down again. They were a tangle of slapping arms and kicking legs until Miren's friends pulled the girls apart, both looking worse for wear.

Kitty laid a hand on her cheek where the video showed she should have a bruise. Her books spilled out of her arms. The video stopped just as the dummy walked out of view.

"Do you still want to say you have no idea?" Principal Shepherd asked.

The room was suddenly sweltering. Kitty's shirt choked her around the collar and her sneakers pinched her feet. Everything was unbearable.

"Miren hit me first," she whispered, staring at her shoes.

"I see that, but it doesn't excuse fighting. We have a zero tolerance policy. You know that."

Kitty stooped down to pick up her books and then settled back into her chair and stared into her lap.

"I'm very disappointed, Kitty," her principal continued. He leaned back in his chair with a heavy sigh. "This just can't go overlooked. I'm afraid this will be after school detention. Three weeks."

"What?!" she cried out again, leaping to her feet. "Principal Shepherd, I didn't—! She—! That's not fair!"

"Zero tolerance means zero tolerance. We'll inform Ms. Patrick of her own punishment when she gets back to school tomorrow. You'll be sitting in detention starting tonight."

"But I have to watch my sister! And I have Homecoming meetings! Please!"

Mr. Briggs stood up and cleared his throat. "Kitty, it appears to me that perhaps...well perhaps Homecoming was a little too much for you to take on. It's a tremendous amount of pressure, I understand. But after this violent outburst, and from you of all people, well I can't let it go ignored. In the best interest of your mental health and the event, I'm going to ask that you step down as student adviser."

Kitty dropped her books again. Her chest throbbed with unspent breath, and her ears rang louder than the groaning computer. "No."

"I'm afraid that's not an option."

"No. Mr. Briggs, please. I swear it won't happen again. Please don't do this!"

He only shook his head. "The decision is final."

Principal Shepherd stood. "You can return to class now, Kitty."

Her feet were planted to the ground and her mouth hung slack. "But—" How could she make him see he was wrong? How could she show them this was all she had? How could she erase their memories of what her dummy did?

I can make him pay. Make them listen.

A flicker of green crossed her eyes, but it was drowned out by the sting of tears that blurred her vision. Kitty grabbed her books with shaking hands, fumbling to keep them in her arms. Mr. Briggs helped pick up the last few notebooks. Kitty wordlessly turned away and slammed the office door shut behind her.

The rest of the day was a waste. Kitty skipped lunch altogether because she was sure she would throw up if she tried to eat. She left a pop quiz completely unanswered and didn't write down any of the day's homework. What did it matter? Good grades weren't going to make her life easier. Anyone could do that. She needed to be someone important, someone who risked it all and got a big job done. Kitty from the Slope instead of Kitty from the Valley. In an instant, her entire plan was stolen from her.

I can make them suffer, said the dark place in her heart. Whenever the cold voice snaked into her thoughts, it overwhelmed her, and Kitty excused herself to the bathroom and cried.

The only time she couldn't excuse herself was when she finally reached the detention classroom. The musty smell choked her as she readjusted her backpack and found a seat in the corner by a window. It looked out towards the sports fields where Kitty should have been. Her posters were up around the school thanks to the volunteers, and now the sale items needed to be organized and labeled with price tags. The volunteers needed tee shirts and make up in school colors under their eyes like the football team had. Everything was perfect in her head, and now Kitty was stuck in a gum stained chair with other eighth graders who looked like they could break her in half just by staring.

From the drifting conversation between a few kids who sounded like friends, they were caught fighting another student too. Kitty hugged her bag in her lap and slipped her hand in to call on her MHD. She looked over the dummy diagram and gasped when she realized it was still active. The energy meter at the top corner of the screen read 87%.

What the actual Heck are you up to, Dummy? Kitty groaned to herself. She locked onto the oration and found it in the Rec Room, which made her pause. At least it could put itself to good use while Kitty was trapped in detention because of it. It wouldn't be in charge of her sister again until she got it just how she wanted it, and she didn't have to worry about missing Homecoming meetings anymore. What more trouble could it cause from doing its actual job?

A man with a crisp button down shirt and pleated slacks walked into the classroom and pulled Kitty's attention. He dropped his backpack on the torn chair behind the desk up front.

"Alright," he said as he pushed his glasses aside to rub the bridge of his nose, "settle down, please." The few murmurs from before ceased. The teacher pulled out a stack of papers and handed one out to each student. Kitty looked over the list of questions as the teacher stepped out briefly and returned with a large cart wheeling an ancient television the size of one of the windows. He pressed a few buttons and slapped it for good measure before it buzzed into life and started playing a nature documentary.

"Answer as many questions as you can," the teacher droned. "No, you can't help each other. No, you can't do your other homework. Yes, you need a pass to go to the bathroom." He made room for himself in the chair and propped his legs up. "Oh, is..." He checked a notepad from his pocket. "Is Kitty Guthrie here?"

Kitty slowly raised her hand. Snickers erupted from behind her.

"Mr. Briggs said he needed your help with a particular project. Now's as good a time as any." For a moment Kitty's heart fluttered. Had he changed his mind? Was she back in charge? The teacher held up a pen with white goop

187

drifting inside and a red permanent marker in the other. "He said he needs you to change the signs up in the school about Homecoming. Putting Angela Smith's name up or something?"

Kitty squeezed the strap of her backpack wishing her hands would stop shaking. She practically snatched the white out and marker from the teacher's hands and stormed out the door to the continued laughter of the classroom.

The walls in the building felt plastered with the signs Kitty created for Homecoming. She could remember almost every email discussing the design and what would best show off the event as the family friendly, cool hang out, community driven fundraiser she wanted it to be. And it would be—because of Kitty's hard work. She ran herself ragged to collect raffle prizes from the community and student body. She researched former students of the Glade Crest public school system to track them down and thoroughly embarrass herself trying to sweet talk them into donating for the cause. Now her feet ached from swaying in front of each sign. Her shoulder screamed from lifting it and pressing the white out to the posters. Every sign announced her name proudly as the organizer of Glade Crest's first Homecoming Dance. Kitty's stomach flopped as her name vanished beneath the tacky white pen, erasing her from everything she worked so hard to accomplish, whiting her out of history.

And who was replacing her?

The red pen marked up each poster in Kitty's curly handwriting.

A-N-G-E-L-A

S-M-I-T-H

Kitty's stiffening arm shook as she finished replacing herself on yet another sign. The pen lingered on the H and started bleeding through the paper. She pressed harder and watched the slim felt tip of the pen widen until it gave in to the pressure and popped against the sign, spattering red ink all over the wall and Kitty's shirt and sneakers. She kept staring, her eyes stinging with tears she hadn't felt creeping up on her.

"Kitty?" April Sullivan's soft voice eased through the shrieking hatred in her brain. "You're done for the day. C'mon, babe. We're gonna watch the Homecoming Game and Capital B Smith has nothing to do with that. But let's get you cleaned up first."

Becka was already rounding the corner with Kitty's abandoned backpack, and Kitty dragged her feet behind her friends who pulled her into the nearest bathroom.

Thirteen

Everyone in the stands screamed and stomped their feet on the metal bleachers, swinging noise makers and ribbons over their heads. The mild evening air echoed with their celebration. The boys in blue and white on the field pumped their fists just as a buzzer sounded. The crowds seated themselves or began the march to the outdoor bathrooms. Most traipsed by without caring which knee or elbow smacked into Kitty's face or back. She groaned and lowered her head into her hands just in time for a flailing hand to yank her ponytail out of place.

April patted her back. "Babe, you've gotta see this isn't the end of the world. You're here to have fun. It's a game and our team is winning! And look how cute Preston looks in that uniform!"

Kitty cautiously peeped through her fingers at the players gathered by the coach. Number 84, Preston Smith.

She couldn't see past the helmet or the blue jersey draped over several pads along his shoulders and chest, but still she felt her cheeks get warm. She covered her eyes again, and April rubbed her back.

"Becks and I still have to help at the merch booth," she said, "or else we'll get detention too. Mr. Briggs is already uptight since someone knocked a cart into something expensive in the Rec Room storage. Whatevs. It's just a nick. But we'll be right back."

Kitty heard the wobbling metallic sound of the bleachers under foot and felt the pressing loneliness of a sea of strangers. It was almost getting comfortable when another familiar voice interrupted her. She heard Will plop onto the bench beside her.

"Someone's been busy ignoring us," he said.

A stirring anger burned in Kitty's stomach. "Go away."

"What's your malfunction? We said we were meeting after school to get this transit worked out."

"Well I changed my mind," Kitty said. "I don't want to be part of it, and I don't want to be a Mage or whatever."

"Whoa whoa. Slow down and breathe. What happened?"

Kitty sat up straight and yelled, "Nothing! Just go away!" Then she buried her face again.

"Alright, I get it. You're mad about...whatever. Girl problems or something. Fine. Be mad. But we need your help with the oration *you* messed up. So I think you need to take a little responsibility, suck it up, and help us get Raquel back wherever she belongs."

Kitty only tutted. She wished Raquel would just disappear. After minutes of ignoring Will's logic and pleas, she felt the tingling of magic at work, and then he was gone. As if afraid he would show up with the whole Alliance this time, Kitty shouldered into her backpack and made her way down the bleachers to the commotion by the merchandise she had carefully picked out. The long line of tables was barely visible past the clusters of students, parents, and alumni demanding attention. Half of the volunteers were talking to each other leaving all the work on the handful who showed up for more than extra credit. Kitty spotted Mr. Briggs apologizing and turning to another guest, while dabbing his forehead with a handkerchief.

Someone bumped into Kitty as they quickly ducked away from the table. She nearly toppled over, only catching herself on the boy's arm. He was holding a squishy vinyl football in blue and white on a short silver chain and ring. A bright red price tag covered the letters GCJH. Kitty glared at him.

"You gonna pay for that?" she said louder than necessary. A few eyes of volunteers glanced her way.

"I did, you stupid liar!" the boy shouted right back.

"Oh really? Then why does everyone else have a nice baggie and no price tag, numbnuts?"

The boy flushed as more eyes collected on them. She waved her arm towards April, about to ask if she handled the boy's order when he dropped the football and bolted for the stands. Kitty picked it up and returned it to the table.

"We could really use a hand," April said. "Those lazy bums aren't doing anything. Even Becka can't scare them straight."

"Hey!" Becka whined. "I already did, but I'm not in charge."

Without thinking, Kitty went behind the table and snapped right between the faces of two chatters. She tapped the shoulders of a few more and started ordering their eyes on specific customers to get the lines moving. The first lines of upset customers cleared in minutes, and Kitty found herself smiling despite the stress. This was what she was good at. This was where she was the most comfortable. Taking charge of this event was all she wanted. The rush of euphoria overwhelmed her as the buzzer sounded to start the next half of the football game.

April tackled her into a chair with another hug. "Kitty Cat, you're the greatest human being in the world!"

"Ugh, April, I can't breathe!" But through her words she was laughing, something she didn't think she would ever do again.

Becka pried April away. "April, you're totally squirrelnuts. But Kitty, that was fifteenth level awesome. Now you just need to lift some weights and you could've punched that kid out. Much faster."

"You're such a caveman sometimes, Becka," April said, brushing off her denim skirt and white lacy blouse. The glitter war paint under her eyes was smudged.

"Kitty, that was like twentieth level coolness!" a fiery redheaded girl piped up, suddenly appearing beside her. Daphne Blair, always shadowed by her friend Sarah White, was in charge of the school newspaper and those two never missed a scoop. Daphne had her cell phone held close to her lips. Sarah, the blond girl beside Daphne, had a professional camera held up to her eye. The flash went off a few times, a blinding light in the dark. "So Kitty, tell us how you made this Homecoming game possible."

"Huh? Oh, I didn't—I mean—"

April pulled Kitty up from the chair. "What Ms. Guthrie means to say is while she didn't make the game happen, she raised a ton of money with these awesome souvenirs for the students and parents, and it's all going to beautifying the school and adding to the after school programs like a new game club and even a fashion club!"

Daphne and Sarah gawked.

"So those surveys weren't bogus? Could we really get a photography club?" Sarah asked.

Kitty fumbled again, but April beamed, "I'm sure Kitty can make that happen. It makes sense to have photographers to take pictures of the hot new styles we're gonna come up with."

The reporters nodded eagerly.

"You know we're in eighth grade and we won't get to be in the clubs, right?" Becka pointed out. "I was gonna ask for a girls wrestling team, but what's the point?"

"I'm sure future lovable brutes will thank you," April said, threading her arm around the muscular girl.

Daphne held her phone towards Kitty. "Anything you'd like to say about Homecoming and your expectations?"

"Uh, well," Kitty looked around at the crew of volunteers slowly breaking down merchandise tables under Mr. Briggs' direction. She remembered she wasn't in charge of any of this anymore. April nudged her in the side with an encouraging smile. Kitty gulped and continued with a paper dry throat. "Well, it's been a lot of hard work. It's been a lot of giving up time with my best friends so I could plan things and go to meetings. But I can't wait to see everyone together at the dance just relaxing and having fun, and to see how much more money we can raise for the school. But it's really about supporting the lower grades *and* the upper grades. We'll be in high school next year, but we'll be ready for it because of our teachers and friends right now so the better we make GCJH for future grades, the better prepared they'll be when they're in our shoes. And I just have to say, I have the best friends in the world who put up with me being totally squirrelnuts to do all of this, and I couldn't have done any of this without them, and I wouldn't be able to get through high school without them. They're the best."

April's lip quivered, and she thrust herself forward to envelop Kitty in another hug. Daphne jammed the back of her hand against her eyes to hold back tears.

"How about a picture of the three of you!" Sarah got up close. Kitty and April dragged Becka back over and smiled. The flash went off a few times before the young reporters thanked them and scampered off.

"We'd better get this cleaned up before Mr. Briggs gets all uppity," Becka said, rolling her eyes. "Maybe you're lucky not to be involved anymore, Kitty."

Kitty didn't agree. She helped with the clean up for a few minutes, showing the students how to unlock the folding tables and making sure only one person collected the money boxes. Then she went back towards the cheering crowd on the bleachers.

"I don't think she planned any of this anyway," Kitty heard from a group of chattering girls. The voice was distinctly Jennifer's. "I told her to ask Mrs. Smith about a Homecoming Queen. Did she? Nope. So useless."

"I heard she got fired for beating someone up," their friend Gemma said. "That's so Valley."

"Exactly! She's such a Valley girl. So trashy. I'll bet she just wanted to do this to get close to Preston. Like she could ever. Oh my gee. Quality boys like him don't deal with trashy druggies like her. That's probably the real reason that cop arrested her."

Kitty's mind went numb, but her feet couldn't stop moving and the conversation drifted into the rest of the roaring crowd. It was a joke. It had to be. Jennifer was her friend. Friends didn't care where the other one lived. They were still...weren't they...? Why would she...? Kitty never said anything mean about her even when she ignored her texts or never helped her with any homework when Kitty jumped at the chance.

She's a liar. Nothing is the same as it was.

"Earth to Kitty!" she said to herself, but her lips didn't move. Kitty stopped short as someone raced to cut her off. It was a girl with her dark ponytail tugged through the back of a baseball cap. Other than Kitty never wearing baseball caps, she looked identical to her, like staring in a mirror. "You hear me now?"

"What—what do you want?"

"I want you to do your part of the transit so I can go home already! Stop being a crybaby about whatever it is you're being a crybaby about and come back to Will's house."

"Leave me alone, Raquel," Kitty shoved past her and felt a jolt up her arm where it made contact. Raquel grabbed her wrist and spun her back around, another sting. She dragged her away from the crowd to a spot past the fence that enclosed the field. Kitty yanked her arm loose when Raquel slowed down. "What the actual heck! I said no! I don't want any more part of this magic junk!"

"And I don't want any more part in being here, but too bad for both of us! Just help us put the diagram together and lend us some energy and I'll be out of your hair for good."

"The sooner the better," Kitty spat, "but I'm not doing it. I'm not doing any more of this ever again. Find another loser."

Before Raquel could snap back at her, she cried out in pain and collapsed into Kitty. The touch felt like holding a live wire, and Kitty rolled her away. Raquel's eyes were half open, staring at nothing. Kitty turned towards the attacker. She was starting to wonder if she would ever need or want a mirror again as a second Kitty look-a-like hovered over them with a metal chair clutched in her hands. A bright red stamp read PROPERTY OF GCJH.

"You've been enough trouble, Raquel," Dummy said. She pressed her foot into Raquel's chest. "Kitty, terminate the oration!"

Kitty stared back and forth between Dummy and Raquel. Coming to her senses, she scrambled toward them to separate Dummy from the other girl. Or other dummy. She couldn't tell anymore.

"Hold on!" Kitty said. "What are you doing?"

"What we need to do," Dummy said. "We have to get rid of her. Then we'll be in the clear."

"No, no, no!" Kitty lifted herself to her shaking knees and pushed Dummy back. "The plan is to send her home."

Dummy scoffed. "Puh-lease. She's just a dummy gone wrong. I know it so you know it. We want her gone as fast as we can. Terminate her or let's just end the oration the fast way. Like Becka says." Dummy raised the chair again.

"Don't!" Kitty dove forward and connected with Dummy's stomach, and the girls collapsed into the chain link fence behind them. It had enough give to bounce them back and to the ground. Kitty wrestled for the chair.

"What is wrong with you?" Dummy grunted. "I'm doing what you asked!"

"I never told you to hurt anyone, not even her!"

Kitty winced sympathetically as she elbowed Dummy in the eye. The girl made of magic screamed and clutched at her face. Kitty pulled back with the chair in her hand now, but a quick thump against her calf knocked her over and left her sprawled on the ground, banging her head against the walkway. Stars burst across Kitty's vision as Dummy loomed over her. She snatched the chair back.

"Maybe I have it backwards," Dummy said. "Maybe you're the double. You're the one we begged to make disappear. I felt it. It was so strong—so important. I wouldn't leave my sister otherwise. I was told to do what Kitty would do so I—"

Kitty flinched as Dummy suddenly became so many motes of blue-white light that flickered in the air. The lights swirled like ribbon loose in the wind until they vanished into winks among the stars. A flood of Dummy's memories washed over Kitty like a recap of a terribly mundane TV show behind a fog of static. Kitty knew they would sort themselves out in time. Seeing what the dummies saw was the only positive part of that oration so far.

Kitty tilted her head as Raquel slowly approached. The lights from the nearby field glinted off of her silver arm band. Kitty thought she might offer a hand, but Raquel just stared ahead where Dummy once was. Kitty rolled herself to her hands and knees.

"Thanks," she said. Raquel didn't say anything. "Uh, I guess that pretty much confirms you're not an oration. How were you able to terminate something I made?"

Raquel stayed quiet for a long time. Finally she turned her glance to Kitty; her eyes were ferocious slits. "Help or don't help," she said. "I don't care. I'll be out of your way soon enough. If you let me live that long."

"Raquel, that dummy was squirrelnuts!" Kitty pleaded. "I would never—"

"If I remember right, you're the one who made the impossible perfect dummy, so who knows what else you could do, Kitty. I guess I'll count myself lucky if I'm alive in the morning." Raquel tapped a few keys angrily and stepped through a small slice in the air.

Kitty buried her face in her hands and bit her lip until it bled, but the tears wouldn't stop. She did wish Raquel would go away, but she would never hurt her. But the dummy oration seemed to think differently, and they were supposed to be the same. Kitty scrubbed at her eyes with the back of her hand. She decided enough was enough.

With new resolve, Kitty launched to her feet and jogged away from the football field where the crowd was letting out a groan. A filter fell over her eyes as she imagined the streets of home and almost instantly her whole body felt the cool splash of breaking through space as well as an eager tug as if the magic knew how desperately she wanted to get away and, for once, was helping her along.

Kitty tore up the steps towards the lonely front door of the Glade Crest municipal building. Every light was out except for a few little blinking colors from the phones at the front desk. Kitty grabbed at the door handle and yanked at it, demanding it slide like it did for Will. It didn't budge. In a terrible mix of sadness and rage, Kitty kicked at the door, beat it with her fists, and then cried as she fell against it and slid to the concrete steps, hugging her knees close.

Please let me in, she begged to no one, but she felt like someone was listening. The air wrapped around her body like a frigid cloak starting to suffocate her. *Please let me in. Please...don't leave me alone.*

Kitty shivered as the cold licked at her arms and legs. It lingered around her body as if fans were suddenly surrounding her, blowing her backwards. More like insistent tugging. Her body was off balance for a split second. She looked up and squinted at the sudden brightness of artificial lights. Walls replaced the sidewalk across the street. A low hum took over for the active night birds and revving cars. Kitty's knees gently sank into a trimmed carpet instead of bruising cement.

It took her a moment to realize people were staring at her. A group of men, women, and other humanoids shared various looks of shock and concern. One of them stepped around the small crowd, a handsome man in a finely cut suit and his once stubbled beard shaved down to nothing but a shadow.

"Kitty?" Leo Baldwin asked. "How in the Hell—?" Leo shook his head and looked at the other Mages, suddenly speaking a different language that sounded like silk tickling her ears compared to his thick New York dialect when he spoke in English. Kitty couldn't make out the words, but they vibrated with feeling. Respectful dismissal of high level peers. The others nodded and filed out of the room, stealing a few more glances at Kitty.

"And don't tell Governor Cohen just yet!" he called out as the last Mage left the room. Kitty didn't know where to look or what to do or say. She just wrung her wrists until the skin turned red. Leo kneeled in front of her with a weak smile. "Why don't you and I have a talk, huh?"

Fourteen

Silence smothered the office as Kitty sat as far back in the egg shaped chair as she could and stared at her hands. She didn't want to see the twisted frown on Leo's face like he was fighting with all of his might to hide his anger or fear. Somehow her transit had taken her directly into his office, which, admittedly, was what she wished for.

"Well, let's cut to the chase, shall we?" Leo finally said. He leaned back in his chair and rocked lazily. "From the looks of it, you just did a transit oration right smack into my office. Am I on the right track, Kitty?"

She slowly nodded.

"Alright. Well if you recall as part of our last conversation, that shouldn't be possible. So you see where I'm at an impasse. Tell me exactly what happened that led you here." Leo leaned forward again and caught Kitty's gaze with unrelenting demand. "This is extremely important, Kitty. Don't leave out anything because I'm afraid you simply can't judge its importance right now. Breaching the Planetary Homestead this way is incredibly dangerous."

Kitty's lips bobbed as she fumbled for words. She scratched her head and then the itch moved to places she couldn't reach as if stealing the only excuse to stall that she had left. "I—um...I got in a fight at school. It's been a really long day, and I just wanted to get away from there. So I jumped—I made a transit diagram. I guess I wasn't really specific about where. I just wanted to be somewhere else. Actually, I just needed to find you."

"So you wished for it instead of properly compiling an argument again," Leo said. There was no question about it, and Kitty lowered her head. "There aren't words in English with enough degree of intensity to explain how important it is that you not tug on the heartstrings of the universe, Kitty, but I'll do my best. You're not just putting yourself in danger, but you endanger the lives of everyone on this planet. Even further out, but maybe that's too grand a scale for a thirteen-year-old to understand. You have a lot of life to live before you get to concepts like that, but I'm afraid I need you to understand something perfectly clear right now. You cannot wish for magic to simply happen as you want it to. You can't."

Leo typed into one of the monitors on his desk and then spun the screen around to face her. It looked like two fuzzy white disks swirling in a black void on either edge of the screen. In the center was a transparent funnel glittering as the disks spun against it on either long, curving side.

"Let me try to make one thing very clear," Leo continued. "I told you the Planetary Homestead, where we are right now, is sitting in an oration called a Dimensional

Hold. It's a buffer space outside of the normal restrictions of any given universe, and it has a dual purpose. One, it allows us to perform extensive orations generally without interference of other magics at work. Two, these spaces provide assistance as well, allowing for continued expansion of neighboring universes and not letting them collide with one another. That's the type of chaos Nefas lives for—My bad, Kitty."

Kitty held her weak stomach and quickly accepted the chilled water bottle Leo pulled out of his mini fridge.

"Transit orations directly to the Homestead can cause inconsistencies in the orations at play here. If we ain't doing our job right, horrible things go down." On the screen, the center funnel shivered and frayed into useless strands. In quick motion, the spinning disks moved through it, intercepted each other, and rearranged into shattering bits like fallen crystals. Kitty bit her lip and gulped.

"These are millions of star systems, like ours with our sun and our perfect distance from it here on Earth to provide life. Millions. Billions. They would be warped, torn, shredded. Natural laws we take for granted would be twisted and cracked in ways they were never meant to know. Do you get it?"

Kitty slowly nodded again. Her entire body shivered.

"Well, you don't," Leo said, returning to his chair and dropping heavily into the padding. "but maybe you have a better idea now. I'm going to see about arranging some time with you personally so we can work on this wishing business. It has to stop."

"I didn't do it again before this. I promise!"

"Then what brought this on? From what you've told me so far, it seems stress induced."

Kitty paused again, shaking hands wrapped around the water bottle. "It's just been a lot to think about with school and all. And I have a big event—" Kitty sighed. "Well I had a big event happening in two days, but my dummy got messed up and turned into a freakazoid."

Leo raised an eyebrow. "You attempted another of those orations? Did Will tell you what I said about that?"

"He did." Kitty's heart raced as she danced around the truth about Raquel. She was grateful she wasn't using the Chameleon Ear. "It's not the same one you said was too much like me. I did a new one, but—I'm just no good at using magic. I don't think I want to keep using it." Kitty pressed her thumb and forefinger around the charm on her bracelet, and it melted away into her MHD. She stood and held it out to Leo.

He shook his head and smiled as he pushed the MHD back into her hands. "Regardless of your choice to join the Alliance, keep your harnessing device. It has a lot of useful information so you can take your own learning nice and slow. And still keep your friends close by. Will can be a tremendous help to you. Not just a mentor, but he's a good kid. Have more people like that around you, the ones who really care about you, and maybe you won't be so stressed."

Kitty remembered Jennifer's words and how much they stung. She thought they were friends no matter where Kitty lived, but maybe it was all a joke for Jennifer's new friends.

"Leo, why did I get this magic junk anyway?" Kitty asked. She looked down at her open palms, and the 'K' charm of her bracelet glinted against the pale lights. "What good is it to me?"

"Ah, well, the first part of that is the easy answer," Leo said. "You're smart, Kitty. You know it. I know it. Most importantly, Vitae knows it. You have the makings of a leader, a person who can change the face of the world. Don't roll your eyes, young lady."

"Sorry," she said as she sat back in the curved chair. "I've just heard that garbage before. My teacher Mr. Briggs told me that when I asked about running our Homecoming Dance."

"He sounds like a smart man then. It's true, Kitty."

"Magic doesn't seem to think so. Every time I activate an oration, it asks me a bunch of questions, and it always asks me why I'm a Mage. Like it doesn't trust me."

"Magic doesn't feel things like trust. The universe you affect does. And so do you. Do you trust yourself with magic? Are you using it for the right reasons? You know what magic is. You know how a spell's use molds the world to be more peaceful. You already have a good sense in your heart for peace, hence that desire manifested itself in you. Unfortunately, you also have the responsibility of being an Empath, which can take that desire and turn it into something terrible. It's your responsibility to understand that. Now that's why you got magic. What good it'll do you is a whole different can of worms."

Leo stood up and crossed back to the window that displayed a breathtaking skewed cityscape at night. The Washington Monument stood stoically, dominating the curved horizon.

Leo turned back towards her. "What good is magic to you, Kitty?"

Kitty was caught off guard. "Well—I mean—I can help people with it."

"You sure can. Is that all?"

"What else is there? That's even what the resource thingy said."

"Who are you helping?" Before Kitty could answer, Leo's brow wrinkled and his eyes turned towards nothing in particular as if he heard something Kitty couldn't. Then he looked back at her. "Kitty, you need to head back to the transit docks right now—damn it."

"What's wrong?"

"No time. You need to leave the Homestead."

"What did I do?"

Leo didn't answer. He jumped up from his seat and jogged to the door. With a snap of his fingers a phone in a thick white protective case appeared in one hand. He swiped his fingers along it for a few seconds and then the door took on a blue-white sheen.

"No more wishes. No more—" He was interrupted by clamoring and banging down the hall. Some rumbling gurgles and screams.

"What—?"

"There isn't time," Leo said. "I made a stabilized transit back to your home. Kitty, go. Now! And no more wishes!"

Her heart slammed against her chest, but she did as Leo said and approached the metal door. It slid aside for her, revealing a familiar, cold, black chasm that felt like a bubble shattering across her face. On the other side she was standing on her fire escape in the brisk evening. Kitty looked out at the horizon as if she could see through the sky to a buffer world that might suddenly go ablaze, and probably because of her.

I'm getting to be a real hoodlum, Kitty thought to herself as she stared down the white slip of paper crumpled in her fist.

Bold ink forever etched into a pink carbon copy somewhere scolded her for being late without notice. She had slept so hard that her mother was a second away from calling an ambulance. But once the fear had passed, Mrs. Guthrie was right back to doling out Kitty's punishment on their way to the school for hitting Miren. Grounded for a month.

The rolling TV shelf was back in the detention room. The other students were half asleep or scrolling Friendville on their phones in the semi-darkness. Kitty rubbed at the red ink on the side of her right hand with a wet tissue. Still it wouldn't come off. At least there weren't any more posters for her to vandalize, but as the second part of the documentary droned, Kitty figured she wouldn't have minded a chore outside of the classroom again.

Whispers picked up around her. Kitty slowly peeked behind her to make sure she wasn't the butt of someone's joke, but every student had their eyes elsewhere. Hushed tones washed over her thoughts, and her ear prickled as the Chameleon Ear perked up. Those whispers weren't for her, but they left trails of feelings in her mind. It sounded like someone calling for help, and still no one was talking except the narrator on the DVD.

"Kitty, you done with being a delinquent yet?" Will's voice made her jump in her seat.

"Jeez! This thing needs a ringtone. No, I'm still in detention. What do you want?"

"Raquel and I found a few more interfering orations to add

to our list," he said. Kitty's stomach dropped. *"Two more popped up. I locked down the spots."*

"...okay." That was the best she could think to respond, forgetting how easily emotions and intentions flowed through the Chameleon Ear. She cringed as her stress and yearning to be free of the mania screeched through that single word.

"Still not willing to help? Fine. Should only take a few days to sew up these tears. Can we at least ask for your help to fuel the diagram?"

Guilt and unease vibrated along the connection. To Kitty's shock, she felt it from both sides. *"Sure, I guess that's easy enough. Then I'm done."*

"...alright. I'll call you in a few days. And Kitty, you'd make a great Magistrate whether you believe it now or not."

The Chameleon Ear shut off. The quiet was louder than the whispering had been. What did Will have to be upset about? His life wasn't the one flipped upside down after realizing he was a Mage. Then again, Kitty hadn't asked him about anything like that.

"Get your head off my desk!" a boy hissed to the girl in front of him, swiping at her skinny, colorful braids. She twisted around in her seat with a scowl on her lips. Her eyes were so narrow they looked closed as if she were flirting with her clockwork lashes. "No one wants to see your junk face neither."

"Why don't you chill?" another girl said as she cracked a bubble of gum in her mouth. Her gold hoop earrings bounced on the sides of her round face with each chew. "You should be lucky a girl is even paying attention to you, numbnuts."

"Why don't you mind your own business?" the boy said with a rude finger gesture just as the girl with braids turned and said, "Nobody asked you, Laina chubs."

Before the teacher could finally notice, the chubby girl was out of her seat, tipping it in the process. She dropped on top of the girl with braids, slapping her and tugging on her hair. The boy threw his head back with a laugh, hitting the nose of the boy in the seat behind him. Immediately the taller kid was on his feet, nose in one hand and slugging the back of the first boy's head with the other. Someone else joined in, throwing himself at the tall boy, a head higher than he was, and soon it was an explosion of screaming, fist and palms finding bruised targets, and the screech of desks being shoved aside and knocked over.

Kitty jumped up just as Laina was pushed into her desk and dented it right where Kitty had been resting her head moments before. The teacher was on his feet, pulling at students' collars and backpacks to get them off of each other, but it seemed he lost his own reservation at times and pulled with enough force to choke someone or lift them off of their feet. Kitty grabbed her backpack and crawled along the sticky floor behind the empty teacher's desk. She waited until a path was cleared to the door. The moment two boys at the front of the room threw each other back into the fray, Kitty bolted.

She didn't realize she had grabbed her MHD until she was searching through a list of spell diagrams to calm people down. Everything she looked at either had permissions tags, demanding consent of the person being affected unless the oration was on the user, or it used up enough energy to drain twenty people along with *cellular decay of amygdala tissue*. Kitty didn't want to handle that.

Magic had to be able to do something.

"Should you be in a class?" a man asked. Kitty hid her tablet behind her back. He was in a too tight black polo shirt and dark pants with his sunglasses resting above his bald head. Beady brown eyes locked onto hers. The security guard lifted an eyebrow.

"Uh, yeah, but—"

A screech and thud against the detention room door stole their attention. A streak of saliva mixed with something darker stained the door as a student lifted himself and dove at someone. The security guard charged inside while communicating to someone over a walkie-talkie. Kitty reached out to Leo through the Chameleon Ear. All she heard was static.

"Leo? Leo, can you hear me?" Only more static. Kitty switched off their connection and thought of Will. She took a deep breath. *"Will? You there?"*

"A little busy," he said. Kitty cringed as if she could see the annoyed scowl, but it shifted as her worry filled the line. *"What's up?"*

"Can you reach Leo? I just get weird static."

A pause followed. Then Will's thoughts returned. *"That's weird. The connection is open, it's just...messed up. I don't know."*

"Uh...I might know a little." She told him what happened after she and Raquel fended off the dummy oration. The crashing and yelling she heard in the Planetary Homestead sounded an awful lot like what was slowly being quelled in the classroom beside her.

"Whoa whoa whoa," Will said as the thought suddenly dawned on him. *"You made a transit diagram that took you*

211

directly into Leo's office? The office in the Planetary Homestead? Where you can't make transits?" Kitty's uncomfortable nod was obvious through the connection. *"Oh Kitty, that's really bad. Something is really not okay about that."*

"I already know that! I didn't mean to!"

"I mean, you say you didn't mean to, but that's exactly what you meant or your magic wouldn't have made it happen. Okay, look. What's done is done. The most important thing now is just moving forward. You take a breather. I'll see about getting to the Homestead and talking to Leo. No wishes!"

"Fine." Kitty sharply disconnected the Chameleon Ear. She'd had enough scolding to last a lifetime.

Kitty looked back at her tablet screen and the impossible spell diagrams. Guilt settled in her chest. Sure she didn't want magic anymore, but if someone needed help, she thought she could use it to do a little good. When she needed it, it fought her or was too complicated for her to do alone. Why had it shown up in the first place if it was only going to make things harder?

Through her open bedroom, Kitty could hear her mom's car beep. Somehow she always knew which beep was hers even when it sounded like every other car in the lot. Edith also knew. The floor shuddered. The patter of Edith's footsteps down the hall and the shrill of excitement would have warned her about her mom's return too.

Kitty looked back at her lap where the white tablet sat quiet and dark. She had been swiping her finger along it for the last hour after finishing her homework. It was strange to have free time. She knew if her plans hadn't changed she would still have free time soon, but this felt different. The guilt clung to her as she stared into space like when she should have been doing something important, but was too tired to do homework or too grossed out to take the garbage to the dumpster.

Stupid magic, she thought, careful to only think it and not activate the Chameleon Ear. She didn't have an excuse not to help get Raquel home other than she was scared. Magic was so wild, so out of her reach. Everything else came naturally to her. At least the things that mattered like homework and being a responsible big sister. She kept the apartment as clean as she could, and she volunteered. Not to be self-centered, but she was great at a lot of really important things.

Magic felt important, and Kitty was far from great at it. Sure, she only had the Magical Harnessing Device for less than a week, but she caused so much trouble in that little time. Or trouble was finding her.

"Kitty?" her mom called out.

With an exasperated sigh, Kitty tossed her tablet onto her made up bed and left the room. Toys were scattered down the hall and into the living room, one of which her mother almost tripped on after tossing her purse on the floor by the front door. Edith was glued to her leg.

"Someone missed you," Kitty said, taking a seat on the arm of the couch. Her mother limped towards her and smacked her knee.

"You know better. Get up, please. I don't need Edith getting any ideas." She was already opening her bedroom door by the time Kitty took a dramatically long while to stand. "I was invited out to dinner with a friend tonight,"

Mrs. Guthrie said as she unknotted her scarf and started pulling bobby pins loose. Soft auburn curls flounced against her shoulders with tasteful fly-aways that showed a hard day's work. Edith kept one arm around Mrs. Guthrie and used the other arm to swat at the tips of her hair. "I know it's very sudden and I didn't prepare dinner. You can make the good macaroni and use the block cheese instead of the canned."

Kitty's eyes widened. "What's the occasion?"

"Just a night out. They're nice to have every now and then," she said through her teeth clenched around the bobby pins. She started to secure her hair into a new updo. "But I know it's sudden so I want to make sure you'll be alright. I don't have to go."

"No, no. You should totally go."

Mrs. Guthrie patted her hair and picked up her lipstick in her favorite rouge. "Is that a real 'totally' or a teenager 'totally'? Because this doesn't mean you can be on your phone. You're still grounded."

"I know. It's a real 'totally', mom," Kitty said, rolling her eyes. Her mom kissed her forehead before reapplying her lipstick and adding a touch of color to her eyes. "Where to?"

"Belladona Bistro on Park Ave," her mother said. Her eyes were glued to the mirror.

"Whoa! That's crazy expensive. What is this, a marriage proposal??"

"Relax, Kitty." Mrs. Guthrie blotted her lips on a tissue, smiled, and turned back to her daughter. Her face looked brand new. "It's just dinner with a friend and I like to get a little dolled up outside of work. Out you go. I have to change. Edith, please let go now."

The younger girl stomped through the door, throwing herself onto the couch. In minutes their mother was back in the living room with a slinky black dress stopping just shy of her knee. She had a pair of heels Kitty hadn't seen in years and a matching black purse with leather fringe and a gold chain.

"Kitty, Edith gets dinner—"

"—at seven. In bed at nine. Duh."

Mrs. Guthrie blew Kitty and Edith kisses and hurried out the door. A strange silence filled the living room. Edith silently walked to the door and pressed her ear to it with a wobbling lower lip. Their mother was a hidden social butterfly. A debutante locked up by work and environment. She was the reason Kitty and Jennifer were friends. Mrs. Murphy still set up hair appointments with Kitty's mom after the move, but now they did private sessions at the Murphy's home. Kitty understood her need to get out sometimes and be like she was before. It just never happened very often.

"Seems like everyone has a bad attitude today. Come here, kid," Kitty said to Edith. She reached her arms out and her sister ran over and plunked her head into the crook of Kitty's neck. "She'll be back to kiss you good morning like always. Let's have special fancy pants macaroni, okay?"

While Edith sang along to her favorite movie, Kitty started preparing the boxed elbow noodles. The routine was peaceful. Kitty hummed while flecks of poorly grated cheese fell on and around the cutting board. Then she had to grate more because she picked at the pile too much.

"Kitty, there's something you should see," Will's voice made her jump and almost knock over the cutting board.

215

"My last wish is gonna be to put a bell on this stupid thing!"
"What?"
Kitty rolled her eyes. *"Never mind. Just send it."*

Kitty squeezed her bracelet charm and laid her MHD on the counter. She selected the messenger icon bouncing in anticipation. Kitty opened Will's message. A wall of text scrolled down her screen.

CRITICAL NOTICE FROM ACTING CHIEF PLANETARY
JUSTICE ROEN CAPLAN

EXTREME CONDITIONS IN EFFECT. INVESTIGATION UNDERWAY TO DETERMINE FACTORS OF EXCESSIVE SPATIAL CONTAINMENT. ACCESS TO PLANETARY HOMESTEAD IS CURRENTLY WITHDRAWN.

DUE TO EXTREME CONDITIONS, BE ADVISED THAT SPELL DIAGRAMS MAY ACT WITH TENTATIVE RELIABILITY. TEMPORAL-SPATIAL AUGMENTATION AND TRANSITORY DIAGRAMS ARE ILL-ADVISED. EXTREMELY DANGEROUS CONDITIONS. CONTACT YOUR LOCAL LIAISONS AND LOCAL ASSEMBLY GOVERNOR FOR ASSISTANCE IN EMERGENCIES ONLY. SEEK THE FAMILY TREE IF A LIAISON CANNOT BE REACHED.

The same message scrolled across the screen on repeat. Kitty read it over and over trying to make sense of it. Everyone was barred from the Planetary Homestead and their Liaisons. Extreme conditions. Transits could be broken. The part about Excessive Spatial Containment confused her.

"Uh, did they just call the universe fat?" she asked.

Will paused a moment, mulling over her words. *"Huh. I think they did."* They shared a relieving laugh. *"But this is what appeared right before I was going to head over to the Homestead. I think it's being sent to everyone. Looks like we'll need to lay off transit orations until this gets resolved."*

"But what about the one for Raquel? And—Will, is this my fault?" She didn't want to hear him say yes, but she also didn't want to be lied to. Those feelings clamored through the connection; she thought she felt Will wince.

"Kitty—I don't know," he said. Kitty could see a big part of him believed it. *"I mean, not being able to reach the Homestead after you fast-tracked there. And the stuff with Raquel having your exact frequency. It's more than coincidence."*

"I didn't mean to..."

"Magic isn't about what you mean—well, no. That's not true. Magic is exactly about what you mean. It's about truth. Okay, so you screwed up. Now what are you going to do about it? Moping doesn't change the fact. Magic is also about action to make things better. It's especially important if you've made a mistake. Own it and fix it."

Kitty absently swirled the macaroni in the pot with the melting cheese and butter. *"I don't know how. And I don't want to make things worse."*

"Then wise up. Read the resources and help me and Raquel. It's not like you're doing this alone. And don't use transit orations until we get Raquel home. I think I've got this mini Dimensional Hold figured out. That should make her transit safer."

"Is she real, Will, or is this a lot of trouble for nothing? She said dummies can't do orations, and I looked it up, and she's right. So—who is she?"

Will shrugged. *"It's your oration. You tell me."*

217

He disconnected the link.

Kitty and Edith huddled on the couch with soup bowls of macaroni and the sequel to Hop-Along Princess on the crinkling screen. As Edith started drifting to sleep, Kitty kept her up long enough to put her to bed in her favorite nightgown with the rainbow sleeves and smiling unicorn on the front. Kitty took one of her satin crown barrettes and clipped it to some of her curls. As she flicked the light switch and shut the door, Kitty shook her head as a crackling filled her ear for a moment, like a persistent bug. It hissed incomplete words and babbled.

Mis—gra—who are you? Will you help? Why are you a Mage? What size shoe—?

Then the whispering stopped. Kitty peaked back into her sister's room, but she only saw the pink haze pouring over the bed from the moon through the window. Her sister was a silent bundle tucked into her blankets. Nothing else moved or made a sound.

Kitty went back to her bedroom and got into her own simple yellow camisole and sweatpants with flaking cartoon cats. She summoned her tablet and swiped along the screen. The shivering symbols in the top corner greeted her as they always did. She saw a message from Will waiting for her. When she opened it, two attachments blinked. One was labeled RAQUEL HOME TRANSIT. The second said FUNKY INTERFERING PORTALS. A small list of coordinates filled the screen along with a familiar magic frequency that twisted into a spell diagram of an interfering transit.

> Caught a few more. Just in case. I hope that's it.
> Thanks.
> -Will

She clicked the first coordinate. A map expanded across the screen with a blot of light right over Mort's Bagel Shop in the Slope, the one she couldn't find before. Kitty minimized the window and tapped on the second line of the list. The map reappeared in the Valley, this time at Hope Creek Church. Kitty cocked her head. The church must have been one of the places Raquel and Will investigated without her. The list wasn't long, but if any of those transits—those tears—were getting in the way—

Kitty shook her head as her ear buzzed again. Those harsh whispers that were now nearly words crackled and stung in her mind like someone snuck into her brain and threw a tantrum. The MHD beeped, just audible past the slowly dying whispers. She minimized the screen back to the list and saw a sixth coordinate pop up, eerily familiar. For a moment she didn't want to touch it; she knew why she had seen it before. How many times had she jumped back to the safety of her apartment?

As perfectly clean as she kept it, her room felt dirty now. Kitty leaped off her bed and checked under it, through her closet, outside her window to the fire escape, anywhere a tear might be. She grabbed her tablet and left her room. The light from the screen helped her avoid stepping in something she shouldn't until she could reach the hallway lightswitch. Nothing on the walls or beneath the couch. The kitchen was clear and so was her mother's room, under the bed, vanity, and all. Kitty stepped out of her mother's room, staring straight at her sister's door. She groaned, but crept inside.

Still her sister lay there in a perfect dream world coated in pink from the curtains. Little shadows fell across her from the stickers on the window and each one felt like tiny tears that might burn her sister's skin. Kitty's heart raced as she used her tablet's light to look around. The bed was fine. Nothing about her closet or dresser was charred or tipped over.

Something snapped overhead, and Kitty jumped. A chiffon drape fell from the top of Edith's canopy bed like a split cobweb. Kitty shined her phone's light at the ceiling. Stretching in a thin line from the top of Edith's bed to the edge of the ceiling was a black split with wispy edges that left the ceiling paint chipped. A few pieces snowed to the floor.

Edith rolled over in her sleep to Kitty's relief. With less grace than she wished she had, Kitty climbed onto her sister's dresser and leaned against the posts of the bed for support. The dresser shook under her feet, and she immediately knew this was a bad idea, but magic was difficult enough. She wanted to use as little as she could until this was over. Kitty reached up with the needle and poked it through the air of Edith's ceiling. As she pulled it back through, she heard a small moan below. Edith rolled back over in her bed. Her face was scrunched and her bottom lip was quivering. Explaining why she was using her sister's bed like a jungle gym would be easy enough to do for Edith, but Kitty would still prefer she just stay asleep.

Kitty carefully continued across the tear. Each time the needle passed through, she could hear another soft groan or cry.

"I'm sorry if you can feel this somehow, Edie," Kitty said mostly to herself. "Just a little more."

The bed rattled and Kitty nearly lost her grip. She

slipped forward and clung to the curling top of the posts. She pressed back with her feet to keep the dresser steady and looked down at her sister.

Edith shook. One of her hands was clenching the bed sheets while the other had a pillow in a vice grip. Her eyes were rolled to the back of her head and her mouth hung limp.

"No, no, sweetie, not now."

Kitty looked at how much of the tear was left. She could always redo it, but it wouldn't matter if her sister would just keep reacting to it. Kitty peeled her burning eyes away from Edith who was gurgling and shaking under the sheets. She stabbed at the ceiling again and again, following the last quarter of the unstable slash. As soon as Kitty knotted off the oration, she terminated it and jumped down from the dresser to keep Edith's head turned to the side. Tears spilled down her cheeks as Edith's stiff body rocked in her arms for another few seconds.

Kitty lay next to her sister for a while longer before kissing her forehead and tiptoeing back to her own bed, thoughts reeling. A fat universe splitting its pants. People acting like bullies and even criminals. Her sister's usual cheer gone and then finding a tear in her room. It took hours, but when her eyes finally drifted shut, she was still sobbing in her sleep.

Fifteen

The last time Kitty fought that hard to get out of bed was four years ago when she learned about her parents splitting up. It was different than the anger she felt when her dad simply didn't come home one day. That was something she never wanted to experience again. Instead, she chose to be better than him. She promised he wouldn't drive her crazy like he almost did to her mom. Every night for months, Mrs. Guthrie sat alone with a bottle in her hand, yelling or crying or both. Every night Kitty sat up with her sister and sang songs or played with loud toys to drown out the sound.

There was a terrible responsibility she felt for her sister and then her mother. The unfairness crashed down on her, threatening to squeeze the life out of her. Then she made a wish to be far away. She dreamed of herself in California where she imagined it was always sunny and warm. A nice old lady who owned an ice cream shop offered her a free cone as payment for her first day on the job. Kitty smiled and eagerly lapped at the scoops of her dripping dessert before it could stain her perfect white apron. The folded paper hat didn't do much to keep the heat off of her dark hair, and the beating sun made her sweat and itch, but she didn't mind too much.

What she minded was the strange swirling circle of blue threads appearing between her and the nice ice cream lady. The wrinkly smile grew further away. Kitty reached an arm out, dropping her cone in surprise. She never saw or felt it splatter.

"I want to go there!" she begged of the disappearing woman. *"I want to be somewhere else!"*

Where? How far? Warm? Sunny? Dry? Raining? Why? Longitude? Latitude? Friends? Strangers? Fears? Joys? Why? Your mother? Your sister? Your father?

The center of the circle grew dark as Kitty threw out as many answers as she could, but the questions never stopped.

Country? Language? Sandy? Coastal? Earth? Galaxy? Universe?

Her heart clenched as she pleaded for the circle to take her anywhere, but even as she reached out, her feet planted to the ground. She didn't dare step forward. Something stopped her, but when her eyes opened, she knew she could have made that wish. She saw the messy blue scribbles in her half crumpled notebook and the waxy crayon nub with half of its body embedded under her fingernails and smeared on her floor.

Kitty didn't want her wishes to come true like that anymore, not when she still struggled with the easy orations. Maybe when she had more time to think about it, she could be a Magus.

But first, she had to get Raquel home. Whatever that meant.

"Kitty? What are you still doing in bed?" Mrs. Guthrie said through the ajar door. Her makeup was done, and she was knotting a white and gold scarf over her hair. "Let's go, baby. C'mon."

Before Kitty could answer, her mother disappeared down the hall. She reached under her covers for her charm and pressed it. Her palm warmed as she closed her hand around her MHD and hid it under the lip of her blanket.

Heat.

Heat area.

Kitty frowned at the range of too simple and over complicated spell diagrams.

Small heat area.

"Score!" Kitty dragged strands of symbols to match a simple diagram. The oration asked every question it could spit out, mostly more questions about Kitty, before it finally felt satisfied. Kitty couldn't see the execution, but her forehead, and neck warmed like a personal spa. Beads of sweat broke out over her forehead.

A few minutes later, Mrs. Guthrie pushed the door open. "Kitty, what's going on? You're going to miss your bus."

"I don't feel good, mom."

"Hmm? My Kitty, sick? That's devil's talk. Did you stay up too late again?" Mrs. Guthrie grinned as she sat on the edge of Kitty's bed and placed the back of her hand against her daughter's forehead and at the top of her neck.

Her hand felt cool on her clammy skin. Mrs. Guthrie's smile dropped as she pulled her hand back. "Oh lord, you're definitely warm. Shoot. Okay. I need to get your sister to Glade Crest General, but I'll swing back here before work to check in."

"I'll be fine," Kitty croaked. "Can I make the chicken noodle soup?"

"Of course. And drink lots of water and get rest, you understand? And still no phone calls. You're still grounded, little miss."

Kitty nodded and snuggled into her covers. Her mother kissed her forehead and left. The shuffling and giggling from the living room eventually trailed out the front door, but Kitty waited for the locks to click into place before getting up.

"Will? You ready?"

A drawn out yawn answered, and the connection through the Chameleon Ear was flooded with bleariness.

"No. What's with you school kids being awake before the sun? Jeez!"

Kitty rolled her eyes and terminated the heat oration before she sweat through her pajamas.

For playing hookie, the day didn't feel like a vacation. There were only so many of the tears the Mages could handle in a day before actually feeling sick. Kitty wasn't thrilled to find herself sneaking back into the Sunday school classroom at the church, peaking over her shoulder every few minutes. Chills left her skin smothered in goosebumps, and any bump or churn from the pipes made her jump. The room was as clean as she left it except the brooms and mops were stacked back in the closet. Sunlight pouring through the windows showed the cloudy spots Kitty missed.

She stepped lightly through the room looking for any signs of the tear. She looked behind the cubbies and the shelves with the bible stories. She checked the closet where she first found Raquel, and she checked it twice more to be sure. She wasn't certain why these tears were showing up, but she didn't think it was too much coincidence that it was happening right after Raquel appeared.

The closet was perfectly normal, mildew stench and all. Kitty backed up towards the bright plastic table, looking around for her next stakeout when a burning pain shot through her foot. She yelped and fell against the rounded chairs, hearing one crack under the sudden weight, and it pitched her against the table face first. The throbbing against her cheek told her she had a bruise on the way. It was a familiar pain, back to the first time she made a wish to take a bruise from her sister. It was nothing compared to the lingering heat against the bottom of her foot.

Kitty pushed herself to a seated position with a groan, never more thankful that no one was around. She looked at her foot and saw a raw scorch mark on her exposed heel. The cracked skin was bleeding in some areas from behind melted rubber threads that remained from her sneaker. Kitty bit back tears as she gingerly laid her leg back down.

"When you guys are done, can you swing by the church tear?" Kitty asked, unable to hide the pain through the connection. *"Yes, I'm alright. Yes, I accidentally touched it. More like stepped on it."*

"Yikes," Will said. A more muted sympathy popped through from Raquel's end, honest but still annoyed. *"Yeah, hold tight. Almost done here."*

Kitty looked back where her foot landed. The plush storytime rug with the Last Supper scene was charred through the middle, sunken into a smoldering crack in the floor. With a quick pull, Kitty tossed the rug aside and saw a fat black tear in the tiling and greedy, wispy edges clawing for more space to eat. It was wider than the one at SportsPlex, and neither Will nor Raquel said anything about theirs being more than maybe six inches wide. This one was at least two feet across and stretched five feet long. Kitty counted her blessings that she stepped on an edge and not right in the middle.

She had her MHD out in a moment, squeezing it to the rhythm of the throbbing in her heel. With her jaw clenched so tight she thought her teeth might pop out of her head, Kitty found the recently activated oration and recreated it. She was grateful not to get bombarded with questions. As she approached the tear, she wielded the needle like a sword. It was so much bigger than the other one.

There was no time to lose. Kitty pressed the tip of the needle to the floor and pushed with enough force to pierce one of April's leather skirts. The needle's tip disappeared into the ground. A smile flickered across Kitty's lips with the thrill of an oration that worked. Her chest swelled with pride. She wished her sister or her mom could see what she was doing. If Mr. Briggs could understand, if Mrs. Smith could, maybe they would give her the respect she deserved.

Kitty brought the edge of the needle back through the floor on the other side of the tear, watching as a glowing blue-white thread trailed behind, and she pulled to stretch it across the gap. Her limbs felt the same tug. Her skin tingled and her blood rushed as if she were starting a race.

As she looped back a few more times, nearing where the tear bottlenecked towards its widest point, her muscles twinged and a line of sweat traced her brow. Kitty paused a moment to breathe. The rest of the tear looked daunting from the middle.

Then let it go, a little voice creeped into her thoughts, one she had become familiar with over the last few days. *Magic didn't help me so what do I owe it or anybody?*

Kitty swallowed hard. She was already halfway through an oration. There was something binding, like a promise, when she started any magic. She was speaking to something, telling it that it was off track and promising to fix it to become better. That didn't sound like a promise she wanted to ignore.

After an unhelpful break, Kitty continued stabbing at the ground and yanking further and further with her crooked strands of oration. As she crested the middle of the tear and pulled, she nearly fell over from the effort. Every muscle in her body screamed and begged for her to let go. To just stop. She was tired and sore, she didn't have enough strength to finish an oration of this size alone. She kept tugging against the weight of an entire universe pulled apart.

"Oh junk," she muttered. "I'm gonna kill myself with this."

"May I? Please say yes and mean it before you pass out," said the girl who had abruptly appeared beside her. Kitty squinted through the white spots forming in her vision. Raquel was holding her own needle and aiming it at the floor beside Kitty.

Kitty nodded and watched Raquel start her own

struggle with the tear while she knotted off her side of the oration. Once the knot was sealed off and the spell diagram was terminated, Kitty fell back against the bundled plush rug behind her and hoped she had energy left to breathe. In a few minutes Raquel joined her, less pain on her face.

"You could've asked for help," Raquel said. "That thing is huge."

Kitty only flopped her arms in a half shrug as she continued to catch her breath. "How'd you get here so fast? No transits, remember?"

"I was only like twenty minutes from here at that pizza place."

"Oh man, I could go for some Fabio's pizza right now. I'm starving."

"First let's see that foot."

Kitty winced, but she slid her leg towards Raquel who sat up and inspected the sole of her shoe, cringing. Raquel tapped a few keys and silently read from her MHD armband screen. She laid her hands by Kitty's foot. A warm sensation coated her, and she sighed with relief as the throbbing stopped. She looked at Raquel to thank her and saw her squeezing her eyes shut, a few tears trapped in her eyelashes. Raquel waved off her concern.

"I do this all the time for my sister," she said. "Before you can change something, you have to know what you're changing. And now I know definitely do NOT touch these things."

A knock on the door made the girls jump, but they immediately relaxed when Will poked his head in. "Good afternoon, ladies," he said, and he shut the door behind him. Kitty was envious of how relaxed he was. She supposed homeschool kids didn't have to worry about truancy laws under the Student Protection Act. "Nursing home is done. Did you guys finish?"

"All done here," Kitty said with as much of a smile as she could muster. Raquel also gave a thumbs up.

"Great, but also, we've got a small problem," he said. "I saw the tear at SportsPlex light up again just as I got here. Looks like it's not out of the way yet."

Raquel groaned. "No way. That thing was nearly invisible when we finished with it. Can something that small still get in the way of my transit home?"

"I don't think so." Will summoned his MHD and started swiping across the screen. "It wasn't a problem until a few minutes ago when I saw it light up again. Oh what the heck!"

Kitty and Raquel shared wary glances as Will went silent. Before they could ask, their MHDs pinged with a new message. In the body was a similar list to the one Will had sent before. One of the other tears was on it, and a new one appeared, but Kitty immediately noticed the blip over her apartment, and her heart sank.

"We have to stop these things for good," Kitty seethed. "I'm not letting that thing show up in my house again!"

"We'll shut them down," Will said. "We just need to take a closer look and see what we missed. This was all a guessing game anyway."

Kitty pushed herself up with unsteady arms. She looked at the small list, furious that the tear over her sister's bed could have reappeared and anxious that someone else could get hurt from the one at SportsPlex. Were they big, clear rips like when she first saw them or were they still thin, but widening? What could make them grow like that?

Will took a seat in one of the upright chairs, scratching at his head.

"Oh wow. I'm an idiot—or rather I overlooked something and I will be much more careful about it in the future." He spoke deliberately, punctuating each word with a more positive attitude. "Okay, so apparently these tears aren't always pinging. The list I made, I nabbed as soon as something popped up. I thought those were the only ones. Looks like even after I save them to my list, they go away soon after. I didn't realize because I was only looking at the list. Right now nothing is pinging. Nothing is getting in the way of the transit for Raquel, but I get a feeling if we wait long enough, something will ping. If that happens after we hit Execute…"

He didn't need to finish.

Mission—gr—Initiate—what are your favorite pizza toppings? How long can you hold your breath under water? Kitty slapped at her ear as the whispering swelled and then washed away.

"You okay?" Raquel asked. Kitty nodded.

"Crap! Where's the tear?" Will suddenly asked.

Kitty was taken back by the desperation in his voice. She and Raquel moved over so Will had full view of the sewn up tear a few feet away. It didn't look like anything more than a slight mismatch of tiles easily hidden by the plush rug. Will kneeled beside it.

"What's wrong?" Kitty asked.

"It pinged!"

They all leaned in as close as they dared, afraid the tear might suddenly burst open and swallow them. A glint from the window was casting smoky light over the kitchenette side of the room. Kitty held her arm in the way of the beam on that section of the floor and saw the sliver of light from hers and Raquel's oration. Just a few millimeters wide, the blue-white thread puckered and between it was a small shadow that could have been the stained grout between the floor design.

"Oh junk." Kitty scooted back, more afraid of what the tear might do. "Oh super junk."

"That really sucks," Will said. "It looks like the tear gets bigger when it pings. This thing is definitely fighting back against our oration."

He fell silent again. The girls watched his desperate swiping and tapping against his tablet screen as his tongue stuck out from the corner of his lips.

"Oh. Oh man. That's...more of a challenge. So hey, I think the tears aren't our problem."

Kitty's and Raquel's MHDs beeped again as Will sent another message. Neither girl was eager to open it. Attached to the mailing was a new scan. The frequency spoke of bursting and shredding, bringing destruction to life as its sole objective. It wanted to break things apart and consume them with its fiery might. Beside her, Raquel's face turned pale.

"Is that...is that a bomb?!" Kitty shrieked. She nearly dropped her tablet in horror. "Will! You said this wasn't the kind of stuff we'd have to deal with!

"I said we probably wouldn't have to," he responded, but his voice was shaky and breathless. "Maybe we don't. If we can get this timing right, we can activate Raquel's transit before another bomb goes off. Maybe there's a pattern.

We'll figure it out. At least we know the tears we sewed up shouldn't be too bad anymore. There's one that looks like it's a house on Crystal Ave if you guys have any energy left. I'll handle the one at the hair salon. Maybe if the place is any good my mom will want to check it out. She doesn't mind long trips for things like that." Will forced a little laugh.

"She should go to Beautician Magicians on Main Street," Kitty said, glad for even a short reprieve from her fears. "My mom works there. She's the best stylist they've got."

"Perfect because that's where this tear popped up. I'll take care of it, but we'll have to wait until tomorrow for the transit. I won't have enough energy left in the tank." He stretched and then dismissed his tablet back into fluttering symbols that vanished into his watch. "See you two tomorrow. We'll get this all taken care of." Will saluted to them and jogged out of the classroom.

Kitty and Raquel looked at their MHDs as well. Kitty's energy meter bounced between 50% and 51%, and she could feel the consequences, but she ignored her aching body for a moment as a thought struck her. She looked at all of the lists Will sent side by side.

Sportsplex Fun Zone
Fabio's Pizza
Mort's Delicatessen
Hope Creek Church
Shady Acres Nursing Home
Beautician Magicians.
Her apartment.

The house on Crystal Avenue...where she used to live in the Slope.

Her stomach wrenched. Kitty covered her mouth, afraid to vomit in front of Raquel again. These were all places Kitty visited often. Not only visited, she had practiced transit orations to these places. That was when she learned she could only go so far without getting sick. Each tear was somewhere she had been, and Raquel showed up in one as well. Kitty started a problem, and something was making it so much worse.

"Well you're almost rid of me," Raquel said. Kitty clapped her hands over her ears at hearing her own voice escape the other girl's mouth. "Kitty, what's the matter?"

She only shook her head and jumped to her feet, wobbling as she got lightheaded. She used the wall for support and shrugged off Raquel's stinging palms from her arm. "We'll get you home tomorrow. First thing. I'm really sorry."

When her head stopped buzzing and the room was solid in her eyes again, Kitty ran for the door. She wished she could make a transit home, but she didn't want to cause any more trouble.

Sixteen

Kitty was painfully aware of every car that drove past her or the few people walking by as she crept up the side streets as long as she could towards the Slope. The tear on Crystal Avenue had no business existing, but it was her fault for clinging to old memories. Now a nice family could be in trouble.

Rather than use the energy for an invisibility oration, Kitty projected a very basic image of a woman standing beside her. She had dark hair pulled into a scarf like her mother and a nice dress and belt. For just a moment Kitty pretended this was a walk with her mom like they used to do. If anyone were to touch the woman, their hand would simply glide through her. It was fine. No one needed to speak or touch the projection. No one in the Slope still cared to.

Kitty hurried to the intersection of Park and Main, hugging her arms for warmth, and tried to look casual as they came up on the cul-de-sac of Crystal avenue. There was the same blue paint and bright white shutters. The golden numbers over the door glinted as they caught the last dregs of sunlight. A walkway lined with miniature lanterns led up to steps and a porch with wind chimes and hanging flower pots. A maple tree stump dug into the front lawn, but the memories of thick lower branches and scraped knees were powerful.

Kitty went around back, ducking below the windows to avoid being seen. The backyard was an expanse of bright green grass that had been well watered over the summer. Dandelions clung to the past season, but the flowers in the garden bed were bright and still attracting little bugs and critters. Kitty's heart always stung a little at the sight of the maintained swing set and slide. Mrs. Guthrie obviously couldn't take it when they moved to the Valley.

The patio had new tables and chairs that fit snugly under the lawn umbrella. The smiling lemon tablecloth was gone, replaced by chiseled glass tops that looked like church windows. The back door that Kitty knew led into the den also had a few hanging decorations to celebrate autumn.

Without checking her tablet, Kitty had a strong idea of where the tear might be. When she used practice jumps to visit the old house, there was a small area of the backyard she could reach without being seen. She crossed the patio to where a line of holly bushes grew close to the house. They partially covered a small window that Kitty used to crawl through. She was never a troublemaker so her parents never thought to seal the little window. Now as she ducked beside the holly bushes, the window that normally looked into a finished basement was just a dark void.

The tear wasn't big, only just encroaching on the frame of the two and a half foot window. The wisps of the tear brushed along the white plastic and ate it in small scoopfuls. Kitty executed the needle oration and watched the thread leading from her chest coil through the eye. Quickly she went to work, sticking the needle through the air and feeling it pop. She brought the needle back around and worked her way across the slit. Before knotting off the stitch, Kitty tugged on her thread and watched the blue glow pull at the tear. It shrank and wrinkled until it was no wider than a butterfly wing. Her head throbbed and her stomach lurched so she knotted the oration there. Leo could clean it up when this was done.

A harsh whisper screeched in Kitty's ears, but quickly faded. For just a moment she saw her work jolt like it was trying to break free. Kitty pulled up the scan for that second oration hidden in the tear. There had to be something she could do so it wouldn't undo all of their work. All of Will's and Raquel's work.

Reading over the diagram showed a series of complicated patterns and words Kitty didn't understand. She made sense of the parts that had to do with bursting. It was like a tiny bomb that was scheduled to go off over and over again. No one could notice something so small without looking carefully as Will had been. Her eyes glossed over an area of the diagram that writhed and darkened for a moment, but as it did, Kitty's throat tightened. She looked away, afraid to be sick again.

Kitty wasn't an expert on bombs, only on dealing with people and their short fuses. Instead, she considered another temporary solution. They just had to hold off long enough to make sure Raquel made it home.

Wherever that is, Kitty thought.

She took the time to carefully search the diagram lists under explosive devices and armor. One oration could withstand the force of ten nuclear bombs, but that would use energy Kitty and the others combined didn't have. The bomb wasn't that big.

Instead, she activated the diagram for an oration that acted like a blast shield blocking the tiny explosion from reaching as far as it was meant to. Sure, it might break down the oration over time, but it could withstand the one day they needed to make the transit for Raquel.

Kitty didn't rush despite feeling her nerves twisting her stomach. She could feel resistance from the oration. Whatever energy had created the bomb was actively working against her. It wasn't very strong, but it was a cruel kind of feeling. If she thought energy could laugh at her, she imagined the cold sneer the bomb would wear as it hid in that terrible darkness. Whoever it belonged to understood that this was an attack. It was a curse, and she was defending herself.

EXECUTE? [Y/N]

Kitty executed her diagram and sat back in surprise as the tear spat out sparks of blue light. The two magics fought one another until the blue overwhelmed the black void and sank in. Then it was quiet again. Kitty checked the diagram and waited, but didn't see the little explosion again. She slipped away with a satisfied smile. She wouldn't be the cause of anymore heartache in that house.

Kitty had to sacrifice a little bit more energy for another lethargic dummy to sleep at home so she could pull off the latest NQC. There was no way her mother would let her stay at April's on a school night when she was grounded, but the sooner she got to school in the morning, the sooner she could help with the transit, get Raquel home, and fix the fat universe problem.

What Kitty hadn't expected—and maybe she should have—was April turning the quiet sleepover into a slumber party with Becka staying the night too. She had been hoping for a bit of quiet like last time, even though it had meant April was annoyed with her. She could use a good rest to restore her energy. Instead, she found herself listening to the other two chat about school happenings that Kitty missed because of Homecoming and magic business. She stared at the pink polish on her toes drying and reflecting sparkles of lavender and mint green in just the right light. She wasn't going to Homecoming anymore. The decoration was more to appease April for going to school early with her the next day. Raquel was going home first thing, and then Kitty was done with magic.

"Mom almost dragged me here before I was out of the shower when I said you were making me a dress for Homecoming," Becka said with a quirked bushy brow. She took another fistful of popcorn with her unoccupied hand while April painted the last nail on her other hand black with a midnight blue shimmer.

"You can't be gross 24/7, Becks," April said. She sat back and looked at her masterpiece. "Voila! That and those black pants with that green top to go with your eyes. Oh my gee I'd kiss you if I were a guy."

"Whatevs," Becka said, blowing on her nails as she was instructed. "Go torture Kitty now."

"Puh-lease. She loves the spa treatment, don't you, Kitty?"

"Mhmm." There was a break in the hum of the two girls' conversation that made Kitty finally look up. They both stared at her with different levels of concern, April's being more dramatic by far. "What?"

"You're mega bummed," April said, "but you're still gonna look way gorgeous in your dress."

"April, I'm seriously not going to Homecoming," Kitty said. She curled her legs back and hugged her knees to her chest.

April crawled over to her, careful to keep her toes off of the carpet. "You have to go, Kitty! This is your big night! You've literally worked your butt off for this and you can't not go."

"I'm a thug now, remember? I'm just Valley trash. I'm not allowed to go."

"Oh my gee, like Mr. Briggs won't be begging you to help after how you handled the Homecoming game. And I swear I will slap you stupid if you ever call yourself Valley trash again. Forget Jennifer. She's a bimbo! We've been telling you that."

"Then maybe I wanted to be a bimbo too. It's better than being Valley—kid," she finished with a wary glance at April's ringed hands.

"If you actually want to be like her, or even be friends with her, then you have a much bigger problem. Real friends don't act like her. You have nothing to prove to her."

"I can do whatever I want and I *don't* want to go to Homecoming. I don't want to see any of them any longer than I have to. It's not my night anymore. I got fired. Angela

Smith can stop harping on everything I do like she's afraid I'm gonna ruin her reputation by breathing. Now she can mess it all up however she wants. Slap her name all over the stupid thing. Or make Jennifer her go to girl. At least she's from the Slope."

"You are fifteenth level out of control. Who cares if numbnuts capital B Smith says she's in charge? And who cares if she likes Jennifer better. They're both monsters. Let them have each other. You did everything and you should see it. You deserve to see it."

Kitty bit her bottom lip, but kept her eyes on her wriggling toes that flashed between colors. It would be the biggest event Glade Crest had ever seen, but that made the heartache worse. She wanted everything to be perfect, and Homecoming would still be pretty perfect without her at that point, but she never imagined Friday showing up without her panicking over silly little details no one but her would notice. She didn't want to care anymore. April didn't know—and Kitty hadn't known until Dummy was terminated—that Mr. Briggs already asked her to attend Homecoming to help run it and he would lighten her detention sentence in return, but Kitty hadn't agreed yet.

"Also," April continued with a raised perfect eyebrow, "we deserve to have our friend back like you promised. And this ain't it, Kitty." She swirled her jeweled finger in front of Kitty's face. Kitty only sank her chin deeper.

"What about your mom chaperoning?" Becka said with another mouthful of popcorn gumming up her words. She was carefully scooping up more with the sides of her palms to avoid ruining her nails and earning April's wrath.

Kitty tutted. Her mom wasn't going because she

wanted to; she already signed up to chaperone as a favor to Kitty. Once Kitty had been grounded for a month for fighting, it was too late to back out.

"Which means Edie will be there," April added. "I remember you saying how much she would love a party like this because of the dressing up and the sparkles and—"

Kitty shot a glare at her friend. "Super not fair, April."

"The whole town shouldn't be enjoying your party without you, Kitty. Homecoming isn't what makes you awesome. You made Homecoming awesome. We still love you with or without your name on it. Or is our opinion not good enough because we're not Jennifer? Or Mrs. Smith? Or whoever has your panties tied so tight you can't breathe? We want to be there with you too. Isn't that enough?"

Kitty didn't look up. Her cheeks burned behind the curtain of hair over her face. She put April's and Becka's opinions before everyone else's for as long as she had known them. Seven years was a long time. Suddenly she found herself begging at everyone's feet except the only one's who offered themselves. Maybe Homecoming wasn't the best idea. She tried to wipe her wet cheek on the knee of her jeans without being noticed, and she felt Becka's hand rubbing soft circles over her back.

"We're not mad," Becka said. Her voice was much softer than usual, her own way of being the sympathetic voice of reason. "April's just annoyingly right like, all the time."

"I am right," April preened. Kitty looked up and saw April approaching from her closet, having gotten up while Kitty was moping. She held the hook of a metal hanger that peeked out of a plastic bag as tall as a person.

It bunched at the bottom as if it were trying to break free of the beige prison. "I'm right that we love you and you're fiftieth level amazing. And the best part!" April slid the plastic from the frame of the hanger and tugged it off in one practiced motion revealing the layers of glittering pink fabric below. Kitty's jaw dropped as she tried to see the entire dress without having to move her head. The bodice was a shimmering satin that connected to a tulle skirt like a ballerina, but draped further than a tutu. The zipper in the back was hidden by satin ribbon that somehow looked like butterfly wings.

Kitty sputtered over her words. "What the actual heck is that? A prom dress?"

"It's your highness' Homecoming dress! I broke two nails making this for you so you are going to wear it, do you hear me? You worked too hard, and whatever it is you have to prove, I swear you've done it already, Kitty. Whoever can't see you for how incredible you are doesn't deserve to be around you."

Kitty forced herself to her feet and walked to the dress. It was like a cloud under her touch as she grazed every inch of it with both hands. She had never been so close to something so outrageously fancy. She bit back tears. April put the dress down on Kitty's trundle bed and wrapped her in a hug.

"You're the best, April," Kitty said into her friend's shoulder.

"I know." They laughed. "Now say that you're going to your dance. I'll sick Becka on Briggs if you want, but say you'll go. It's going to be an incredible night."

Kitty took another moment's pause as she honestly

considered it. Maybe it was the soothing lavender and rose scent of April's shampoo or the warmth of finally being around the people she loved most, but Kitty gave a small nod. "Yeah, yeah."

"Perfect!"

Behind them, Becka crunched on another handful of popcorn. "Oh junk," she muttered. Kitty and April turned around, and Becka snapped her hands behind her back. April tensed.

"Rebecca Abigail Hutchinson, you little monster, what did you do to your nails?"

"Nuffin'..."

"That color was so hard to find! Don't you run from me!" Becka bounded out the door, only pausing to snatch the bag of popcorn from the ground. April's mile long legs kept her at Becka's heels. Kitty sat on the guest bed next to the glowing dress.

Not too shabby for a Valley girl, she thought with a smile. In just one day, everything would be back to normal.

Seventeen

Of all the days to wake up well before her alarm, Kitty's brain was wide awake on the one day she was already getting up earlier than anyone should for school. She stared at the ceiling through the dim light as the sun slowly rose through April's vaulted windows. Her stomach flopped as conflicting feelings tugged at Kitty's mind. There was excitement and anxiety for sure; that was how she imagined she would feel when Homecoming finally arrived. Sadness and longing crept in as she wished things had turned out differently, that she was still leading the parade and everyone would applaud her and shout her name. Warmth radiated in her from her real friends who would stand by her no matter how things turned out.

Then she remembered the most important part of the day. Raquel was leaving. Whether it was a complicated transit diagram to send a dummy back to her Magical Harnessing Device or to send a girl from an identical world back home, Kitty didn't care. She wanted to help get Raquel home safely after the trouble Kitty had caused her and a lot of people. Maybe no one would ever know how much she wanted to prove she could fix this mess. Not without revealing so much more than she wanted to. It was fine. Once Raquel was home, Leo could close the tears, shut down the bombs, and then Kitty would dance the night away with her friends.

It was going to be a good day.

She quietly showered and dressed in what she realized too late were clothes she hurriedly grabbed from her closet the night before. Her reflection was a sad sight of an ill-fitting gray tee shirt and a pair of jeans with a hole in one knee covered by a heart-shaped patch. Kitty unbraided her hair and used the hair tie to bunch the bottom of the shirt until it could pretend like it fit her narrow frame. At least she knew how to take away the bruise that finally darkened on her cheek. She quickly brushed out her hair and returned to April's room where her alarm had abruptly woken her groggy friends.

Within the hour, the girls were fed and buckled into the back of Mrs. Sullivan's van. April was clutching an armful of dresses and a pair of sleek black pants. Her backpack had quickly been discarded to the floor.

"Today is gonna be the slowest day ever!" she moaned.

"Flower," her mother said, "what did we say about whining?"

April rolled her eyes and mouthed along to her mom's quoting, "Adults learn to handle their problems by talking through them, not whining about them."

Mrs. Sullivan dropped them off at the front of the bus

lane, nearest the school entrance. "Have a great day, girls! Flower, I'll be right back here 9pm sharp or else daddy will, okay?"

"Okay mom. Love you! Later!" She closed the door and hurried with Kitty and Becka to the school.

At their lockers, April stored their outfits for the party with more care than any school books would ever see. As they started towards the Before-Hours Care center, Kitty excused herself.

"Just need to run to the bathroom," she said before darting off.

The halls were eerie without the normal bustle of students. Kitty only passed a janitor on her way. He was too busy to look up from mopping and bouncing to the song playing through his earbuds. As she reached a stairwell on the far side of the building, she made sure no one was watching and ran in, taking the steps two at a time until she reached the lonely metal door to the roof. It was a forbidden area for students and, according to Will, a perfect place to meet and send Raquel home without interfering with anyone's day.

The door creaked as it swung aside, grating over the cemented roof top and a few loose pebbles. Everything seemed normal other than a student being on the roof. The sun was peeking over the tree line and the sky was shifting much quicker from the velvety purple of daybreak to a pale blue. The far off streetlights were fading over the Valley as stores opened and more cars took to the streets. Everyone was having a perfectly normal, even somewhat exciting Friday. Kitty wondered how many people in the city were already preparing to be under the roof of Glade Crest Junior High School that night.

"Good morning," said a tired, friendly voice behind her. Kitty shrieked, and she was sure all of Glade Crest heard it. She spun around with one hand on the wall for support and saw Will holding a steaming foam cup, rich with the scent of coffee, and clutching his stomach from painful laughter. "Oh my god, don't make me laugh like that this early."

"What is your malfunction?" Kitty asked as she slid down the wall to sit. Her heart was racing so fast she thought she might faint.

"I'm just grand," Will said. He took a slow sip from his coffee cup and sighed with delight.

Kitty glowered at her mentor from the wall and crossed her arms. She regretted looking so childish as Raquel came up the steps shortly behind him. Immediately her eyes landed on Kitty and then rolled. She followed Will towards the edge of the roof where he settled his cup beside him. In a moment his tablet was in his hand, and he was scrolling across the screen with his tongue jutting out from the corner of his lips.

"Wait 'til you ladies see this masterpiece I've been working on. It's gonna blow your minds!"

Both girls scoffed in the same tone. Behind Will, a light flashed. He grinned and turned, sipping his coffee like a winner's trophy. The air wavered in a familiar way, but rather than the darkness Kitty expected to see from her recent transits, the bright sky seemed to widen, soft clouds forcing themselves into the little split until it was a fluffy square framing Will's body. He hopped to his feet and stumbled for a moment, catching himself against the ledge. The girls barely withheld their squeaks of terror.

"Whoa," he said. "Okay, okay. What have we learned? Don't stand up right after making a Dimensional Hold. Nope. Okay. I'm good." After another quick swig from his styrofoam cup, he stepped up onto the ledge.

"Why did you have to make it all the way out there?" Kitty asked.

"I'm glad you asked, my young pupil." Before either girl could say something, Will kicked his leg out and hopped off the side of the roof. Two identical shrieks echoed across the platform, met by one unabashed laugh as Will's feet landed firmly at the edge of the square of clouds. All that was missing was a pair of pearly gates and some halos.

"Oww! I shouldn't make myself laugh this hard so early either," he said between ragged breaths. Kitty's face twisted in a scowl, and she stormed across the platform. In a swift motion, she slapped the coffee cup from his hand. Some of the steaming contents spilled onto Will's arm, but the rest drifted below with the cup, whisked by the wind a few times as it dropped. Will gaped. "What was that for?"

"For being a numbnuts," she said. "Do you ever take things seriously?"

"As a matter of fact, this is super serious," he said, pointing behind him to the mounds of clouds that held him over the school lawn. "I was looking up more about Dimensional Holds and quickly learned this is not the kind of oration you want to breeze through. You have to be careful where you make these. They could be a worse interference with spell diagrams than those mini bombs. They could even mess with everyday life."

"Did we really need it then?" Raquel asked. "What if it gets in the way of my transit?"

Will shook his head. "This won't. Not the same way. I already added in the calculation for the new space—the much less crowded space, mind you—for your jump. Those mini bombs are in our universe. We won't be."

"That's...so..."

"Squirrelnuts?" Kitty offered. Raquel only shrugged. "This sounds way out of our league, Will. Are you sure about this?"

"Sure I'm sure. You've gotta trust your mentor, Kitty. I'm not gonna let you fall. Scout's honor."

She tutted. "Then stop messing around and let's get this over with."

Raquel's small huff from beside them warned Kitty to mind her words. Will squeezed the bridge of his nose, but Kitty could see him fighting a smile as he feigned his heavy sigh. "Women. The nuances you'll just never understand. That's alright. Come up and check out this beautiful oration I've been working on all week."

Will held his hands out to Kitty and Raquel. Raquel immediately took it and hopped up on the ledge. She paused for just a moment before stepping over onto the cloudy platform where Will stood. Her body tensed as if not believing her feet were actually touching anything solid. Will turned to Kitty with that same goofy grin. She helped herself onto the ledge with shaking hands. She knew she could trust him and his oration, but a week still wasn't a lot of time to completely convince herself of anything.

Except how fast I can ruin nine months of work, a little voice in her mind creeped in and startled her.

Kitty shook her head and laid her hand on Will's. His grip was firm, and she half expected him to yank her across the small gap of air between the ledge and the cloudy terrace. She shifted in place, his hand moved with hers, and then she gasped as she jumped across. A jolt ran up her spine as she landed harder and sooner than her eyes believed. Will steadied her, but one arm flew out to catch what looked like a wall. Up close, she could see the clouds clearly. As fat and fluffy as they looked, they were actually a smooth, thin surface like a two dimensional doorway. It was the part of the Dimensional Hold she had never seen when she visited the Planetary Homestead, covered in its facade of an office building.

Once everyone was steady on the platform, Will turned back to the wall of clouds and walked forward. His body was outlined in a brief spray of sparks, and then he was gone. Kitty and Raquel shared a wary glance, but they followed. They met the familiar splash of something chilly breaking across their faces and then appeared in an almost painfully bright space. Kitty could just make out edges and flat, vertical surfaces that still looked like they had been swallowed by a sea of cotton balls. Little lines of white hot light glowed to indicate all of the geometric edges, and it formed a space no bigger than Will's bedroom.

Will plopped down on the ground, and a ripple of light fled from him like disturbed water. Each footstep created waves of light. Kitty and Raquel sat down as well while Will swiped along the surface of his MHD.

"Okay. Let's bring out the monsters one more time," he said.

Kitty heard a ping in her ear. She pressed the dangling silver charm on her bracelet between her thumb and index finger. It glowed briefly and then became a bright spot in her palm that shortly revealed her tablet. She found the oration they had worked so hard on for hours last weekend only to be told there were orations interfering with it—an extra step that prevented Raquel from getting home and caused so much more chaos than anyone might have guessed. The whole situation felt absurd, Kitty could barely understand it.

It doesn't matter anymore, she thought. The diagram appeared on her screen and together with the others, she pressed activate.

The air filled with tangled knots of blue lines from the oration demanding to be heard and understood. The Mages could immediately recall the dread of seeing the almost never ending lines of oration piled on top of themselves. Kitty's stomach clenched. She gripped her tablet until her knuckles turned white, but soon she remembered that the diagram was already complete. The threads were where they needed to be according to the picture on each of their screens. All they needed was Kitty's third of the energy to fuel this monstrosity.

"No one pulled an all-nighter, right?" Will asked.

"Honestly, I'm surprised I got any sleep at all," Kitty said.

"Well it is a big day for you." Will paused at Kitty's raised eyebrow. "Your party is today, right?"

"Oh. Right. It doesn't matter."

Will cocked his head to the side. "You were gonna tear Dino's head off, and now it doesn't matter?"

"No. It doesn't matter. So shut it already," she snapped.

Will raised his hands defensively. "Whatever. Ready when you guys are."

Kitty and Raquel nodded, and they all hit EXECUTE.

Nothing happened.

"Oh come on!" they all shouted. Their words bounced through the box around them with a terrible echo.

Another red exclamation mark popped up on their MHDs. Kitty tapped it, and it expanded into a red box with white text scrolling a warning.

DESTINATION UNAVAILABLE. INPUT PROPER
COORDINATES.

Kitty looked at Raquel whose eyes scrolled across the screen over and over. Her lips quaked and her hand slowly formed into a fist that started to beat against the floor. The slick surface flashed on impact, turning into a small laser show. Kitty and Will watched her in silence until she wore herself out and buried her face in her hands.

"Raquel, this doesn't mean anything except we need to take another look," Will said.

"Why is Nefas doing this?" she whispered. Kitty held herself steady against the ground as the world tipped for a moment. "Why can't I just go home?"

"It's all about the chaos. If you being here has anything to do with these tears showing up, of course It would want you here."

Kitty's heart froze as Will spoke. Had they figured out that this was all her fault? Across from her, Raquel slowly shook her head and then lifted her face from her wet palms. Her eyes were rimmed in red.

Silence fell over the Mages for a long while. Kitty looked at the error message, wishing it would just explain

253

itself. She was tired of piecing things together like it was a test with the worst consequences. Orations didn't have to be easy, Kitty appreciated a good challenge, but she wasn't expecting to flounder like she needed a remedial class.

Kitty opened her tablet to the spell diagram. The destination section was grayed out after Will helped them divide the diagram into thirds. Kitty double tapped the grayed out third belonging to Raquel. She would have known the destination best. A new wave of sensation poured over her that she hadn't felt since Will showed them the diagram. Questions piled up before her, waiting impatiently for a response as they started asking bits of the world to change. Who were they to judge what was better or worse, asked the air around them.

They were Mages, and they understood that there was something better. Something to look forward to—or to look back towards. They understood that there was a natural state of being where tears in the seams of the world didn't happen on purpose and people could talk to each other with much less convincing and much more trust.

Things had gone so wrong. Who thought it was smart to ask a thirteen-year-old with her own problems to handle everyone else's?

Raquel cleared her throat. "Okay, so what's wrong? Why aren't the destination coordinates working?"

Will could only flop with a shrug. "Something might've shifted when we were working on this last time. Let's take it apart and see. We'll do it as fast as we can."

Something else about the diagram clawed at Kitty's brain. It felt like it had shifted, maybe as Will said. It felt bigger somehow. The sensation reminded Kitty of when she would play with perspective to entertain her sister some nights. She would have Edith sit on Kitty's window sill leading out to the fire escape and then take one of her stuffed animals and hold it all the way at the front door across the apartment. Edith would gasp at how tiny Mr. Bearington had gotten, and Kitty would pretend to gobble him up to her sister's wave of laughter. But then she would pretend to spit the bear back out and bring him back to sit right in front of Edith's nose, and she would shriek with delight at how big Mr. Bearington grew.

"He's right," Kitty said. "It can't be that big a change, and at least those stupid tears aren't the problem now. We can find out what's going on."

Raquel turned to her with a confused frown. "You're helping now?"

"I'm already a thug at school," Kitty said with a weak laugh. "I got dropped from Homecoming planning. I'm back to being some nobody from the Valley. And I beat up a girl for probably no real reason. What have I got to lose by skipping classes?"

Raquel's laugh was clearer.

"Kitty, you shouldn't get in more trouble over this," Will said. The girls looked at him, eyes widened. "Seriously. Magic isn't your whole life. It's just one thing you can do because you can see the difference between what's important and what's not. Your regular life is still important. Go to class and I'll call you when we need your energy boost."

"You're kicking me out?"

"No, I'm being your mentor. You did your part of the oration and you helped close up the tears. Go have a normal day. You've earned it. And I recommend you still go to your party tonight too."

Kitty's mouth twisted into a grimace. "It's literally the last place I want to be tonight."

"I think you're a big fat liar," Will said, but a ghost of that grin played on his face. "You'll go. You'll dance. You'll eat. It'll be great. And...if you decide you still want to know some stuff about oration when this has all blown over, you still know how to reach me."

Kitty had almost forgotten she swore off of magic business while all of this was going on. In the thick of the panic, it seemed like the right call. She was still sure this was above her understanding, but maybe a few tutoring lessons wouldn't hurt later.

Eighteen

The day was a blur of useless lessons, a cruel pop quiz, and conversation. Kitty didn't want any part of it. Every time someone asked her about Homecoming, Kitty wished she had stayed on the roof. Her lips felt sewn shut as she tried to briefly direct student questions to Mr. Briggs. Everyone thought she was just keeping exciting secrets. Becka tried to talk down the event whenever it accidentally slipped into conversation. Even April tried her best to not bring up Homecoming, but it was the lingering feeling in the air no matter where they turned.

About an hour before classes let out, a message streamed through the speakers in each room. Kitty buried her face in her hands. The students given permission to miss their last class for Homecoming preparation grabbed their bags and bolted. Kitty only looked up again when April nudged her.

"They called you," she whispered while beaming.

Kitty didn't understand, but she took her books and followed the trail of students to the gymnasium. Mr. Briggs was immediately grouping students with a harried look and dabbing his forehead with a handkerchief. A few other adults were helping to keep everyone situated.

"Oh Kitty, come here please," Mr. Briggs said. A ghost of a smile formed on her face. "Could you direct this group to where you said this equipment is?"

Kitty helped send students she recognized to different areas of the gym and described with perfect detail what they should look for and how everything should be placed. She felt back in her element. When she cracked the whip with a few overzealous sixth graders, she still smiled. It didn't take long for everyone to be in their assigned spaces.

"Thank you," Mr. Briggs said as everyone went to their tasks under the watchful eye of the other PTO members. "We just needed a little direction and you obviously know your own notes best."

"That's fair," Kitty said. "I appreciate you still letting me help with this."

Mr. Briggs dropped his gaze and blotted his head again. "Oh no, Kitty. Your punishment stands. That's an order from the higher ups. I'm sorry if there was confusion."

"Oh." Kitty fumbled for words as her cheeks burned. Her forced smile was tight and painful. "Of course. Duh. Obviously. I'm just glad to help however I can. I know I made a mess of things. Probably just got a little overwhelmed, but I've learned a lot the last few months, and I definitely know better than to let my frustration get the best of me."

Mr. Briggs cleared his throat, but gave Kitty a curt nod. "I'm very glad to hear that. You're a bright girl, Kitty. You'll go far. Just remember to take things in manageable chunks. As the old saying goes, 'When eating an elephant, take one bite at a time.' But I will see you tonight as we talked about, yes?"

Kitty slowly nodded as Mr. Briggs clapped his hand on her shoulder and walked back into the gymnasium, now a much more organized chaos. She watched wistfully as all of the equipment she ordered and all of the tables she labeled were carted back and forth. Banners were hung and more of the P.A.L.S. kids were screwing large platforms together to form a stage. All of her hard work was coming together, and she couldn't do anything more than watch from behind the window of the gymnasium doors.

"Excuse me!" a short boy piped up as he tugged on one of the doors with his free hand. His other hand was filled with posters, unscathed by red marker. As he scampered into the gym, Kitty laid her hands on one of the hung posters she had designed. These had been reprinted, as if to mock Kitty further for making her change the other signs by hand. Clearly budget wasn't an issue anymore with the PTO President in charge.

Tears stung in the corner of Kitty's eyes, and she scrubbed at them furiously. Ignoring a few stray student passersby, Kitty tore the poster from the wall, crumpled it into a painful, spiky wad, and hurled it down the hall as the bell rang to end the day. It was the end of the worst day of her life and the start of the worst night.

◆

"If you keep crying, I can't finish your eyes," April said as she leaned back from Kitty's face. She reached for another tissue from the stack on the bathroom sink and gently pressed it below Kitty's lower lashes. Some pale gold shimmer bled and smudged. Kitty's lips pursed as she fought another sudden wave of sadness. She took a shuddering breath and let it out before sitting still again. April leaned back in and laid her forehead to Kitty's.

"I don't care what numbnuts PTO president says. You're the Homecoming queen tonight. She can't take that from you."

April sat back. Her brown eyes were somehow a deeper chocolatey color than Kitty had ever seen. Her cheeks had a slight rosey tint and her lips were deep purple. Every black curl was pinned in place and April managed to do that to herself with just a half hour before Homecoming started.

When April finished touching up Kitty's eyes, she stepped back. "All better. Think you'll make it through the door this time?"

Kitty looked at her ankle boots and fidgeted with the lace of her dress. April smacked her hand away and guided her out of the bathroom. They returned to the gym where Angela Smith was still welcoming the students from her perch on the stage with uneven streamers and boasting the success of her efforts from the last few months. For the students, of course. For Glade Crest.

Kitty wormed her way through the crowd behind April who was tall enough to find Becka. She was at one of the round tables along the edge of the dance floor. A welcome breeze drifted in from the back doors of the gym that were propped open. A teacher and a few parent volunteers were helping tack up one of the banners caught in the wind. Kitty hoped her mom was alright. She had almost missed a text message that she was stuck outside in the car with Edith who wouldn't stop throwing a tantrum every time they got near the school doors. The girls sat together as Mrs. Smith finished her speech. As the track lights shone above, she was a blinding glare of gold sequins and waxed heels that gave the disco ball a run for its money.

"And to kick off the year right, not only are we celebrating our great city with this event, but we're celebrating the great students and making sure they get the well rounded education they deserve. Here is just a sampling of new extracurricular activities we'll be bringing to Glade Crest Junior High at your request! I was so thrilled so many of you responded to our surveys!" She patted her blonde bob while she waited for a teacher to hand her a sheet of paper.

Kitty nearly lost it again. She let her face fall to the table. April and Becka patted her back or smoothed her hair. A burst of applause and cheers filled the room when Mrs. Smith was finished.

"Everyone enjoy the party!"

The dance was underway. Kitty didn't move, willing herself not to cry again. Song after song streamed through the off center speakers. Students passed by munching on snacks and talking about some of the gift baskets that looked interesting. Kitty was finally able to prop her head up after some coaxing. Everything still looked beautiful. Nothing was quite right, but no one was complaining. Everyone dressed to impress. Parents and alumni stood aside and chatted or danced along the edges of the gym. There were students that Kitty didn't think knew what a comb was who had their hair slicked back, spiked or pinned. She spotted

Miren Patrick in a black dress and polished boots with some of her friends, and even she was smiling, patched up nose and all.

A fast song blared across the gym, one of the songs that never stopped playing on the radio, and the entire room echoed with students' cheers. A flood of bodies reached the middle of the gym and nearly drowned out the speakers with poor singing. No one was thinking about who made this happen for them. They were just dancing.

"Shall we, lady-fellas?" Becka said as she stood.

April was right behind her, and Kitty let her brief lapse of angst drag her to the dance floor. They danced until their feet were numb. They sang until their throats were raw. They danced with each other, spun around, and were suddenly dancing with other friends from their classes.

"Kitty, we figured out what's happening," Will's mildly panicked voice cut through all of the noise and sank directly into her brain. She scratched at her ear, not recognizing why until she remembered the Chameleon Ear that she never unhooked. *"So skipping over all the science junk, wherever Raquel's transit leads is moving."*

"Wait, what? How?"

"Beats me. Probably the universe always expanding and all that junk I said I was gonna skip for you. Anyway, we can fix the end coordinates, but then we need to get the oration moving right after so it doesn't have time to move too far out of sync. Can you get here?"

Kitty spun right into a well dressed boy whose brown hair was gelled stiff. Preston Smith caught her as she lost her balance.

"Sorry!" they both shouted over the music.

"Sorry," Kitty said again. Preston cleaned up nicely. She was sure his mother had a say in that since her reputation was at stake. The top two buttons of his dress shirt were undone and his navy tie was loose.

"No worries!" He smiled. "Awesome party!"

She stopped dancing for a moment, just long enough for someone nearby to bump into her and toss her towards Preston. She fell flat against his chest, and he held her up, lightly swaying so they could avoid the other moving bodies around them.

"Sorry," she blathered again.

"I'm good. Homecoming is twentieth level awesome. Good job with all this."

Kitty shook her head. "Don't look at me. Your mom is the PTO President. It's her name all over this."

"So what?" he said. Kitty wasn't sure she heard him right. He took her hands and tugged her to the side as another group shimmied dangerously close to her. "My mom doesn't care about all this junk. She was real mad when she had to take over because you got detention. What was that about?"

"Nothing really." She blushed furiously and hoped the lights and lasers didn't show her face.

"It was enough to get student soldier Kitty Guthrie fired," Preston said. "What, did you kill somebody?"

Kitty looked at her boots. "No. Just...punched Miren Patrick in the nose and broke it."

"Whoa! That's sick!"

If Kitty's face got any hotter, she was sure she would burst into flames. "It was stupid. And I'm a thug now. I even forge bus passes. So, I don't know about all that."

Preston shrugged, but he kept smiling. "Nah, she probably deserved it. And the party is awesome. So, you know, it probably takes a pretty awesome person to do all this. Not my mom. She is way not awesome. She's the worst sometimes. But yeah, cool party, Kitty. Later!"

Preston jostled his way through the crowd to the snack table where some of his football buddies were launching cheesy puff balls at each other to catch in their mouths. She didn't realize how long her grin lasted until her cheeks started to hurt. Someone knew she put this together. Preston Smith knew she put this together.

"Kitty? You coming or not?"

"Oh, sorry. Gimme a second."

"Kitty Guthrie, if you're here, please make your way to the gymnasium front doors," the student DJ said. "The front of the gym, please, Kitty. Thank you. Keep rockin' everyone!"

Kitty looked towards the doors. A parent chaperone was moving aside as two men in dark uniforms and glinting badges pushed their way in. One man had dark skin and very sharp features. His chin was angular and his cheekbones were high, making his eyes look like tiny dark pinpricks. His partner was taller and wider than him. He was nothing but muscles stretching his uniform to pucker between the buttons of his shirt. It was hard to tell if he wore a white shirt underneath or if the dancing lights that fell on him made his fair skin look even more pale.

One thing they shared was that they made Kitty shiver. It reminded her of when those cops harassed her and Will the day they met. As the two men glanced around the gymnasium, Kitty wanted to slink away and hide, but she also felt her hands balling into stubborn fists. Kitty slipped through the crowd on the dance floor. As it thinned out by the door, she saw Mr. Briggs looking around like the officers until he spotted Kitty and waved her over. If the officers were Hostilia like the others were, maybe she could at least get them away from the dance before they turned into monsters.

"You're Kitty Guthrie?" the taller officer asked. Up close, Kitty could see the muscles of his upper arms threatening to rip his sleeves. His thick eyebrows were knit into a frown. Kitty nodded. "Alright, sweetheart, I'm Officer Sanders. I'm gonna need you to step outside with me for just a minute. My friend and I need to ask you a few questions."

"Did I do something wrong?"

"We can talk about it outside." He opened one of the double doors with one bulky arm and gestured towards Kitty like he meant to wrap her in a bone crushing hug. The officer looked at Mr. Briggs. "You can go back and enjoy your party, sir."

Mr. Briggs placed a hand on Kitty's shoulder. "In the absence of Kitty's legal guardian, she's under the care of the Glade Crest educational system. As her faculty adviser for this event, I am her legal caretaker for the evening so I need to be present."

"This is police business," Officer Sanders said again. To his side, his partner had his hands resting on his belt that had every type of intimidating object someone could carry. His fingers tapped to the beat of the next song against a sleek black rod with grooves on the hand grip. The twirling rainbow of lights flashed across his badge that read 'Officer

Martin Keynes'.

"I'm afraid that doesn't matter here. I can't let any of these children out of sight of an authorized chaperone."

"Listen, buddy," said the smaller man, "what don't you get about us being officers of the law? You don't spout off to us what we are trained to know. Want me to recite the Transference of Guardianship addendum in the case of a minor needed in police custody to investigate criminal activity?"

Kitty turned to Keynes in time to see the taller officer hit his arm with one of those enormous fists. "Criminal?"

"Don't worry about it," Sanders said. "Just come on out with us. We've just got some questions. Nothing more."

Kitty's thoughts raced through her memories to find anything she might have done that could have been seen as criminal. The music was too loud and the colored lights were spinning too fast. Mr. Briggs never took his hand from her shoulder as he continued to insist staying with Kitty if she went with the officers.

"I understand full well that you are both officers of our great city and you uphold the law, but you're not beyond it," Briggs said. "You can't speak to this child without a guardian present!"

Mr. Briggs moved to stand between Kitty and the officers. His missing hand left a chilly spot on her shoulder. Then everything happened so quickly. Officer Keynes suddenly had a hand around a sleek black shape with a trigger and a crackling blue-white line at the far end that he pressed to Mr. Briggs' chest. He fell, shaking and groaning. Officer Sanders grabbed for Kitty's arm. Kitty crawled under the officers and shoved the door open with her shoulder. The growling she heard from both officers made her run faster as they gave chase.

"Will, I need help!" she screamed into the link. *"Two cops. Not cops. Hositilia! First floor!"*

"Get to the stairs! I'll be right there!"

Kitty dared to look over her shoulder. The men weren't so much running as they were hunched and lumbering after her. Kitty touched the bracelet on her wrist and her Magical Harnessing Device appeared in her hands. She tried to find an oration that could help, but she couldn't read anything as she ran towards the stairwell to the roof.

Kitty pushed through the door and took a split second to execute one of her saved orations she hoped she would never need before darting up the stairs two at a time. Her hands glowed with a blue sheen three inches thick. She never heard the lower door open as she hit the second platform, but suddenly heard the slapping of polished shoes hitting the stairs, and the officers were only half a section behind her. Black mist seeped off of them like sweat.

Someone at the top whistled. Kitty saw Will jump, and she shrieked until he landed in front of her, unharmed like a superhero in a movie scene. She could see a distinct glow of magic at work around his hands and feet. She and the Hostilia were unimpressed with his antics. Both officers charged at Will. He shoved Keynes back into Sanders and they steadied themselves with the railing.

Officer Keynes pounced again, diving into Will's stomach. He fell back onto the landing, beating at the creature with his fists. Sanders was around them in a moment and storming towards Kitty.

She didn't know how to fight. She never needed to

know how to fight. Her mother kept her away from nasty areas of the city, and she never wanted to see what she was missing. Sanders grabbed for her arm, and she batted his hand away with her invisible gauntlet. He looked down where she struck and watched the black smog that coiled around his skin. Then he looked back at Kitty. His eyes were nothing but red pin pricks in a black sea staring at her.

Both arms snapped forward faster than Kitty could react, forcing her against the steps. She kicked at him, but she couldn't push away his enormous form crouched over her like a rabid dog. Just past his bulk she could see to the lower platform where Will struggled with Keynes for a moment and then headbutted him. It was enough to throw the officer loose. Will jumped up and threw his arm wide just as Sanders leaned towards Kitty and blocked her sight. His smile was nothing more than razor teeth in his darkening mouth.

"You were warned."

Kitty's body reacted before she could think straight. She leaned her head back and then threw it forward. She felt a nasty crunch and stinging against the top of her head as she collided with Sanders' nose. Her headband pushed into his eyes and her scalp.

He cried out and stumbled backwards into Will who grabbed him. Will threw his arm wide and connected with the Hostilia's face. The creature slammed into the wall of the stairwell and vanished into a dark cloud. Will was by Kitty's side in an instant, covered in some oily stains.

"Are you okay?" he asked. Kitty slowly nodded, and Will helped her stand. "Then come on. Let's get this transit executed and get you back to your party. Or whatever it is you were gonna do in that dress tonight."

A terrible screeching echoed through the stairwell. Without waiting for their unwelcomed guests, Will took Kitty's hand, and they ran back up the stairs. Dark shadows seeped from the walls and clawed at them. They slapped away any straying limbs and gnashing teeth. Raquel called through the link.

"Will, we've got company! Hurry up!"

"We're on our way!"

A few of the shadows melted completely from the walls. They were human-like by their silhouette, but they only had red pinpricks for eyes and their bodies were smoke-covered ooze in the shape of two arms, two legs, and a head. Will smashed the Hostilia with his gauntlet hands, clearing the path to the top. They dove through the door and held it shut behind them. Anywhere a shadow tried to snake through, one of them shoved it back. Kitty activated the shield she used for the mini bombs and expanded it to the size of the roof so none of the shadows could creep through the walls. The sudden expense of energy made her hands tingle.

There was the cloudy threshold to the Dimensional Door. Raquel stood below it, hands aimed like a pretend gun, shooting at a few wobbling shadows that made it through before Kitty completed her oration. A blast of light pulsed from her finger tips, and her targets quickly became clouds of smoke.

"Transit is ready!" she said.

"Careful with that oration," Will said. "It can drain you—"

"Blah blah blah. Kitty is your student, not me. Now hook into this already! It's too big!"

The roof door jostled as bodies crashed into it from the other side, and Kitty was thrown to the gravelly floor from the force. When she looked back, expecting a barrage of shadowy creatures, she just saw the bumping door, sealed and fighting a bright haze where her oration was locked in. Will whirled around, grabbed Kitty's arm, and tugged her to her feet. Kitty could barely keep up as they sprinted across the rooftop to the ledge and jumped without hesitation into the cloud room.

Raquel handed them cords, and Kitty saw the two others connect the plugs to spots on their MHDs. She didn't know if it mattered, so she just picked one and prayed the screeching monsters didn't find their way in. Raquel hit execute and the transit's diagram lit up. The chains of magic latched to one another, and everything within their boundaries filled in like spilled ink. Kitty felt a breeze that rustled her skirt and hair. It took a minute to realize the breeze was going towards the diagram. Kitty tripped over her feet. The others started flailing as well, throwing their arms out for balance.

"What the—" was all Kitty could say before she was lifted into the air. She heard Raquel shout with surprise and saw Will soaring towards her. The transit grabbed the Mages and sucked them inside.

Nineteen

Kitty felt a splash against her face as she crashed forward through the darkness. She was falling like she had been shoved off of a cliff, and there didn't seem to be a bottom. The black tunnel was silent. She couldn't even hear the screaming she thought she was doing. She could hardly feel herself breathe.

After what felt like a lifetime, the black void turned dark gray, and the gray lightened as it flung Kitty out onto asphalt. She somersaulted a few feet before coming to a harsh stop. The world around her was too bright and still spinning. A few groans nearby told her she wasn't alone anymore. Kitty looked over to see Raquel face down against a chipped street and Will a few feet away rubbing his neck as he turned to lay on his belly.

"That...was weird," Will said.

Whatever Kitty was expecting to see through the transit, this wasn't it. They were in some type of city with a few buildings Kitty would dare say looked familiar in a way. These buildings looked incomplete, mostly white with slivers of gray. Some parts seemed to be missing altogether, missing corners of rooftops or jagged holes below and through windows. The buildings were low, and a few had grates pulled down over their entrances. Kitty rubbed her eye as it blurred every now and then until she realized she was seeing hazy spots drifting along the shattered sidewalk. She looked up to find some sort of landmark. All she found was a strange, broken horizon like looking through shattered glass that kept twisting and dancing in front of her.

"This isn't where you're from, right Raquel?" Will asked as he pushed himself to his feet.

"Definitely not," Raquel said.

"Well, there's one way to find out where we are." He took out his tablet and swiped his finger along the screen. The light blinked a few times before bursting into life. He frowned for a moment, but continued looking for the resource he wanted. Then another pause. "Since when is a location unauthorized to view?"

He sent Kitty and Raquel the search results. Finding a location on a map and taking those coordinates for an oration was as simple as a few keystrokes. Kitty looked at the warning sign as the coordinates remained hidden. A small permissions tag flashed in the corner from a very important Justice.

"But is this where the transit let us out?" Raquel asked. "I was so sure we did it right. Once I knew it was changing, I timed it right. I know I did!"

Kitty kept looking at the street. Something in her mind

filled in some distant trees behind the stout buildings. A few ghostly men with bobbing cigarettes could have been standing across the road from her.

Raquel's cry of pure frustration broke her thoughts. "Dang it! Now what? If this is it and we have to make another stupid jump home, how do we do that without the coordinates? We're stuck! We are freaking stuck!" Raquel slammed her fist against the street. She grabbed her bruising knuckle with another hiss of pain.

Will looked back at his tablet with a thoughtful frown. After a few swipes, he showed the others his screen with a list of active spell diagrams. The enormous transit was still there.

Kitty sat back. "How is that—?"

"That's the million dollar question. If the transit is still active, where is it? This is the best and the worst part of being a Magistrate. Time to go to the weird web."

Will sat down, fingers flying across the screen as he scrolled through articles. Kitty and Raquel watched him in silence. Everything in the pale, broken city was quiet. Every sense felt smothered.

"Aha! Here we go," Will finally said. His sudden voice was like a gunshot through the still air. "Says right here that transits have something like a fail-safe. If the oration gets interrupted after it's executed, there's a built in fail-safe to protect the Mage that executed it. The diagram sorta splits in half, like what we did to it when we activated the diagram in the first place. It gives the lost Mage a path to follow instead of—" His face paled. He lowered his tablet and scratched at his head with half a grin. "Let's not get stuck here."

"Gladly," Kitty and Raquel chorused.

Kitty bolstered herself. "Well if the transit split in half, we can just track down both halves and be done. Easy."

"Except no map, remember?" Raquel said. "We're not supposed to be here—wherever here is. It's unauthorized."

The group fell silent again. Kitty hugged her knees to her chest as she spied the nearby ghostly store fronts. Part of her expected some elderly men to push open the noisy grates and give them a hand or yell at them to stop loitering. In fact, one of the buildings with the fewest cracks and shatters in it reminded her of a corner store near Beautician Magicians that Kitty would run over to sometimes with Edith when her mom couldn't get a sitter for the night. Kitty would scrounge out the quarters she collected over time from change for school lunch to buy bubble gum or a chocolate bar.

The memory brought a smile to her face. Kitty pushed herself up, sucking in a sharp breath as her hand caught on a craggy edge of the concrete street. She must have hit harder than she thought. A sunken outline of her legs were imprinted into the street. When she leaned in to look closer, the edges of the concrete seemed to slightly curl as if it were aiming to wrap around her legs. Kitty shuddered.

"We really shouldn't hang out here long," she said. Kitty brushed off her skirt and walked towards the building. "It looks like Carlo's Corner Store. I mean, I guess it could be any city corner store, but..."

"What does your gut say?" Will asked. "You're a Mage."

Kitty bit her lip, but stepped up onto the sidewalk. There were a few broken wooden slabs nailed over a shattered window frame. The red graffiti tag was split in half by a glowing white fracture. Without warning Kitty jogged down the long road that seemed to endlessly flow into a too bright horizon. The wig store. The beauty supply store. A few burger chain restaurants and the place with the overcooked chicken nuggets. She slowed down in front of a wide building, normally painted over with a faded yellow, now it was just a haunting gray. A strange sense of pride and sickness swirled in Kitty's chest.

"It's a copy of the Valley," she exclaimed almost completely out of breath as Will and Raquel slowed their chase. "It's like a copycat world that looks like home!"

"Copycat world?" Raquel stared at the yawning street in both directions. "Like a Dimensional Hold?"

Kitty shrugged. "Maybe. I guess this isn't part of your oration, huh Will?"

"Nope," he said. "This place looks...huge. It would probably take hundreds of Mages to put something like this together. But why make a copy of Glade Crest? Unless it goes further than that and we just happened to fall into the part that looks like home. It could be like a Dimensional Hold, but I don't understand why our transit would get mixed with a Dimensional Hold like this."

Raquel ran her hand over the wall of the beauty salon, a ghost of what it copied. "If the diagram said to take me home, and it dropped us here in the copycat world instead, it'd make sense that we'd be close to home. If we start with that, can't we just walk to where the other end of the transit would probably be? I'm sure I orated right. It ought to be right in my backyard."

Kitty went up to the door and tugged on it, and it gave

way with a little extra pressure. The foyer was empty. Parts of the wall that normally had shelves of beauty products in different scents and brightly colored plastic bottles were now just jagged white cracks that led to a painful bright nowhere like staring into a frozen lightning bolt. She walked further in towards the partition that separated the foyer from the salon chairs, dryers, and the waiting area for the customers. The chairs were bent at strange angles, and then Kitty realized they weren't bent. The salon chairs were crooked in mid air with parts of the seat jutting out from other jagged lines. The mirrors were embedded too far into the walls that seemed to grow over them. Tiles in the floor were cracked and twisted against the pattern while some were entirely angled to raise up from the floor on a tilt with one corner lost in whiteness.

A shiver ran through Kitty's entire body. Somewhere behind the wall she heard a scratch and something heavy falling over. Incessant whispers buzzed through her ear and made her scalp itch deeper than she could reach. Kitty quickly backed out of the salon, nearly running into Will who was waiting right outside the door.

"What's the matter?" he asked.

"Uh...maybe if we're gonna go we should go."

"Is something in there?"

"I don't know," Kitty said. "I thought—maybe something fell. It's fine. Let's just go."

Kitty led the march up what she now knew was Main Street, channeling the courage and authority her boots demanded. She needed it more than ever. The walk wasn't long, but it was eerie. Every street they passed had more cracked gray buildings. The number of those jagged lines seemed to drop the further they left Beautician Magicians behind. Every street was quiet as if smothered by a blanket of snow. No wind, warm or cold, found them as the crowded industrial section widened into what would have been greenery around the stubby one floor homes that guided Main Street uphill.

Eventually they gave way to little parks and fields, boutiques, and larger, cleaner versions of the same chain convenient stores that were scattered throughout the Valley. The Slope was just steps away, but it felt like worlds apart. The Mages followed the road for almost half an hour before Raquel led them down an intersecting street. The muscle memory in Kitty's feet let her follow as she tried to keep from shaking too badly. Her most recent memory of coming down this road reminded her of that policeman's warning. Stay out of trouble. Don't make waves. Behave. He turned out to be a Hostilia, and Kitty couldn't tell how much she was fighting for what was right and how much she was actually causing trouble.

Further down, the houses on the block had more of those cracks and splits than the ones a few blocks over. It made Kitty shudder again and wrap her arms around herself. They turned onto Crystal Avenue and walked up towards the cul-de-sac where the rows of houses looked as if someone chopped them to ribbons with a terribly sharp kitchen blade. Everyone paused for a moment, just staring at the mess. One house seemed to radiate with the first sensation the Mages had felt since arriving: cold. A breathtaking chill. Raquel moved towards that house, and Will followed. Kitty could only stare for a few moments longer, her feet glued in place.

This should still be my house, that dark voice cooed in her mind. *It's not fair.*

"Kitty?" Will's voice snapped her from that strange place. "You alright?"

"Yeah," she said. "Just thinking whoever made this place could probably use some more practice."

"Or me as a mentor," Will offered. "It really does look a lot like a Dimensional Hold, but that could be seriously bad news. Let's not stick around longer than we have to."

Kitty nodded, and the two jogged to catch up to Raquel who was crossing the lawn, stepping around the white lines that left half blades of grass floating in the air, separate from their roots. The backyard was just as Kitty remembered. It was wide and clear, sectioned off from the back neighbors by a small metal fence with some smaller plants twisting between the chain links. The glass patio furniture was tilted in mid air. Some pieces were speared by those cracks. The backside of the house was lined with a few tall holly bushes, but the outline of the pale leaves were faint when everything around it was just as light.

Raquel made her way to the holly bushes and ducked down.

"Of course," Kitty mumbled to herself.

"Guys! Something is here!" Raquel said, waving them over. "Tight squeeze, but I can get to it for sure!"

Kitty and Will joined her by the line of trimmed greenery that looked unassuming next to the house. They peered behind it in the foot-long gap between the spiky leaves and the wall panels. The oration was the first bit of color—or lack of color—they had seen since falling into the copycat world. The transit was a glaring black spot against

278

the siding, a few feet from a small rectangular window. The edges wavered, looking uncertain unlike the transits Kitty had made before where it starkly parted the air and waited to be used.

"Are we sure that's not another tear?" Kitty asked. She didn't feel comfortable taking her eyes off of the black spot in case it suddenly got bigger and tried to dissolve the rest of her.

"I guess not," Raquel said. "It doesn't look...as deadly..."

Will crossed his arms and his tongue jutted out, his usual way. "It doesn't have those weird creepy crawly edges like the tears did. I've never seen a transit look like that before, but I guess I've also never seen an oration cut in half. I think this was a smart call, Raquel."

Raquel smiled. She pressed herself against the side of the house, testing the fit. The leaves behind her snagged in her hair and against her shirt, but she could easily pull past them to slide between the bushes and the house. She gave the other Mages a thumbs up. Kitty and Will returned the gesture.

"Hold on," Raquel said, stopping her shimmying. "Can't go without a goodbye. Even if you were being a pain in the butt, Kitty."

Kitty flushed and turned her head aside. Her face must have been beet red against the painful grays and whites around them. She heard a rustling, a small yelp and thud, and then Will calling out, but by the time she looked back, she only saw Will starting to make his way between the bushes.

"Something grabbed her!" Will grunted. He quickly

slid forward and dropped in front of the window, which Kitty now saw was open and had small specks of red along the track. In a moment he vaulted through feet first.

"Careful! There might be some shelves there!" Kitty said as she heard another thud and some softer tings of smaller objects being knocked to the ground.

The leaves didn't phase her, just as they hadn't when she snuck through that crawl space as a kid, and in moments, Kitty was through the window and dropping to a low table in dim grayness. She could feel hanging lace against her leg where her dress hadn't fared as well as her. Will had his hands wrapped in the shape of a finger gun, aimed at a group of dark figures surrounding Raquel. The other Mage had propped herself up with one arm and swung a metal rack from a toppled shelf at the looming figures. They looked like people: clearly defined heads, arms, torsos, and legs. But they also stood out even in this darker shadowy gray. They were painted pure black and hunched like animals, batting at the shelf in Raquel's hand. They hissed and stared her down from a safe distance with pinpoint red eyes.

One shadow person, a female it seemed from the bust and the angle of the stiff material swooping from her waist, screeched and dove for Raquel, but quickly took a metal rack to the side of her head. She was knocked off balance, but still reached her arm out to grab Raquel's leg. Will let off a few quick blasts at the others, a mix of men and women and a few people possibly as old as the Mages. The shorter people skittered towards Will. Each blast that soared from his fingertip left the creatures reeling, but still clawing forward, driven by some deep-seeded hatred of these people they had never met.

Kitty grabbed another free standing shelf and dragged it from its nook before pushing it ahead. The boxes that had been stabbed through with jagged streaks of light held firm in mid air, but the metal unit dropped, catching two of the people under it with solid cracks to their heads. The shelves creaked and fell further as the Hostilia melted into slick black puddles. Will quickly put the last one down, panting and wiping his forehead.

"Leave me alone, you stupid monsters!" Raquel screamed and scrambled to her feet. The woman trying to wrestle with her was now an oily stain on the ground beside her. Four more Hostilia charged into the room with wild eyes. Raquel backed away towards Kitty and Will. "How many could there be?"

"No idea," Will said, "but you need to get home."

"What? How? They're not just gonna let me walk out of here. None of us!"

"I don't care if they want to try to stop us. We'll keep them here. You get to the transit."

Raquel stared blankly at him. A Hostilia cried out and beat his hands on the ground. He bolted forward, and Will landed a well timed punch right between his eyes. With a sickening crunch, the Hostilia lost his footing and collapsed to the ground, melting into an oily cloud.

"Get out, Raquel!" Kitty said. "Once you're home, at least we know things won't get worse. The universe won't be fat anymore."

"What?"

"Just go!"

Kitty looked back at the remaining group of Hostilia that looked like rabid animals waiting for a moment to strike at a careless prey. She pressed the charm on the silver chain around her wrist and let her MHD appear in her palm. As Will stood in front of her, allowing her time to find the diagram he sent, she felt two arms wrap around her, slightly burning, but she could tolerate it.

"Thanks, Kitty," Raquel whispered. Then the arms released her and she could hear the soft, quick steps of Raquel climbing back up to the window and crawling out.

The Hostilia shrieked again and dove, regardless of Will who let out blast after blast at them, sometimes letting a weak one get close so he could slam its face with his unseen gauntlet to save energy. The two Mages ducked out of the way of the largest in the group, a round figure that seemed to move in spite of his body's limits. From behind another free-standing shelf that Will guarded, Kitty activated the diagram and immediately felt the questions roll off of it. With an urgency and authority she didn't know she had, she answered the questions and then shut them up by speaking over them, telling them exactly what she needed of the part of the diagram involving her own hands, body, and energy. Kitty executed the oration and felt her hands tingle as the diagram reappeared like a lacy glove.

Kitty popped back up and felt the warmth of her hands charging with energy. Her fingers created the 'L', and she pressed down her thumb, watching a mound of blue-white light bulge over her index finger and then rocket towards a creature. It skidded past its shoulder and singed a half shattered washing machine.

"Nice shot, dead-eye," Will said with a laugh as his own bolt landed true against the Hostilia Kitty had aimed for.

"Oh come on! I'm new to this!"

"Get better, and fast!"

Kitty's hands started to shake, but she took a deep breath and let loose two more shots. One snapped a shelf in half. The other sank into the midnight black creature swiping at Will. It melted before a meaty fist could catch Will in the side of the head. She turned her attention to the other two who were slamming their fists into the ground like riled up apes. Her heartbeat drummed between her ears, and a haze crept along the edges of her vision, but she used her left hand to steady her right and kept firing. Each shot left her a little more shaky than the last as her own energy pelted the creatures, slowing them down. Two well placed shots finally dropped the Hostilia into pools of black muck.

"Better," Will said with a pop of his eyebrows. He received a swift smack on the arm as Kitty passed him by.

"Come on. They might have friends and that was pretty loud."

Kitty pushed herself up to the window, but dragging her body the rest of the way felt like doing a hundred push ups at one time. She clenched her jaw and pulled until she felt Will's arms wrap around her legs. She squeaked in surprise as he lifted her up, nearly knocking her head into the ceiling.

"Watch it!"

"Sorry, sorry. Just go already! You're not a feather!"

Kitty pulled herself back through the window and shimmied past the bushes towards the yard. Will followed closely behind, but stopped just where the bushes began.

"What?" Kitty asked. He was too tall, and the space was too narrow to peak past him.

"Well either Raquel is a lot shorter than I remember or that transit is smaller than I remember." He stepped out of the way, and Kitty saw what he meant.

The edge of the circle cutting into the side of the house was at least a foot thinner all around than it had been when they first arrived. Kitty stared in horror. "What does that mean for our end of it?"

"I don't want to wait to find out. I figure our end should be where we started. Back at the school."

Kitty shrugged. "Makes sense to me. As much as any of this can make sense."

"Then let's go—"

A howling from the street cut him off. It was followed by more cries, both humanoid and animal. If those were all coming from Hostilia, how far gone were these people? Will took Kitty by the arm, bringing her back to her senses. He held a finger to his lips in warning. They climbed the backyard fence to the neighbor to avoid the prowling Hostilia, and started their way up to the Crest.

Twenty

The streets were no longer abandoned. Kitty and Will ducked behind every car and tree, into every yard they could reach, and still had too many close calls with the Hostilia that looked like untrained soldiers. Some still looked very human. They whipped around at every sound with manic eyes and darted in and out of the streets with seemingly no reason. Others looked warped, hunched into squat, spiky lined animals. They stopped and sniffed the air with grunts and snorts. On their legs, they still didn't stand tall anymore. Their arms bowed at an odd angle, and they seemed more comfortable scouting on all fours.

Kitty led the way while they traveled through the Slope, but Will kept a hand securely around her elbow, ready to pull her at his pace to a new hideout. Kitty and Will cut through as many backyards and treks of untamed trees as they could before they had to change directions to get nearer to the school. That meant taking to the streets.

They started with the smaller roads even though it easily doubled the time. By the time they neared the Crest, Kitty could barely stand the ache in her knees from crouching behind pale topiary.

"This is going to take forever," Kitty moaned into the Chameleon Ear as brutish Hostilia stomped past them mere feet away. *"Our end of the transit could be closed by now! Then we'll be stuck!"*

"Relax, would ya?" Will flipped his tablet screen towards her, showing the active diagram list where their transit was marked right above his oration nicknamed 'Cowboy'. *"We've still got time."*

Seeing the listing didn't help ease Kitty's mind, but she shut the connection before she bothered Will further with her worries. Something in her gut told her that the transit wouldn't wait much longer for them. While she couldn't see the school from where they were, Kitty and Will were approaching the Crest, and at least it wouldn't be much further than that.

Another howl made them both jump. What was once feet away was now inches as clawed hands struck through the thick bush, ignorant of spiny branches and pricking needle-like leaves, and clenched down on the bottom of Kitty's skirt. Kitty pulled back in a panic as the Hostilia used her as leverage to pull itself clumsily but ferociously through the destroyed bush. Its red eyes sat on a small round face. The fangs protruded from pouty, childlike lips, but its grip was as immense as its hatred. It was the smallest Hostilia she had ever seen, nothing but a kid. It yanked the satin pink layer of Kitty's dress until most of it tore from the bodice, leaving only a flouncing petticoat. Will's hand flecked with blue light as he gripped the Hostilia's hand and squeezed. It cried out in pain as the fingers bent inwardly. Then he pried Kitty loose. They darted towards another yard, but the howls of the pained beast only drew more attention.

"Crud, this is NOT going to work!" Will fumed. "We need to disappear!"

"Over here!" Kitty boosted herself over the picket fence into the neighbor's yard.

"They'll find us!"

"Shut it!"

Will bounded over the fence with more grace than Kitty had managed, but as soon as she was over, she opened her used orations, suddenly glad she hadn't done many that week. The projection from the night before was near the top. Kitty executed it, praying that the appearance didn't mean much. The spitting image of her mother in her dress and perfect silk scarf stood beside her.

"Run!" she told it. Her mother wasn't athletic, preferring strength of mind over other things, but she could move when she needed to. She watched the projection turn on her heels and dash into the street, stretching her legs as far as the dress would allow. Kitty and Will waited in tense silence, listening to more howls and shrieks as the Hostilia chased after the projection. The ground vibrated as it seemed a small army took off in the opposite direction. "That won't last long. And there's probably more the way we're going."

"Then let's stay off the streets," Will said. He pointed toward the abandoned road, but before Kitty could question him, he was already back over the fence and dashing to the center of the street. He crouched over a manhole cover.

"Oh junk and a half," she muttered. She hoped the copycat world muted smells the way it muted other senses.

With almost no effort, Will set the grate aside and motioned for Kitty to join him. Reluctantly she obeyed, darting into the street and hurrying down the ladder into the crushing dim gray below. She didn't think this world knew how to be any darker than that until Will shut the manhole cover and left them in its own version of pitch black.

"Hang tight," Will whispered. In a moment his watch gave off a warm glow that illuminated the narrow well around them. Kitty saw the slick muck on the rungs of the ladder and tried not to think too hard about what it was copying as she kept climbing down. The sound of her boots on the metal echoed in her eardrums, and she was certain the entire city could hear them. She wouldn't know which way to run anymore as long as they stayed underground.

At the bottom, Kitty's feet dropped into half a foot of water. She moaned as her feet squelched in her boots. They were definitely going to be ruined after this.

Will's watch still only lit most of what was above while he made his way down. Kitty clung to the wall and waited as the light seeped in and stretched ten feet all around them when Will touched down beside her. He pulled up a map of Glade Crest's drainage system with a deepening frown.

Kitty started to ask what was wrong, but she lost her balance and found herself tumbling into the water next to Will. A shadowy lump was slowly rising, staring at them through glowing red pupils. Her soaking hair dangled along the sides of her face. She snorted into the air and held her side with a twisted hand while the other hand curled into a fist.

Will's arm shot up, but Kitty slapped it aside, "Wait!" The pellet of light struck the wall. The Hostilia screamed, long and agonizing.

"Kitty, what the hell! It's a monster!"

"She's just a kid!"

"We don't have time to sort this out!"

The child-like creature ran at Will as best she could, splashing through the water with unpracticed steps. Will easily shoved her aside, but didn't raise his arm to fire again. He led Kitty down the remainder of the tunnel and turned another corner just as they heard more splashing join the small Hostilia's chase.

"Great, now the whole crew is back!" Will said.

"You can be pretty heartless, huh?" Kitty puffed her retort through aching lungs. "She's only a kid."

"Don't scold me for saving your life."

Will stopped as they approached another tower of rungs anchored into the slimy wall. He motioned for Kitty to go first.

"I'm wearing a dress! No way!"

"Kitty, I'm not looking! Just climb!"

She blushed as she heard her own ridiculous complaints, and she dragged her tired legs up the ladder. She was too afraid to look back down as she quickly reached the edge of Will's light. Before she could call to him, the light started to follow her. Each footfall on the metal sped one after the other. Will was moving quickly, and she needed too as well. Kitty climbed until she could finally see the roof of the well, but she held on with all of the strength in her burning muscles as the ground below rumbled. It vibrated all the way up the passage, and Kitty cringed.

"I hope that's not breaking things down worse," Will mumbled, now directly below her. "Hold tight. I'll get the cover."

As he squeezed past, Kitty finally looked down. She couldn't see all the way to the bottom as dust wafted upward and blurred the rungs below them. She knew Will was right about the Hostilia. By this point, they were just deadly, aggressive beasts. They couldn't see reason over whatever anger and fear fueled them. Still, she thought something similar about her own family on some dark days. But her mom came back to her. At the very least she got herself back to work and kept a roof over her daughters' heads. She found the light again.

Kitty started climbing back down, ignoring Will's calls. She held her breath as the dust choked her. The slap of her boots hitting the water was lost to the splashing of cement and brick collapsing into the tunnel. Kitty created her own little light with the glow of her tablet, but there wasn't anything to see. The tunnel was destroyed, and if she dared to look closely, she was sure there would be inky stains swirling in the drain water.

Could they have been saved? Maybe she was trying to make up for the week she didn't help when she should have. Just a touch of hope.

"Yoooooouuuuu...." a little voice hissed in the wreckage. Kitty tried to follow it. She started grabbing at stones and chucking them aside. She finally revealed a small black arm grasping at her. With renewed purpose, Kitty dug at the collapsed pile until she could pull out the limp body of the Hostilia and drag it to a clearer spot. It sputtered, and the crimson pupils fell on her. It swiped at her face weakly, still catching her cheek and temple.

"Stop that!" Kitty said sternly, and batted at the Hostilia's hand. It hissed again and tried to turn, but it was clearly hurt. Its ankle was twisted and one arm hung limp at its side. "I know you can hear me, young lady. You do not hit people who are trying to help you."

The Hostilia tilted its head, the red of its eyes flashed as if blinking. It let out a low growl like a dangerously wary animal.

"You're hurt," Kitty said. "Let me fix that leg, and then you go home where you belong. Your mother is probably worried sick."

Kitty expected the Hostilia to leap at her at any moment, scratching her eyes out or shoving her head under the murky water. Until it did anything actively against her, she would treat it like any little girl throwing a tantrum. Whether or not she could use powers, she knew for certain she could handle a child with a bad attitude. Kitty gently lifted the twisted ankle and received a quick batting on her hand. A few thin red lines bubbled up across her skin, and she lifted a stern eyebrow at the creature.

"I know it hurts. Let me make it better or you'll get stuck down here. You wouldn't want to be alone down here, right?"

Kitty dragged one of the discarded slabs of cement towards her and let the Hostilia's foot rest on it. Then she turned to her MHD for help.

"I don't know about doctor stuff," she admitted as she scrolled through the diagram search engine. She tried a few different forms of her search. Healing twisted ankles. Healing broken ankles. Links and resources that looked like anything she could have found with a normal tablet popped up, almost guiding her hand to the exact information she had asked for. Still it was a bit over her head and all very intimidating. Leo's words came to mind.

"...one of the key concepts when using magic is understanding what you're changing."

Some of these answers made her worried she might pass out from pain. "I mainly know about broken capillaries. I learned about it in science class. That's where bruises come from. It's a bunch of blood under your skin. What you've got looks like it just needs some time to heal up on its own. Think you can rest a while?"

It didn't answer her, but it also didn't scratch or scream. Kitty smiled.

"Okay then. Now we're cooking. To help it heal, I'm gonna give it a..." she looked at the screen again for the right vocabulary, "...a splint. So I just need to bandage it next to something hard so it won't move when you're not thinking about it. This might hurt a little bit."

Kitty examined the pile of rubble around them, but all of the bricks were too thick or jagged. Then she had an idea. She activated the gauntlet diagram that she could quickly orate like a big sister rather than the ones she had been dealing with the last few days that felt like giving a speech to the presidents of million dollar companies. The diagram appeared over her hands, this time more solid as if these unseen gloves were made of stone. She walked back to the metal rungs, lifted one foot to the wall of the tunnel, and tugged at one of the lower bits of metal. With just a little extra force, it creaked and dislodged from the wall. Kitty placed it beside the Hostilia's foot. It continued to watch her, its head flicking from side to side.

"Now we just need something to wrap it with. Oh! Oh. April is gonna kill me." With a sigh, Kitty grabbed a fistful of her underskirt and yanked it, hearing the fabric easily tear apart. She pulled all the way around twice until she had a long enough piece of material to wrap around the Hostilia's little leg a few times. It was stiff enough to get the job done, although she wasn't entirely comfortable with how much was left of her dress. Still Kitty only smiled as she kneeled down in front of her patient again and slid the material under the Hostilia's foot. The metal rung didn't perfectly fit at the ankle, but Kitty continued to wrap the skirt bandage around as many times and as tightly as she could without getting too much hissing.

"Okay. We'll tape it down and be done," she said. Kitty reached up to where her hair was falling out of its pins. Her finger grazed one of the hair ties April used. Kitty wormed the section of hair loose from the rest and unwrapped the tie. It stretched around the Hostilia's flattened foot, more like a sneaker that had become part of her body, and plunked into place. Kitty removed a few pins and pinned the cloth together to be sure.

"It's not perfect, but hopefully it'll stay put," Kitty said. "Try not to move until it's all healed, okay?"

The Hostilia leaned forward, the red pupils bouncing between Kitty and the makeshift bandage around its ankle.

"Yoooooooouu...." it said again.

"I'm Kitty. Do you have a name?"

The Hostilia didn't answer. It slid to the side, rolling off of the stump of cement and edging into the water. Slowly it stood, clearly favoring its good leg as it backed towards the opposite wall. Then it turned away from Kitty and the pile of rubble and hobbled down the tunnel, disappearing into the first intersection. Something about seeing its lopsided gait made Kitty smile. At least it was able to move at all.

A hand on her shoulder made Kitty jump.

"It's just me," Will said. "You okay? Said your goodbyes to the Hostilia?"

"...yeah." She looked at the rubble. "They were people once, y'know?"

"Yeah, I know." His eyes were distant for a moment, but he led her back to the ladder and helped her up.

With some careful movement, the two were back to the top. Will pushed the manhole cover open just a crack, and when he was satisfied that the coast was clear, he slid it further aside. Kitty felt a rush of cool air, after the stagnant feeling from the tunnel. It was so refreshing that she started to laugh as Will pulled her up behind him.

"That feels so much nicer!" she said. She helped put the manhole cover back in place. "Air hasn't felt so good since we got here! Actually, I haven't felt anything since we got here." A lump formed in her throat as she quickly remembered there weren't proper sensations in this world. It was only a copy. It played pretend to protect what it wasn't.

"I don't want to burst anyone's bubble," Will said, "but I don't know if this is a good thing."

"No, I don't think it is," Kitty agreed. "I wonder if this is the air from home. It sort of feels like a cool fall night."

"Then maybe we're close to getting back. So we should be just a couple of blocks—oh crud."

"Oh junk."

Both of them turned towards the ghostly version of Glade Crest Junior High. It was mostly hidden behind pale, crooked houses and wilting trees. Only the upper stories of the building could be seen, but the Mages quickly realized that was all they needed to see. On the roof that looked like the spot Kitty, Will, and Raquel had created their Dimensional Hold, a towering black stain clung to the sky. Its edges made it look like a crushed circle pawing at the air with spiraling arms to fill itself in.

Both Mages knew their exit was somewhere near that thing, if it hadn't been eaten already.

Twenty-One

For being so bright out, the school had never looked creepier. It was a four-story, unstable brick tower with enormous gashes dug into its belly. Parts of it were just crumbled brick specks caught in mid air like a morbid painting of an explosion. All across the grounds were shadows of people and animals patrolling for any unwelcomed guests. Most seemed to know to hop over any of the scattered cracks against the gray grass. Some faltered and howled in pain when any part of them touched the lines. That answered some questions that the intruders never wanted to know.

It seemed that the sentries had all of the entrances blocked and were waiting out their prey. In due time the transit would close, unused, or the Mages would have to reveal themselves.

Crouched behind the line of trees just past the football field, Kitty and Will watched the Hostilia rove about. Kitty had a feeling Will could dash for the back entrance leading from the gymnasium. It would be nothing for him to reach the gate of the field, and either go around or hop it and sneak through the bleachers. Then he just had to go up the path, with little to no cover, and in through the gym's double doors. Kitty, on the other hand, wasn't a track and field athlete like him, but Will wouldn't go without her; he never left a gap more than a few feet between them.

I'm slowing him down...

Will cut off the incessant cruel voice in her ear. "I don't know if the Hostilia know what they're doing or if they just happen to be good at patrolling, but I can't see a way past all of them yet. I don't think just being invisible will help either." One of the passing groups heading back towards the front of the building paused to sniff at the air and then kept moving.

"The less oration the better too," Kitty said. Her eyes were drawn back to the roof, and she had to wonder if someone—or something—was waiting for them.

"It's your school. You know any secret underground passages?" Will leaned against the pale tree and slid to the mossy ground.

Kitty shook her head. "I don't spend a lot of time outside the building. Honestly, preparing for Homecoming is the most time I've spent near the football field."

"You? No! Surely you're the cheerleader type." Will laughed quietly. Kitty rolled her eyes. "That's alright. Most of those girls are nice, but way insecure. If I've learned anything while being a Mage, it's that those kinds of people are on the fast track to wearing a shadow suit." He nudged his thumb towards the Hostilia.

"Really?"

"Sure. Like I said, they're nice, but it always seems like they're after the next bit of praise from someone. *Anyone.* Probably daddy issues. Get too desperate and who knows what you might be willing to do to keep yourself popular?"

"I have a friend who's a cheerleader. Well, she *was* my friend until we moved out of the Slope." Kitty grabbed at a desaturated twig and ran it across the weak blades of grass. In her head she could see the green they were meant to be, and she felt the missing yellow and orange touches on the fallen leaves around them. The Dimensional Hold was becoming more and more like their world.

"If that's all it took to ditch you, doesn't sound like much of a friend."

"Maybe, but she'd probably know what to do here. She's always on the field either for cheering practice or probably making out with Preston Smith or whatevs." She pulled a sour face

"Jealous?"

"Ew, no! Gross!" she said. Still she kept her face away from him. "I was just saying. I only had to come down here to store the merchandise for the Homecoming game and see what size tables we could use. And even then, everything got stored in the Rec Room storage—oh! I'm such a numbnuts!"

Kitty jumped to her feet and ducked through the trees until she could see past the bleachers on one end of the football field. The Hostilia were patrolling everywhere on the grounds leading up to the doors of the main building. The Rec Room's storage shed was nearly hidden from the rest of the building. A short, confusing set of steps led to it from the Meyers-Patel Rec Room that was previously an unfinished, unleveled part of the basement floor of the school. It was down an adjacent hall to the new art studio where she had borrowed supplies for Homecoming.

"If we can get down those steps, there's a door that'll lead inside," Kitty told Will. "It doesn't look like anything so the Hostilia probably aren't thinking to guard it!"

"Good spotting! It shouldn't be hard to wait out the next patrol. You're right. They're definitely not paying attention this far over."

A group of four humanoid shapes crept along the edges of the bleachers, stooping to look underneath and looking up at the higher rows of metal benches. Seemingly satisfied, they kept moving, disappearing around the curve of seats.

"I don't run as fast as you," Kitty blurted as Will crouched down with his eyes on the stair.

"I don't know why you keep putting yourself down like that," he said, "but you're not doing yourself any favors. Just run. Move as fast as your legs will go and I'll drag you the rest of the way if I have to. I'm not gonna leave you behind."

She bit her lip, but looked back at their destination. The coast was clear for now so they needed to move fast.

"Ready," Will said. "Set—" He took Kitty's hand, and for a moment she flinched, ready to draw it back. Instead she squeezed to make sure he kept his promise. "Go!"

Will sprinted from the tree line, and Kitty pushed her legs to move as fast as they could bear and then a little faster than that. Her breath came out in small, useless puffs, but Will tugged her along. In the distance, she could see some shadows still peering around the streets and getting dangerously close the trees, but they didn't turn towards the Mages as they reached the stairs built into the ground some ten yards from the main building. More stairs opposite them led back up and towards the building, but they stopped at the lower platform where a door was set in the wall. Kitty and Will grabbed the handle and tugged. They heard something snap out of place, and the door slid towards them with a rusty screech. A sound far too close, like a scream of pure rage, made the hairs on Kitty's neck stand on end. She and Will dove inside the dark room and yanked the door shut behind them.

Will took out his cell phone and turned on the light from his camera flash. The darkness was much heavier than before as the Dimensional Hold fell apart. Kitty took his arm and followed him through the cavernous room that echoed each of their footfalls. Tubs of rubber balls were split in half horizontally by streaks of white. A few balance beams against the wall seemed mid fall into one another. There were white folding tables haphazardly piled in a corner like a dump site. Kitty shook and hurried them to the far door. It led to a short flight of steps, up to a dimly lit hallway with an intersection to some other newly constructed rooms, and then back to the gymnasium. As they pushed open the door, the sudden brightness stung at the Mages' eyes, but they wouldn't complain. They made it inside.

The gym looked like a war zone. There was just as much white as there was faded yellow-brown wood on the ground. The bleachers were pushed against and through the walls. Overhead, the ceiling barely existed, just shards like metal teeth ready to chomp down on them. Kitty and

Will carefully skipped over the lines of white and pushed past the gymnasium doors.

"Be ready for more unfriendlies," Will said. He folded his hand into the finger pistol, and Kitty saw it glint again, thrumming with energy they could barely afford to spare. Letting the Hostilia get too close wouldn't be good for them either. She followed suit as she led him into the hallways.

Patrol was much lighter inside. Kitty and Will only needed to get past one hunched over man who spent most of his time looking down to avoid the cracks. The Hostilia probably couldn't manage to get around all of the jagged wasteland that the hallways had become. She brought Will the long way to the stairwell and tugged the door open. She wasn't surprised to find it carved up like a piece of art her teacher had shown them with sideways and upside-down stairs.

Will approached the base of the steps and started testing what was left for stability with his foot.

"Hope you took some rock climbing in gym," he said, stepping up onto a jagged ledge where steps used to be.

Kitty's knees thrummed with pins and needles. Her heart pounded in her chest making breathing difficult. Static and white noise filled her ears. All Kitty could do was drop to the floor and hold her clammy face in her hands, biting back the scream that wanted to rip from her throat. Her breath came out in shuddering bursts and whimpers.

She felt Will kneel beside her. "Hey, c'mon. We're nearly there. You can't quit on me now."

"I'm not—just—would you just gimme a second?!" Her cry bounced around the stairwell. The anxiety of sneaking around and being attacked piled on top of the physical exertion of running and hopping around cracks became one moment of overstimulation. She broke down.

"If you knew how bad this was, you'd know we don't have a second," Will said. His tone wasn't cruel, but it was direct.

"I get it. The transit is closing. I know. I just—"

"Do you know?" The urgency was clear and yet he still sat down in front of her. He leaned a hand against the door to the stairwell and Kitty felt the tingle of magic making her skin itch a little. A lock clicked into place. "You know we're in a Dimensional Hold, right?" Kitty nodded. "Good. And you know we got here from trying to get Raquel back home, right?"

"Yes, I know," she said with an exasperated breath. His words made sense, but it was all tangled in the white noise.

"And you know what Dimensional Holds do, right?"

"Will, what the actual heck do you want to hear? Yes, I know. They're little buffers for universes and the Planetary Homestead—"

"And here we are inside of one that's falling apart. One that got in the way of the otherwise pretty straight path of getting Raquel home with a jump. If she wasn't a dummy oration you could terminate, where do you think she went? Where do you think she went that would take us through a Hold to get her there? A hold that buffers universes!"

Kitty's hands dropped as quickly as her heart did. Will sat crossed legged in front of her looking fairly sick himself. Leo had shown her these exact consequences if someone— Kitty, for instance—messed with the orations surrounding the Planetary Homestead. The scrolling warning had said it too. The universe was too fat. One person in two places at once. Kitty's perfect dummy.

"Raquel is from—!!"

Will slapped his hand over Kitty's mouth. She simply sat there, frozen. Her wide, teary eyes stared off at nothing. Kitty's oration brought a second Kitty into the universe, and the universe split its pants because two Kittys was too many. All so she could shirk a few duties and see her friends whenever she wanted to. So these powers could be used for something fun just once.

"But she's back in her universe," Will said. His voice through the Chameleon Ear was powerful, fighting back the lingering fear with overwhelming calm and duty to his adjudication. *"You helped get her there. Now we have to get to ours and get the Hold fixed. We're almost there, Kitty. Stand up."*

Still shaking, Kitty accepted his hand as he lifted her to her feet and guided her back to the stairs. Spears of white ran the length of the steps to the next platform. Will grabbed onto the railing and hoisted himself up, finding footing on the bars. One foot over the other, he worked his way to the first platform and gave Kitty a thumbs up before he crawled over the corner railing and dropped onto the second set of steps. With a useless breath to steady herself, Kitty made sure her feet only stepped wherever she remembered Will's feet touched. She clung to the metal bars until her knuckles were white and shuffled up the railing. Will helped her over the corner and down onto the steps.

"Nice," he said. "Just...three more times until the top!"

"But we have to get above the fourth floor," Kitty said in a moment of a clarity.

Will only shrugged. "Looks like this stairway only goes to a third floor." The ceiling was a mess of white streaks. Kitty wouldn't be surprised if the fourth floor had fallen apart somehow. They would just have to go as high as they could.

They continued climbing along the railing, only stopping if one of the jagged edges cracked the bar. Kitty knew Will could leap over and stay standing, but he never said a word. He just took her hand and helped her onto the stairs. At the third floor entrance, they carefully opened the door.

Kitty's eyes crossed from the piled up distortion. The walls of the hallway were crumpled like paper, jammed against the entrance the Mages were about to step through. Instead of hundreds of feet across, it was just a couple of yards over uneven ground and toppled, crunched lockers, doors, and shattered windows. But on the other side was a single door with a crash bar.

"This place is twentieth level messed up," Kitty said.

The Mages carefully stepped forward, trying to find flatter ground to stand on. The floor wasn't entirely steady. Some peaks sank against a stray foot and some flat surfaces dipped. Will lead the way, and Kitty did her best to follow his tracks again, but the floor didn't stay the same. One peak that flattened under Will's weight nearly stabbed straight through Kitty's boot, while another flat surface almost entirely gave way like wet paper. Will's last jump had him on the toes of his sneakers against the metal trim below the door. He tested the ground with his heels and stepped back with a sigh of relief. He held his hand out to Kitty who was still testing his last step.

Kitty mumbled a quick prayer in case God or Vitae was listening and then jumped towards Will's waiting hands. She grabbed on, but only one foot reached the solid ground, while the other punched through the floor. She started to drop. The fall was cut short with a quick yank on her arm. Kitty saw Will's face twisted with strain as one hand was gripping the crash bar and the other was throttling her wrist. He swung her towards solid floor, and she snatched at the crash bar before sinking to her knees, hiding her face between her sore arms.

Will laid a gentle hand on her rocking shoulders. "You're alright. You made it."

Kitty could only shake her head until the tears stopped. "Sorry."

"Don't be. But you've gotta get up. Let's get out of here."

Kitty dragged herself to her feet, and they slowly pushed the door open. More painful brightness stabbed at their eyes, but they squinted through it until they could adjust. They saw the paved roof with its stray bits of gravel, somehow more solid than any other spot in the school, but also pierced along its ledge by an enormous tear as tall as Kitty and Will combined. Beyond that the clouds over the cityscape were like spears against the faded gray that slowly melted into a velvet blue directly above the roof. Right at the edge of where they stood, being torn through its center, was a solid black hole in the air—the transit home.

"Sorry," came a voice that made Kitty hold her throat, but she hadn't spoken. It was then that they saw a girl with mousy brown hair in an oversized tee shirt and jeans. She scrubbed at her eyes beneath the shadow of the enormous pocket of darkness. A silver band stretched the length of her right forearm. "It looks like we're all stuck here."

Twenty-Two

Kitty ran across the gravel rooftop to Raquel with Will easily falling into step. She was almost afraid to touch the other girl now that she knew where Raquel had come from. She wasn't lying about being real. Every science fiction movie about traveling to a different universe and meeting a copy of yourself sprang to mind, especially the ones that warned against it. Things could explode or you could stop existing. In their case, the universe got fat.

"What happened?" Kitty asked. "Didn't you get through the transit?"

Raquel nodded slowly, but her eyes were trained on the oration and the terrible gash running through it. Dark gray streaks cascaded from her eyes and stained the backs of her hands as she wiped them away. "I just fell out up here. Must've been too late..."

"No, it's not. Tell her, Will. What does the failsafe thingy do? How does it work if one side of the transit is gone?"

Will scratched at his head and looked back at the mess of dark pools intertwining. Chilled air spilled from that side of the roof and left goosebumps all across Kitty's skin.

"It said—uh—the top priority was getting the Mage to a safe place," he said. He started walking towards the tear and the transit. The size of it made him look small for the first time. "If one side is gone, the other side should be pretty secure, and it should lead wherever it's supposed to lead. So if we were too late on Raquel's end, this should be a direct way to our side at least. Then we can give it another shot."

Raquel slowly nodded and took a deep, shuddering breath. "O-okay. Okay, that's fine. I guess—uh—I guess we go through and—start again—"

Will patted her tense shoulder. "Exactly. Spoken like a true Mage."

Kitty looked between the two of them and marveled at their calm. Her heart was pounding in her chest and her clammy fingers twitched. She couldn't ignore the trouble that bringing Raquel back to their world would bring. How many Hostilia were waiting on the rooftop or right back in the cracking Dimensional Hold?

No amount I can't handle, came a low voice that scratched against her brain. *Not when I've got power like this. I could do whatever I want and stop this whole mess...*

Then Raquel's head sprung up, eyes growing wide, staring at nothing with irises as dark as her pupils. Kitty's stomach lurched. Her throat became sandpaper, and she doubled over to dry heave. The feeling wouldn't subside. Her body continued to revolt until she was lightheaded and clawing at the rooftop, praying for relief. A swarm of Hostilia appeared in the doorway, the ones who could manage to dodge the cracks. People-like figures of different shapes and sizes lumbered out. They charged across the roof, some with arms stretched towards Raquel, and others with sights on Will. He turned around and grabbed Kitty's arm, yanking her to her feet. Her knees felt numb, and her stomach still tensed.

Running is useless. I have to take what's mine.

"You've gotta focus," Will said. "We need to get the tear shut!" He pulled her towards where Raquel was letting off blast after blast at the creatures. Her arm shook, but her aim was true.

The cloud over Kitty's mind cleared just enough to hear Will and the tremor in his voice. The tear. The transit. The way home. A green screen dropped over Kitty's eyes. She hadn't meant to do it; it appeared as naturally as blinking. Will didn't take the time to scold her as a bright arc of light reached around the Mages creating a dome that encompassed the three of them and the transit home, strong as a bomb shelter. A wave of dizziness swept over Kitty, and she fell to her knees again.

Will kneeled beside her. "Alright, it didn't need to be that big, but I appreciate it."

Panting, Raquel stepped back from the wall of the dome where only oily patches of unfortunate Hostilia made it inside the barrier. The Hostilia growled, almost inaudible, and slammed their fists against the wall. Kitty's head lightly thrummed from their efforts, but it was easily forgotten as the world inside the dome was muffled and, for just a moment, seemingly peaceful. The beating blended with another distant rhythm swept in from the cold of the tear.

"Okay, so we start sewing?" Raquel asked, bunching the material of her torn jeans in her fists. Her voice quaked as if it took everything in her power to keep control. "Great. Fine. Good. Oh my gee. Okay."

In the next breath she was tapping furiously on her screen, and the familiar giant needle was in her hand with a threaded eye from the glowing strand in her chest. Raquel crawled up to the ledge and shoved the tip of the needle against the air. Her arms shook as she continued to press inward with more force than they needed before. When it finally pierced the air, they all jumped at what sounded like cracking glass. Kitty thought the Hostilia had penetrated her dome, but it was only the fragile air they were shattering. In a practiced motion, Raquel turned the needle and brought it back through the air on the other side of the rip, and they all cringed as the air cracked like smashed ice.

"We'd better help her," Will said. He kept his voice low, and still it sounded like he was trying to be heard from across the roof. His voice competed with the steadily growing wind tunnel and the blended sounds of the voices it carried. Some scents wafted through, an odd mixture of baked goods and floor polish that reminded her of the gym at school. "That thing is gonna need all of our energy. You okay?"

Kitty took a shuddering breath and started to nod just as another voice in her head told her, *I'm not okay*. It sounded like her, like she was trying desperately to make herself understand she couldn't take on a curse of this size. More cracking echoed around the shield as the sky snapped and broke under some invisible pressure. Kitty's skin itched as the air seemed to crumple and push her towards something.

I'm so much closer to home than I even know. The voice returned and spoke with words she felt, but didn't understand. An endless sea of voices whispered in her ears like the whispers plaguing her all week. They cried out and begged for help. Fear and powerlessness strangled their words that weren't so much voiced as they were simply existing and haunting her. They came from two far off places, but so similar in feeling. Each plea spoke of enormous, crushing weights that were never meant to meet as they barreled towards each other. The line separating them cracked and chipped, falling apart and drifting into space like spilled diamonds. In her mind she could see stars of far off galaxies and stars of her own world that slowly blinked out. An impossible explosion tore the vacuum of space, and she felt the tremendous shockwave and swore her heart stopped at the foreseen final moments of two entire universes.

But it wasn't real. At least not yet. It was her magic as an Empath hearing every little voice and every tremendous echo that others weren't cursed to hear. Power she never understood, but she had asked for it. Why?

"Kitty, come on," Will said. He was already at the ledge with a needle in hand. As he waved her over, another voice flooded her mind. Somehow it was just as gigantic as the voice of the universes screaming against her skull. From the sudden wide-eyed stare of the others, she wondered if they could hear it too.

"Kitty, sweetheart, we have to talk," a man said. He had a smoothness to his voice that drew you in, and Kitty could imagine he must have had a rich, hardy laugh on better

days. One that could make anyone around him smile. Now it sounded almost saddened. Hurt. But nowhere near as hurt as Kitty. Her lungs seized up in her chest, and she could hardly stand for shaking. Her stomach wrenched, but the queasy feeling didn't compare to the rage, the sadness, the pent up feelings that scared her as they broke the surface of her thoughts. She didn't dare crane her neck around to see him. He had a face she didn't want to remember, a voice that was sweet poison spilling over her brain.

"No," was all she said. It was barely a whisper, but it traveled in the dome. Behind her she could feel that strong presence her father always gave off. It was cold now, everything was icy around her, and she couldn't stand to look at him.

"Kitty, I've hurt you," he said, his voice only slightly muffled behind the barrier. Kitty clenched her eyes and balled her fists so tightly that her nails stung her palms. "But my god, look how you've grown. Look at this power you control. No one will hurt you again."

"No," she said again. Her words smoldered. "Definitely not you."

His words revealed his smile, "Definitely not me. You let me walk away, and you've been chasing me ever since. Well now I'm here. You don't need to chase me any further. You don't need to obsess over me anymore. Look at them dragging you through crap you never asked for. You don't need anyone else commanding you, not with the strength you possess. Haven't you seen how your powers command others? Wherever you travel and make your magic known, people's true nature is exposed to you. Everyone lives on their fear, their desperate need to survive. They bow to you because only you can control them and help them survive. You're an Empath. Your heart is all you need, and you know where to turn your eyes." In her mind she saw the arm of her father lift and point towards Will and Raquel who were both furiously stabbing and tugging on the their threads.

If Kitty had never made the too real dummy oration, Raquel would never have wound up here. Let her leave. Kitty didn't want her around anyway. And Will. He brought her to Leo. He showed her the spell diagrams. He wormed his way into her head that this was some kind of gift, but it was only a curse. The weight of the whole world—the whole universe—sat on her shoulders, and she never wanted that.

Curse...

"Kitty, come on!" Will shouted. "We need you on this or we can't get out of here! Ignore him!"

Her eyes flew open. She felt the wetness on her cheeks with her trembling hands. When she pulled them back, her fingers were stained black like faded watercolor. The image of Miren Patrick and her bloodied nose crossed Kitty's mind. That stupid goth wannabe running her mouth about Kitty's family. Righteous fury burned her cheeks. She glared at Will who had abandoned his needle and leaped from the ledge back to the rooftop.

"Go home," she told him.

He stopped just inches in front of her. "Nope. Not without you."

"I'm not joining the Alliance."

"You don't have to. You're not joining Nefas either."

Instead of the sudden urge to vomit, she only felt a pulse of heat in her belly. Kitty clicked her tongue. "Who are you to tell me what to do? I barely even know you!"

"True," he said. A ghost of that lopsided grin returned to his cheeks, but worry still shone over everything. Worry for her? He was only out to trick her into doing more work she didn't want to do. She shouldn't have had to do any of it. "I really should have done better with that, being your mentor and all. I don't know what that guy did to you, but it doesn't matter anymore."

"You don't know what you're talking about," Kitty said, overlaid by the man's voice behind the dome.

Will paused for a moment, shrinking back and eyeing Kitty. His eyes darted between Kitty and something behind her. "Who is that? Your dad?" Will asked. Kitty's eyes dropped for a moment. "You think him walking out screwed everything up?"

"It did!" She shoved him back with shimmering hands, smirking at how he stumbled from surprise and fell to the ground. Her presence over his, towering and powerful, was everything she wanted. She was in control, and she could take what was hers. "He disappeared and suddenly my home was gone. My friends were gone. My life was ruined. I could've just sat there and let my mom scream and drink us out of every last penny, but I didn't. I stood up. I did everything, but I shouldn't have needed to. I took care of our house and my sister after she got hurt. My sister..."

Will didn't say anything. He didn't stand or move. His eyes caught hers and waited.

"I ruined you," her father's voice trailed in her mind.

"He ruined us. Ruined everything. And all I wanted was to have my life back. I want—I want everything to be like before. Then I'll be a better me. Not this numbnuts Valley girl."

"Kitty," Will finally said, "you're crying black gunk. That's not better. I know orations are new to you, and being an Empath doesn't make it easier, but you're so smart, and I know you've got the answer just sitting in your brain. The way you jump head first at challenges like new orations, the way you think of creative ways to get around a problem. I've seen you work, student soldier. Just look at him. Look at the guy trying to tell you that wallowing in the past is the better answer. You can't be the girl you were yesterday *and* be better because that other girl isn't better than you. Just turn around."

Kitty furiously shook her head. "Screw him! I never want to see him again!"

"Don't see him. Face him," Will said. He staggered to his feet, rubbing his stomach where Kitty had shoved him. Kitty wondered for a fleeting moment if she had hurt him badly. "Tell him to go die in a fire and then move on with your life. No wonder you have trouble with magic. Who's the one calling the shots? You or your dad?"

"Me! You're all just scared of me. I don't need a stupid tablet to do magic, but you tried to make me use it."

"I mean, you're pretty powerful for a Magus, I'll give ya that, but you can't convince life it's supposed to be something different if you don't even know who you are."

"I'll make it do what I want," she spat. "And you."

"And everyone you love will suffer because of it. Your sister too."

"Shut it!" Kitty slammed her fists towards his chest, but Will caught her arms and held firmly. "I would never hurt her! I did everything *for* her!" Every shrieking word felt pitiful against Will's calm voice. Why didn't he flare with rage like she did? Why wasn't the weight of every fear crushing his chest until he screamed and broke everything around him just to expel it all? She could hear more whispers calling out, but they flocked to him more than her. They craved the warmth of his understanding. She shivered in her own icy shell.

The air beyond the dome splintered further. Chips of sky cracked and dissolved into white streaks. Everything pushed closer to them and to the tear. More whispered screams of terror clanged in Kitty's head, all looking for help, for a figure to turn to. Somewhere in there was the unusual scared feelings of the boy standing in front of her. The girl who was from the far off place. Students who were celebrating one of the best nights of their young lives. A mother with more worries than most, and a sobbing young girl in pain as the rips in the air crept wider and wider. Those voices all turned to her, still the stronger presence. They would do as she said.

Will shook his head. "Maybe you did do it all for your sister, but listening to Nefas means you're doing everything for yourself. You can't change that your dad walked out or that your sister got hurt." Kitty bit down on her lip. "But you can be better than the Kitty that let one really bad thing ruin a lot of really great things, Homecoming Queen."

Kitty looked back at Will. Her lips tugged, trying to glare and smile at once. The weight of the presence behind her faltered. Her eyes flickered towards the dome again. Will held his hand out, it didn't demand anything of her. She could feel him as protective as an older brother, as protective as the dome around them.

"But how do I get what I want?"

315

"Depends on what you want. You might not," Will said, his grin returning, "but if you need help getting whatever it is, you can always just ask."

The whispers swirled in her head, each feeling holding some unknown renewed hope that some powerful Mage was finally listening. Kitty grabbed his hand and squeezed as they both turned around. The small army of Hostilia were still slamming their fists against the unseen surface. The dome gently pulsed on contact. They viciously shoved each other aside or climbed on the backs of the fallen, anything that put them closer to their prey in their minds.

Behind them, almost entirely blocked except for a quaff of smooth brown hair flicked to the side, was David Guthrie. Kitty remembered how his hair was always soft as a cloud when she would sit in his lap and snuggle against him, patting it down and smoothing it back with her small hands. She could almost feel it now. Instead of riding the sensation, she grabbed at what was left of her skirt and let the scratchy material keep her in reality. Behind those monsters, Kitty thought he might be smiling a grim smile or frowning with grave disappointment. Either way, it hurt her. It was just like the last time she had ever seen him. He was masked by the door frame and her mother wishing him goodbye. And then that was it. He simply didn't come home again.

"Kitty," Mr. Guthrie said as if he stood right beside her. "I've hurt you. I walked away. I left you alone. Don't you feel it?"

Kitty took a labored breath. "I do. You won't do it anymore. Sorry...Nefas." Kitty's lips fumbled over the name, and Will pat her shoulder and smiled down at her. All of his cuts and bruises were like so many badges of pride. She wasn't sure she would ever fully understand how he could be so positive all the time. It seemed like a much better power than being an Empath, but she took a moment to bask in his appreciation. Not because she needed him to side with her, but because she was lucky that he did.

A sudden jolt, like a heavy fist to her gut, made Kitty drop to her knees gasping. She was almost sick again. When she looked back up, the man who had been entirely obscured by the Hostilia before was now front and center at the edge of the dome, rearing his fist back and letting it collide with the shield of magic. His face was blurred like a smeared painting as it grew into a flat black mask. The dome flashed like lightning in a hazy sky, and Kitty cried out.

"C'mon!" Will said, pulling her to her feet.

"You're making a mistake, little Magistrate," Nefas said as if over a cup of tea. The avatar in the shape of Kitty's father hurled his fist against the barrier again, and Kitty stumbled as she and Will approached the tear. It was pulled up from the bottom of the transit behind it by about a foot thanks to Raquel and Will. A sheen of sweat covered Raquel's face as she held the end of her thread, trying to knot it off with every ounce of strength she had left. Will grabbed the remains of his thread. The brilliant blue-white light trailing from his chest to the needle's eye returned. Another crack echoed within the dome as he punctured the sky.

Kitty fumbled with her MHD, squeezing it to her chest as Nefas made contact with the dome again. She crawled to the edge where Raquel had her oration pulled taut and picked up where she left off. Creating the diagram felt like a mile run, but she jammed the needle into the air right above the ledge and stood on shaky feet to draw it out through the air over the rip.

Another fist into the dome. The flashing continued, and Kitty nearly lost her footing. Raquel grabbed her wrist, barely acknowledging the sting. "I've got you. Keep going."

Kitty tugged the needle back around in a messy whip stitch. In the back of their minds they could feel the growing anger that revealed the truth in Nefas' smirk. It was a roiling hatred to not have his way. That someone would dare stand up to his brute force was the most vile insult. Every contact, every cry Kitty couldn't contain, it was a show of control. Power over others.

Even with Raquel keeping her on her feet, Kitty struggled not to collapse under the force of Nefas' battering. Just as she thought her bones would break, a terrible scream raked through the air. The Mages spun around. Nefas' avatar was grabbing at his face and the two little arms wrapped around it. They were pale gray and ended in claws that sank into the eye holes of that black mask. Its legs wrapped around the squared body and kicked back and forth with one sneaker and one splinted foot.

"What the heck?" Raquel muttered. "What's that Hostilia doing?"

"She's changing her mind," Kitty said.

Will snapped his fingers at the girls. "She's giving us time. Hurry!"

One tug after another, Kitty brought her needle around with Raquel holding her around her waist so she didn't fall or tug too hard. She held onto hope for as long as Nefas remained distracted. For a minute, the weak slapping of the Hostilia was all they had to contend with, and Kitty finished more than half of what remained in the tear. Soon after, the horrible shriek of a child and the pulsing agony that was suddenly still told Kitty that their free time had run out. Still, it was enough, and Kitty tearfully promised to say a prayer for that girl next Sunday at church.

As Will finished up, the beating worsened. Each flash revealed cracks that lingered as the diagram broke down. Spots of oily black clung to the cracks and dripped like rain. Kitty's chest ached and her arms grew numb. Will stood behind her to prop her up just as her knees gave out. Half sitting on Will's shoulder and half pulled along with Raquel's arms, Kitty wound the thread of energy a few more times.

"Wait," she said breathlessly. The weight on her chest was like a boulder crushing her lungs. "I can't tie it off."

"You've got to," Will said. "You're so close."

"I can't breathe." The Chameleon Ear beeped with warning. *Energy levels critical. Functions activated to prioritize vital organs.* Kitty cried out as Nefas continued to pummel the barrier to a chorus of shattering.

"I've got you, Kitty," Raquel said, taking the needle from her now limp arm. Kitty fell back against Will and hoped it wasn't disappointment on his face. She didn't want to disappoint her friend when she had come so far. She felt the fizzle of her oration terminating. The thread she had created dangled from the still gaping tear, and it quickly started dropping, the weight pulling apart the untied line. "Will, get ready to run."

"Huh? What are you talking about?"

Already Raquel's hands flashed with an oration at work. The needle returned to her trembling hands, and she hopped back up onto the ledge. "I'm gonna pull the tear the rest of the way up. At least enough for you to get through. I don't think I can do much more than that before my heart just stops."

"Raquel, I promised you were getting out of here."

"Then maybe be more careful about your promises," she said, but she was smiling. She shoved the needle back into the air, and her shaking hands started to loop it around. Kitty's cries and coughs became more frequent, and the jagged etches along the face of the dome started to block their vision through it. The patter of oily cursed droplets was almost soothing. "As soon as there's enough room, get through. I'll bolt once the shield is down."

"Bolt where? That's insane!"

"It's our only choice." As she said that, she gave a great heave on the needle. The world seemed to fold on itself leaving the Mages reeling, but the tear lifted. There was just enough space to crawl through into the transit. "That's all I've got. Go!"

Kitty wanted to speak. She wanted to protest as loudly as Will was. His voice was tired, but adamant. Kitty couldn't twitch her fingers to take Raquel's arm and pull her down with them. The argument ended as a thunderous crack echoed through and around the dome. The frigid wind swept outward, spraying the black droplets across the rest of the roof. The roar of the Hostilia was palpable now, and it shook the Mages to their core. Nefas let his riled army storm ahead.

"Please go!" Raquel said.

"I'm reopening it once we're through."

With that, Will stepped up to the ledge and slid Kitty forward. She felt the familiar splash of the edge of space across her cheeks as the darkness swallowed her. Then she was bombarded with a terrible bright light. By her feet, she heard Will gasp and groan with pain, but he was hovering over her and helping to sit her up again.

"Will?"

"No time. C'mon. You've gotta try to stand."

He pulled her to her feet that may as well have been jelly beneath her, and he half led, half dragged her across the blinding white miniature Hold. Kitty dared one peak behind her and saw a shriveling black spot along the shining wall. It couldn't decide if it wanted to shrink or grow, but sparks flared around its edges, battling against bruised looking splatter.

"Jump on three," Will ordered. Kitty could barely understand the words, but as he counted down, he tensed beside her, his arm wrapped around her waist. "One. Two. Three!"

Twenty-Three

Kitty knew the motion for jumping. She bent her knees, but once she did, she didn't have much energy to spring back up. Will did the same and leaped with strength for the both of them. They tumbled through a wall of white and into twilight, landing hard on a gravel-spattered ground. The force jarred their legs. They fell, rolling to ungraceful stops. Will's hand flashed as his tablet reappeared. With another quick keystroke, the flat plane of white clouds shivered and faded away like a misty breeze, and the black hole seemed to dissolve with it.

Ringing silence deafened them for a minute. Kitty could feel her heart pounding against her ribs like it was trying to escape the torture she was putting it through. Certainly it wasn't expecting a workout in a party dress and boots. As the ringing subsided, Kitty could hear night birds chirping from the trees around the school grounds. Some wafting chatter rose from people in the parking lot.

Spotlights painted the dark sky welcoming those who were attending Glade Crest Junior High's biggest event ever planned. Kitty's event.

They were back home.

Kitty pushed herself up to her elbows and looked over at Will, still lying flat and staring up at the sky. She could see the steady rise and fall from his chest. Kitty rolled onto her stomach and lurched to her hands and knees, testing the weight on her sore limbs. Shaking arms and legs brought her across the roof to sit down next to Will. He was battered and bruised, but still he kept smiling. He turned his head towards her, eyes a little glassy in the moonlight.

"You're dumb," he said.

Kitty gaped. "That's what you have to say to me?" she said. "You're a real jerkface."

"I just know if the situation was reversed, you'd be the one in that Dimensional Hold." He fell silent as he sat up and stared at the space where his mini Hold had been. She knew he was really looking past it into a shattering world where Raquel stayed behind to make sure they got home. Kitty had a few ideas of how she would avoid those Hostilia if she were in Raquel's shoes. Those thoughts let her believe Raquel had similar plans. She had to have gotten away. Kitty had to believe it.

"She isn't a dummy," Kitty said. Her hand rested on her wrist over a small silver chain and its dangling charm. "She's...she's good people. I wish I could've said goodbye."

The air where the transit once hung began to wave like heat lines spurting out from nowhere. Kitty's front felt hot where she faced the air that started to blister before her eyes. Wherever the blisters popped, she saw light and smelled something sharp like smoke. They popped faster. A sheet of light seemed to be pushing through until the air looked like a pot of boiling water.

"No," Will said. His eyes were wide in panic. "No no no!" He jumped to his feet and pulled Kitty with him as she begged for an answer. "The oration. The one we couldn't get to. We never got to it!"

"So what? What's happening?" She ducked as a larger blister belched out a spray of light that burned.

"It's setting off the bombs!"

Will held Kitty close to him with one arm, and Kitty saw the flash of his MHD appearing in his other hand. Behind them, the air popped like an overfilled balloon. A shockwave crashed into their backs and threw them forward. They covered their heads as they were pelted with bits of gravel and stone. The sound of snapping concrete made them dare to look, but there was nothing to see except dust and heavy slabs flying about and light that was blocked as they quickly dropped backwards and then straight down. Their screams were drowned out by the sounds of crashing, snapping, twisting, and breaking. Metal, stone, pipes, wires, tiles, everything fell into itself as the roof caved in and crashed down through the third floor of the school and beyond. Every inch of Kitty's skin felt something. It was scratched or battered or squeezed or pinched. She was knocked around or being wrapped in warm arms. Her head clamored as a green filter dropped over her eyes.

Please protect everyone! Make them get out of the way! They don't deserve to get squashed or turned into monsters! Not even Miren or Jennifer!

An incredible patchwork of blue threads weaved across the darkness. They asked many questions but the urgency was clear, and the crashing world respected that.

Will may have spoken, but Kitty couldn't know. The entire world slammed into something else solid that finally bore the weight of a universe and a quarter of a school. More stone crumbled and dropped or slipped from unstable perches. Then finally all that was left after an unknowable time was the sound of a pebble plopping from higher up to wedge between larger bricks and slabs.

Kitty wanted to cough as she slowly came back to consciousness, but her chest hurt. She was afraid to open her eyes. She was surprised she could think at all when she was pretty sure she was supposed to be a goner. Something dripped on her face, and she peaked one eye open. In the dim blue light of a struggling oration, Will was kneeling over her, his face clenched, bruised, and bleeding from a gash along the side of his forehead. There was a droplet hanging from the tip of his nose that wobbled and then landed on her cheek. A few tears trickled down his nose to join the last one. His arms were shuddering like he could barely keep himself up. Then she looked past him where a light blue sheen hovered around both of them a foot past Will's back.

"Will, hold on," she said. "I'll help."

He peaked one eye open. "Oh yeah? How?"

That was when Kitty noticed her own situation. They were both pinned in by a wall of rubble lying on top of the dome. The glossy wood beneath them showed one string of light from a crack between the slabs just past Kitty's head. Even if she could slide towards it, her right arm was only halfway inside the shield Will must have thrown up at the last second. It was pinned between a few large slabs, which meant her tablet was too. Will's MHD had skid to the edge of the field, but his hands shook just to hold himself up let alone to move and grab it.

"I can wish us out of here. I know you don't want me to. I know I'm not supposed to, but what else is there?"

"One. Wrong. Move—" He didn't have to finish the sentence.

Kitty closed her eyes again. Immediately her racing heart was struck with the labored drumming from Will's chest less than a foot apart from hers. His fear was barely contained by the sheer focus on each aching muscle that stayed as still as he could get them. The distant murmurs of panic from anyone alive outside of the rubble hummed in her chest too, and soon she was breathing in the clamor of the city. The green screen dropped over her eyes. Kitty watched streams of blazing blue ribbon wrap around her forearm and the flat stones with mangled piping wedged between them. It spread all along the ground beneath her and Will. Cool air sneaked past their clothes and stung at their cuts. Her fingers began to tingle under the pressure of pushing her oration and answering more and more questions.

How heavy? How far? What is the weight per square inch traveling with target—?

"Just move!" She felt the words in her head and tearing past her lips.

"Kit—ty—wait…" Will puffed. They heard the groans of shifting rocks, and Will's shoulders quaked. The air around them wavered with heat lines, and Kitty felt a fire against her back. She ignored it, pushing through the screaming questions that would lead her to the safety of the fire escape outside of her bedroom window.

"Kitty, stop! You have to stop! The transit isn't safe!" His voice crashed through the Chameleon Ear. The cap on his fear was blown away. Each panicked syllable spoke of bombs going off in the space right outside of their world. Each bomb they encountered burst and seared the molecules surrounding it, setting off devastating chain reactions. The constant explosions trapped them in their own world until they all ran their course, and the rush made Kitty freeze and drop the oration.

The tower of rubble shifted again. Will cried out, and his arms buckled for a moment. He dropped to his elbows, and the shield followed him, shifting rocks and boulders above. They slid along the path of least resistance, one of which was slamming into the rocks hovering over Kitty's arm. They pushed down with a new, tremendous force that made the thin slabs cave in. The other shifting boulders pulverized them, leaving room for the bigger stones to plummet directly onto Kitty's forearm.

She didn't know what was happening for a second. The light couldn't reveal much. Then a searing pain like nothing she had ever felt exploded up her right arm. She screamed. It was all she could do. She didn't have room to move and curl up and flail like her body tried to do. So instead, she screamed.

"Kitty, stop! Look at me! Damn it, look!"

The sight of him was swimming in front of her eyes. White splotches started creeping along the edge of her vision. The pain wasn't going away, but suddenly it was the norm. It couldn't be so horrible if it was everything she knew. She had a strange urge to scratch some itch on her wrist as if the annoyance was nothing more than her bracelet rubbing her the wrong way.

"Kitty, I need you to stay with me. C'mon, please. I'm gonna take the pain away. I promise. I'm sorry I couldn't hold it. Let me fix this."

"No…" she mumbled. She wasn't sure why, but her cheeks flushed with embarrassment while everything else felt cold.

"What? Kitty, stay with me. Stay awake. Just let me help you. You have to give me permission."

"…what?"

"Let me help you, please! This wasn't your mistake. This was mine. You've done enough. Let me help already!"

"Oh…" The white blotches were persistent. She wondered if Will could make them go away. It was hard to see him. No matter how scared he might get, he always looked brave and handsome. She felt her lips curl into a smile as she hoped he never heard her say that. Kitty felt warm again, like wrapping herself in her favorite winter quilt. Her brain stopped jumping from thought to thought without stopping for air. The pain melted away, but she felt lightheaded. Will dropped another inch and groaned. His breathing was heavy, and each breath in was more of a gasp while each breath out was like a cry.

"Start moving," he said. "But DO NOT use your right arm. Just start crawling. I'm following right beside you."

"What are you talking about? You can't move!"

"I swear to god if you don't listen to me I will drop this whole effing roof on your head!"

Kitty blinked, but nodded. She rolled slightly to the right, but a hiss from Will made her stop.

"Don't even look. Just move."

Now Kitty wanted to look, but Will's twisted face scared her enough to keep moving. He was right that her arm was free even if she couldn't feel it because she could use her right elbow for balance instead as she propped herself up and started to slide back. Will shuffled along on his knees, struggling over a dark streak beneath them that made the ground slick. They could hear more crashing above them as the stones behind Kitty were shunted aside and the ones over them fell without the shield to hold them. Will could only move so fast, but the more they moved, it seemed there was less and less weight as stones fell away.

Finally Kitty's back nudged past a rock and into open air. Sensations overwhelmed her. There were sirens and men shouting orders. Whirling white and red lights poured in from the partially destroyed wall leading to the sports fields. Everyone's attention seemed to be on helping other people and they didn't see Kitty peek out from where stones were somehow sliding aside.

She looked back at Will whose head was hung low. It was the most pitiful sight she had ever seen, but then he looked up at her. His eyes were tired, but determined. His bangs stuck to his forehead hiding some of the cuts. And he was smiling. It was sad, but he didn't seem scared.

Before she could speak, the stones dropped again and the small hole Kitty had crawled from was caved in with concrete boulders half her size. She tried to reach out to him, but she fell into a whirlwind of confusion. Someone else called out to her and pulled her aside. She saw a concerned dark face, once perfectly pinned hair now falling to the side. Her hazel eyes were wide with terror as a sudden, unbearable pain shot up Kitty's right arm. It was one thing too many, and the white cloud over her eyes won out.

Twenty-Four

There were times in her life Kitty had felt more than tired. She didn't know the word to describe it. It was just more than tired. She never looked it up because she never thought describing that feeling would be important. Two times in a row Kitty woke up with that feeling after Homecoming, and both times she was blinded by fluorescent bulbs in the ceiling. She couldn't see much else because turning her head was far more energy than she could imagine using. For a moment she thought about a time she looked in the mirror and felt that way. Then she remembered it wasn't exactly a mirror—it was a dummy oration. Like a magical spell.

Spell? What am I, squirrelnuts?

Just out of her peripheral vision she could see white curtains drawn all around her and long beds with handles on either side. A few men and women in baggy teal pants and shirts were holding charts and speaking softly to other people in beds. Kitty's skin felt too tight on her, especially by her right arm where it throbbed with pain. She saw it sealed up in some flesh colored brace with netting over it, squeezing her bones until they felt ready to snap. Beneath the brace, all of her forearm and wrist were covered, but just past it she saw her hand had swelled up and took on a mean shade of purple with crusted bits of red between her fingers.

One of the women in the teal clothes walked by her bed and smiled at her. She mouthed some words and stared like she was waiting for a response. Kitty only blinked. Then the woman picked up a chart at the end of Kitty's bed, shook her head, and replaced it. She patted Kitty's foot over the stiff white blanket and mouthed something else before walking away. Surely she wasn't that bad. She was alive with a banged up arm. It could have been a lot worse. Her eyes started drooping again as someone new looked into the room that had somehow emptied between blinks. A tall boy with a sheepish look that didn't suit him at all approached her bed. She thought she knew him. Her heart felt heavy. Something terrible must have happened to him. Maybe he could tell her. He sat in the chair and pushed sandy brown bangs out of his face, talking without words.

Maybe if she spoke up, she could set a good example, and everyone else would speak louder.

"Hi. I'm Kitty. I'm fine if you're wondering," she said. The boy kept talking as if he didn't hear her either. He took a white device from out of nowhere and started tapping it. "Hello? Oh fine. I'm going back to sleep. Later."

The boy rested his chin on the railing as Kitty drifted back to sleep. A warm blue glow and an itch she couldn't reach invaded her dreams. When she opened her eyes again, she was in a different room with bright lights and only a single bed this time, and she wondered if someone shrunk the room while she was asleep.

"Kitty? Baby, are you awake?"

Again, moving her head was tiresome, but her eyes slowly wandered to her right. Her mom was on her feet in an instant, hovering over the bed, face scrunched in worry and relief all at once. She was framed by flowers, cards, and chocolates on the nightstand beside her that all shouted in bold letters: GET WELL SOON! Parting her lips felt like yanking tape. Her mom reached for a cup of water and let a few drops fall against Kitty's lips. She didn't realize how thirsty she was until the droplets landed on her tongue.

"Oh my god, Kitty. Oh thank god. Good morning, sweetheart. You scared me half to death!"

"...sorry," she croaked.

"No, this is not your fault, baby. There will be hell to pay with the DoE, but don't you worry about a thing except getting better. Some of your friends came by. April and Becka were here. A certain Smith boy too." Mrs. Guthrie brushed Kitty's hair back as she laughed. "I'm just so glad you're okay. Even your arm! You're a miracle child, you know that? The doctors were trying to tell me they couldn't help you. They said there was nothing to operate on. Like your bones were just dust. Idiots. They probably just get more money for chopping people's arms off. Vultures, all of them."

"What?" Kitty looked back at her arm that was in a full white plaster cast with her puffy fingers twitching at the end.

"Mommy, can Kitty play now?" Kitty perked up at the sound of her sister's voice. She tried to turn faster than her body would allow.

"Soon, baby, but she was in a bad accident and she has to get better. And for all we know, we might be homeschooling you from now on." Her mom muttered the last part.

"Now she's like me!"

Mrs. Guthrie patted her youngest daughter's face and kissed her forehead. "I'll go find a doctor and let them know you're up, Kitty. I will be right back. Come on, Edie. Let's see if your friend Hannah's foot is better. She's had a bad few weeks too. Don't worry, Kitty. I'm not going far." She gave Kitty a kiss on the forehead too.

"Sure, mom."

Her mom led Edith from the room. Kitty watched the door and tried to figure out how long she had been sleeping. She had enough weird dreams to last a year. A year of sleep would be horrible. She wasn't ready to be a freshman in high school yet. And what would her friends have been up to for a year without her? How many more orations would Will have learned to show off?

Who? ...Will...

The fog started to fade, and Kitty remembered the night of Homecoming. She remembered the dance and then the chasing, the transit and shadow people, and the evil. Everything caved in and Will protected her. She dreamed of him, but she almost wished she would forget. Had anyone found him under those rocks? Was he in the hospital too? Horrible guilt stabbed Kitty's belly as she wondered what else she could have done to help him.

It would be easier to forget with time. That's what her mom would say if she ever told her. When her mom and sister returned with a woman in a white coat, Kitty was too weak to wipe away the tears that had formed. Her mother laid a hand on Kitty's cheek while the nurse approached with a stethoscope and wheeling a small monitor.

"Are you in any pain, Kitty?" the nurse asked, offering a tissue to Mrs. Guthrie. Her mother started wiping her tears and murmuring reassurances. Even if they were for something else, they set Kitty's mind at ease for a moment as the nurse hooked up another small bag of pain medication.

"Mom," Kitty said as another thought seized her mind.

"What is it, baby? What do you need?"

"...I lost the bus pass you signed."

Her mother cocked her head to the side. It took her a few seconds before she broke into sad laughter. "Oh Kitty, it's fine."

"I'm sorry I yelled at you."

"And I'm sorry I lost my cool." Mrs. Guthrie kissed Kitty's forehead again. "I love you, sweetheart."

"I love you too, mom."

A week had passed. That's what the TV in the living room was announcing as Kitty hugged April and Becka goodbye at the front door of her apartment. It was still strange celebrating a week's worth of lazy Saturdays with the school shut down.

"So we definitely need more time over here," Becka said. "I don't care how gourmet April's dad can cook. It doesn't beat Fabio's pizza. Like, literally ever."

"She's not wrong," April said as she slipped her arms into her pink leather jacket. They laughed. The twinkling sound filled the apartment, and the tears and stains seemed to matter so much less. "Okay, c'mon. Mom's gonna freak. Later, Kitty cat!"

"Later!" She watched them walk down the buzzing hall, talking about the movies they watched on their last day off from school before it opened after inspection and maintenance. A school gym collapsing on a bunch of students was big news, and it picked up media attention across all of New Jersey. Kitty's mom told her a few news reporters were trying to get into Kitty's room for an exclusive interview, but she nearly put them in the hospital for trying. She said it all while smiling.

Kitty shut the door behind her. The apartment was quiet, and it made her skin crawl. The cast covering her right arm all the way up to the elbow was particularly heavy and itchy. That strange fear crept up since leaving the hospital. Magic had a way of worming itself into her mind like banging pots and pans, and when she stopped thinking about it to get on with normal life, the clamoring was still there to remind her. She needed to have someone in the room with her nearly all the time. Going to the bathroom made her anxious. She had sleepover princess parties with her sister four nights in a row and worked up the nerve to invite Becka and April to the apartment just to have company. She had enough of the questions about how she was feeling, but it was better than the silence.

Kitty laid back in her bed. As she feared, broken whispers interrupted her thoughts; ideas of using magic to scratch the itch under her cast or to tidy the apartment further crept through her brain. At least they were helpful considerations. She never wanted to feel that deathly cold grip around her heart again. She could blame Nefas all she wanted—she could even blame her dad if she wanted—but the reason wouldn't matter if she acted in any way that would make the Cursed Boss happy. A lot of people could get hurt, and she couldn't imagine being the cause of that. She hated the thought of being used for something so awful. Worse yet, she hated the thought of wanting to do awful things.

An idea struck her. Kitty slid out of her bed and ducked down, pushing her sheets aside. Unused notebooks sat piled near the wall below the headboard. She frowned at them for a minute. A number of excuses rattled through her mind, not the least of which was she couldn't use her writing hand. Deeper than that, she couldn't ignore how stupid it felt to write thoughts down and not actually do anything about them. Still, she picked up the top notebook, grabbed a pen from her desk and plopped back on her bed.

The page stayed blank for a long time, and the intrusive thoughts grew louder. Kitty shook her head and touched the pen to the page. Her shaking hand began to scrawl.

I feel

How did she feel? Lonely? Scared? Used?

I feel dumb. I feel afraid. I'm afraid using magic will make me hurt people, but even worse I don't want to hurt people I care about. I already did. I don't want my friends to hate me if they know what I can do. I'm scared of seeing It again. What if I listen to It? I don't want to die.

Someone knocked on her window, and Kitty's heart leaped into her throat. A boy a few years older was crouched on the metal grating of the fire escape and waving through the glass. Kitty threw the notebook under her bed and sprinted to the window. The sun was dropping, and the sky was dribbling with pinks and faded yellows. It was beautiful and ordinary, right where she left it two weeks ago when Will showed up at her Homecoming meeting. There was Will destroying that calm yet again.

Kitty opened the window and shimmied through it into the brisk autumn air. Will helped her the last few steps when she struggled with her cast. She stared at him, still questioning if he was real or if she was mourning her new friend buried under tons of stone and plaster. She took a few steps along her balcony and then punched him in the arm.

"Ow! What the heck, Kitty!"

"What the heck yourself!" Tears stung the corners of her eyes. "You couldn't message me? Call me? Just tell me you're freaking okay?"

"You were unconscious for a week, and I had adjudications and other things."

Kitty shoved her hands on her hips and realized how hard that was with a cast on one arm. "Whatever, jerkface,"

"Sorry you're learning the world doesn't revolve around you even if you are an Empath."

"Whatevs." Kitty rolled her eyes, but it was just an excuse to look less hurt than she felt. She crossed the balcony to the twang of her sneakers on the metal. The trees painted a bleak shadow across the property, and the railing was icy against her uncovered palm. She was glad he wasn't hurt, but the racket of magic returning left her shaking worse than the chill. She couldn't form the words that she had to say now that he was here.

"I'm just on an adjudication from Leo. He needs the Chameleon Ear back since—" Will shrugged. Silence fell over them. Kitty scratched as far into her cast as she could reach. "I mean, I also wanted to make sure you were alright obviously."

"What about Raquel," Kitty finally said as the terrifying memories flooded back.

"She's fine. I debriefed with Leo when I got out of the emergency room—dude, Governor Cohen got involved. Some Mages were sent back to find her. She was hiding at some pizza place or something, but they got her to the other side safely. So—okay, you're seriously not gonna join us? You're really gonna ignore magic?"

Kitty jumped at the sudden change in his voice, but lowered her eyes again. "Will, I can't-"

"You can."

Kitty turned to face him with a stomp of her foot, much less powerful in her sneakers. "It's my choice!"

"It's the wrong choice!"

His words were like slaps to the face. Mentor Will never told her she was wrong; he suggested other options. Will distractedly scratched at his head and hopped up onto the railing, holding the vertical bar.

"Well I already made my choice so deal with it," Kitty said. She slipped the thin wire from around her ear, tossed it towards him, and went back to her window. Then she paused; April would be furious if she stormed off from an upset friend. "It's just too much," she said through a sigh. Her cheeks burned, but she was glad for the excuse to talk. "I can't do all the things I already have to do and be responsible for everyone in the whole world. I don't want to be. I thought I finally found something that was just for me. Not about my mom or Edith. Homecoming was supposed to be this cool thing I did that was just mine, and magic was supposed to be this even cooler thing that was just mine. But Homecoming blew up—literally—and magic is just... not what I was expecting. It's not bringing my dad back. It's not making me better. People got hurt, maybe worse, because of me and this cruddy wish granting. It's just one extra—thing."

*   "Magic isn't here to make you better," Will said. "It's proof that you understand things better. You're not responsible for anybody, but yourself, but you do have to live with knowing you could be helping other people be better. Setting an example for people to follow."

"I feel like it's supposed to be my job. If people can't do magic and they get into trouble, who helps them? Who else was going to stop the people in the church or Reverend Al at the deli. Who else could sew up space?"

"Mages will handle the magic stuff, but people will help themselves and each other. You're not a superhero; you're a Mage. It's a fine line between doing what's right for the people around you and doing what's actually right and leaving people alone. Not everyone squares off with Nefas on the regular. That's a Mage problem. Quotists deal with things like annoying parents and fighting with friends. It's normal and it's not on your shoulders."

"Maybe..."

"I get that you're scared. I sure as hell was. I'd never seen Nefas before."

Kitty perked up, ignoring the twinge in her stomach, and stared at him. His eyes were soaking in the city past the fire escape. "Really?"

"Really. I read all about where It's from and what It wants. But hearing that voice in my head? That was freaky. And seeing how he could take a good kid and turn her into... whatever was happening to you—dang. It also reminded me of why I chose to side with the Alliance. I can look at things like that—" he pointed to the sky "—and I know I helped somebody, sometimes just me, enjoy that sight. And when I see my folks and my friends, and they're happy— like, really happy—I know I'm at least not making them unhappy. They're not thinking about it, but I do. Makes me feel pretty great, but it's not about me."

Kitty looked out at the sunset to avoid his eyes. Will rested his face in his hands, then looked up again with a crooked smile.

"I guess I didn't do my job so great as a mentor. Believe me, I tried everything to make this easier for you. Maybe I should've told Leo more of what we were doing, but, I mean, c'mon. We thought we were dealing with a weird dummy oration. Until we weren't. Still, you handled it all really well." His shoulder flopped with a shrug. "What a waste. I guess if you need anything, you know where I live."

"Right."

A flustered whisper in her ear made Kitty itch. Will nodded just as the sounds stopped, and he hopped down from the railing.

"Can't ignore this call," he said. "Leo and Governor

Cohen wanna finishing debriefing with us—with me, I guess." He stared at his watch in silence for a moment. Kitty waited for the warm sensation and slight itch of a transit oration activating, but it never came. Finally Will said, "I think I'll walk." He started down the steps and waved over his shoulder.

Kitty watched him go. Each distant sound of sneakers on the metal grates was a sad note plucking at her heart. Words were hard to find, but Will was something like a friend. It wasn't the normal way she made friends. It was like one of those short-lived whirlwind hookups the popular kids at school got to have. It was sudden news, it was fast and exciting, and it ended in an instant. Somewhere deep down, Kitty hoped he wanted her to take him up on his offer to stop by. She could finally see him crossing the lawn towards the side of the building.

"Later!" she called out from her balcony. He turned around with that goofy smile and flailed his arm in an overdramatic wave. Kitty's smile was strained as he rounded the corner into the streets of the city.

She didn't realize how long she had been staring at that spot until a breeze picked up and chilled her through her blouse and skirt. The sky was a velvet purple that barely let her see past the property line. Kitty slid back inside and waited for her mom's return. Chores. Chores were good distractions. Kitty cleaned dishes in the sink, folded laundry, and picked up Edith's toys. She made quick work of the glass recycling, pausing only to note how few bottles there were, then started a stack for paper when she picked up the newspaper article April brought over a few days ago.

SCHOOL LEAVES UNANSWERED QUESTIONS AS
TRAGEDY STRIKES EVENT OF THE YEAR.

*When it comes to our children, we expect the
safest place for them is under the watchful eye of our
renowned teachers. This was the hope of young Kitty
Guthrie (13) as she planned the first Homecoming
Dance of Glade Crest Junior High School history.*

Kitty stared at the picture of her with April and Becka
from the Homecoming Game. She read and reread the
quotes Daphne included, mostly summarizing April's rant.
Even though the article focused on the mysterious roof
collapse, it still told the truth about her that she thought
everyone forgot. Kitty folded the clipping and set it on her
bedroom desk until she found a good frame for it.

The living room was as clean as it had ever been as her
mother and sister came home. She heard the lock shake a
few times and heard Mrs. Guthrie groan on the other side.
Edith laughed. Kitty would have helped, but she might
have broken her arm again if it got in the way of the door
her mom finally threw open.

"Okay, sweetheart, play with your sister. Mommy has
to get dressed. Kitty, please make dinner. But also play with
Edith. But not at the same time."

Kitty raised a hand to speak, but her mother had already
torn through the living room and slammed her bedroom
door shut. Kitty looked at her sister who was wiggling in
place like she was practicing a dance she learned at her
therapy group. Sounds of banging and softened swear
words filled her mom's room.

"What bug crawled up her butt?" Kitty asked as she held her arms out for a hug. Edith quickly obliged.

"She's gonna go out."

"But weren't you just out?" Kitty said, holding Edith back at arm's length. She kept wiggling, strong for being so petite. "Mom doesn't have work tonight."

"She's gonna go out!"

"Okay, okay. Well I guess we need to get dinner for you. C'mon little princess."

As Kitty grabbed instant macaroni and cheese from the cupboard and started preparing it, she saw her mom leave her room. She was wearing a dress Kitty knew she had never seen in her closet before. It was a stretchy red material with golden hoops over the cut out shoulders. An attached belt jingled as she undid the work Kitty had put into cleaning the living room.

"Where are those dang shoes?" she muttered. Kitty let the noodles cook and leaned against the kitchen doorway.

"Mom...what are you doing?"

"I'm running late is what I'm doing. Those know-it-alls at the clinic didn't want to interrupt a breakthrough they were having. Oh please!" She crouched down to look under the coffee table again and then came into the kitchen to look under that table too—then to look on top of it. "My daughter is no different than the first day she went in there. She's happy as can be—which of course is all a mother could ask for—so they just keep taking my money and I just keep handing it over. All because she could talk about God and the devil? She learns that in Sunday school! For the love of Pete!"

Her mom nearly slipped in her tights along the kitchen

tiles, but she steadied herself on the door frame and went back to her room.

"She's happy," Edith said as she kicked her feet in the kitchen chair. Kitty had to agree.

The difference between her mom on a warpath and her mom filled with anxious excitement wasn't clear to most, but her daughters had seen every layer of it. Her mom hadn't acted so high strung since she went in for the final interview for assistant manager at Beautician Magicians. Kitty remembered hearing her mom sob with joy when she came home that day. When she had opened the door again, she was a ball of sunshine and not a tear to be seen.

There was a knock at the door. A muffled censored swear exploded from the bedroom. Edith clapped. "He's here! He's here!"

"He?" Kitty looked at her sister

"I got it!" her mom shouted, but the bedroom door remained shut and Kitty heard another *THUD* from the room.

"Nope, I got it," Kitty said mostly to herself.

She went to the front door and looked through the peephole. Someone was standing there facing away. Normally she wouldn't answer the door if she didn't know the person, but her mom was clearly expecting someone. A 'he' no less. Kitty unbolted the door and slid it open. A man turned around and smiled down at her. He had salt and pepper hair pulled back in a sleek ponytail and light stubble across his naturally tanned chin. His eyes squinted as he smiled. The collar of his tucked in button down shirt was slightly relaxed and brought out the navy pinstripes in his nice pants. His polished shoes caught the hallway lights buzzing around them.

"Oh hello!" He had a hint of a Spanish accent in his voice. "You must be Kitty. Lyddy has told me so much about you. It's an honor to finally meet you. I'm Emanuel."

Kitty saw his outstretched hand, but could only stare. There was really a man standing at her front door waiting to see her mother, and both of them were dressed to impress. Her stomach turned at the sound of the old pet name for her mom that she hadn't heard in over four years. She never thought she would hear it again.

A door behind them bounced open, slamming into the wall and nearly bouncing back to hit Mrs. Guthrie. She hopped out of her bedroom while slipping her second black pump over her heel. Her hair was pinned to the side and her makeup was done. Despite her harried smiled as she jogged to the door, she was glowing.

"Manny, I'm so sorry. I'm running a little behind tonight. I'm ready now. Oh, this is my oldest daughter Kitty. Kitty, this is Manny Ramirez. We're going to dinner. No big deal. I'll be home by eleven the latest, but Edith—"

"—is in bed by nine. I know…" The words were on autopilot. Her mom hugged her and kissed the top of her head.

Manny immediately complimented her and left her giggling like a schoolgirl. It was a little scary. She could still hear her mom laughing after she shut the door again. That was even scarier, but seeing her mom so happy was a huge change. She was…going on a date.

That'd be worth falling out of space and time to see, she thought without realizing the words were scrolling through her mind so easily. She paused at the door. It was worth falling through space and time. Seeing her mom choose to move forward and not stay stuck was worth fighting with dummies, jumping through transits, and feeling tired but satisfied with an oration well done. Her mom being able to choose that happiness was worth everything it took to fight for that happiness. Kitty could see the fear of the new in her mom's eyes, but she looked stunning and she looked ready.

"Kitty! The noodles are dancing!"

Kitty gasped and ran back to the kitchen, not sure why she was laughing too.

———————◆———————

Kitty leaned against the wall in the long hallway, tugging at the end of her skirt. The fingers on her right hand were still stiff through the cast. She felt a clammy sweat under her sweater, and she wanted to go back home. She wanted a lot of things to be different, but they weren't. That didn't mean she couldn't make things better. Kitty lifted her arm towards the metal door, but lowered it again. She took another deep breath, but decided to lean back against the wall.

You're being a numbnuts! she berated herself. *No one is going to bite your head off! Well, there could be aliens and they might do that. No, that's not right.*

Kitty squeezed her eyes shut and pushed away from the wall. She scratched at the cast, but it was more to stall than to be effective in relieving her nervous itch. Finally she threw her left hand at the door. She heard the hissing of a vacuum seal releasing before she could make contact. When she unclenched her eyes, two people were staring at her from beside an L shaped desk littered with monitors and

347

wires. The centermost monitors were buried in a hidden compartment of the desk, and a man's face smiled at her from beneath a thick moustache. In a spinning, egg-shaped chair was a boy just a little older than her who brushed his bangs aside.

"Uh…" Kitty said. "Can I come in?"

"You'd better," Leo Baldwin replied in his thick New York dialect and gestured towards the seat beside Mage Will Cavanaugh. Kitty hurried to a seat and plopped down. Leo lightly tossed a small wire and bud towards her and Kitty wrapped it around her ear. "Your input is invaluable, Kitty. And since you're here, I'll get a Mage from R&D to replace your Chameleon Ear with a NAP. Much better for Alliance members." Leo turned back to one of his monitors to pull up some information.

"Welcome back," Will heard at her.

Kitty smiled. It was nice to be around family. Sometimes it popped up where she least expected, but where she needed it most. The banging and clanging of magic surrounded her like music to her ears, and she leaned forward to listen to Leo guide her through it all.

Acknowledgements

This book has been over a decade in the making, dreamed up by a girl who clung to books when she didn't have people to cling to. Now there is an abundance of people who have helped bring this dream to life. So much more than just the writer goes into the creation of a book.

Thank you to my parents who have always encouraged me to pursue any endeavor. I wouldn't be anywhere without them. And to my brothers who have their own mountains to climb, but always reach a hand back to their little sister.

Thank you to my first writing friends and supporters on FictionPress when this story took place in another universe. I kept the reviews and I'm still cheerleading. And thanks to my new writing friends and supporters on Twitch, Patreon, and all across social media. The Virtual Write In gave me the space and encouragement to create, and it brought me to people who are both friends and teachers. The people I've met through Twitch have been simply invaluable to my writing victories, big and small. Twitch subscribers, tippers, and Patreon backers, you literally funded the creation of this work and future works, and I simply can't thank you enough.

And lastly, thank you to the girls—now women—who were my best friends when I stood in Kitty's shoes. Circumstances created distance, and I'm sorry for that, but I carry you forever in my heart.

More from the Author

To stay up to date on future fiction and so much more, subscribe to my monthly newsletter and follow the behind the scenes blog! Meet the woman behind the words, and we'll celebrate our victories together!

www.authorbrenna.com

Want to see how this book and other stories were written? Need a friendly place to make your own projects come to life? Join the daily Virtual Write In Monday through Friday for live writing, workshopping, and community! No more excuses. Your future novel is waiting for you!

www.twitch.tv/BrenNailedIt

Patreon VIP supporters are an integral piece to the publishing puzzle. Become a Patron and get exclusive content, mini stories written just for you, and complementary ebooks of my published work! You guys are dream builders, and I can't thank you enough!

www.patreon.com/author_brenna

About the Author

Brenna R. Singman is a fiction author and online writing coach. She was born and raised in NJ before transplanting herself to Atlanta, GA in pursuit of a life of teaching theatre—which still wound up revolving around writing. She has been writing fiction since childhood, but never dreamed of pursuing writing as a career until adulthood when she couldn't deny her passion for it any longer. Now, apart from novels, she writes collections of flash fiction pieces and short stories of various genres and hosts a daily writing group on twitch.tv where she gets to do what she loves most among fellow authors on a similar journey. When she's not writing, Brenna is likely baking, playing board games, or taking long walks with her brother while contemplating the vicissitudes of life.

Made in the USA
Columbia, SC
16 January 2021

31047052R00217